Coastwalk

Also by Andrew McCloy

Land's End to John o'Groats

COASTWALK

Walking the coastline of England and Wales

ANDREW McCLOY

Maps by Benedict Davies

Hodder & Stoughton

British Library Cataloguing in Publication Data

McCloy, Andrew
Coastwalk : walking the coastline of England and Wales
1. Coasts – England – Guidebooks 2. Coasts – Wales –
Guidebooks 3. Walking – England – Guidebooks 4. Walking –
Wales – Guidebooks
I. Title
914.2'04859

ISBN 0 340 65739 1

Typeset by Palimpsest Book Production Limited,
Polmont, Stirlingshire
Printed and bound in Great Britain by
Mackays of Chatham PLC, Chatham, Kent

Hodder and Stoughton
A division of Hodder Headline PLC
338 Euston Road
London NW1 3BH

For my parents

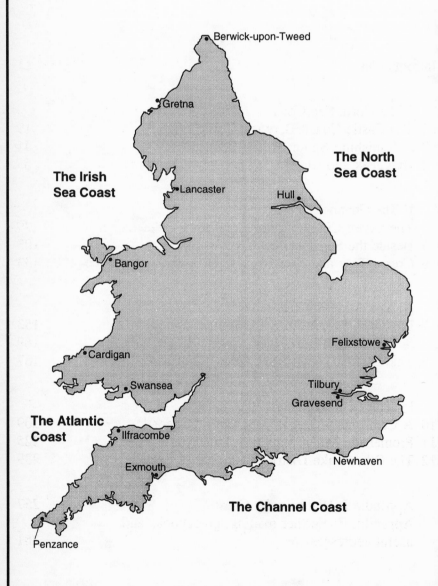

The Irish
Sea Coast

The North
Sea Coast

The Atlantic
Coast

The Channel Coast

Berwick-upon-Tweed

Gretna

Lancaster

Hull

Bangor

Cardigan

Swansea

Felixstowe

Tilbury
Gravesend

Ilfracombe

Newhaven

Exmouth

Penzance

Contents

Acknowledgements

The author and publishers would like to thank A.F. Kersting for providing the pictures of Bosham, Chesil Bank, Golden Cap, The Lizard, Lantic Bay, Bedruthan Steps, Tintagel, St Non's Bay, Whitesand Bay and the Ribble Estuary; Northumbria Tourist Board for the photographs of Bamburgh Castle (taken by Michael Busselle) and Dunstanburgh Castle; Cumbria Tourist Board for supplying that of St Bees Head; Lancaster and Morecambe Newspapers for the picture of Morecambe promenade; Ian Johnson for his picture of Staithes; Walt Unsworth for the picture of Arnside; and Mark Button for his picture of Rhossili Bay. All other photographs were taken by the author.

Maps were expertly drawn by Benedict Davies.

The author would like to record his special thanks to Margaret Body for her advice and encouragement over the last three years. Also to Katherine, for her patience; and last but certainly not least to Jenny, who spent the first year of her life in a camper van visiting various coasts – and didn't complain once! Thank you.

Maps

Introduction

A few years ago I was walking along the dark, burly cliffs south of Saltburn on Day 3 of the Cleveland Way. Pounding the high turf on my own, quite glad to have swapped the moors for the sea, I drew alongside a local family enjoying an afternoon's stroll. They were a friendly lot: Dad, maybe late forties, three or four lively kids, and a dog. He began chatting the moment he noticed my boots and backpacked frame, and I soon learned that Mum was at work, the children were on school holiday, and he was simply doing what he did every afternoon for the last few years, ever since he was laid off from the nearby pit. 'Do you like walking?' I asked, a little uncertainly, since he didn't really look the rambling type. He nodded happily. Oh yes, it kept him in shape (albeit a rather round shape); and, he added thoughtfully, it was good for the soul.

Hippocrates would have agreed with my friend from Loftus. As far back as 2,000 years ago the wise old sage was recommending walking, when enriching the soul and mind was more important than analysing cholesterol levels or gauging the release of endorphins. Artistic folk of every hue have sought inspiration ever since from walking, and there's no better place to get the creative juices flowing than by the sea. Coleridge, Turner, Du Maurier, Betjeman – they were all drawn to the coast, whether by hidden creeks or majestic cliffs, or simply by awesome seascapes that seem to stretch the land and sky to its limits.

But it's not just Dickens who had to have a view of the sea. There is a lure, a pull, that is almost inexplicable. Children get excited when they near it; old folk retire to die beside it. It has been estimated that no one within England and Wales is any more than two hours' drive from the sea. Of course, much depends on how fast you drive, but what do you do when you get there? A surprising number of people seem quite happy just to sit in their cars and stare at it. Others are a little more adventurous, making it to the beach, or the promenade deckchair. But if you have any sense, you go for a walk.

Where excise men and coastguard lookouts once patrolled the cliffs, now ramblers enjoy the same tracks. It is hardly surprising that coastal walking is popular. It is not a specialised art and no expensive equipment or exceptional navigational skills are necessary. Cliffs or bays, marsh or sea wall, you can wander for an hour or tramp for a week. Although few people walk the 600 or so miles of the South-West Coast Path in one go, there is an almost endless selection of day and weekend walks. In a recent survey 44% of all holidaymakers to the South-West of England said that the existence of the coast path was a factor in visiting the area, even though nine out of ten only walked for a day or less, and a third of those for less than one hour! Our varied coast offers so much scope, and the attraction of an amazing range of terrain. From the wild, sandy miles of Northumberland to the popular pebbles of Brighton and Worthing; from the awesome Atlantic cliffs of Cornwall and Pembrokeshire to the flat and deserted sea walls of Suffolk and Essex.

The good news for walkers is that many local authorities are waking up to the benefits of walking, whether it is for reasons of health and fitness, or for the good of the local economy. Recently opened long-distance footpaths have embraced some or all of the coasts in Cumbria, Lancashire, County Durham, Suffolk and North Wales, and another may follow in Somerset. Of course long, continuous coast paths have existed for some years in Devon and Cornwall, Dorset and Norfolk, the Pembrokeshire peninsula and part of the Cleveland coast; and in some of Kent (and unofficially in parts of Northumberland, too). With some coastal trails still being developed and others on the drawing board an intriguing scenario begins to take shape. It is not stretching the realms of fantasy too far to imagine that in a few years' time it may be possible to walk all the way from Sefton, north of Liverpool, to the Scottish border at Gretna (Sefton Coastal Path – Lancashire Coastal Way – Cumbria Coastal Way). Or how about this for a mind-blowing continuous coastal walk: Emsworth, by Chichester Harbour, along the Channel coast to Land's End, then around the shores of the Bristol Channel to the Gower (Solent Way – Bournemouth Coast Path – South-West Coast Path – Severn Way – Seascape Trail – Gower Coast Path). Sure, the idea of extending the Severn Way beyond Bristol is only vague, and Cardiff Ramblers' idea of a South Wales Seascape Trail is in its infancy, but what a prospect!

Away from official paths the coast road or prom often rules the shore, as in much of Sussex and southern Lancashire. But this is all part and parcel of the British coast, eminently walkable and sometimes quite interesting, if not always terribly scenic. Aside from official long-distance routes, there are other, shorter paths and tracks that are equally walkable, and often just as fascinating. Have you ever heard of the Carmarthen Coast Path, the Headland Walk at Flamborough, or the Peter Scott Walk along the edge of the Wash? Here, at last, they are all pulled together into one volume for you to choose from the whole of the coast of England and Wales.

Making the most of the coast
This is a book for both casual ramblers and long-distance walkers. Whether you are inspired by a pub lunch and a gentle afternoon stroll, or the dragon-slaying feeling of notching up 20 miles in a day, the following pages cater for both. The route is described in a continuous, rolling fashion that can be picked up or put down at any point. Few people will want or be able to walk the whole of one of the four 'coasts' that I describe, but the key is to dip in and select the piece that takes your fancy. Or if good fortune lands you near the sea for a while, use this book to check out the perambulatory possibilities. It may read like a long-distance journey, but the day's mileage is yours to decide.

Coastwalk begins at Berwick-upon-Tweed and works its way around the whole coast of England and Wales in a clockwise fashion to end by the Solway Firth just over the border at Gretna. Where islands occur I have examined all those that the mainland walker can reach by bridge, and mentioned those not too far offshore that are worth exploring. But there is no room here to do proper justice to the Isles of Wight and Man, both of which have good walking routes across and around their attractive countryside and shores, and separate guides are available for each.

In the case of rivers and estuaries, I have looked to the first bridge or safe fordable point, or, where practical, to a ferry. This may be a bone of contention to some purists, and I have heard fellow long-distance walkers argue that stepping on to a boat is no different to catching a bus. If you are walking the coast, then it should be foot only, they say. All very well, perhaps, but refusing the five-minute ferry from St Mawes to Falmouth adds over 30 miles to the South-West Coast Path, mostly on roads. And do you really want to trudge all the way around the industrial mouths of the Tees, Thames and the Mersey in order to reach the first bridge or foot tunnel? If you're planning a long-distance walk along the coast, consider what decisions you might be forced to make.

Although I have researched and recorded every mile of the way some sections are examined in more detail, purely because of the fact that the cliffs of Pembrokeshire are more attractive and interesting than the bungalows of Worthing. At all times I have described the nearest route to the sea that is both safe and scenic. Sometimes this means a long-distance path; at other times it may be the sea wall, promenade, foreshore, or else the nearest practical public right of way. There are a few sections where there is simply no feasible walking route by or on the shore (small sections of Teesside, Essex, South Wales, the Dee estuary, and others). The likelihood is you will not want to walk next to an oil refinery or petro-chemical works, but I have outlined the best way to get around these obstacles anyway, just in case, say, someone wants to walk the entire seaboard of their home county, or indeed their country.

The record breakers
Land's End to John o'Groats is no mean achievement, clocking in at somewhere around the 1,000-mile mark (if you stick to footpaths for most of the way, which any sane person would). But a feasible walking route around the entire coast of England and Wales is almost three times that distance, and then by the time you've tacked on Scotland it comes to something approaching 7,000 miles for the entire British coastal walk. Of course it's been done, and done several times now. The first person to walk the whole coast of England, Wales and Scotland continuously was John Merrill in 1978. In an extraordinary walk of 6,824 miles he suffered a fatigue fracture to his foot caused, quite simply, by walking too far too quickly (3,300 miles in just 126 days – an average of over 26 miles per day). Equally remarkable was the feat of 'Granny' Vera Andrews who between January and December 1990 walked 7,318 miles around the shore of the British mainland; and in 1994 a woman called Spud and her mongrel dog Tess notched up 4,500 miles (they caught ferries across river estuaries). Meanwhile,

seventy-five-year-old Robert Steel set off to walk around the 'perimeter' of Great Britain (4,444 miles by his route) in order to celebrate the sixtieth anniversary of the National Trust in 1995.

The first man to walk around the coast of the British Isles – and that includes the whole of Ireland, of course – was John Westley. He completed this remarkable feat between 1990 and 1991, walking a total of 9,469 miles and wearing out nine pairs of boots. See Appendix II for details of their published accounts.

Presuming that you are not entering the realms of the superwalker, and would like to enjoy a comfortable, sensible and pleasant (rather than gruelling) coastal walk, Appendix I also has practical points on tides, weather, footwear and so on.

Meanwhile, at the end of each of the book's twelve sections I have picked out what I think is the best day and weekend walk from that stretch, in terms of scenery, quality of walking and local points of interest. Wherever possible these begin and end at a railway station or are on or near a bus route, so a round day or weekend excursion is feasible; and some of the walks are actually circular. For details on guidebooks and maps see Appendix II.

Finally, you may be forgiven for thinking 'why not Scotland?' I know it exists, but it's very difficult to walk around – as those few who have tried have found out. There's a lot of it, much of which is indented, very rough and extremely difficult to walk; and some is simply very awkward to reach. The odd coastal path does exist, such as around Fife and along some of the Lothian shore, but even here it is piecemeal and at the moment largely unwaymarked. There is much glorious walking to be had in Scotland – but, with a few exceptions, it is mainly to be found inland.

Two hundred years ago doctors began sending their patients to the seaside for health and relaxation. Not that much has changed today, although thankfully we are not encouraged to drink seawater any more. But George Trevelyan, former Master of Trinity, Cambridge, did not bother with physicians. 'I have two doctors,' he said. 'My left leg and my right.' Go to the coast and enjoy a walk!

I THE NORTH SEA COAST

1 THE CASTLE COAST
Berwick – Hull
284 miles

2 A VANISHING SHORE
Hull – Felixstowe
299 miles

3 BY CREEK AND MARSH
Felixstowe – Tilbury
280 miles

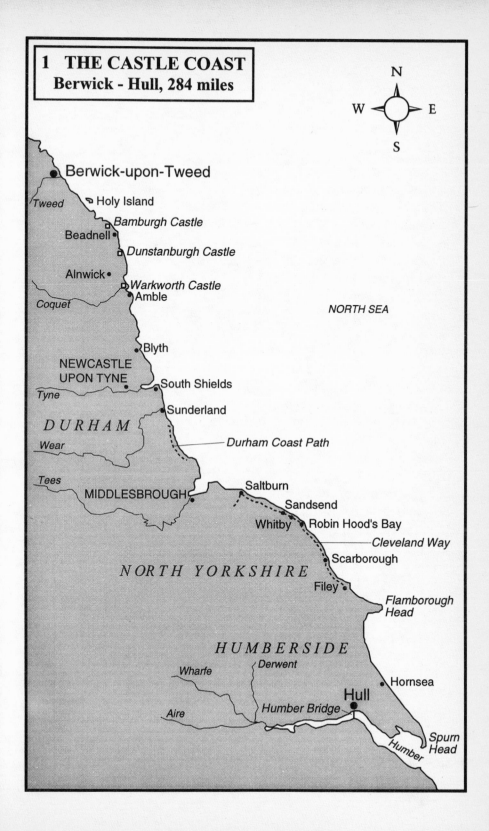

1 THE CASTLE COAST
Berwick - Hull, 284 miles

N
W — E
S

Berwick-upon-Tweed

Tweed

Holy Island

Bamburgh Castle

Beadnell

Dunstanburgh Castle

Alnwick

Warkworth Castle

Coquet

Amble

NORTH SEA

Blyth

NEWCASTLE
UPON TYNE

South Shields

Tyne

Sunderland

DURHAM

Wear

Durham Coast Path

Tees

Saltburn

MIDDLESBROUGH

Sandsend

Whitby

Robin Hood's Bay

Cleveland Way

NORTH YORKSHIRE

Scarborough

Filey

Flamborough
Head

HUMBERSIDE

Derwent

Wharfe

Hornsea

Hull

Aire

Humber Bridge

Spurn
Head

Humber

SCOTTISH BORDER (BERWICK) – BEADNELL (28 miles)

Let's be exact, shall we? The precise starting point of a clockwise coast walk around England and Wales is about four miles north of Berwick-upon-Tweed, on a pleasant if rather inaccessible piece of cliff near Marshall Meadows Bay. The distance to Gretna, where the Scottish Border meets England's West Coast, is about 85 miles by road. Follow me around the whole of the coast and we'll clock up an impressive 2,970 miles.

From the border with Scotland a clifftop public right of way extends south around the golf course into Berwick, and despite the proximity of the East Coast Main Line it's still an enjoyable route. Cross-border walkers may also be interested to know that a 40-mile coast path is being considered which will link Cockburnspath, the eastern terminus of the Southern Upland Way, with Berwick-upon-Tweed.

Berwick is most certainly in England – its most northerly town, in fact – but the Scottish influence can be detected in the accent, the money, the buildings, and even the mouthwatering pies and cakes in the shops. No wonder, since the gritty walled town above the Tweed was one of the four original Royal Burghs of Scotland, and the football team still plays in the Scottish League.

Of the two road bridges that cross the river, the old one dates back to the 1620s, and was built after James I (James VI of Scotland) is said to have complained about the dodgy old wooden affair that he was forced to use. Once you have left the swans on the Tweed and the houses of Spittal the Northumbrian coast settles down to what will be the recurring theme over much of its length: long, low and mostly empty stretches of sand and beach, interspersed with a little gentle cliff and marshland, and the occasional town and fishing village. Northumberland is one of the least populous counties in England, and its national park one of the least visited. All the more reason to explore, therefore, and where better to start than on the long sweep of the castle coast?

For many people the highlight of this remote shore is Lindisfarne, or Holy Island, where St Aidan established a priory in the seventh century and which was later made famous by St Cuthbert. Given the right conditions it's possible to walk all the way along the shore to it from Berwick, via tracks and paths through the dunes and along the edge of the links; and from Goswick to Lindisfarne Causeway there is a public footpath. But beware – use only the causeway and do not stray too far on to Goswick Sands, which at low tide seem to stretch forever. There are perilous patches of quicksand, and when the tide turns it races in with such speed that walkers can soon be cut off.

There are many good reasons to spend a day or more walking around Holy Island, not least that it's small and attractive, commendably undeveloped, and easily accessible on foot. In addition, endless fun can be had sitting at the end of the causeway watching hapless and frankly stupid motorists believe that they can beat the incoming tide and drive across. The refuge box, sitting high on stilts above the water halfway across the causeway, is not just there for decoration. The road is impassable for roughly half of each tide, so it goes without saying to plan your own trip carefully.

Virtually nothing remains of Aidan's original priory, finally destroyed by marauding Vikings in 875, but Benedictine monks founded a new abbey here two centuries later. The castle was even later still, built as a fort around 1540 and restored as a private residence at the turn of this century. Perhaps fortified by a drop of Lindisfarne Mead, first brewed by the monks, take a wander beyond the castle to the north of the island. As with the other island seat of British Christianity, Iona, from where Bishop Aidan came, if you get away from your fellow visitors for a while you can sense how removed and peaceful this place is, and perhaps why Aidan and his monks chose this spot. The Gertrude Jekyll-designed walled garden is a particularly peaceful nook.

Back on the mainland the shoreside footpath veers inland to Fenwick, and with no legitimate coastal track it is then probably best to follow a combination of minor roads and linking paths via the farms of Fenham-le-Moor and Elwick to regain the sea just past Waren Mill at Budle Bay. There are several access points in between, leading to some superbly unspoilt coastline; but all of this shore is a designated nature reserve and you must stick carefully to permitted rights of way and access points.

Firmer and continuous paths begin once more at Budle, on the south of the bay, and from here onwards there are few problems sticking to the shore. With Holy Island's castle to the north, follow the sea edge or duneland track to bring you out underneath the next impressive pile, that of Bamburgh Castle.

King Ida of Northumberland is believed to have erected a wooden defence on this huge, dark lump of rock, but the present building was begun by Henry I. It has played its part in a number of historical struggles, from the England–Scotland tussles to the Wars of the Roses. Although now in private hands, the castle is open to the public, and there are displays of furniture, art, armour, and some terrific views. The village also has a museum dedicated to the memory of Grace Darling, who made headlines in 1838 and aged only twenty-three by helping her father row out and rescue a number of men from the stricken steamer *Forfarshire*.

The unfenced coast road south from Bamburgh to Seahouses is a reasonable walking option if the tide is high, otherwise the best route is along the lovely clear sands and rocky platforms below the dunes. Visible a few miles out to sea are the Farne Islands, a scattering of up to twenty-eight small islands and reefs that represent the eastern end of the Great Whin Sill – the same basalt outcrops that give Hadrian's Wall such a dramatic roller-coaster ride west of Hexham. A boat trip to the Farnes is an unforgettable experience, and I can still remember the captain of the small boat that we took all those years ago pointing out to me Manx shearwaters, Arctic skuas, razorbills, terns and, of course, those silly fat little puffins flapping across the water, their amazing technicolour beaks full of fish. St Cuthbert lived on Inner Farne as a hermit for eight years, and he, too, was something of an ornithologist, insisting that nesting eider ducks should be properly cared for (they're still occasionally known as Cuddy's ducks around here, and hundreds continue to nest on the islands). The Farnes are also home to a large colony of grey seals, as well.

The tiny amusement arcades of Seahouses always seem rather out of place, but it does have a damn fine fish and chip shop and an attractive harbour from where you can board boats to the Farnes or relax in the Olde Ship Hotel. It's a place you're through in a few minutes, anyway, and beyond Snook Point you can either ford Annstead Burn at low tide or use the safer road crossing before following the beach to Beadnell.

BEADNELL – AMBLE (22 miles)
Despite the odd caravan site Beadnell remains an attractive place. No one-armed bandits here, but a sprawling and quiet village with

a 2-mile crescent of glorious sand at low tide and the haunting shape of Dunstanburgh Castle on the southern skyline ahead.

There is a public footpath behind the dunes leading around the rocky points off High and Low Newton-by-the-Sea (the Ship offers refreshment at the latter) to Embleton, and another sheltered beach. From here grassy tracks lead up to the ruins of Dunstanburgh Castle, isolated on a low, rocky headland that juts out moodily into the North Sea. Begun by Thomas, Earl of Lancaster in 1313, it suffered attacks by the Scots and later by the Yorkists in the Wars of the Roses when John of Gaunt strengthened the fortress. Like Bamburgh, its original builders took advantage of the Whin Sill so that the basalt cliffs on the north side made a curtain wall unnecessary; and despite falling into disuse as long ago as the sixteenth century much of the original structure can still be seen today.

A gentle path descends through pasture to Craster, kipper capital. Visitor information and parking is provided in one of the small quarries or heughs, since the hard, local whinstone is popular as an ingredient of tarmac and can also be found in London's kerbstones. But it is the humble herring that has made this tiny Northumbrian fishing village famous, for here a hundred years ago thousands of fish were brought to be gutted, washed and smoked every day, and exported not just to Billingsgate but to places as far away as Russia. The secret, of course, is in the smoking. Traditionally, smoking only takes place between June and September, when the fish are plump and their oil content is high. A few smokehouses are still active in the village, where pretty ordinary-looking herrings (now caught off Scotland and not locally, it must be said) continue to be hung on what are known as tentersticks over smoking oak sawdust, to emerge around ten to fourteen hours later as tasty, reddish-brown kippers.

South of Craster there is a path along the top of the dark, folded cliffs and reefs to Boulmer, although beware cliff erosion and be prepared to follow any waymarked diversions – one already exists from Rumbling Kern to Howick Burn. Occasionally there is access to a sandy inlet, and before long either tracks across Alnmouth Common above the golf links or along the wide sandy beach will take you into Alnmouth.

A sedate, respectable kind of place seemingly, so you may be surprised to hear that John Wesley once described Alnmouth as a 'small seaport famous for all kinds of wickedness'. Certainly the village once had as many as six pubs; and in 1895 the shocking 'Alnmouth Riot' occurred, when a bunch of fishermen from nearby Amble arrived on a rowdy pub crawl. Jack Richardson, constable for Alnmouth, made the mistake of apprehending one of the group, and was beaten up for his pains. Reinforcements were called from Alnwick, but more fighting followed, Jack's house was smashed up and his canary killed. Peace was finally restored when further police arrived and all the miscreants were arrested.

The safe way to cross the River Aln is to follow the road upstream to Hipsburn and back, returning via a bridleway to the National Trust's Buston Links. The not so safe way is by foot across the mouth of the Aln, fordable for about 1½ hours at low tide, but you *must* find out the time of low tide first.

Church Hill, on the southern bank of the Aln, was once connected to the rest of the village until a ferocious storm in 1806 changed the course of the river. From here to the mouth of the Coquet the sands and dunes are unspoilt and unbroken, but since the Coquet can only be crossed by bridge upstream at Warkworth you may choose to leave the sea by bridleway at Birling Links.

Today the famous Percys of Northumberland have their family seat in Alnwick, but for a long time they also used the splendid castle at Warkworth. Centrepiece of the compact town, it sits in a tight loop of the tree-lined Coquet. Here Henry Percy and his son Harry Hotspur plotted to overthrow King Henry IV, later dramatised by Shakespeare who set some of his play at the castle. To regain the coast at Amble simply follow the roadside path from Warkworth Castle.

AMBLE – BLYTH (18 miles)

From Amble onwards the Northumbrian coast changes, and as far as the freedom-loving walker is concerned it changes for the worse. Until now the wild and unfettered shore – designated both as a Heritage Coast and Area of Outstanding Natural Beauty – has been free of the blight of heavy industry that has so spoilt the North-East coastline further south. But now the occasional opencast coalfield and power station appear, and the seaside throngs of Whitley Bay and the urban sprawl of Tyneside approach. But the threat to Druridge Bay, above all else, typifies the precariousness of Britain's natural coastal beauty.

From Amble, a popular if not overly pretty harbour town with a flashy modern marina, there is a choice of beach or dune route along the shore opposite Coquet Island, variously occupied by the Romans and Benedictine monks. Then, turning gradually south, Druridge Bay opens up and seven miles of glorious, pure white sand are revealed. There are tracks and lanes behind the dunes if the going gets hard, but most people come here to enjoy the uncrowded beach. In addition, there is a country park (reclaimed from a former opencast mine), two Sites of Special Scientific Interest and four nature reserves along its length, some of which is owned by the National Trust. All the more appalling, therefore, that for the past thirty years heavy lorries and diggers have been at work regularly extracting huge amounts of sand from the beach for the building trade. Up to 1.5 million tons have disappeared since the Government allowed digging to begin, dramatically altering the level of the beach, accelerating erosion, and jeopardising plans of local wildlife trusts to create new habitats for otters, bitterns and marsh harriers. If this wasn't bad enough, in 1978 local people discovered that Druridge Bay was being considered as a possible site for a new nuclear power plant. These plans have since been revised, but the nuclear authority refuses to return the land to public ownership, and the ghastly spectre remains. If you visit Druridge Bay – and you should, since it is still very beautiful – give your support to the Druridge Bay Campaign to save one of the most beautiful beaches on the East Coast.

At the southern end of the bay is the small village of Cresswell, after which you must take to the road to negotiate the industry at Lynemouth. Immediately after the power station, however, you can join an uninspiring public footpath into Newbiggin-by-the-Sea, or alternatively follow the shore around the golf course (but this is not a right of way). The sand at Newbiggin Bay is discoloured by sea coal, and like elsewhere on this seaboard it is not unusual to see coal being collected from the beach by hand.

From Newbiggin the clifftop path to the mouth of the Wansbeck has succumbed to the sea in places, and it may be easier to keep to the road until across the river. From here to Blyth the Cambois power station rather dominates things, although the coast road and beach are both walkable. If you follow the latter and walk into North Blyth you will have to take the ferry to reach Blyth proper. Once a busy coal-exporting centre (up to 4 million tons annually at the turn of the century), with the demise of the local industry Blyth is now much quieter.

BLYTH – SUNDERLAND (20 miles)
South of Blyth you can beach-walk as far as Seaton Sluice, whose harbour used to be periodically drained, ploughed up, then cleansed of the accumulated silt by water released by sluice gates built upstream across Seaton Burn. Then there is a pleasant public footpath along the cliffs past St Mary's Island, with its distinctive brilliant white lighthouse that is now a visitor centre, until the boarding houses and Glaswegian holidaymakers at Whitley Bay take over.

The next few miles up to and over or under the Tyne are predictably urban, but the inquisitive pedestrian can still find much of interest. Two saints are buried at the seventh-century Tynemouth Priory, once one of the richest in the country, and after uninvited Danish visitors arrived in the Dark Ages this site has been defended ever since – even as late as the Second World War. A short distance away is the Watch House, built by the Tynemouth Volunteer Life Brigade. This unique band of volunteers was set up in 1864 after devastating storms the previous month had wrecked five ships in three days, several the result of the treacherous Black Middens rocks by the mouth of the Tyne. Over 140 men came forward to offer their services, and still today the TVLB offers a back-up service to the Coastguard. More details can be had from the Watch House Museum, which also includes the original breeches-buoy, the land-based rescue device.

With Newcastle's urban grip firmly felt, walkers can cross the River Tyne by either the Shields Ferry or Jarrow foot tunnel, and the sea is soon regained at South Shields or, as the tourism planners would have it, 'Catherine Cookson Country'. Born in 1906 at the foot of Simonside Bank, Tyne Dock, the undisputed queen of the clogs and shawls saga has written more than ninety novels set in this locality, though the tourist pamphlet has to admit that 'Our Kate' didn't actually start writing until she had left the North for Hastings, where she spent forty-six years.

Most of South Shields is luckily not plonked on the shore so, beyond the South Pier anglers, the chips and a noisy funfair, you can swiftly stride on to the Leas, a welcome strip of low cliff and rough grassland. This gives way to Marsden Bay and the red-and-white striped Souter Lighthouse, on Lizard Point (a different Lizard). It is all part of the National Trust's three-mile-long holding, and culminates in the landscaped grassy slopes of Whitburn Coastal Park, formerly a colliery. Look out for Marsden Rock, in particular, a huge limestone stack off the cliffs that is popular with kittiwakes and fulmars, and over 100 pairs of nesting cormorants.

When the rifle range at Whitburn is not active it is possible to follow a public footpath along the clifftop to Whitburn Bay, and then a sand and promenade walk into Sunderland. Along here you will find the Bede Memorial, remembering the venerable Anglo-Saxon scholar and historian who was born in Sunderland but spent much of his life at St Paul's monastery by the Tyne at Jarrow, and where today he is celebrated by something called Bede's World.

SUNDERLAND – SALTBURN (42 miles)
Much of today's Sunderland grew up after Second World War bombing, although prior to that the port had only really taken shape after it gained the coal trade from Newcastle as a result of siding with Cromwell in the Civil War.

Although there is a low tide beach to the south of Sunderland the clifftop right of way that once led from Hendon into County Durham has largely eroded away and the authorities have been forced to close the path – don't try and walk it! Start at Seaham, instead, where the Durham Coast Path begins. This new 11-mile trail runs along a shoreline ravaged by the effects of coal mining, and yet with the industry's recent demise – all the coalfields along this County Durham coast have now closed – has come gradual natural regeneration. Coal-blackened beaches are slowly becoming lighter, and the effects of years of abuse are slowly being turned back. This may not be immediately apparent as you follow a road and bridleway landwards of Dawdon Colliery, closed in 1991, where an artificial beach was created at Nose's Point by the daily dumping of slurry, spoil and slag. This has now ceased, and the mile-long thick crust of detritus that had formed is slowly being eaten away by the waves. There is even a new sewage treatment works here to deal with another aspect of man-made coastal pollution.

Soon the railway-side path reaches Hawthorn Dene, owned by the National Trust and Durham Wildlife Trust (a short diversion inland of the railway is necessary here). The viaduct is a Grade

II listed building, and includes the second largest brick arch single span in Britain.

At the time of writing the Durham Coast Path is not waymarked, but the route is mostly obvious and the explanatory leaflet clear enough. Some of the ground is rough, although not especially difficult, and watch out for clarts in the denes (not a medical condition, you'll be glad to hear, but local terms for wet/muddy areas in the wooded gorges).

Beyond Beacon Hill the path leaves the side of the railway and takes to the low, rocky seashore and passes former collieries at Easington and Horden. Easington's Welfare Ground contains an avenue of eighty-one trees planted to commemorate the eighty-one miners killed in an underground explosion at nearby Ducks Bill in 1951.

South of Horden is Castle Eden Dene, a fine area for two reasons. The beautiful, 4-mile long wooded valley is a national nature reserve renowned for its yew, beech and oak, and the rare Durham Brown Argus butterfly. It so impressed historian Arthur Mee that he was inspired to write: 'It is indeed an Eden.' Another reason is that further upstream is Castle Eden Brewery, where decent real ale has been produced for 200 years.

The coast path continues alongside the natural arches and stacks of Blackhall, consisting of 18m-high reef limestone, to finish at Hart Station, inland of Crimdon Park. At the latter is a large and unlovely caravan park, and from the public car park on its southern side there are rather unappetising views of Hartlepool and industrial Teesside beyond. For those set on Hartlepool there is at least a path across the rough grassland and golf course of Hart Warren.

St Hilda was once abbess at Hartlepool, where the double monastery catered for both monks and nuns. She later, and more famously, set up a similar operation at Whitby, but in Hartlepool Hilda is remembered by the twelfth-century church that bears her name and which can be found on what is known as the Headland, which overlooks the new marina and waterside developments. Here you can visit the Historic Quay, with its full reconstruction of life in an eighteenth-century North-Eastern seaport.

But, let's face it, Hartlepool and industrial Cleveland are unlikely to figure in a walker's top ten. The Durham Coast Path is new and shows promise, while ahead the Cleveland Way's glorious cliff miles beckon, but in between it's not just unattractive – it literally stinks.

Although Seaton Sands stretches in an uninterrupted fashion to the mouth of the Tees, any further progress is in turn blocked by a nuclear power station, an oil terminal, and a chemical works. A turgid tramp along the A178 is the only answer for a dogged long-distance walker, but at least you get to cross the Tees at Middlesbrough on the famous transporter bridge, a towering, blue-painted Meccano-like construction that whisks you silently across the river on a platform held by cables (pedestrians are charged 20p for the privilege).

From Middlesbrough to Redcar any sane person would catch a bus and wind the window up tightly; but accepting that walkers are a breed apart you might like to consider the merits of the final stage of the Teesdale Way, a newly created long-distance footpath that follows the river for 100 miles. High up in the wild North Pennines the trail visits High Cup, Cauldron Snout, High Force and a number of other delectable locations. Downstream from Middlesbrough the Teesdale Way's final ten miles include the so-called Black Path, a remarkable track once used by sailors to reach their work and which passes through a nightmare of smelly, smoky, and quite simply massive industrial installations. At night the so-called Teesside Lights of the steelworks and ICI chemicals plant present a fascinating spectacle, but seen by day it is a different matter. Even the author of the Teesdale Way guidebook is forced to admit that these miles 'will be unlike any walking you have ever experienced before'. For the curious or the deranged (and for a route out to South Gare Breakwater) see the title listed in the Appendix for more details.

As the British Steel works slowly diminish behind you (who on earth chooses to stay at the caravan site next to it?) relax and walk into Redcar, admiring the distinctive scars that spear out into the waves. At low tide the sands around Redcar to Marske-by-the-Sea (note the Ship Inn) and Saltburn can be walked, and there are clifftop tracks, too. The RNLI's museum at Redcar includes the world's oldest surviving lifeboat. Built in 1800, 'Zetland' saved over 500 lives in the sixty-two years that it saw service off this coast.

SALTBURN – WHITBY (17 miles)

The sands eventually come to an end at Saltburn-by-the-Sea, a neat, unshowy place with a simple pier (its original length of 1,250 feet was halved in 1924 after the close attentions of a wayward ship). At the southern edge of the resort is the Ship Inn, once a haunt of smugglers and nowadays home to the Saltburn Smugglers Heritage Centre; while on the opposite side of the road is a tiny, well-preserved mortuary dated 1881. (Is there a connection?)

Here at Saltburn the 110-mile Cleveland Way National Trail meets the sea, having stomped around the North York Moors from Helmsley. For the next 50 miles or so you will share its mostly high and heady miles, as it clings to the cliff edge virtually all the way south to Filey. It's a stimulating and invigorating walk, but since these are the first heavyweight cliffs of the North Sea Coast that you will have encountered don't overstretch yourself – and take something to keep the wind out!

For the most part the trail is well-defined and obvious, but watch out for occasional erosion and some steep, towering cliffs. Rock Cliff, near Boulby, is in fact the highest on England's eastern seaboard (203m). Until recently the area around Skinningrove and Loftus was also notable for the mining of ironstone, and potash is still extracted near Boulby – from deposits lying over 1,400m below the surface. Before this, alum was mined, since alum shales lay close to the surface. The Boulby cliffs were worked until about 1850, and some old workings are still evident on the clifftop.

All of a sudden a narrow defile in the cliffs opens up and there nestles Staithes. An attractive old fishing village (Clovelly of the North, according to some), it was here that the young James Cook, Cleveland's famous son, had his first job, working in a grocer's shop. Within five years, however, the lure of a life on the sea had drawn him to Whitby – but that's still a few miles away. Make sure to visit the Captain Cook and Staithes Heritage Centre in the former Primitive Methodist Chapel (1880).

Past the well-named Cod and Lobster pub, head steeply up a lane through the village to regain the clifftop path. The route is obvious and well-waymarked, especially where erosion has forced diversions – to the north of Port Mulgrave, for instance.

After rounding Runswick Bay you eventually drop down to Sandsend, and the long, sandy approach to Whitby. If both weather and tide are favourable there is a lot to be said for walking the foreshore, preferably bootless.

WHITBY – ROBIN HOOD'S BAY (15 miles)

What do you look for in a seaside town? Probably a beach and some cliffs, maybe a busy harbour and a swing bridge, possibly a couple of amusement arcades and fish and chip shops; or how about a ruined abbey, clifftop church with fine boxed pews, and old, narrow streets lined with shops selling locally worked precious gems? For all of this, Whitby fits the bill. It even has a huge whalebone arch, reflecting the time when this was the country's leading whaling port, and it is reckoned that almost 3,000 had been landed by the time its whalers stopped for good in 1837. Since then Whitby has become better known for its shiny black jet, usually worn as jewellery but once burnt by the Romans who believed that its smoke cured hysteria. Technically, jet isn't a gemstone at all, but the compressed remains of wood from around 200 million years ago. Bram Stoker even set some of his famous *Dracula* in Whitby, and the quayside Dracula Experience tells more, situated next to the Ship public house (Vaux brewery).

Near the whale jaw arch there is also a statue of the good Captain Cook, who went to sea for the first time from Whitby's quayside in 1746 as apprentice seaman on a collier. Ten years later he joined the Royal Navy, and embarked on a series of famous voyages exploring the South Seas and discovering Australia which were brought to an end by natives in Hawaii who had him for supper.

The Cleveland Way resumes its clifftop passage southwards beyond the Abbey, which St Hilda founded in 657, and where Brother Caedmon is credited as writing the first English hymns.

The next seven miles to Robin Hood's Bay are straightforward. At Maw Wyke Hole, where a small stream falls into the sea below a caravan site, Wainwright's popular Coast-to-Coast route reaches the North Sea after its 190-mile trek from St Bees on the Cumbrian coast. It then joins the Cleveland Way across field edges for the short distance to Robin Hood's Bay, where custom dictates that Coast-to-Coast walkers rush into the North Sea to complete the baptising of the leather (a sure way to ruin a good pair of boots). This is another attractive East Coast village that, like Staithes and Runswick Bay before it, seems to be clinging on to the rocks in order to avoid slipping into the surf. There again, some vessels don't do much to help the situation. So close to the water is the Bay Hotel that in 1893 the bowsprit of the brig *Romulus* went clean through its window! As to the name, Robin Hood is no more likely to have lived or visited here than any of the other dozens of locations around the country associated with his name. One legend has an ageing Robin leaving Sherwood Forest for a safer place, with a boat kept handy should a quick exit be called for (Robin Hood in a seaside retirement bungalow – surely not!).

ROBIN HOOD'S BAY – SCARBOROUGH (16 miles)

A mile or so southwards the coast path passes Boggle Hole Youth Hostel, then climbs back on to the high cliffs at Ravenscar. The views back across Robin Hood's Bay are stunning, with low rock ledges extending out into the bay at low tide. Ravenscar may take its name from invading Danes of the third century, who according to the sagas bore the image of a raven on their standards; and before this the Romans built a signal station on the headland. In more recent times developers tried to build a resort here at the turn of this century (roads and drains were constructed, and a few plots of land sold), but the windy and exposed position didn't find many takers and the plans failed.

The coast path now continues along the sometimes slipping cliffs to Scarborough, negotiating a number of scenic indentations known as 'wykes'. Hayburn Wyke is the best, where the babbling Hayburn Beck tumbles into the sea. The cliffs afford the wooded glen shelter, where ash, hazel and hawthorn scrub, plus numerous mosses and ferns, are all to be found in a National Trust nature reserve leased by the Yorkshire Naturalists' Trust. It is a particularly pleasant spot, that benefits (as does much of the Cleveland Way's non-urban seaboard section) from the absence of a coastal road.

SCARBOROUGH – FLAMBOROUGH HEAD (20 miles)

As far as resorts go, Blackpool may be bigger but Scarborough is the oldest of the lot. It certainly enjoys a more pleasing setting, huddled tightly about the sloping cliffside around a bulky, castled headland, rather than stretched out along a flat coastal plain like its Lancashire rival. Scarborough's two beaches are separated by the remains of an 800-year-old castle, besieged six times and blown up once, following the Civil War, in 1649. But it was medicinal reasons that saw the town expand into today's size and shape and become Britain's first resort. Scarborough's spa properties were expounded as early as the 1620s, when water from a local stream was described as 'a most sovereign remedy against Hypondriak, Melancholly and

Windiness'. Forty years later a Dr Witte claimed that Scarborough's seawater 'dried up superfluous humours' and 'killed all manner of worms'; and so it was that – like Bath, Buxton, Epsom and Harrogate – Scarborough developed into a popular spa location but, unlike the others, its coastal location meant its long-term development would be very different. Not everyone received the miracle cure, however, and Anne Brontë died while staying here in 1849 and is buried in St Mary's churchyard.

From Scarborough it's only a short hop to Filey, although at the time of writing a diversion is still in force around the grounds of the former Holbeck Hall Hotel on the southern side of the resort. In the full gaze of the public the building tumbled unceremoniously into the North Sea in 1993 when the ground on which it stood became unstable. Considerable relandscaping has taken place, and the national trail should soon resume its original course above South Bay.

There is some very pleasant, shady woodland before the popular sands of Cayton Bay open up; then it is clifftop all the way to Filey Brigg. Beware, however, for the grassy path sticks seawards of several caravan parks and at times the distance between fence and cliff edge is narrow enough to concentrate the mind on other things than the view. Watch your footing!

According to legend, the thin, dark cliff finger of Filey Brigg was the beginning of a bridge that the Devil planned to build to join Yorkshire to Europe. There is a sort of monument/sculpture on the clifftop to mark the end of the Cleveland Way and the beginning of the Wolds Way. The latter runs for 83 miles across the Yorkshire Wolds via Market Weighton to the Humber – earmark it for another day if you haven't already sampled its quiet pleasures. At your feet the gentle curve of Filey Bay sweeps out to the impressive cliffs of Bempton and Flamborough Head. It's an enticing prospect, but first descend to the unspoilt sandy seafront of Filey, from where traditional East Coast cobles, tough little boats flat-bottomed for beach landing, are still launched. The likes of Charlotte Brontë and Frederick Delius enjoyed the quiet surroundings of Filey, and there's plenty more history waiting to be unearthed in the Folk Museum.

At low tide you can walk the lovely sands of Muston and Hunmanby all the way to the boulder clay outcrops at the foot of Speeton Cliffs. From here climb steps up to a track to Speeton, but before reaching the village turn left for a superb clifftop route to

Flamborough Head. (A very high tide or poor weather may mean a diversion inland around the series of clifftop holiday camps.)

Now you are back on the soaring heights (up to 130m), and they don't come much more impressive than north of Buckton. Here, and along at Bempton, the huge chalk cliffs support England's largest breeding seabird colony, and Britain's only nesting gannets. Until earlier this century men used to be lowered down the sheer cliff face on ropes in order to collect the eggs of guillemots, kittiwakes and razorbills, a practice known locally as 'climming'. As many as 300–400 eggs were collected daily, and then sold locally for food, or sent to the West Riding for use in the patent leather trade. Remarkably few men were ever injured, even though their crash helmets consisted of a cloth cap stuffed with straw. Since 1971 the RSPB has managed the site, with an information centre and wheelchair access, and there are fabulous views from the track that runs the length of the clifftop. The screams of up to 200,000 birds can make it pretty noisy, too.

A steep slipway affords access to the sea at North Landing, after which the path continues along the heritage coast to Flamborough Head, with its fine white lighthouse that is often open to the public. An older, chalk version built in 1674 can also be seen, and remains the oldest surviving light tower in England (although some maintain that it was simply a lookout tower). Shipping is also alerted to the dangers of the cliffs by another means, as a sign explains for visitors on foot: 'The public are advised that a fog signal emitting a very loud noise may be sounded in this vicinity at any time without prior warning.' A short distance inland is Flamborough itself, a pleasant village that boasts two pubs most appropriately named the Ship and the Seabirds.

Nearby is a toposcope, claiming that Land's End and John o'Groats are both 362 miles away. It was erected in memory of a naval battle fought off the headland in 1779 during the American War of Independence. The American privateer John Paul Jones, considered the founder of the United Sates navy although actually born in Scotland, led three ships in an attack on a British convoy, and although he eventually captured HMS *Serapis* and claimed victory his own ship sank and he fled to the Netherlands.

FLAMBOROUGH HEAD – HORNSEA (18 miles)

Occasionally signposted as the Headland Walk, the clifftop route

now swings westwards, and beyond the Heritage Coast Visitor
Centre up the lane at South Landing it slowly drops down via
Sewerby into Bridlington. Local fishermen used to have boats at
both North and South Landing, either side of Flamborough Head,
and sail from the one which had the most favourable conditions in
terms of tide and wind.

Further on you descend a steep valley mouth and cross the
southern end of Danes Dyke, a mysterious, 2½-mile bank and
ditch that cuts off Flamborough Head from the rest of England.
Dating from some time in the Dark Ages, or possibly as long ago
as the Bronze Age, no one is quite sure what purpose it served,
although most experts agree that it probably wasn't anything to do
with the Danes. More baffling, still, is the fact that after sacking
Flamborough seven times Danish Vikings did settle here, and that
the peculiar local accent that lasted until quite recently earned
Flamborough the title of 'Little Denmark'.

Not so much Scandinavian as the broad vowels of Leeds and
Bradford fill the streets of Bridlington, a popular resort which still
retains a busy harbour with 300 berths. It was here on 10 February
1871 that a great storm suddenly blew up, catching unawares
dozens of mainly coal-carrying vessels plying between Newcastle
and London, which often sought shelter in Bridlington Bay. Despite
the heroic efforts of the two lifeboats as many as seventy men
were drowned, including six of the lifeboatmen, and thirty ships
lost. As a direct result of the tragedy Samuel Plimsoll introduced
a new law requiring all merchant vessels to make a mark on their
hulls indicating their cargo loading levels, which became known
as the Plimsoll line. Should you want warning of rough weather
today there is a storm cone on the South Pier which is hoisted if a
gale is imminent: peak upwards signals a northerly gale, and peak
downwards for a southerly.

South of Bridlington there is a long and uninterrupted sweep of
sand all the way to Skipsea, and should the tide be safe it is perfectly
possible to walk by the waves the whole distance. There is also an
intermittent public right of way along the clifftop, but since this is
crumbling into the sea on an alarmingly frequent basis you are likely
to have difficulties. For instance, the clifftop campsite at Ulrome
that we stayed at had recently repositioned its border fence back
from the cliff edge, but yet again it was under threat. The local
authority estimates that as much as 7½ feet of land is lost to the

sea each year along this seaboard, and since Roman times the shore has retreated by almost two miles and up to twenty-three villages have disappeared.

From Skipsea the low tide foreshore may still be walked, but the safer route is along the road to Atwick and then back via the sand to Hornsea.

HORNSEA – SPURN HEAD (31 miles)

Hornsea is worth pausing over, for in addition to its pottery and folk museum there is Hornsea Mere, Yorkshire's largest natural freshwater lake, where as many as 170 bird species are recorded each year. It is an important refuge for waterfowl, plus migrants like whinchats and whitethroats, and wayward foreign visitors such as the blue-headed wagtail. Hornsea is also the eastern end of the Trans Pennine Trail, a 200-mile 'multi-user' route via Hull that finishes on the West Coast at Southport, Merseyside.

South of the town the sandy strip continues, but if the army firing range is active you must stick to the coast road. From Aldbrough onwards there is a continuous public right of way along the coast to beyond Withernsea. Again, the soft, boulder clay cliffs are prone to erosion and walking tracks can disappear, so that the sand and shingle shore may be a better bet. However, for the most part this long, straight and flat Holderness coastline is pretty featureless and fails to inspire. Fine, perhaps, for exercising the dog or idling away an afternoon with children; or maybe for a few hours moodily spent staring at the sloppy grey waves and thinking profound thoughts, but give me the bold chalk cliffs of Flamborough any time.

There's not a lot to hold the attention at Withernsea, from where a cliff track runs to just beyond Holmpton, at which point you will have to join a lane in order to pass landwards of Easington gas terminal. Much of our North Sea gas comes ashore here, via the large BP and British Gas installations, but gradually the sea has edged nearer as the cliffs have fallen, finally forcing the authorities into remedial action. South of Easington village you can regain the shore and follow the narrowing spit of land all the way to the far tip of Spurn Head (but bear in mind, of course, that you will have to walk all the way back again).

SPURN HEAD – HUMBER BRIDGE (37 miles)

Strange though it may sound, there have been four previous Spurn

Heads before the present-day one that you see dwindling out into the mouth of the Humber. Previous versions have all succumbed to the sea, taking with them the earlier settlements of Ravenserodd and Ravenser. The former was thought to have begun as a landing-spot for the Vikings (hence the 'raven' in the name), and was where Harold Hardrada limped off home after defeat at Stamford Bridge in 1066. Ravenser was its port, and at one time they were important enough to return Members of Parliament. Both are now somewhere a couple of miles out to sea. It's quite possible that the present Spurn Head may change location, as history shows that there is a regular 250-year cycle of disintegration and regrowth. The spit is formed from boulder clay deposits washed down from the Holderness coast, and its fragile position is constantly shifting as new drifts accumulate, and periodic breaches are made by storms.

It's not a place you can easily get lost either. The narrowing thread of land includes a concrete road often partly covered by blown sand, and here and there you may see iron railway tracks embedded in the ground. They belonged to the Spurn Railway, which ran from Kilnsea to the Head and was built some time around the First World War for military purposes. Although it had its own locomotives, the line was frequently run solely by wind power, and speeds of up to 40mph were achieved. Bizarrely, the wagons used for this had no means of braking, and the men had to resort to primitive methods such as throwing a sleeper on to the track before the front wheels.

There are several waymarked trails (Spurn Path, Seaside Path) that usefully keep you off the vegetation and duneland used by nesting birds and rare landfalls from the continent. Pallas's warbler, hoopoe and even a yellow-billed cuckoo from North America have all been spotted on Spurn. Oh yes, twitchers by the bucketload here. But at the far tip there is a tiny human community, involving a coastguard tower, café, lifeboat station, and the Humber Pilot Service which helps guide an endless convoy of massive craft bound for Immingham and Hull. There was even once a school for the children of the lifeboatmen and other workers. Altogether it is an odd, desolate and yet fascinating place; so if you want to see Spurn Head for yourself, here's your chance before it disappears.

The river before you is a monster by any standards. Technically the Humber is not so much a river but a confluence of the River Trent and the Yorkshire Ouse. It drains almost 30% of the land area of England, and in its catchment live around 11 million people; it includes some of the country's most industrial and urban centres, like Leeds and Birmingham. On the south bank its mouth and lower stages are tarnished by Grimsby and Immingham Docks, but on the north Spurn Head gives way to an empty shore of marsh and mudflat that extends almost as far as the edge of Hull. It's fairly walkable, too, but although there is an embankment track from Kilnsea to Stone Creek it is not technically a right of way, and although walkers have used it without objection in the past you may be better advised to follow lanes via Skeffling and Patrington. Return to the Humber at Stone Creek, after a wander through the vast, reclaimed farmland around Sunk Island, and now there is a continuous public right of way along the river edge all the way to Paull.

The grassy picnic site at Paull is a tremendous place to view both the city of Hull and all the antics on the Humber. A BP plant and docks hamper immediate waterside progress, so some pavement is necessary to enter Kingston-upon-Hull (to give the city its proper title). There has been a settlement on the River Hull for about 800 years, and its name comes from the granting of its first charter by Edward I in 1299. As a port it predates even Liverpool, and has maintained Britain's trading links with the major Baltic and Scandinavian trading centres. Today many of the older docks have vanished, and Hull's seven miles of waterfront now also sport new offices, shops and housing, plus a large marina, the latter being the final resting place of the well-known Spurn lightship which was decommissioned in 1975. In the Old Town near the River Hull is the birthplace of William Wilberforce, where relics of the slave trade which he helped to topple, plus personal effects and mementoes, are on display.

From St Andrew's Quay, former home of Hull's fishing fleet, there is a riverside path to Hessle, and despite the close attentions of the A63 it is hard not to avert your gaze from the awe-inspiring Humber Bridge that is gradually expanding before your eyes. Incidentally, the waterfront route through Hull to the bridge is part of the Trans Pennine Trail, which we encountered at Hornsea, and it is mainly through the strenuous efforts of its Development Officer that the city centre waterfront route is now open and accessible to walkers.

Although it seems just an extension of Hull, Hessle in fact dates from Anglo-Saxon times. The Ferry Boat Inn is testimony to the river service to New Holland that only ceased when the bridge was opened; and Hessle Haven was for a long time an important shipbuilding centre. By now the wide and well-walked riverside track will have taken you up to the bridge, at which point you can choose which side of the bridge to walk, or else continue underneath for refreshment and education at the Humber Bridge Country Park.

Pick of the walks

BAMBURGH – AMBLE (30 miles): superb weekend walk along wide, unspoilt beaches and low, dark outcrops. A quiet and delectable heritage coast of fishing villages and castles.

FLAMBOROUGH HEAD CIRCULAR (5–8 miles): with Flamborough village as a base, it's a straightforward stroll via South Landing to the lighthouse, then north to seabird city and towering cliffs before field paths back.

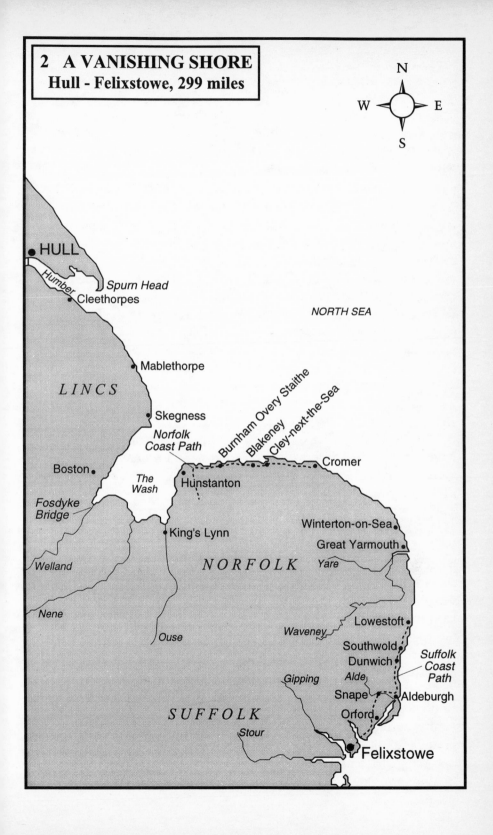

2 A VANISHING SHORE
Hull - Felixstowe, 299 miles

N
W · E
S

HULL

Humber

Spurn Head
Cleethorpes

NORTH SEA

Mablethorpe

LINCS

Skegness

Norfolk
Coast Path

Burnham Overy Staithe

Blakeney

Cley-next-the-Sea

Cromer

Boston

The
Wash

Hunstanton

Fosdyke
Bridge

Winterton-on-Sea

King's Lynn

Great Yarmouth

Welland

NORFOLK

Yare

Nene

Lowestoft

Waveney

Ouse

Southwold

Dunwich

Suffolk
Coast
Path

Gipping

Alde

Snape

Aldeburgh

Orford

SUFFOLK

Stour

Felixstowe

HUMBER BRIDGE – CLEETHORPES (28 miles)

To walk the Humber Bridge from one end to the other is an absorbing exercise. Not the quietest 1⅓ miles you will ever face – the wind is too keen and the vehicles too close to the walk/cycleway for that – but the views are fantastic, and if you take it slowly there is a palpable sense of floating way above the muddy river. As all the tourist bumf at the visitor centre on the north bank will tell you, when the Humber Bridge was opened by the Queen in 1981 it became the longest span suspension bridge in the world (the main span is 4,626 ft or 1,410m). Mug, T-shirt, car sticker – we got the lot, and possible collectors' items they may be, since the bridge is soon to lose the record to a new Scandinavian effort, and will then be eclipsed by some huge new construction in the Far East. Perhaps all the Humber Bridge merchandise will have to be altered to something like 'Once the world's longest span suspension bridge'.

On the southern bank former clay pits at Barton-upon-Humber have been turned into wildlife refuges, and where twenty busy yards once worked the alluvial deposits to produce bricks and tiles now the likes of grebes and coots go about their business. The Romans' Ermine Street crossed the Humber near here, which explains Barton's origin, although then it was possible to ford the river at low tide. Much later a ferry service developed, but not all its passengers were impressed. In 1725 Daniel Defoe described Barton as 'a town noted for nothing that I know of but an ill-favoured dangerous passage, or ferry'. But perhaps his discontent was not surprising, as his boat took an incredible four hours to complete the rough crossing, plus he had to share its confines with twelve cows, fifteen horses, 'and about seventeen to eighteen passengers, called Christians'.

The 141-mile Viking Way begins on the waterfront at sleepy Barton, initially following the Humber upstream for a few miles before turning towards the Lincolnshire Wolds for a twisting journey south to Oakham. Your direction, however, is east, back out along the Humber to the sea and for the first few miles this is straightforward enough, along the bank of the river to New

Holland, where the railway and pier once served a ferry to Hull; and then around what's been called the Humber's elbow to North Killingholme Haven. This is also the route of the Nev Cole Way, named after the late James Neville Cole, well-known local rambler, tireless champion of walkers' rights, and founder of the Wanderlust Rambling Club who pioneered the route. But by now the scene will be rather dominated by the chimneys, pipes, massive oil container tanks, jetties and the other assorted paraphernalia of Immingham's heavy industry. It's not very pleasant at all. The docks will need a long road detour if you insist on continuing, although the river bank can be resumed for the rest of the way into Grimsby. But it's not a pretty journey.

From being the country's largest fishing port fifty years ago, Grimsby has successfully transformed itself into a major food-producing centre, although its fish market is still among the largest in the country and in 1995 Grimsby celebrated a seafood festival. The past is well-preserved and expertly presented at the National Fishing Heritage Centre, on Alexandra Dock, where life both on board a trawler and back on dry land is brilliantly recreated – sights, sounds, and even the smells of a North Sea journey to Arctic fishing grounds are all evoked. Among the odd fishing facts that come to light is that many trawlermen cannot swim, reasoning that if the sea gods want you they will take you. Also, if a bird taps on the bridge window of a ship it signifies an impending death; and never utter words such as pig, egg, clergyman or rabbit when aboard a trawler, since these are meant to spell bad luck!

CLEETHORPES – MABLETHORPE (23 miles)
Ahead are the broad sands and marshes of Lincolnshire, providing an easy if flat journey south towards the Wash and East Anglia. It begins with the popular and noisy resort of Cleethorpes, a rather unremarkable place whose main claim to fame is that the Greenwich Meridian – zero degrees longitude – passes through it. The plaque on Marine Parade celebrating this fact also relates that it is 9,895 miles to the South Pole and 2,513 miles to the North Pole from this spot.

Once Lakeside and all the other run-of-the-mill attractions have been left behind follow the sea wall southwards. A short diversion up the Louth Canal to Tetney Lock will be necessary before returning to the low, indistinct coast and a public right of way out to Donna Nook. MOD warning notices describe the boundaries of the offshore bombing range and what might happen if you stray too far: 'Danger – when access allowed do not touch any military debris. It may explode and kill you.' At Donna Nook you may actually see the fighters zoom in and take pot shots at targets out on the sands. The planes come in very close and not surprisingly the noise is absolutely deafening. But this still doesn't deter a fair number of visitors who get the folding chairs and flask out of the boot and dig in for an afternoon's planespotting. Very odd.

An official from the range assures me that unless otherwise indicated the sea wall/marsh-edge track can be walked south from Donna Nook to Saltfleet, and indeed is a popular route. Despite the occasional noise from the sky the mile upon mile of sand and saltmarsh, which at low tide seems to make the sea vanish, is home to an array of birds and other wildlife. Sea lavender flourishes and marsh orchids can be found, while the Saltfleetby-Theddlethorpe Dunes nature reserve is noted, in particular, as an important home of the Natterjack toad. Off Saltfleet are vast beds of marsh samphire, or glasswort, a small herbaceous annual with thick green stems. Once burnt to provide ash for use in the glass-making industry, samphire is also known as Poor Man's Asparagus. It is best washed and soaked in cold water to remove the saltiness, then boiled for a few minutes in a small amount of water and served with a generous knob of butter and lemon juice.

Saltfleet was originally a Roman port, and marked the eastern end of the Fosse Way, the mighty Roman road that led via Lincoln all the way to Exeter. Nowadays it is a quietish little place with a tin hut of an amusement arcade and a few bored-looking holidaymakers. If the conditions are right stick to the track above the shore and continue along the seemingly endless sands all the way into Mablethorpe.

'A traditional family resort, offering all the facilities you would expect' the rather candid tourist leaflet admits. The bulk of Mablethorpe shelters behind a huge terraced concrete promenade designed to keep the North Sea out and the popular golden sands in place. The donkeys do good trade here, and in the early evening are shepherded home at some pace along the prom by a young man on a bicycle.

MABLETHORPE – SKEGNESS (15 miles)
The Romans were among the first to start repelling the North Sea

and developing new, rich tracts of farmland; but sea walls and other man-made defences have been breached too often to allow the inhabitants of Lincolnshire's low-lying coast to rest easy. We have seen erosion at work already on this vulnerable East Coast, and there will be more still in Norfolk and Suffolk, but over the years Lincolnshire has suffered as much as any from storm surges and high spring tides that have regularly inundated the land, sometimes with disastrous results.

In the great floods of 1953, forty-three of the 307 people killed lived on this next section of the coast, between Mablethorpe and Skegness. Three further floods have hit since, and coastal defence work continues in an effort to try and protect the land. The current project involves depositing millions of tons of sand to create new, higher beaches – but most of this will be washed away in ten years' time!

After the floods in 1953 Sir Winston Churchill launched a policy of 'No Surrender' to the sea, but recent official thinking seems to be placing more emphasis on defending significantly populated areas rather than low-value farmland, and a move away from large, expensive projects involving mile upon mile of concrete wall. Indeed, one school of thought is that the coast should be left to evolve naturally, and that the huge sums of money spent on trying to shut out the sea are ultimately a wasted exercise. Experts at English Nature have spoken of 'managed retreat', and of 'soft defences' allowing penetration by a regulated amount of seawater that in turn will encourage the growth of new saltmarshes to act as a buffer against rising sea levels generally. These have been caused by global warming, as well as the fact that Great Britain continues to tilt south-eastwards as the land mass recovers its equilibrium following the last Ice Age. Managed retreat is an interesting idea, not least because the cost of rebuilding just one mile of artificial sea defences is usually well over £1 million, and it is reckoned that up to 200 miles of England coastline needs attention.

All this means that you might occasionally face some disruption should you wish to walk the coast between Mablethorpe and Skegness, but it is unlikely that your route will ever be blocked. Linking many of the small holiday resorts ahead – Sutton-on-Sea, Chapel St Leonards, Ingoldmells – is a high concrete promenade, with the option of many well-walked tracks and, of course, the beach. Acre Gap, near Sutton-on-Sea, was the proposed site of a handsome new Edwardian resort to be called Woldsea, but in the end the plans were scuppered by the outbreak of the First World War, and only the Grange and Links Hotel and a few other buildings were ever built.

A little further on, at Huttoft Bank, huge chunks of rocks brought over from Norway defend the shoreline. From here it is necessary to switch to the broad, safe beach, past Chapel St Leonards and Ingoldmells (I have learnt lately that a huge theme park is being planned for the latter). Then stay seawards of the golf course and stroll the wide, welcoming golden sands into what many people know simply as Skeggy.

I doubt that many of the tens of thousands of holidaymakers that arrive every year realise that the name actually comes from the Scandinavian word 'Skeggi', meaning 'the bearded one'. It's likely that Skeggi was in fact a Viking leader, whose force invaded and settled, although their original settlement was washed away some time later. Modern Skegness is, of course, due to another wave of incomers. Once the railway steamed into Skegness in 1863 and the first excursion passengers arrived from King's Cross, London, a few years later, visitors began to come in ever-increasing droves. 'Skegness is so bracing' boomed the famous railway posters. The area is known to many as the home of the first Butlin Holiday Camp, which was established at Ingoldmells (site of today's Butlin Funcoast World) as far back as 1936, and one of the original chalets that has been carefully preserved is now a listed building. The holidays were specifically targeted at large, low-income working-class families, and advertised with slogans such as 'A Week's Holiday for a Week's Wage'. The theme of the camps is captured in a verse from the 'Butlin Buddies Song':

> *Leave your shop or factory, your office or your home,*
> *Give yourself a holiday beside the shining foam,*
> *Come on all you scholars now and put away your studies,*
> *Come and join the happy band that's known as Butlin Buddies,*
> *Hi-ya fellers, we are Butlin Buddies.*

Who could resist that?

SKEGNESS – FOSDYKE BRIDGE (35 miles)

South of the resort you can follow the lane across Bramble Hills to the picnic site at Gibraltar Point. There is a visitor centre for the nature reserve, and fine views south over the massive expanse of the Wash.

However, should you want to continue further south the lack of public rights of way means that you will have to detour briefly inland, via Wainfleet St Mary, before a minor road leads to New Marsh and from there an embankment path returns you to the shore. The sea wall path then leads all the way south via Freiston Shore to the mouth of the Witham, and up to Boston. It is likely to be a solitary but stirring walk, with miles of reclaimed farmland one side and the vastness of the Wash the other. The sky seems immense, and you may find yourself gazing endlessly at the cloud formations.

Lincolnshire's fragile boundary with the sea is in the process of being mended along this stretch too, and sea defence work has temporarily made some sections of the sea wall between Skegness and Boston impassable. However, public rights of way should not be affected in the long run, but it may be wise to check with the relevant local authority before setting off.

Eventually the endless sea wall reaches the Haven, and the man-made banks of the River Witham. Visible upstream is Boston's famous Stump, a navigational aid for many centuries and quite handy for the walker who may be seeking reassurance amid the sea of featureless marshland. At the newly created Havenside Country Park is a memorial to what became known as the Pilgrim Fathers, who set sail from near this point, now known as Scotia Creek, in September 1607. They didn't get very far first time, mind you. The small Puritan community from Scrooby, just over the county border in Nottinghamshire, bribed a Dutch captain to take them to religious freedom overseas; but, instead, he informed the authorities and the whole lot were returned to Boston, several ending up in the cells in the Guildhall. A second attempt was more successful, and after living in the Netherlands for several years, they then set sail in the *Speedwell* to join the *Mayflower* at Southampton for a voyage to North America. But the rest of that story can wait for a few pages.

The so-called Carol Williams Walk takes you into Boston itself, an old and very likeable place with a tremendous church. Back in the Middle Ages the well-off citizens of this prosperous wool staple port decided that the way to enter Heaven's Gates was not to flaunt their wealth by building a huge cathedral but instead construct a humble parish church. But, of course, St Botolph's, begun in 1309, turned out to be the largest parish church in the country, with a 83m-high lantern tower to boot. There is a small charge to climb the 365 steps to the top of the Stump, but the views over the county and out to the coast are splendid. The 'Stump', incidentally, may refer to a spire that was never built on top of the tower.

An embankment path along the south side of the Haven leads back out to the sea (although it is likely that all you will see is never-ending saltmarsh), then along the Welland's channelled banks to cross at Fosdyke Bridge. On the opposite bank is the Ship (Bateman's – 'Good Honest Ales'), from where the waterside path leads back out and around the Wash.

FOSDYKE BRIDGE – KING'S LYNN (33 miles)
To walk the sea wall around the Wash is to walk through a scenery as flat as anything you will find in Britain. Inland are the Fens, where the drained farmland even dips below sea level. Several hundred years ago most of this was covered by the North Sea, that distant pool of water that at spring high tides surges up to the sea wall, and then retreats leaving an expanse of mud that could swallow a small town. It is a land of horizontals: fields, dykes, banks and sea stretch the vision wide; it presents seascapes of incredible space and emptiness.

Towards Gedney Drove End there is an offshore bombing range used by planes from RAF Holbeach. Periodically they scream in and take aim at two bright orange marker ships moored out in the water, and when this occurs – more often on weekdays than weekends – observe official signs and red flags, and be prepared to modify your route.

Follow the Nene Outfall Cut inland to Sutton Bridge, and back via the river's artificial eastern bank. Signs warn that the path may flood at high tide. The mouth is guarded by a lighthouse on each bank, built to commemorate the opening of the Nene's outfall in 1831 rather than as a navigational aid, curiously enough, and the eastern one before you was where the naturalist and artist Peter Scott lived between 1933 and 1939. This champion of British birdlife is remembered here in several ways. The Wash National Nature Reserve is dedicated to his memory; and, from here to King's Lynn, the grassy sea wall path has been named the Peter Scott Walk, a ten-mile stretch that affords good views of the low, wooded hills and sandy beaches of north-west Norfolk, and, like the miles before it, provides an ornithological feast for the quiet and observant walker. The Wash supports more birds than any other estuary in the whole of Britain; in winter the number of wildfowl and waders can exceed 400,000! Despite forgetting our binoculars, in the space of a few miles our list of sightings on a cool May afternoon included redshank, shelduck, oystercatcher and terns, plus skylark, goldfinch and yellowhammer. A passing twitcher drew our attention to a male marsh harrier, gliding over the fields in the distance; and then there was a common seal or two out on the sandbanks – the Wash supports Europe's largest group, in fact. Nearby, about a mile or so offshore, is a tiny, artificial island rising out of the mud. It was built in 1975 as part of a study into the construction of freshwater reservoirs, but proved so popular with seabirds that the Fenland Wildfowlers' Association made it a permanent nesting site in 1987. (In order not to disturb the birds, and also because tidal marshes are dangerous to walk upon in general, it is advisable to stay on the sea wall path at all times.)

The Peter Scott Walk – or the Wash Coast Path, as the leaflet guide also calls it – finishes at West Lynn, where there is a year-round passenger ferry across the Great Ouse to King's Lynn, or else a bridge a little further upstream.

An important port from as early as the eleventh century, Lynn (as the locals call it) continues to receive shipping, although pilots are necessary to navigate the hazardous channels and sandbanks of the Wash. Rather unusually the town has two separate market places, and also two medieval guildhalls, one of which (now the town hall) is decorated in fine chequered flint.

KING'S LYNN – HUNSTANTON (18 miles)
As inviting as it may seem on the map, there is technically no right of way along the shore to Snettisham Scalp from the mouth of the Great Ouse, so if you are a law-abiding walker you will have to make an inland trek via the Norman remains of Castle Rising and perhaps Sandringham Country Park before rejoining the sea at Shepherd's Port. From here to Hunstanton and beyond stretch inviting golden sands or firmer tracks back from the shore.

The RSPB's reserve south of the caravans and chalets at Snettisham Beach is worth pausing over. There are saltings and mudflats, plus shingle banks and former gravel workings that now house a visitor centre and hides. Among the winter attractions are divers, long-tailed duck and red-breasted merganser.

Hunstanton's claim to fame is that it is the only East Coast resort where you can watch the sun setting over the sea – because it faces west over the Wash. A popular Victorian resort, its open spaces, flower borders and rather haphazard street planning give it a relaxed air. An interesting but fast disappearing visitor attraction is its striped cliffs, comprising bands of red and white chalk and deep brown carstone, which can be inspected from below at low tide – but do keep a safe distance from the cliff base.

HUNSTANTON – BURNHAM OVERY STAITHE (15 miles)
Either walk the beach or green above, past the lighthouse, and out via the old town. If you are keeping to the sand you should eventually cut inland on a clear public footpath. Otherwise stick to the signs for the Norfolk Coast Path National Trail, which runs for a total of 44 miles between Hunstanton and Cromer, and is joined by the ancient Peddars Way near here at Holme-next-the-Sea. It is a path not always lavishly waymarked with national trail acorn signs, but since the route is by and large obvious it really doesn't need to be. Forget the boots and packs of the Cleveland Way, the crowds of the Pennine Way, or the horses and bikes of the South Downs Way – this is one national trail that is quiet, unspoilt and quite simply *relaxing* to walk.

From Old Hunstanton it follows a firm footpath landwards of a golf course, then takes to a rolling boardwalk through Holme Dunes Nature Reserve. Look out for sand fescue and the deep-rooted sea holly. Behind the visitor centre at The Firs is a distinctive clump of Corsican pines, where hides overlook Broad Water and other sheltered pools; and then the path follows a creek full of small boats in varying states of health to Thornham.

For the short distance between Thornham and Brancaster there is no coastal walking route, and the official path deviates inland. If you want to visit Titchwell Marsh RSPB reserve stick to the A149 instead. Here reclaimed pasture was returned to saltmarsh following the 1953 floods, and since then avocets have begun breeding, and warblers and bearded tits nest in the reeds.

The coast path resumes at Brancaster, where the Ship Inn makes another appearance, but the vessel in question is none other than the *Victory*. A couple of miles along the road another pub is simply called the Hero, and all is explained by its sign which depicts Horatio Lord Nelson, born nearby in Burnham Thorpe. Follow the track along the edge of Brancaster Marsh and out along the sea wall to Burnham Overy Staithe. Whelks and mussels are still farmed at Brancaster Staithe, which also used to handle coal and grain.

BURNHAM OVERY STAITHE – CLEY-NEXT-THE-SEA (17 miles)
Leave the flint-decorated buildings beside the quiet, picturesque creek for a sea wall walk out to the vast area of saltings and sand dunes towards Gun Hill. In high summer sea lavender provides a purple carpet, while in autumn it turns red with samphire, a delicacy often on sale from local shops.

To the west is Scolt Head, a wide and wild site of shingle and saltmarsh and dune, while ahead is yet another national nature reserve bordering Holkham Bay (this part of the Norfolk coast is more or less one gigantic nature reserve). This one is in fact the largest in the country, stretching from Burnham Norton as far east as Stiffkey, and most of it belongs to the Holkham estate. The centrepiece of the estate is the Palladian Holkham Hall, which sits amid woods and parkland inland, and is the ancestral home of the Earls of Leicester.

Keep to the established track through the dunes and by the lovely pine woods of Holkham Meals. The trees were planted at the end of the last century in one of the earliest attempts to stabilise sand dunes and so protect reclaimed agricultural land from windblown sand. Lately birch, oak and willow have all been introduced to provide a better environment for birdlife. Over the years the shelter afforded by the Corsican and Scots pines has attracted an array of migrants and rarities, including a yellow browed bunting in 1975.

As with so much of this shy, gentle Norfolk coast, so little spoilt by human hand, the unhurried and inquisitive walker has treats in store. Time it so that you wander from Burnham in the late afternoon or evening sunshine, and take any one of the deep, sandy tracks through the cool, peaceful woodland and discover Wells beach. When the old wooden huts have closed their doors and the crowds have romped off to scoff fish and chips on Wells quayside this is an exquisite spot, a place to linger and contemplate life.

When you've done with contemplation follow the high-tide bank into Wells, past a huge caravan and campsite. A plaque explains that the bank was built in 1978 following a surge tide that completely flooded the area – a small ship was even deposited on the quayside during the gales. The high-water marks for both 1978 and the devastating 1953 floods are shown, and are quite staggering.

Wells is a busy but very likeable little place, with a small harbour that is home to yachts and a few fishing boats. Some bigger ships do still tie up here, but gone are the days when they would load up with malt, corn and barley for the brewing industry. In fact there were once three brewers and four maltsters in the town itself in order to satisfy the demands of the forty local inns, and it is recorded that some of the workers at the maltings were occasionally paid in beer! Follow the road past the chandlers on to the grassy sea wall towards Stiffkey. Seawards are extensive saltmarshes, and should you wander across one of the tracks to the dunes the only sound to disturb the peace will either be the wind or the black-headed gulls that nest here in their thousands.

Stiffkey, a quiet little spot that sometimes pronounces itself 'Stukey', had a most engaging rector in the 1930s. Revd Harold Davidson became known as the 'prostitutes' parson', since he spent much of his time away from the village trying to reclaim the souls of those who worked in Soho. Defrocked for his efforts, he ended up in a barrel on Blackpool's Golden Mile as a one-man show berating the church, and then more bizarrely still moved to a Skegness amusement park where he sat among lions, until one of them decided to eat him.

At Morston Marsh the National Trust has a small information centre, with an observation balcony. There are boat trips to Blakeney Point to see the seals, although this massive shingle spit is better known as Britain's most important site for nesting terns. Common, little and sandwich terns can all be seen at close range from the National Trust's hides. Access is from Cley Eye, further on along the path near Cley-next-the-Sea, which is reached along the sea wall path via the attractive flint and brick village of Blakeney. Do not attempt to wade across the creeks or channels, by the way, even at low tide. Apart from the fact that you will probably disturb the wildlife, the mud is often soft and treacherous and the incoming waters can rapidly overtake a stricken pedestrian.

CLEY-NEXT-THE-SEA – WINTERTON-ON-SEA (37 miles)
From the well-preserved brick tower windmill at Cley follow the

Beach Road out to the sea at Cley Eye ('eye' is Old English for island and Cley rhymes with it). Turn left for a long shingle crunch to Blakeney Point, or right for an even longer shingle crunch to Weybourne. The latter is the course of the coast path, although the actual right of way is at the foot of the rather firmer inland side of the shingle bank. This is just as well, for a prolonged walk along pebbles can be exhausting, even where like here they are fairly tightly packed. Your feet tend to slip, ever so slightly, at every footfall, which inhibits a relaxed gait and after a while can become quite infuriating.

To take your mind off things gaze at the waves and the open sea, which you will not have seen close up for some time now; or inland over Cley Marshes, truly a mecca for twitchers great and small. Over the far side of the coast road they congregate at the Norfolk Naturalists Trust's visitor centre, but they will also pop up before you on the coast path, zoom lens straining for a sight of an avocet or a bittern.

Passing Weybourne the marsh and duneland give way to rising brown cliffs that continue to Cromer and beyond. But these are not stable cliffs, and in stormy weather or after heavy rain take appropriate care, since the path keeps to the cliff edge all the way into Sheringham. Weybourne Hope, incidentally, offers seaborne traffic both the shelter of the cliffs and deep water close to the shore. It was feared that this could be used by an attacking force, and from the days of the Armada came the verse:

He who would old England win
Must at Weybourne Hope begin.

More recently fears were expressed that Nazi submarines could also use this place to mount an attack.

Smoke and whistles are likely to belong to the North Norfolk Steam Railway, which terminates at Sheringham, and beyond the pleasant little resort the official coast path reaches Cromer after a lengthy inland circuit via Beacon Hill in order to avoid a ghastly nest of caravans that has colonised the clifftop of East Runton. However, a far better option enjoyed by many holidaymakers is to walk the sand and shingle beach below the cliffs between the two resorts. Cromer's very own Beach Inspector recommends the walk, but *only* when the tide is low or falling.

And so to Cromer, the most genteel of Victorian resorts,

home to tasty crabs and one of the few remaining end-of-pier
theatres. However, a few years ago an unfortunate event made the
Pavilion Theatre rather difficult to reach. On 14 November 1993
a contractor's rig broke free from its moorings and literally sliced
through the pier, marooning the theatre out at sea. Thankfully, all
has now been repaired, and the Cromer and Sheringham Operatic
and Dramatic Society can once more belt out *The King and I* to
eager audiences.

Long-distance path baggers may now want to turn their back
on the sea for the pleasures of the 56-mile Weavers Way, which
winds its way through the Norfolk Broads to Great Yarmouth. It
is a component part of the so-called 'Around Norfolk Walk', which
from Great Yarmouth utilises the Angles Way westwards to near
Thetford, followed by the Peddars Way north towards Hunstanton,
and so back along the Norfolk Coast Path.

The crumbling cliffs continue to Mundesley, and as far as
Overstrand there is a walkable clifftop path. But, as with the path
before Sheringham, signs such as 'Dangerous cliffs: continue at
your own risk' and another helpful one saying simply 'Path ends'
(where it clearly disappears over the edge) indicate the instability
of the ground. In addition, there is a real danger from flying golf
balls as the path skirts several fairways, so my advice is if the tide
is out stick to the wide, welcoming sand!

At Overstrand large boulders (or 'rock armour', as engineers tend
to call them) are being positioned to try and reduce the impact of the
waves and preserve the foreshore. Whether they will halt the overall
erosion is open to debate. The cliffs contain many springs, which
makes them intrinsically unstable, and when last I visited part of the
promenade was fenced off due to a recent fall. The man who has
run the beach café for the last twenty-six years recalls that when he
started here the level of the sand was virtually up to the promenade.
Now it's a drop of nearly twenty feet. He regularly serves parties
of schoolchildren who walk up the shore from Mundesley during
the long, low tides that this coast often enjoys. This should be
your route if at all possible, since the alternative is along the edge
of the B1159.

Mundesley sports a Ship Inn and several red brick hotels that are
testimony to the efforts to develop the location into a fashionable
watering place when the railway was built in 1898.

Now follow the low and unswerving shore via Bacton and

Walcott to Happisburgh. You may want to follow the road through the massive British Gas terminal at Bacton, built in the 1950s to handle the natural gas piped in from fields under the North Sea. Rather incongruously, a very short distance away – and in sight and certainly in smell of the terminal – is a large caravan and chalet park.

The cliff-edge track into Happisburgh, a waymarked public footpath, is via a small caravan site. How long the sometimes precarious path will remain intact is anyone's guess, and whether a new one will be reinstated if it disappears is even less certain. Whichever way you reach it, be sure to take a photo of the glorious red-and-white striped lighthouse, sitting safely back from the cliffedge. It was built after Norfolk experienced a ferocious winter storm in 1789, which claimed seventy ships and 600 men. Happisburgh, Norfolk people will delight in telling you, is not pronounced 'Happisburgh', but 'Azeburr'. Beyond the lifeboat station the village is in the process of losing some of its clifftop dwellings to the sea, and a fieldside path is rapidly going the same way, so, if the tide is in, stick to the roads and inland footpaths.

If the tide is out, the firm sea-edge sand or the low concrete sea wall can be walked all the way south via Eccles and Sea Palling to Waxham. There are some tracks among the high dunes (although the going can be soft and slow), and these give views over the Broads to the south. At Sea Palling a plaque commemorates the completion in 1959 of 8 miles of sea defences between Happisburgh and Winterton, following earlier floods. But, as we have seen, sea defence work on the East Coast is never finished. On 31 January 1993 the sea broke through and completely flooded seven villages. The present, long-term project involves building sixteen artificial offshore reefs parallel with the shore 'to reduce beach volatility and periodically replenish the beach to acceptable profiles with material obtained from offshore sources'. The first few reefs are now in place.

A brief diversion inland via Waxham and back to the shore at Horsey Corner may cut out some monotonous dune- or beach-walking, and then there is a long public footpath via Bramble Hill and the edge of Winterton Dunes National Nature Reserve into Winterton-on-Sea. Do stay on established tracks and watch out for adders in dry weather. They are not particularly big nor are they at all fierce but, as I found, it is very easy to almost step on one when both parties are taking in the sun and not paying much attention to anything in particular. This is the largest dune system in East Anglia, and as you wander through the marram grass pause and point your binoculars at the beach for a sight of nesting terns, as well as common and grey seals.

WINTERTON-ON-SEA – LOWESTOFT (18 miles)
The dune paths of Winterton lead to Hemsby, then California (the Norfolk one). The elements are slowly forcing this gruesome, miniature world of chalets and burger bars into the sea, which is no bad thing, so much so that the road down to the beach finishes in mid-air and when I was here scaffolding and steps had to finish the job. The public footpath along the low cliffs south from California indicated on the most recent OS Landranger map (1993) has disappeared, although I was told that you may walk through the caravan site to pick up the dismantled railway into Caister; otherwise stay on the beach if the sea is out.

From Caister-on-Sea, a one-time walled Roman port, walk over the wide and mostly empty sands and marram grass past the race course into Great Yarmouth. Until the nineteenth century Yarmouth (it became 'Great' after Henry III's charter in 1272) faced west, over the estuary of the converging Bure, Waveney and Yare Rivers, but since then tourism and latterly the North Sea oil and gas industry have taken over from fishing. Once Yarmouth had the largest herring fleet in the country, and produced the famous Yarmouth Bloater (a full herring slightly salted and smoked). Strange that a fish so unremarkable in size and appearance as the herring, like the once-important pilchard off Cornwall, was at one time the mainstay of East Coast fishing. Herring wars long predate cod wars!

In the town centre are a number of narrow, parallel alleys called the Rows. Specially constructed wheelbarrow-like carts known as trolls pulled goods along these tiny passageways, the narrowest of which was No 95, Kitty Witches Row, just over 2 feet wide at one end. The Rows were home to the less prosperous merchants and the poor, and they were built at right angles to the sea to aid ventilation. Altogether there were 145 rows, stretching for a total distance of 7 miles, but many were destroyed in ruthless World War II bombing that wiped out much of the old town.

Cross the old bridge in the centre of Yarmouth and follow the riverside track to Gorleston beach. Watch out for low-flying golf balls from the links, along what should now be a public footpath via Hopton and Corton all the way along the coast to Lowestoft. But periodic erosion, especially at Corton Cliffs, may mean that yet again the easier option for walkers is the beach.

Lowestoft is the most easterly town in Britain, a fact emphasised by its coat of arms which features a rising sun. It is a place strongly connected with the sea, and like Great Yarmouth its fortunes mirrored the rise of North Sea herrings and trawl fishing. The biggest boost of all came with the opening up of the Dogger Bank fishing grounds in the mid-1800s, and in the years before the First World War as many as 1,000 boats were employed in the local industry. The first lighthouse erected by Trinity House in England was built here in 1609, and when Lowestoft's own lifeboat station opened in 1801 it predated the founding of the RNLI by twenty-three years.

LOWESTOFT – DUNWICH (17 miles)
For the next 60 miles or so the route is along the quiet and often remote Suffolk Heritage Coast, a flat land of dunes and shingle banks, low crumbling cliffs and marshland. It's a place where the land is actively surrendering to the sea, and where birdlife usually outnumbers human visitors. Suffolk County Council's official coast path runs between Lowestoft and Felixstowe, a pleasant and mostly obvious route except for an inland diversion after the River Alde which misses out Orford. Needless to say, we will be sticking to the coast.

As with the preceding Norfolk miles, the serious problem of coastal erosion continually threatens the coastal footpath, let alone the land and property of those that live in view of the sea. And as soon as the semis of Lowestoft begin to thin the problem is immediately apparent. Following serious erosion over the last three years the clifftop path from Pakefield to Kessingland has been closed, and since a new path through the holiday camps and caravan sites seems unlikely it is either a question of walking the beach at low tide (a safe option – but *only* at this time) or an unpleasant tramp along the A12.

Beyond Kessingland the coastal path, with the agreement of the landowners, follows the foreshore to Southwold. Since some of this may be impassable at high tide there are several places where you can cut inland and continue the walk via paths and lanes. Observe local notices and try and consult tide tables in advance. These are quiet and attractive miles, and the broads at Benacre, Covehithe and Easton are popular with wildlife; but at the same time the crumbling coastline is all too evident. Off Sole Bay in 1672 a combined English and French fleet fought a long and inconclusive battle against the Dutch. A number of the English ships had less than their full complement, since the enemy's surprise attack left many sailors marooned in Southwold taverns. They were probably grateful, as for many months afterwards corpses from the battle were washed up on the shore, and local people could earn a shilling by recovering and burying a body.

Southwold's distinctive white lighthouse rises from the rooftops and serves as a beacon for this handsome little town. In particular, seek out the Sailors' Reading Room on East Cliff, which has a store of nautical relics and stories. Adnams beer is also worth seeking out, especially as it is brewed in the vicinity. The pleasant mix of architectural styles and scattering of greens throughout the town is partly due to a great fire in 1659 which destroyed almost everything bar the fifteenth-century church dedicated to St Edmund, the last King of East Anglia.

In the summer months the ferryman will row you across the narrow mouth of the River Blyth for the princely sum of 25p; otherwise it's a short walk upstream past the landing stages and moored boats to an iron footbridge. From Walberswick, on the far side, a high shingle bank curves gently around to Dunwich, then low cliffs extend to the futuristic shapes of Sizewell power station. Although the shoreside route is well-walked to Dunwich it's not technically a right of way, and the official coast path takes a far more interesting and attractive route across marshland and around the edge of Dunwich Forest.

In the Middle Ages Dunwich was one of the foremost towns in England, and the capital of East Anglia. Now it is a thin and unremarkable-looking village, although it still manages a pub, called not surprisingly the Ship. The culprit for the demise of Dunwich is, rather predictably, the North Sea. The splendid, privately run museum in St James's Street tells the story. As far back as the second century the Romans used what was then a large harbour, and in Saxon times St Felix spread the Christian word from his base at Dunwich. By the twelfth century the town was half the size of London. But a series of violent storms and the action of the sea silted up the harbour and destroyed the sandy cliffs. Dunwich literally fell into the sea, and the inhabitants departed. The last of the nine churches was lost to the waves in 1913. They say that you can still come across old bones from the abandoned churchyards when the cliffs take one of their still frequent falls.

DUNWICH – SNAPE MALTINGS (18 miles)
The next stretch south to Aldeburgh is long, low and straight, on clifftop and shingle. It passes shorewards of the RSPB's important Minsmere Reserve, with 1,500 acres of reedbeds, woodland, lagoons or 'scrapes' that attract bitterns, marsh harriers, avocets and warblers, and flocks of eager ornithologists. Strange, therefore, that only a couple of miles down the coast from this wildlife haven is Sizewell nuclear power station, which the coast path passes seawards. In January 1995 Sizewell B became Britain's newest nuclear power station, and the first using the American-style pressurised water reactor. Its dour, harsh shapes are relieved by the bloated white golf ball perched atop; but, as Paul Theroux remarked of Windscale during his journey around Britain's shores a decade ago, 'something so new, so huge, so heavily fenced-in, on so distant a beach *had* to be dangerous'. As with so many of the other nuclear power stations, it seems a crying shame that they are located in or close by some of the most unspoilt and uncluttered coastal scenery. Sizewell, Bradwell, Dungeness, Hinkley Point, Sellafield – if the damn things are so safe why on earth wasn't Sizewell B built in Surrey?

From the small settlement of Thorpeness, originally built as an Edwardian holiday village, wander the dead straight, flat shore into elegant Aldeburgh. A stroll along the prom, past the Yacht Pond, Moot Hall and fishermen's huts, introduces you to a string of delightfully individual and eccentric residential buildings, including a tiny, pink-washed house called 'Paradise' which stands isolated, a Hansel and Gretel-type home. Aldeburgh was once well-known for building ships, with Drake's *Pelican* and *Greyhound* constructed here; and fishing smacks for the rough seas around the Faroes and Iceland were built at nearby Slaughden. Some of Aldeburgh's shipwrights were nothing if not hopeful. In 1870 a local man came up with the idea of drilling holes in the side of his ship, so that the hold would fill with water and the newly caught cod stay alive until the return to port. Before the advent of modern lighthouses, local people burned barrels of tar on the tower of the church to guide returning fishermen (the ones that made it).

You can follow the narrowing shore a little further south as far as the Martello Tower at Slaughden, but unless you are interested in the long spit of Orford Ness you must then walk the embankment of the River Alde around Aldeburgh Marshes before joining the road eastwards. After a short while turn left on to the Sailors Path (the official coast path once more, which has bypassed Aldeburgh), and this heads through Black Heath Wood and fields to reach a lane into Snape. Unless you want to visit the village immediately turn left, down a path to the Alde's northern bank, and along to the bridge at Snape Maltings.

In 1840 Newson Garrett began a malting business here, achieving both commercial success and ten children, including Elizabeth Garrett Anderson, Britain's first woman physician and woman mayor (in nearby Aldeburgh), and well-known suffragette Millicent Garrett Fawcett. But Snape Maltings is today better known for its music, since Benjamin Britten's Aldeburgh Festival moved here in the 1960s, and the 830-seat Concert Hall centrepiece is located on the site of the massive grain-drying hall where the malt was dried in kilns before shipping out to London, Norwich and the Continent. Britten, born in Lowestoft, took the character of Peter Grimes for his popular opera from a poem by Aldeburgh's famous son George Crabbe. The modern Snape Maltings complex also has a rather bewildering array of craft shops, galleries, and knick-knack parlours, plus a quayside where sailing barges still tie up.

SNAPE MALTINGS – FELIXSTOWE (25 miles)
From Snape Maltings follow the scenic track around the marshy edge of the Alde via Iken Cliff picnic site to the hamlet of Iken. St Botolph's Church, which once stood on an island at high tide, dates from around 1300, but a late Saxon stone cross built into the tower suggests that it could have been the site of St Botolph's Monastery which is recorded as being founded at 'Icanhoe' in AD 654.

The Suffolk Coast Path now goes wandering off through Tunstall Forest, which I find a little bit odd, since, although there is no access from Iken Church to the waterside, if you follow the lane to High Street (but don't expect anything more than a farm here) you can regain the sea wall at Short Reach and follow what is now a legitimate public right of way along the whole of the firm, continuous sea wall into Orford.

If you climb the ninety-one steps of Orford Castle's splendid Keep (all that remains of Henry II's original fortress) the windy but panoramic views help you to understand the curious phenomena that is Orford Ness. Until the 1500s Orford was a busy fishing port, but a distinctive shingle spit developed and the harbour became less and less accessible. Now the spit, Orford Ness, extends almost ten miles from Slaughden to North Weir Point, and is one of the largest and most important of its kind in the country. The National Trust bought the site from the Ministry of Defence in 1993, and since 1995 there is what is described as 'informal access' for walkers from Slaughden as far as the lighthouse, with more organised arrangements to follow. However, the far tip remains a national nature reserve and the rightful preserve of shingle-loving birds and plants. Elsewhere on Orford Ness, a squat, grey building surrounded by a nest of transmitter masts is where the BBC World Service sends out its messages; and the bizarre concrete pagoda-like structures were built by the military for the testing of atomic detonators (the thinking being that if something went badly wrong the pillars would collapse and the heavy roof would crash down and seal the mess).

The sea wall path leads south from Orford, opposite avocets and little terns on Havergate Island, then cuts back across fields to join Gedgrave Lane which you should follow down to the Butley Ferry. However, since the Butley Ferry is little-used and anyway only consists of one man and a very small boat who only turn up on demand it is perhaps wise to try and make contact beforehand, otherwise you will have a long detour via Chillesford. There are oyster beds at Butley, and the produce can be sampled at the Oysterage in Orford where the menu includes Angels on Horseback (grilled bacon and oysters on toast).

Presuming you have successfully employed the services of the Butley Ferryman continue along the river embankment around Boyton Marshes and out to the sea, although the end of Orford Ness still disguises this for a while yet.

Now follow the sea wall and shoreside south to Bawdsey, at

the mouth of the River Deben. It is a bleak, open landscape of flat lines. At the appropriately named Shingle Street a few houses huddle rather forlornly by the grey water; but the most striking feature is a line of Martello Towers. Almost 200 of these remarkable defences were built around the coast of Suffolk, Essex, Kent and Sussex in the late nineteenth century, as the fear of a French invasion mounted. You may have already seen one near Aldeburgh. They are low, round stone towers, thick-set and impregnable, with guns, magazines and basic living space for a handful of defenders inside. The name comes from an original fortification built, rather ironically, by the French at Mortella Point on the island of Corsica, which impressed the British command after it repulsed a two-day attack by British warships. The 200 or so English Martello Towers stretched from Aldeburgh to Newhaven, but since Napoleon's invasion never materialised none of them ever saw any serious military action. Instead, they were employed in the fight against smuggling, and often occupied by coastguards. Many have crumbled over the years, and although some were reoccupied during World War II, only forty-three remain. There is a Martello Tower Visitor Centre at Folkestone, but most are private residences – such as along this part of the Suffolk coast. Around here, by the way, Martello Towers were endearingly known as 'Mr Pitt's Pork Pies'! Overall, they are a curious, rather eccentric feature of the South-East Coast, like giant concrete sandcastles that the sea has not managed to wash away.

Continue along the foreshore past Bawdsey Manor, owned by the military since 1936 and where modern radar was invented. The Bawdsey ferry operates at weekends from May until July, then daily until September. Before the 1930s, when a motor boat took over, the ferrymen were required to pull the chain ferry across the river by hand, and not surprisingly turnover of staff was high. The alternative to the ferry is a long inland walk to Woodbridge and back through the Sandlings, close to the famous Anglo-Saxon ship burial site at Sutton Hoo. From the fine, restored tide mill in Woodbridge, the return to the sea is along the Deben's southern bank and is waterside almost all the way. From Felixstowe Ferry continue along the sea wall past a couple more Martello Towers and a golf course and into Felixstowe.

Pick of the walks

HUNSTANTON – BLAKENEY (31 miles): a gentle shoreline of beach and dunes, mudflats and saltmarsh, rich in wildlife and with a string of quiet, attractive villages.

PETER SCOTT WALK (10 miles): also known as the Wash Coast Path, this deserted and evocative sea wall route teems with birdlife, ending near King's Lynn. Take your binoculars!

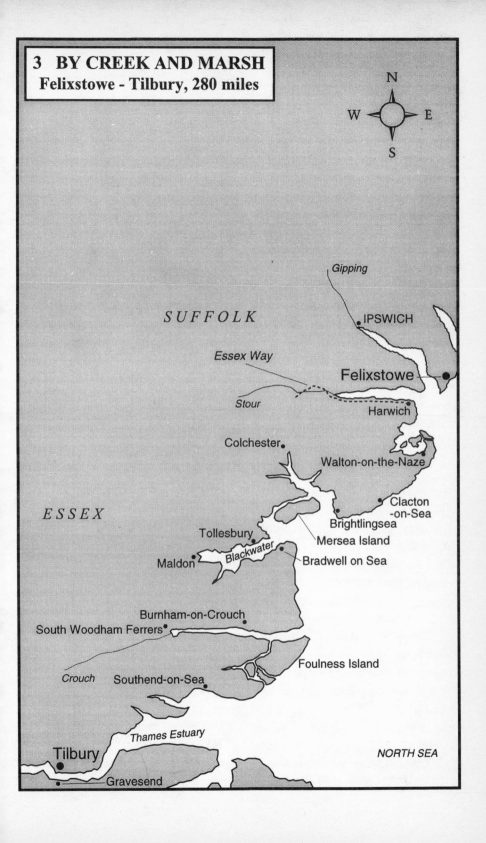

3 BY CREEK AND MARSH
Felixstowe - Tilbury, 280 miles

N
W   E
S

Gipping

IPSWICH

SUFFOLK

Essex Way

Felixstowe

Stour

Harwich

Colchester

Walton-on-the-Naze

**Clacton
-on-Sea**

Brightlingsea

ESSEX

Tollesbury

Mersea Island

Maldon

Blackwater

Bradwell on Sea

Burnham-on-Crouch

South Woodham Ferrers

Foulness Island

Crouch

Southend-on-Sea

Thames Estuary

NORTH SEA

Tilbury

Gravesend

FELIXSTOWE – MANNINGTREE (35 miles)

Once upon a time there was a regular passenger ferry from Felixstowe to Harwich across the harbour, but now that this has been discontinued it is a very, very long walk around the estuaries of the Orwell and the Stour. Mind you, some of it is extremely pleasant, especially along the edge of the Stour; but there is no continuous shoreside walking route for the whole distance so that inevitably a fair amount is on tarmac, and you will have to plod almost into Ipswich. If you hanker for the company of the sea then resume the coastal walk at Harwich.

Felixstowe is the largest container port in the country (a million or so of the things pass through every year) and despite a nature reserve and seventeenth-century fort Landguard Point is overshadowed by the docks and it is unlikely that you will dally – unless you are a container. However, the beach towards Landguard Point is famed for its semi-precious stones, including carnelian, amber, agate, Whitby jet, chalcedony, jasper and quartz. There is a waterside track along Trimley Marshes through a Suffolk Wildlife Trust reserve as far as Levington, but inevitably it then has to be roads if you want to join the A45 for the grand sweep of the 1982 Orwell Bridge high above the river. Alternatively respite is offered by an estuary and cliff path either side of the construction in Orwell Country Park, with other attractive walks possible through Bridge Wood and Piper's Vale; but even here industrial land denies further access upstream into the centre of Suffolk's county town.

The road journey back along the opposite shore from Ipswich allows access at Freston Park, and the Elizabethan folly of Freston Tower, and a track from Woolverstone to near Chelmondiston via National Trust woods. Cat House near Woolverstone Marina takes its name from an old practice of placing the silhouette of a cat in the window to let smugglers know it was safe to land. Interestingly, in the early days smugglers were known as 'owlers', since they communicated with each other by imitation hoots and calls while carrying out their illegal pursuit. (The owl and the pussycat . . . ?) A little further on you can join a continuous embankment route around Shotley Marshes, an important breeding site for waders such as snipe and redshank. Shotley Point is also known as Bloody Point, since this is commonly thought to have been the location for several Viking landings and confrontations. At Shotley Gate return via Erwarton Ness to Stutton. A public footpath leads back out to Stutton Ness and up as far as Cattawade where the river is crossed not far from Flatford Mill.

MANNINGTREE – CLACTON-ON-SEA (37 miles)
Cattawade is the eastern terminus for the Stour Valley Path; while just over the river at Manningtree you can join another long-distance path, the 81-mile Essex Way, for the journey back out to the coast. Manningtree was the home of Matthew Hopkins, the notorious seventeenth-century 'Witchfinder General' who condemned nearly 200 so-called witches to death in just three years and hanged them locally on the village green.

With no shore access after Mistley the Essex Way diverts inland for a while, via Bradfield. Here, in 1871, the new rector of St Lawrence's Church caused consternation when he brought with him a massive organ to have played in his new church. It took ten railway trucks to transport, some of the church had to be demolished to install the thing, and when it was finally played the vibrations caused even further damage.

Returning to the Stour at Jacques Bay, bear in mind that the river is of course tidal here – there is a sandy shore and beach huts to remind you – and high tides may cover part of this route temporarily. A footpath leads around most of Copperas Bay, which is named after bisulphide of iron (copperas) which was formerly dredged from the Stour's mud and transported to Harwich for use in the making of inks and dyes. From the waterside chestnut trees you must now turn inland to cross the railway, and either follow the Essex Way via Ramsey to the coast at Dovercourt, or a track and then roads via the busy ferry terminal at Parkeston Quay to Harwich.

In 885 King Alfred saw off the Danes near Shotley Gate, and Harwich has had an important seafaring tradition ever since. Edward III's fleet assembled here before knocking out the French at Sluys in the first serious naval confrontation in the Hundred Years War; and when Samuel Pepys was MP for the town the King's navy was even moored here. In the Elizabethan era the likes of Hawkins, Drake and Frobisher sailed from Harwich on expeditions; and when Elizabeth

I visited in 1561 she described it as 'a pretty place and wants for nothing'.

Back by the sea once more after too many land-locked miles, but effectively only a couple of miles further down the coast from Felixstowe! The Essex seaboard is a frustrating place for long-distance walkers, with so many creeks and tidal inlets, and mud and marshland. There are certainly some attractive places to explore, and I suggest that this county's coast is best suited for the day or weekend walker.

As if to prove the point, the public footpath along the sea wall south of Harwich gives up the ghost and retires to Little Oakley. Footpaths cut corners off the B1414, but the 5,000 acres of marshy islands and saltings of Hamford Water and Walton Backwaters necessitate a wide diversion. However, between the disued Beaumont Quay and just past Kirby-le-Soken the embankment may be followed, which allows an excellent chance to study the birdlife of the national nature reserve at close hand, and to appreciate why eighteenth-century smugglers liked this place so much. Arthur Ransome also took to Hamford Water, and set his children's book *Secret Water* here, with Skippers' Island renamed Mastodon Island.

You will have to follow the B1034 into the centre of Walton-on-the-Naze before picking up the well-walked embankment path by the Naze Fish and Chip Shop on Hall Lane. Once clear of some tightly packed caravans the path wanders around a nature reserve by Walton Channel to the Naze itself, which like the word 'ness' derives from the Old English 'naes' (nose). Near the distinctive tower, built by Trinity House in 1720 to aid mariners, is the Naze Links Café and some welcome refreshment. Now begins a long and popular stretch of first low cliff (almost unique in Essex!), then beach and prom that extends as far south as Clacton, with a solitary break in the houses at Holland Haven Country Park. In between is Frinton-on-Sea, a demure and respectable sort of place that seems worlds apart from its brash neighbours of Clacton and Southend. Frinton's Connaught Avenue has even been described as the Bond Street of the East Coast. In 1851 Frinton sported just thirty residents and three farms, but sixty years later there were houses and hotels, a railway station and county primary school, and even electric street lighting.

Clacton-on-Sea, on the other hand, is a loud and popular family venue, but still retains the trappings of the old-time resort. Like Frinton, the modern tourist settlement was purposefully developed, but the old area, known as Great Clacton, has a twelfth-century church and until 1872 staged an annual fair by the Ship Inn for almost 700 years.

CLACTON-ON-SEA – COLCHESTER (29 miles)

From Clacton to Mersea things get a little problematic. If you want to stick rigidly to the shore then follow the line of Martello Towers south-west along the unswerving shore to Colne Point, where you will have to head back inland towards St Osyth in order to avoid a large nature reserve. A short road walk via Point Clear leads to the mouth of the River Colne at St Osyth Stone Point; but unless you employ a helpful dinghy to negotiate Brightlingsea Creek you will then have to retrace your steps to where the road crosses St Osyth Creek. From here a public footpath crosses meadows to the west of a ruined priory, named after Osgith, daughter of Frithewald, King of the Angles. As was rather common around the time of the seventh century, invading Danes turned up and ran amok and beheaded poor Osgith. But according to legend she then carried her own head back to the church where she is buried. (And if you can do that you deserve having a priory named after you.) The path emerges on the road to Hollybush Hill, after which an embankment and track leads into Brightlingsea.

Brightlingsea boasts the oldest occupied building in Essex (Jacobes Hall), and is where you may see Thames sailing barges, smacks and other old seagoing craft in action. Brightlingsea was once a Roman port, and in the Middle Ages was prominent as the only member of the Cinque Ports set-up outside Kent and Sussex – but this will be looked at more closely once we have crossed the Thames.

Follow the Colne along a former railway line upstream to Aldboro Point. There is a low-tide ford across the mouth of Alresford Creek which I am told is firm despite the mud; otherwise walkers will have to change direction and follow a track then minor road as far as the church on the B1029 where you should turn left. Soon join a track along the northern bank of Alresford Creek in order to resume a waterside route via Wivenhoe and Wivenhoe Park, home to the University of Essex since 1964, and then into the centre of Colchester. Wivenhoe, a pleasant enough fishing village, is notable for being the epicentre of an earthquake in 1884 which was strong enough to damage the church.

Established around the first century BC by the Trinovantes and touted as 'Britain's oldest recorded town', the Romans called Colchester Camulodunum but saw their fine hilltop settlement sacked by Boudicca in AD 60. Some of the remains were incorporated in the huge Norman castle that followed a millennium later, and which boasted the largest keep in Europe (almost 30m or 100 ft high, 150 ft long and 110 ft wide).

COLCHESTER – TOLLESBURY (33 miles)

When the buildings of Colchester cease a riverside track can be followed downstream to Rowhedge and Fingringhoe, where at Fingringhoe Wick Essex Wildlife Trust have turned old gravel workings into a commendably diverse nature reserve, including a lagoon and area of birch-oak wood. However, beyond this the army's large holding at Langenhoe puts a sizeable area of creek and marsh out of bounds and requires a tarmac trudge as far as Salcott. For the inquisitive and dedicated a wander down the B1025 brings you to Mersea Island, connected to the mainland by a causeway called the Strood, and worth a brief inspection, not least because there is a walking route around virtually the whole of its shore and which takes in Cudmore Grove Country Park. There are close-up views of the shipping entering and leaving the Colne, and larger vessels offshore heading for Harwich and Felixstowe; while along the northern banks is Pyefleet Channel, home to the famous local oysters. Another reason to visit Britian's most easterly inhabited island is that East Mersea's rector from 1870–81 was hymn-writer Sabine Baring-Gould, author of 'Onward Christian Soldiers'. Apparently 'Now the Day is Over' was written to fit the five chimes of West Mersea church.

From Salcott a long stretch of mostly empty and undisturbed sea wall walking begins that takes in the wide Blackwater estuary, and the sinuous and penetrating Crouch and Roach. Essex has a total of around 400 miles of sea wall between the Stour and Thames estuaries, a surprisingly high proportion of which is accessible to the coastal walker. It can be as empty and bleak as anything to be found in Lincolnshire or Suffolk, and all the more confounding due to the lengthy twists, turns and doubling back that the tidal tentacles demand. Many people find it an unlovely landscape, especially with the lack of elevation and perspective, the occasional firing range and a nuclear power station along the way. But even here, at Bradwell, you will find a seventh-century chapel, and a wealth of unfussed wildlife along and off the shore.

From Salcott the embankment route (a proper right of way) encircles Old Hall Marshes and wriggles past Tollesbury until it joins the Blackwater by Tollesbury Wick Marshes Nature Reserve.

TOLLESBURY – BRADWELL-ON-SEA (34 miles)

Wander into places such as Tollesbury on a sunny Sunday and the marina will be full of enthusiastic nautical types generally up to not very much at all. Sailing has always been popular here, but Tollesbury is also known for its fishing, and at one time over 100 smacks operated out of Woodrolfe Creek. The catch brought ashore here included sprats, scallops, crabs and oysters, and even starfish, which were used for manure.

As the Blackwater bites deep inland, the wide marsh and mudflats south of Tollesbury and Goldhanger provide a winter home to huge numbers of dark-bellied Brent geese. Up to a quarter of the world's population fly into Essex each October after summer breeding in Siberia and the Arctic, and feed on eel-grass along the shoreline as well as farmers' crops. Approaching Maldon is Osea Island, sitting in the middle of the wide channel. Earlier this century the island sported a drying-out clinic for alcoholics (they were known as 'gentlemen inebriates'), although it is said that local boatmen made more money rowing over illicit liquor at night than they did from fishing!

At Heybridge Basin, virtually the head of the Blackwater and once a Roman port before Maldon grew up on its present site, you join the route of the Maldon Millennium Way, a newly devised 22-mile circular route centred on the town and celebrating the anniversary of the Battle of Maldon. On 11 August 991 a Viking force led by Olaf Trygvasson sailed up the Blackwater, camped on Northey Island, then attacked and after several days of desperate fighting defeated the resident Saxons under Byrhtnoth, Ealderman of Essex (although Maldon itself was never sacked). The event was described shortly after in the epic Saxon poem 'The Battle of Maeldune'. The modern walking route passes the site of the battle, near South House

Farm on the river's southern bank opposite the National Trust's Northey Island.

From here the sea wall path extends all the way back out to the open sea, via Maylandsea and the caravans of Ramsey Island. During World War II Maylandsea boatyard was where a large number of Motor Torpedo boats and Fairmile Motor launches used to hunt enemy submarines were built in secret. Near Bradwell-on-Sea the path passes waterside of the nuclear power station, opened in 1963 and one of the oldest of its kind in the country. It's due to be pensioned off any time now, and at the time of writing there are dark mutterings about a successor.

As if in direct contrast to this crude and inglorious lump, a couple of miles further on is one of the oldest surviving churches in England. Built on top of the site of the Roman fort of Othona, St Peter-on-the-Wall is a simple and very humble barn-like construction, built in AD 654 by Bishop Cedd who travelled from Lindisfarne to instruct King Sigbert and the East Saxons. The church can only be reached on foot, and such is its appeal that an ecumenical pilgrimage is held here each year on the first Saturday in July. It has even become the eastern focus of a 45-mile walking route from Chipping Ongar, called the St Peter's Way. However, for a time the building was used by farmers rather than worshippers, and the high walls bear crude, patched-up doorways where hay wagons once entered.

BRADWELL-ON-SEA – SOUTH WOODHAM FERRERS (32 miles)

The sea wall continues from St Peter's Church past Bradwell Bird Observatory, quite properly hidden away among the bushes. Stay on the top of the exposed, unswerving path above Dengie Marshes. The bare, flat scene has been accentuated over the last twenty years by Dutch Elm Disease which has robbed the peninsula of its once-dominant trees.

Eventually the embankment swings around for a mighty detour up the River Crouch and back, followed soon after by another around the Roach. If you insist on sticking to the coast southwards all the way to the Thames Estuary it will take more time than you think – and you will need a lot of patience. Perhaps, like Mersea Island and possibly Dengie, this is another section that lends itself to an exploration in its own right.

Burnham-on-Crouch has been called the 'Cowes of the East

Coast' and is the focus of nautical activity in Essex. The London Sailing Club from Hammersmith and the Royal Corinthian Yacht Club from Erith, Kent, first established themselves here towards the end of last century, and today there are four clubs based at the town. The highlight of the year is Burnham Week, a popular festival of sailing held every August that culminates in a regatta in which Class 1 yachts compete for the prestigious Town Cup. Needless to say the high street boasts the Ship Hotel.

From Burnham the river wall can be followed as far as North Fambridge, from where a short diversion must be made across the railway then back to the sea wall and through Marsh Farm Country Park until eventually the Crouch is crossed past South Woodham Ferrers at Battlebridge.

SOUTH WOODHAM FERRERS – SOUTHEND-ON-SEA (43 miles)

And so back along the Crouch once more. The north bank is a tantalisingly short distance away, and you may reflect that a polite word with a boat-owner at Burnham might have saved you a long and not especially interesting walk to Battlebridge and back.

As Burnham approaches on the far bank the river wall twists inland towards Canewdon and arrives at Lion Wharf. If you continue east a public right of way leads on to the bare and unappetising Wallasea Island, but ultimately comes to a dead end. The best option is to continue along the embankment track around Paglesham Creek and Clements Marsh and trace Paglesham Reach as far as Rochford. It's a clear if little-walked track all the way.

From Rochford things get rather messy. A lane to Butler's Farm then a public bridleway around Barling Marsh takes you back to an embankment path alongside a succession of wriggling creeks. Opposite are a host of low, featureless islands, culminating in Foulness Island. A refuge for wildfowl maybe, but on the OS map most of this is plastered with the ominous words 'Danger Area', and together with the fact that there are few rights of way and Foulness looks as attractive as its name I suggest you stick to the mainland and trot into Shoeburyness and Southend for a first real look at the Thames Estuary.

SOUTHEND-ON-SEA – TILBURY (37 miles)

Today it is difficult to imagine Southend as a sleepy hamlet once known as the South End of Prittlewell. Now with 7

miles of seafront, it overflows with pubs and take-away food
bars, jellied eel stalls and bingo, and boasts the longest pleasure
pier in the world. Not that the 1.34-mile-long pier has had an
easy life, however. Originally built in wood, the present iron
structure was finished in 1889; but since 1830 as many as
fourteen vessels have breached it and fire has swept through
four times, most recently in 1995 when a blaze in the bowl-
ing alley gutted the front complex. Presuming it's still standing
when you visit, the walk out to the end and back is a must.
Ignore the miniature train (originally a horse-drawn tram) and
concentrate on the compelling views of Sheerness docks, the
chimneys of Canvey Island, and the power station on the Isle
of Grain.

Like many of the Sussex resorts, modern Southend-on-Sea
seems to go on forever, swallowing up Westcliff-on-Sea and
Leigh-on-Sea, but when the houses finally recede follow the
road down to cross the Fenchurch Street–Shoeburyness Line at
Leigh Station. On your left is Two Tree Island, a former tip
that has been turned into a nature reserve with public access;
while ahead the sea wall continues parallel with the railway
across Hadleigh and Benfleet Marshes. This surprisingly wild
and unspoilt strip between Southend and Canvey Island is given
over to grazing animals and walkers, and was once a wooded
Royal hunting ground before being cleared in the fourteenth and
fifteenth centuries. It is backed by the low, partly wooded ridge
of Benfleet Downs. Hadleigh Country Park is a miniature oasis in
drab south Essex, and has as its centrepiece the remains of a castle
first built in 1230. From this modest height the views across the
busy if not altogether beautiful Thames Estuary are both extensive
and fascinating.

Approaching South Benfleet Station at the far end of the
marsh you can skip over the creek and follow a path into
the houses of Canvey Island if you wish. The small, densely
populated island lies below the spring tide level, and it was
here, above all, that the floods of 1953 had some of the most
devastating effects in terms of loss of human life. In the early
hours of 1 February the sea broke through the sea wall in
forty places, and in such quantity and so quickly that in just
fifteen minutes the water level was above the window sills of
most buildings. A total of fifty-eight people perished. Some

inhabitants drowned in their beds; others died from exposure as they huddled above the icy water on rooftops. After the disaster the clay sea walls, originally built by a Dutch engineer in 1620, were rebuilt and strengthened by the insertion of a fence of steel sheet-piles.

If we're honest with ourselves, though, a walking tour of Canvey Island has only limited appeal, particularly since the vast oil refineries of Coryton and Shellhaven necessitate a return via the busy A130 for a long and grim roadside walk around Basildon to regain the shore near East Tilbury.

The final few miles to the Tilbury ferry are on a thankfully uncluttered and direct footpath along the north bank of the narrowing Thames. This stretch from East Tilbury to Gravesend is part of the London Countryway, a 205-mile orbital walking route around London devised by Keith Chesterton – the walker's M25 but without the cars! From the remains of Coalhouse Fort, built by General Gordon of Khartoum in 1869, the coastal path concludes its Essex journey above ugly marshland and waste ground to end just past the old coal power station at Tilbury Fort. This excellently preserved three-acre seventeenth-century naval fort possesses a unique double moat landwards, while behind its low, solid walls are underground magazines and a parade with modern 12-pounder guns that the public can fire for a small fee. Although the fort never had to repulse an enemy attack, bloodshed occurred with a most bizarre incident. Following a cricket match between Kent and Essex in 1776 a fight broke out, and Kent players stole a gun from the guardroom and shot dead an Essex player. Then an elderly invalid was bayoneted and finally the fort's commanding officer was also killed, before all the players hurriedly left the scene.

A short hop across the river is Gravesend and Kent, and the enticing prospect of the English Channel and the South Coast. Apart from a few creeks and marshes in north Kent the shoreline will now take on a more bold and uncomplicated direction. And if you have forgotten what real cliffs look like then you will soon be reminded in glorious fashion.

Should you not want to take the regular Tilbury–Gravesend ferry then it's a painfully long, tarmac plod past the vehicle-only Dartford crossing as far as the foot tunnel at Greenwich.

Pick of the walks

MERSEA ISLAND (12 miles): low but energetic ramble around the entire island, with views over the Essex marshes and North Sea water traffic.

BRADWELL-ON-SEA CIRCULAR (6 miles): out to the isolated St Peter's Chapel, then the sea embankment south and a farm track back across fields to the village. Flat, and very peaceful.

II THE CHANNEL COAST

4 THE SEVEN CINQUE PORTS
Gravesend – Newhaven
220 miles

5 BESIDE THE SEASIDE
Newhaven – Exmouth
275 miles

6 CREAM TEAS AND SMALL BOATS
Exmouth – Penzance
248 miles

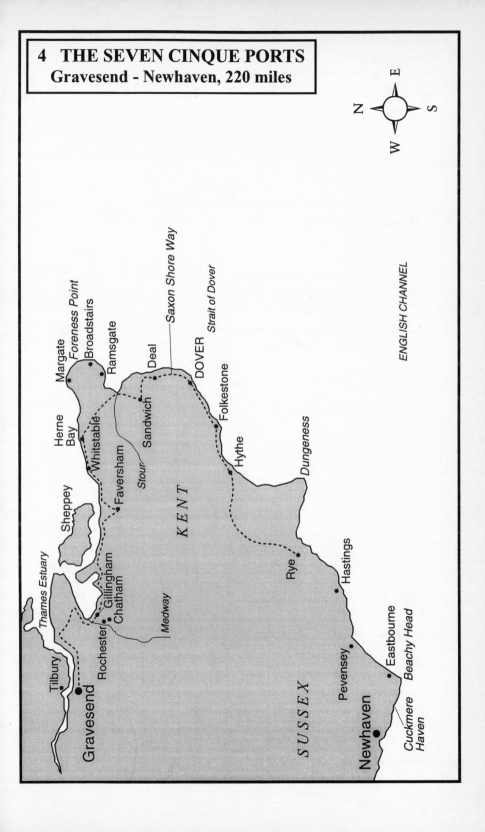

4 THE SEVEN CINQUE PORTS
Gravesend - Newhaven, 220 miles

N · E · S · W

ENGLISH CHANNEL

Thames Estuary

Foreness Point
Margate
Broadstairs
Ramsgate
Saxon Shore Way
Deal
Strait of Dover
DOVER
Herne Bay
Whitstable
Sandwich
Folkestone
Faversham
Stour
Hythe
Sheppey
Dungeness
KENT
Medway
Gillingham
Chatham
Rochester
Rye
Hastings
Tilbury
Gravesend
SUSSEX
Pevensey
Eastbourne
Beachy Head
Newhaven
Cuckmere Haven

GRAVESEND – GILLINGHAM (32 miles)

The ticket office at Gravesend sells a booklet on the history of the Tilbury–Gravesend ferries called *The Five Minute Crossing*. It's not a particularly long work. Also available is a 25p postcard depicting the current vessel, which bears the name *Great Expectations*. This is not the ferry operators having a quiet chuckle at the expense of south-bound passengers, but reflects Kent's association with Charles Dickens, who lived nearby and used many features from the surrounding landscape in such classics as *Pickwick Papers* and *Great Expectations*. But more shortly.

The name Gravesend has nothing to do with the burial of London's plague victims, or the dumping of bodies at sea, it seems, but probably comes from the Saxon word 'Greva' (small wood or grove); or possibly from 'portgereve', an ancient term defining the boundaries of the local officer. Here the Thames Estuary finally narrows and the approach to London really begins, and in Gravesend Reach Folkestone and Harwich pilots are replaced by river pilots. As long ago as 1401 Gravesend was granted the sole right to ferry passengers to London and back, and the four-hour journey to Billingsgate was completed on special 'tilt' boats. Nowadays sturdy tugs wait for business – as many as four are sometimes required to shepherd just one supertanker – and there is an endless passage of container ships and barges. All the activity on what is the UK's busiest river can be viewed from Gordon Promenade, which is located beyond the Port of London Authority's headquarters and the old Custom House. Behind the Promenade is New Tavern Fort, which up to 1918 crossed fire with the guns at Tilbury to defend the upper reaches of the Thames, and has a large underground magazine complex. In 1932, as a sign happily points out, the Fort became a public garden.

At the far end of the Promenade take the bridge over the former Thames and Medway Canal, a short (and short-lived) waterway that was opened in 1824 to assist shipping plying the naval dockyards at Woolwich, Deptford and Chatham. High tolls and tidal problems led to its swift demise, and the canal was purchased by the South

Eastern Railway who subsequently converted the 2-mile long Higham Tunnel for the use of trains instead of boats.

Your route is now that of the Saxon Shore Way, a 143-mile walking trail around the coast of Kent from Gravesend to Rye that follows the course of the former shoreline – before silting joined Thanet to the mainland. Its waymark is a red winged helmet; and in places (such as the next mile or so through an industrial estate) this will prove useful.

Returning to the river bank pass the Ship and Lobster pub, believed to be the Ship in *Great Expectations*. Dickens sets the scene at the beginning of that same book: 'The dark flat wilderness beyond the churchyard [believed to be St James's Church at nearby Cooling], intersected with dykes and mounds and gates, with scattered cattle feeding on it, was the marshes; and that low leaden line beyond was the river; and that distant savage lair from which the wind was rushing was the sea.' Ahead of you are miles of low, featureless marsh, plus reminders of the river's strategic importance with the ruins of Shornemead Fort, originally constructed in 1868 by General Gordon, and two miles further on Cliffe Fort. The landscape is bleak, certainly not beautiful, and at times it can be eerie and rather mysterious. There are also some odd bedfellows around here. Riverside refineries and quarries sit side by side with caravans, while the marshes and flooded pits near Cliffe Fort attract both trail bikers and twitchers.

The Saxon Shore Way now leaves the Thames and heads across the fields eastwards, via Cliffe, Cooling, High Halstow and Fenn Street, to join the River Medway near Hoo (about nine miles). This basically lops off the Isle of Grain, whose combination of empty marshland and heavy industry doesn't endear it to many walkers. However, the ten miles from Cliffe Creek to Allhallows-on-Sea along the low, uninterrupted sea wall allow views across the widening Thames, albeit to the refineries of Shellhaven and Canvey Island, but also inland to the undisturbed birdlife of the marsh and reeds. This section, above all, is for the loner. Beyond Allhallows the unlovely power station at Grain and nearby refineries make progress on foot difficult, and I suggest threading your way back on paths and lanes via Lower Stoke and North Street to rejoin the Saxon Shore Way as it reaches the bank of the Medway just to the south-east of Hoo St Werburgh.

Now follow the shingle and mud beach or rough riverside path

westwards via Hoo Marina to Lower Upnor past ruined forts and
an endless line of jetsam and driftwood, although bear in mind that
water may block your passage for an hour either side of high tide.
At Lower Upnor everything seems geared to the river: boatyard,
yacht club, venture centre and pub (the Ship, predictably). An
official notice near the Medway Yacht Club warns river-users
of the 'potentially harmful diseases which may be present in the
water'. It advises: 'do not touch dead animals, especially rats' and
'do not put wet objects such as fishing tackle into your mouth'.

Go around a small military depot and back to the riverside by
the Elizabethan Upnor Castle (open to the public from Easter to
September). On the opposite bank the clamour from the dockyards
and industry of Chatham is now audible. The route proceeds below
Tower Hill and across a field into Frindsbury and Strood.

The official Saxon Shore Way guide describes an intricate
walking route that connects Strood with Gillingham, via Rochester
and Chatham (*A Picturesque Walk Through the Medway Towns*).
It will eventually bring you out at The Strand, the first walkable
piece of waterside since you crossed the Medway, and with it the
approach to the Isle of Sheppey.

GILLINGHAM – FAVERSHAM (44 miles)
Rochester-upon-Medway comprises Strood, Rochester and Chatham,
but they are all likely to blur into one rather built-up sprawl. The
Romans called Rochester Durobrivae, or the stronghold by the
bridge; but it is the Norman influence that has lasted longest, with
the fine cathedral (its crypt contains an altar to Ithamar, the first
English bishop) and powerful castle, which has the highest Keep
in England (34m), and walls up to 13 feet thick. Charles Dickens
knew Rochester and Chatham particularly well. He was five years
old when his family moved to Chatham from Portsmouth, his father
employed in the Navy Pay Office in the dockyard, and many of
the places and faces that the young Dickens got to know appear
in his novels. Rochester is called Cloisterham in *The Mystery of
Edwin Drood*, a book he was still writing when he died in 1870,
having for the last fourteen years lived at Gad's Hill Place, a few
miles away near Higham. More details can be found in the Charles
Dickens Centre, on Rochester High Street.

Chatham, meanwhile, is rooted in the annals of British maritime
history, and for 400 years the naval dockyard produced such famous

ships as HMS *Victory*. On the hillside above the preserved dockyard is Fort Amherst (open daily), a massive Napoleonic fortress with a vast labyrinth of underground tunnels and batteries. But modern Chatham can be full of bustle and fumes; and there is no pedestrian access through the new docks or riverside developments, so head out east past the Royal Engineers Museum and down to the riverside at the Strand Leisure Park.

Here you will find a short but popular promenade, while across the creeks and marshes of the languid reaches of the lower Medway the Isle of Grain shields the Thames from sight; and it will be some time yet before the mouth of the Old Father is regained.

Follow the bankside tarmac path through the Medway Cruising Club's yard and inland around an old factory. Soon the path returns to the edge of the saltmarsh through Riverside Country Park, a pleasant 125 acres of marsh, meadow, pond and grassland. The wild flowers and shrubs of Eastcourt Meadow used to be a landfill site, and the short spit of land known as Horrid Hill was once part of a cement factory. A visitor centre at Sharps Green has more details about the worthy developments that have taken place on this site over the last twenty years. Horrid Hill, by the way, is supposed to have come by its name when prison ships were moored here during the Napoleonic wars, and the French prisoners were forced to endure dreadful conditions.

Soon Saxon Shore Way signs direct you on to a high grassy bank and then the short road to Motney Hill. At the far end, by the sewage works gates (not a place to linger), a stile to the right leads the intrepid walker through fields and back southwards by Otterham Creek. The quay was once important for brickmaking, and there is a track around the shore (not a public right of way); otherwise the more direct route is via footpaths and lanes, and past extensive orchards around Upchurch to return to the waterside at Ham Green. Near here, in Halstow Creek, the Romans picked oysters; and at Lower Halstow they produced brickwork and pottery. Roman tiles can be found in the walls of the nearby St Margaret of Antioch, a Saxon construction. Beyond the village you must either walk Raspberry Hill Lane or parallel footpaths through fields before veering left towards Chetney Hill for a tour of the deserted Chetney Marshes. Nearby Stangate Creek was once used by the authorities for holding incoming foreign vessels placed under quarantine restrictions, and the construction of an isolation hospital, never actually completed, was begun on Chetney Hill. In addition, and at the extreme tip of the marshes, is Deadman's Island, which was where sailors who died from deadly diseases while in quarantine were buried. As you swing back south-eastwards the buildings of Queenborough on the Isle of Sheppey become closer, and at Kingsferry Bridge – the Island's only contact with the mainland – there is the opportunity to nip across the Swale and investigate further.

Sheppey, or the 'Isles of Sheep', actually consists of three separate islands: Sheppey, Elmley and Harty. On the north coast, overlooking the Thames, are Sheerness, Minster and Leysdown, and a string of ugly caravan sites and holiday camps in between. In contrast, Sheppey's southern, Swale shore is a bleak and mostly deserted place, the domain of sheep and birds. There are nature reserves and miles of rough grazing and marshland, with a few paths and tracks for the curious.

Kingsferry Bridge cost £1 million when it was built twenty-five years ago, and if you are into concrete minimalism then this must be the pin-up for you. Its high, brutal shapes rise starkly from the flat marshes next to Swale railway halt. Now follow the banks of the Swale until the path detours inland to avoid Ridham Dock. Across the water is the RSPB's Elmley Reserve, a haven for wintering wildfowl, such as wigeon, teal and Brent geese, and breeding birds include shoveler, pochard and redshank. Seven species of birds occur in internationally significant numbers (what a splendid term!) on the mudflats and saltmarsh islands of the Medway estuary; but occasionally there are rarer visitors, such as the ruff, a wading bird that has only fairly recently begun to breed again in Britain. The male has a distinctive ruff of bright feathers around the neck, like a Tudor courtier.

Back on mainland Kent head up the bank of Milton Creek by the tracks of the Sittingbourne and Kemsley Light Railway. This narrow gauge line (2 ft 6 in) originally served the paper mill, but now its steam locos pull tourists between Easter and mid-October. To regain the Swale and eventually the open sea you have to continue into Sittingbourne then back out via the houses of Murston. Soon the flat, grey marshes of Sheppey reappear across the Swale. Immediately to your right are Murston Lakes, originally excavated for industry and now flooded and enjoyed by wildfowl. Further inland, towards

Teynham, north Kent's fruit-growing empire resumes. Henry VIII often visited the area to sample the orchard produce, and in the words of Mr Jingle, in *The Pickwick Papers*: 'Kent, sir – everybody knows Kent. Apples, cherries, hops and women.'

The straight and purposeful flood wall is punctured by Conyer Creek, popular with nautical types and where the ubiquitous Ship Inn does good business. This one dates from 1642, and has variously been a bakery, blacksmith's shop and smugglers' haunt. Beyond Conyer the Swale's bank extends for 9 miles or so to Faversham, an uncomplicated and easy passage. Inland are the derelict buildings of Uplees Explosive Works, and just before you turn into Oare Creek for Faversham is the slipway of the former Harty Ferry. A ferry crossing was recorded here as long ago as the Domesday Book, and until 1946 a rope-drawn ferry carried passengers to the Isle of Harty's bare fields on Sheppey's south-eastern corner, and specifically to the isolated Ferry Inn. It is told that until the 1930s the landlord would even provide a boat for mainland customers wishing to cross the Swale for a drink. Today there is an information centre for visitors to the Oare Marshes Nature Reserve, with details of not just birds but also plantlife found in the area, such as water parsnip, frogbit and the highly aromatic sea wormwood, a greyish plant with woolly leaves and small, yellow flowers.

FAVERSHAM – HERNE BAY (17 miles)
On a sunny, summer's day, the centre of Faversham is a very nice sort of place. The market stalls are out, the traffic is kept at bay, and it is very tempting just to wander about with an ice cream and to take life slowly. (The presence of the Shepherd Neame brewery may also hinder acceleration.) The Chart Gunpowder Mill, one of the oldest of its kind still in existence, is testimony to the town's former pre-eminence as Britain's explosives capital. Gunpowder was first produced here under the reign of Elizabeth I, and Faversham powder saw use at Trafalgar and Waterloo. At one time there were four factories on the nearby Uplees site, but an explosion in 1916 killed over a hundred workers.

There are a large number of old, half-timbered buildings in Faversham, and some of the most attractive are to be found near the quay. Thames barges still lie idly by the wharves, sometimes tied two abreast, their pencil-thin masts creating a nautical forest that bobs gently up and down on the water.

The coast path resumes along the raised, grassy embankment. Slowly the Swale gives way to the wider waters of the Thames Estuary, and the Isle of Sheppey is finally left behind. Follow the embankment path around Nagden Marshes, where a line of overhead pylons seems to cut a mighty swathe through the empty reedland and pasture. Nagden and Graveney Marshes border the South Swale Nature Reserve, and information boards explain that the saltmarshes and reedbeds along Faversham Creek support sedge and reed warblers, with sea purslane, sea aster and golden samphire all found in the area. In front of you a wide and uninviting expanse of mud and sand called the Oaze stretches across the bay to Whitstable. Nearby a stern-looking sign advises that shellfish must be thoroughly boiled before consumption.

At Seasalter follow the private road over the railway, recrossing it almost immediately by a public footpath that leads via a small golf course into Whitstable. The town's fame mainly rests on the oyster beds that lie offshore, famous since Roman times but now sadly depleted through over-fishing and pollution. The Oyster Company building and museum, plus various seafood restaurants, provide a taste of the past.

Beyond the town signs relate that Tankerton Slopes, above, contain the rare hogs fennel, also known as sulphur weed, a tall perennial from the carrot family and closely related to cow parsley, celery and parsnip. But it doesn't look that great. At Swalecliffe there are huge notices declaring that Canterbury City Council does not condone naturism on the beach. Unfortunately, as hard as I looked, I found nothing to condone, or even frown upon.

After another small bay of soft mud and silt the headland at Hampton is rounded and Herne Bay arrives. Out to sea container craft trundle in and out of the capital, while inshore a few small yachts or a jet skier may be exercising themselves. When evening falls the lights of Southend twinkle across the water. But perhaps the most arresting spectacle is much closer to hand, even though it cannot easily be inspected. Herne Bay's original pier was partly demolished in World War II, and more was destroyed in subsequent storms. All that remains nowadays is the final, lonely stump of the pier-end stuck out on its own in the sea.

HERNE BAY – RAMSGATE (17 miles)

Leave on a pleasant track above a low, grassy landslip, where there are signs not just for the Saxon Shore Way but also the Wantsum Walk, a local recreational route. The first cliffs for a very long time appear, and a wide track along the top leads to the distinctive towers of Reculver. This started life as the Roman fort of Regulbium (part of the foundations are still visible), housed an Anglo-Saxon monastery, then became a parish church. Due to coastal erosion, the church has been relocated, but the massive twin towers were retained as a guide for mariners. More details from the fascinating interpretation centre nearby.

The sea wall heads straight for Birchington, a stretch particularly popular with cyclists. However, there is much to recommend the unhurried inspection that the pedestrian enjoys. The owners of the fish farm to the right recently found three fifty-year-old experimental bouncing bombs at the bottom of their pools. They were apparently used by aircraft training for the World War II 'Dambuster' raids, when the pilots used the sea wall as a mock dam during practice runs. Now look out to sea. If the weather is clear you should be able to make out a number of odd-looking objects sitting far out in the water. These are the little-known Thames Estuary forts, built originally to repel the German Luftwaffe who used the Thames as a route guide into London. They were fixed to the sea bed, and look like spartan, miniature oil rigs. After their Bofur guns had stopped blazing (they were pretty ineffectual) they lay idle until the 1960s, when pirate radio broadcasters took them over. All kinds of adventures and escapades ensued, including tragedy (drownings and a shooting), and nowadays the rusting platforms are slowly decaying and dropping into the sea.

For the next 17 miles to Sandwich Bay you will be walking around the Isle of Thanet. This, of course, is no longer a true island, since the Wantsum Channel has long since silted up. It was on the Isle of Thanet that St Augustine landed with 40 monks in AD 597 and spread the Christian word, founding the see of Canterbury.

From the petite but attractive beach at Minnis Bay there is a continuous coastal walking route all the way to Margate, either along the concrete embankment or across numerous sandy bays. After Birchington, bungalow capital, comes Westgate-on-Sea, a small but popular burst of golden sand to enjoy on summer days. But the real crowds are reserved for Margate. Early visitors came for medicinal reasons, seeking the fashionable watering places of the day and pursuing some of the far-fetched remedies. The Royal

Sea Bathing Hospital was built at Margate, and the classic bathing machine was designed here, with so-called 'modesty hoods' to conceal lady swimmers. As Margate's reputation grew, more and more Londoners made the short journey, initially via sailing packets or hoys (cargo boats) from the East End. Passage was cheap, but the vessels were cramped and in rough weather the journey was sometimes known to take two to three days! The hoys were replaced by passenger steamers, and then, of course, the railway followed. Margate's popular appeal endures, and on August bank holiday, when the place heaves, it is hard to spot a spare piece of sand on the main beach. But – and Margate is not alone in this – walk a few minutes in either direction and there are pleasant, mostly uncrowded beaches that the herd never seems to reach.

From the harbour there is a beachside walkway underneath the cliffs (best at low tide, since it is not continuous), or better still a quiet and airy surfaced track along the grassy clifftop. Go past the smart hotels of Cliftonville, and at Foreness Point begin the slow swing south towards the English Channel. As you round a small golf course the mock turrets of Kingsgate Castle come into view. Built by the man who introduced the bank holiday to Britain, it stands high on the cliff edge above Kingsgate Bay, but has, not surprisingly, suffered from an irresistible urge to slip into the sea. Concrete supports currently keep the rather over-the-top edifice in place. Beyond is Joss Bay, from where a clifftop route can be followed around North Foreland and into Broadstairs. The smart, squat lighthouse to your right alerts shipping to the dangers of the Goodwin Sands (beacons were first lit here as long ago as 1636). A lightship also blinks out its warning of the treacherous Sands which lie about 5 miles offshore and stretch for a total of 12 miles. Their location shifts daily, which must be rather alarming for the Ramsgate harbourmaster since the general trend is a gradual move westwards.

Broadstairs is a smart little resort which would probably be fairly unknown were it not for the fact that Charles Dickens spent many years here, completing many of his most famous works. Not surprisingly, the massed tea shops have rather cashed in on this fact, and it is even possible that you will see men and women strolling along the promenade in Victorian dress, such is the enthusiasm for the eight-day annual Broadstairs Dickens festival every June.

Follow the promenade along the foot of the cliffs past Dumpton

Gap and into Ramsgate. At certain times the port's artificial marina and harbour can seem positively Mediterranean, although many people's memory of Ramsgate today will be a fleeting glimpse from the window of a hovercraft, or from the ferry to Dunkirk. In 1940, however, up to 80,000 soldiers entered the port from the other direction, after evacuation from the Normandy coast.

RAMSGATE – DOVER (23 miles)

Now the Thames Estuary is finally left behind and the South Coast beckons, although at first the mud and wet sand of Pegwell Bay make it a roadside affair until Sandwich, after which the sea is a constant companion once more.

Beyond Ramsgate's noisy hovercraft terminal the Saxon Shore Way can be rejoined as it wanders along the River Stour's western bank behind the unappetising Richborough Power Station. Nearby is Pegwell Bay, which in times gone by was quite a popular landing place for visitors to these shores. It is believed to be close to where Julius Caesar first landed in 55 BC, since Richborough Fort, on the other side of the main road, was the first fortified Roman garrison in Britain, and was built to defend the southern end of the Wantsum Channel. Then, forty years after the Romans left, Hengist and Horsa's Jutes and Saxons came ashore at Ebbsfleet (a replica Viking longship, rowed over from Denmark in 1949, sits on the clifftop above the Bay); followed finally by St Augustine and his monks 150 years later.

Now for a more modern but equally true story. John Montagu, an eighteenth-century earl, was so addicted to gambling that he could not bring himself to leave the cards for the meal table. So he concocted a sort of cold, fast food, by putting cooked beef between two slices of bread – and so the Earl of Sandwich unknowingly launched the Great British snack. Today the town of Sandwich is a small but elegant affair, but in medieval times, before the silting of the River Stour, it was a thriving maritime centre. Sandwich was one of the original Cinque Ports (traditionally pronounced 'sink' in this context), which before the days of the Royal Navy lent ships and men to defend the Crown in return for special freedoms and privileges. The other members of the Confederation of the Cinque Ports were Hastings, Romney, Hythe and Dover. Rye and Winchelsea joined later, and were known as 'Ancient Ports' (thus doing away with all the bother of changing the organisation's name to 'Sept Ports', I suppose). The original five, the so-called 'Head Ports', drew support from a network of surrounding towns and villages which made the Confederation all-powerful. Gradually the effectiveness and influence of the Cinque Ports waned as their harbours silted up and new ports grew, such as Southampton and those in the South-West that benefited from the opening-up of the Americas. The final blow came when a permanent navy was established, and nowadays Dover is the only one of the original Cinque Ports that retains any sea-faring importance.

Leave Sandwich by the Stour and follow the waymarked Saxon Shore Way across the famous Royal St Georges Golf Links, a venue of the British Open Golf Championship, for a walk along the coastal bank above the shingle into Deal.

Deal is a flat, stretched-out place, with narrow alleys and old, bunched-up buildings, and the minimum of gaudiness. Both Deal and nearby Walmer Castle were built by Henry VIII in 1540 in order to protect his fleet when they anchored in the Downs (the odd name for what is in effect Deal Bay). Beyond the ruined beach huts of Kingsdown follow the clear footpath up the cliff path past a small firing range and golf clubhouse.

Now the cliffs truly soar, and the walking is invigorating. Keep to the obvious clifftop path until above St Margaret's Bay there is a long flight of steps down to the tiny seafront below. Most of St Margaret's at Cliffe is actually up on the massive chalk cliffs above, but at least the Coastguard public house is by the water's edge. The large house at the eastern end of the bay once belonged to Noël Coward, who rented it out to 007-creator Ian Fleming. (Fleming, by the way, was a keen ornithologist, and he chose the name James Bond after an author of a book on birds.) St Margaret's Bay is the point of departure for many cross-Channel swimmers, since France is just about at its closest here (roughly 22 miles away). The first man to swim the Channel was a Merchant Navy captain, Matthew Webb, in August 1875, and his statue is to be found on Dover's East Cliff promenade, three miles away. He had a distinctive approach to swimming, to say the least, crossing the Channel without goggles by breaststroke, and spending a total of nearly twenty-two hours in the water. Captain Webb is believed to have actually swum as much as 38 miles in order to make the crossing, and is reported to have kept out the cold by doses of cod-liver oil, beef tea, brandy, coffee, and strong old ale. Eight years later he tried to swim the rapids below Niagara Falls and drowned. (The Channel has since been swum in under eight hours!)

Follow the steep (and only) road up the hill and after a couple of left turns regain the clifftop. This Deal–Folkestone stretch is Kent's only piece of official Heritage Coast, separated into two parts by the port of Dover, and it is surprising how handsome and under-walked these white cliffs – in fact *the* White Cliffs of Dover – turn out to be. Don't just gaze sentimentally at them from a ferry, but instead put your boots on and explore. Here, from the cliffs at South Foreland, it is possible to see Cap Gris Nez on a clear day, and gaze at the busy shipping – the Strait of Dover is the busiest sea lane in the world. The two clifftop lighthouses on South Foreland originally used coal fires to warn shipping of the Goodwin Sands, and later became the first in the country to use electricity. Neither is operational today.

At Langdon Bay, and with Dover approaching, follow the higher of the tracks across ground presently being grazed by Exmoor ponies in an effort to reduce the coarse grass and encourage chalk-loving wild flowers. You will want to pause by the National Trust café at Langdon Cliffs picnic area, since the hubbub of Dover's Eastern Docks below is captivating. The port is a hive of unending activity, with ferries and hovercraft zipping in and out every few minutes. The noise, alone, is astounding.

Dover's importance stretches back 2,000 years. Julius Caesar considered landing here, but was deterred by the sight of some natives haranguing him from the clifftop. He soon made Dover a chief port, however, and the remains of the earliest Roman lighthouse (or 'pharos') in Britain can be found next to the imposing castle, which itself dates from the time of Henry II (twelfth century). Behind the castle in a field is the flat granite shape of a plane, marking the spot where Louis Blériot landed in July 1909 after the first flight across the Channel. In addition, the castle grounds also contain the entrance to the newly opened Hellfire Corner, 3½ miles of tunnels dug into the cliffs over the last 200 years and from where Admiral Ramsay coordinated the evacuation of Dunkirk. There's a lot to see around here.

DOVER – HYTHE (15 miles)

The most important development in Dover's recent history is, of

course, the Channel Tunnel, and one by-product is a large seashore
dump of tunnel debris near the Western Docks which has been given
the name Samphire Hoe. At the time of writing it is being landscaped
and should eventually be 'returned to nature'. Maybe a new walking
route in years to come? Another result is inevitable road construction, and this, too, is sadly evident as you leave the port. From the
centre of Dover, opposite the White Cliffs Experience, climb steps
to Western Heights, which contain the remains of a large Napoleonic
fortification. Then cross the South Military Road and drop down
through fields to pass below the new highway which roars into
Dover from the west, and take the path up on to Shakespeare
Cliff where a scene of *King Lear* is set, complete with samphire
gatherer off stage below. Oh, how the bard would have cried! What
were once peaceful meadows behind this famous landmark are now
full of the sound of speeding vehicles. Perhaps the blinded Earl of
Gloucester might succeed in jumping this time. There is a stone
plinth by the path which indicates the distances to London, Paris,
and a few other places, but it's not terribly inspiring.

However, don't despair. The erosion is short-lived and there is
another stretch of bracing cliff walking ahead. You may be joined
not just by Saxon Shore Way walkers but also by those finishing
the 153-mile North Downs Way (which arrives at the Channel coast
near Folkestone). And it is just possible that some walkers from the
Continent may be stepping out for the first time on British soil, since
it is hoped that one of this country's first E-paths (European walking
routes) will begin at Dover, and then follow the North Downs Way
towards London.

Continue west along the clifftop path. Soon the Dover–Folkestone
railway emerges from a tunnel beneath you, occupying a tiny ledge
above the shore; then the huge natural landslip of Folkestone Warren
opens up, which is where the soft gault underlying the chalk has
slumped. Although this is rich in fossils and wildlife, ignore tracks
down to the Warren, since the views are better from up top and
there is a handily placed café near Capel-le-Ferne. In addition,
the new Battle of Britain Monument that is situated virtually
on the path is well worth pausing over. It takes the form of a
gigantic propeller set into the ground, with a statue of a young
pilot contemplating the skies. At the western end of the Warren
leave the North Downs Way and descend to a wide, grassy strip
containing Martello Tower No. 3, now a visitor centre, and the

admirable East Cliff Pavilion Café. Below lies Folkestone, once described by Defoe as a 'miserable fishing town', which is a little uncharitable. The five miles from Folkestone Harbour to Hythe are built-up and uninteresting, apart perhaps from Sandgate Castle, one of Henry VIII's coastal defences.

Hythe, an original Cinque Port, is a nice enough place with one highly unusual visitor attraction. If you want to inspect the crypt of St Leonard's Parish Church you may come across a collection of 8,000 human thigh bones and 500 skulls from the fourteenth century (it is thought that they may have been exhumed from previous graves). Meanwhile others come to the town to ride on the Romney, Hythe and Dymchurch Railway, a miniature, 15-inch gauge line that runs for 14 miles along the coast to Dungeness. Like the Ravenglass and Eskdale Railway in Cumbria (which you will meet much later on this coastal walk) the microscopic size of everything takes a little getting used to – you expect Alice in Wonderland to squeeze out of one of the engine sheds that hold the one-third full-size steam engines.

HYTHE – RYE (26 miles)
According to the early nineteenth-century writings of Thomas Ingoldsby, the world is divided into five quarters: Europe, Africa, Asia, America . . . and Romney Marsh. Ingoldsby was the alias for local rector Richard Harris Barham, who warned of the likelihood of still finding the occasional witch 'weathering Dungeness Point in an egg-shell, or careering on her broom-stick over Dymchurch wall' (*Ingoldsby Legends*). Frightening stuff indeed. But wander Romney Marsh in the brooding darkness of an incoming storm, or when the mist and rain is swirling, and the imagination can run riot.

However, it has to be said that while there are paths and lanes across Romney Marsh itself the actual shoreline is not to every walker's taste. From Hythe the rather featureless and dead flat shore curves slowly out to the exposed point of Dungeness. There you come face to face with Dungeness A and B, two nuclear power stations, and beyond this the MOD's forbidding Holmstone Lydd Ranges, necessitating a detour inland. So I suggest you walk from Hythe or Dymchurch to Dungeness and then take the narrow gauge railway or lanes across the marsh back; or perhaps go as far as Littlestone or Lade and then cut off the promontory by taking public footpaths across the marshes south-west to Camber.

If the red flags of Hythe Ranges are not flying you are permitted to walk the foreshore; otherwise via the pavement of the A259, or go one stop on the railway. Then from Dymchurch Redoubt all the way around to Dungeness you can walk along the sea wall or shore. There are several Martello Towers, a few hopeful fishermen, and towards Dungeness an interminable string of rather forlorn-looking bungalows and curious single-storey dwellings, including old railway carriages. Even the pub at Dungeness, the Britannia Inn, was originally a couple of low military block houses joined together. A jewel in the crown is Romney Bay House, on the northern edge of Littlestone-on-Sea, a handsome and sumptuous 1920s building designed by Sir Clough Williams-Ellis (architect of the Italian-style North Wales fishing village Portmeirion) for the American actress and columnist Hedda Hopper. Today the house takes paying guests, but the passing walker can still enjoy a lavish high tea in luxurious surroundings.

If Dungeness is the chin of Romney Marsh, jutting out into the English Channel, then the nuclear power stations on the end are like a couple of unsightly pimples. It is a desolate and windswept place, with a vast shingle headland (the largest accumulation of the stuff in Europe) where even the miniature railway gives up and goes home. Its very wildness is an attraction to wildlife though, and Dungeness Bird Sanctuary is a convenient landfall site for migrating birds. Gulls and terns also nest on specially created islands in flooded former gravel pits. Unless visiting the reserve, or the pub, coastal walkers making for Rye should leave the sea at Lade and strike west to Lydd, where the tower of the medieval All Saints Church is visible for miles around. Then, staying north of the indelicately named Jury's Gut Sewer, rejoin the shore at Camber Sands, popular with runners, windsurfers, energetic children and film directors. The World War II epic *The Longest Day* was one of many films to use this venue, in this instance recreating the massive Normandy beach landings of 1944 (although what John Wayne and Robert Mitchum made of Romney Marsh is sadly not known).

Since there is no access across the mouth of the River Rother, follow the pleasant public footpath along the floodbank of the Rother beside the golf course all the way into Rye. However, the Saxon Shore Way traces a very different route from Hythe to Rye, along the edge of the rising ground of Romney Marsh's north and west borders (via West Hythe, Aldington, Ham Street and Appledore), which in effect was the former shoreline in Roman times. The SSW also borrows the odd mile from the Royal Military Canal towpath. This 28-mile waterway was built as part of Britain's hasty defence against the anticipated French invasion, which also included the construction of Martello Towers and plans to flood Romney Marsh in the event of a landing. (The idea of a 30-foot ditch halting Napoleon's mighty armies, especially after having just crossed the Channel, is perhaps a little optimistic.) Today the Royal Military Canal is being developed as a waymarked walking route between Hythe and Rye.

Rye is not strictly on the coast any more, but it is still the first place upstream that the Rother can be crossed. One of the two additional Cinque Ports, Rye's timbered houses and cobbled streets continue to attract many visitors, although not all have been friendly. The French came over for a day or two in 1377, and rather impolitely fired the town and stole the church bells (both the museum in the Ypres Tower and the Heritage Centre on Strand Quay have more details). Predictably enough, the lads from the Cinque Ports went straight over and ransacked Boulogne. Some things never change.

RYE – HASTINGS (14 miles)
Return to the shore at Rye Harbour via road or a footpath along the edge of Castle Water, a former gravel extraction pit now nature reserve near the ruined Camber Castle. At Rye Harbour refreshment is provided by the William the Conqueror, a comely Shepherd Neame pub, and the Bosun's Bite café. From the information kiosk a small lane runs to the mouth of the Rother and a track along the shore to Winchelsea Beach. Rye Harbour Local Nature Reserve includes the Ternery Pool and Wader Pool, whose attractions are self-evident.

At Winchelsea Beach the robust sea wall leads to Cliff End and Pett Level. A mile inland is Winchelsea, which like Rye once enjoyed a seaboard location until river silting and reclamation drove the waves back. Now the small, sleepy town sits marooned on a hillside above the River Breda, gazing forlornly at the distant sea. Of course we've already seen coastal erosion at work on the East Coast, but the ability of the elements to alter the face of the landscape permanently is evident even on this relatively benign stretch of South Coast. The original settlement of Winchelsea lay near present-day Camber, but was wiped out by the sea in a succession of storms in the thirteenth century; and more recently, a ferocious gale in 1827 swept masses of shingle across the original mouth of the River Rother at New Romney, diverting the flow to the sea at Rye and helping create the marshes of Romney that we see today.

A stern red sign at the end of the sea wall at Cliff End barks: 'Warning. No exit from the beach for the next three miles. Check tides before proceeding.' A glance at the high, impenetrable cliffs ahead should be enough to convince Hastings-bound walkers to take a clifftop and not a seashore route, so follow the road inland for a few hundred yards, past the Market Stores, until a small sign for the cliff path leads up a track on the left. Soon this emerges on to the National Trust's Fairlight Cliffs, a brief but invigorating and windy half mile that represents the first real cliff since Dover.

All too soon the path descends into the leafy but uninteresting Fairlight Cove, along an unsurfaced road by a house with the splendid name of 'The Haddocks'. Unfortunately other properties nearby are not faring too well. Some are literally falling into the sea, and since the cliff-edge lane has already done this follow a brief diversion inland before returning via Cliff Way for an alleyway (right), then left along a part-surfaced lane past dormant houses. This leads into Bramble Way, and at the end turn left and on to Channel Way.

Back to the sea views once more, and when the buildings end the heathy slopes of Hastings Country Park take over. For over 3 miles the jaunty coastal track skips across rolling heathland and cliff, and dips through sheltered, wooded glens. The 640 acres of the unspoilt park play host to song- and sea-birds, butterflies and crickets, and there are plenty of paths and tracks to explore. At the eastern end of the country park is the Firehills, a large area of heathland that possibly takes its name from the bright yellow gorse that grows in abundance and flowers in April and May. The ancient woodland of Fairlight Glen, meanwhile, is full of the small white flowers of wood anemones and rich carpets of bluebells, plus there is also access to the beach. The path finally finishes beyond East Hill at the top of the cliff railway looking directly down on Hastings.

A steep but surfaced path leads down to the Tackleway and into the attractive, old part of the town. The fishing boats, or luggers (a name derived from the distinctive four-sided lugsails that these

Northumberland castles: Bamburgh (*above*) and Dunstanburgh (*below*)
have had to endure many centuries of wear and tear.

Staithes nestles in a cleft in the rocks east of Saltburn-by-the-Sea and offers welcome respite from the windy clifftop for Cleveland Way walkers.

Flamborough Head (*above*) is popular with both ramblers and seabirds; but much further south the Norfolk cliffs are less stable (*below*) and extreme care must be exercised.

Shingle Street (*above*) lives up to its name, and gives the Suffolk Coast Path a distinctive feel. The flat scenery continues in Essex, where St Peter-on-the-Wall, Bradwell-on-Sea (*below*) has been the focus of worship since the seventh century.

The towers of Reculver dominate the Saxon Shore Way on the north Kent coast (*above*); while the South Downs provide an attractive backdrop to Chichester Harbour at Bosham (*below*).

The formidable shingle bar of Chesil Bank, which stretches as far as the Isle of Portland (*above*). Golden Cap from Stonebarrow Hill, near Charmouth, the high-spot of the South Coast (*below*).

Near Kingswear, at the richly-wooded mouth of the River Dart in south Devon (*above*); while the cliffs of the Lizard (*below*) are often covered in an array of wild flowers.

A rugged stretch of coastwalking at Lantic Bay, near Polruan, Cornwall.

boats originally used) are pulled up via rollers high on the wide, shingly beach, and their catch is auctioned early most mornings, then sold over the counter in the former net shops nearby. These tall, narrow sheds date from the early nineteenth century and were built to store fishermen's nets and ropes, and their peculiar shape was simply due to a shortage of space on the beach. Along from the net shops is the Fishermen's Museum (formerly the Fishermen's Church), and the Shipwreck Heritage Centre, Britain's only museum specialising in shipwrecks, which includes the remains of a Roman ship built about AD 150, one of the oldest known seagoing sailing ships from northern Europe. Then of course there is Hastings Castle, and something called the 1066 Story, a modern, audio-visual interpretation of the fateful events of that year. But that tale can wait for a moment.

HASTINGS – EASTBOURNE (15 miles)

Hastings loses a little of its charm the further west you proceed along the seafront, as the gaudiness of the modern resort and the drabness of the modern high street become stronger. Imperceptibly Hastings merges into St Leonards, once a posher spin-off of the former. Marine Court, a high, elegant block of flats that from head-on looks like a gleaming ocean liner is one of the few points of interest. Approaching Glyne Gap the railway muscles its way to the front, but there is space on the shore for the walker, and a surfaced cycle/footpath leads from Galley Hill into Bexhill.

I doubt many tourists or intrepid coastal walkers will be particularly inspired by the first sight of Bexhill: blocks of ugly, featureless flats line the seafront, making you wonder whether punishment and not retirement is the order of the day (over half of Bexhill's permanent residents are senior citizens). Things improve, however, the more you explore. Bexhill Museum is worth a visit, and the graceful shapes of the De La Warr Pavilion are particularly fine. Designed in 1933 by the architects Erich Mendelsohn and Serge Chermayeff, this Grade 1 listed building was the first purpose-built seaside entertainment complex in the country, and its balconies and colonnade built in the international Modernist style of the time overshadow most seaside architecture designed since.

The high, gently sloping shingle shore continues to Cooden, where the tarmac lane behind the pebbles may offer easier walking until it veers inland. This is Norman's Bay, part of Pevensey Bay, and it is around here that William the Conqueror is believed to have landed on 28 September 1066.

Harold was an unlucky sod. He agreed to step in after the death of Edward the Confessor looked likely to leave the country in the hands of a boy named Edgar, then was immediately faced by two serious invasions. Harald Hardrada and his Viking hordes arrived in the autumn of 1066 and rampaged around Yorkshire until Harold was forced to send his crack troops north to end the fuss at Stamford Bridge. Three days later the strong winds that for six weeks had been keeping William's forces at bay relented and the Normans crossed the Channel. Harold's exhausted army rushed back southwards and met the Normans for the showdown on a hill 6 miles north-west of Hastings, where the present-day village and Abbey of Battle stand. Even though Harold's men were tired and depleted it was still a close-run thing, but eventually the Norman cavalry and archers won the day. William, Duke of Normandy, was crowned at Westminster on Christmas Day 1066.

As you crunch along the shingle of Pevensey Bay past Martello Towers and caravans the welcome (or perhaps daunting) sight of Beachy Head looms larger, appearing like a gigantic beached whale beyond Eastbourne, although you will have to deviate inland around a new harbour and housing development before entering the resort. Before you do, consider the merits of a brief excursion inland. The ruined, medieval castle staring at you across Pevensey Levels was actually built on the site of a Roman fort, but its importance is given away in the reference on the OS map: 'Traditional site of the Landing of the Normans, 1066'. The present-day village of Pevensey was then a small port, with the sea washing over today's bare pasture, and it was here that William and his 14,000 men established camp before moving on to construct a more robust fortification at Hastings and preparing for battle.

Next to the entrance of Eastbourne's pier there is an important if rather inconspicuous notice entitled 'Walking for Health': 'Brisk walking helps decrease body fat; increased exercise levels help to lower blood pressure; walking is ideal exercise for all body shapes and abilities; brisk walking makes the heart work more efficiently.' I smiled smugly and jotted down these valuable facts, musing on official confirmation of what I had known all along – that walking is jolly good for you and that everyone should be out doing it. Only when I looked up did I realise that I was being met with stares of suspicion and alarm by almost everyone around me. Clearly these unhealthy fat Londoners, devouring ice cream and chips, were not getting the message. But I decided to be prudent. Conversion could wait for another day. So I put my notebook away and hurried off along the prom. This was a good move, because here I found a useful little building that imparts valuable information for any walker contemplating Beachy Head and the Seven Sisters. Eastbourne's attractive, tiered promenade incorporates a tiny meteorological station that displays up-to-the-minute data on local temperatures, rainfall, pressure, and so on, with handy short-range forecasts.

Most appropriately, Claude Debussy composed *La Mer* while staying in Eastbourne in 1905. But was he into brisk walking?

EASTBOURNE – NEWHAVEN (15 miles)
Eastbourne is the starting point for the South Downs Way National Trail, a 106-mile route that rides the crest of the lovely Sussex Downs to finish across Hampshire's border in Winchester. It's by and large an easy and certainly a scenic journey, and would be a fine choice of route for the uncommitted coastal walker who wants to shun the urbanised Brighton–Bognor stretch. At Winchester you could then join the 27-mile Itchen Way as it wanders southwards to Southampton, and so rejoin the coast for the Solent Way to Milford-on-Sea. However, such an extensive diversion would miss a sizeable strip of the Channel coast, including Chichester Harbour. And do you really want to forego Brighton?

The beginning of the South Downs Way is at the far western end of Eastbourne's seafront, where there is an official noticeboard at the foot of a very steep slope. You will not be surprised to learn that the former points walkers up the latter. Why the South Downs Way begins like this is unclear. Perhaps it is for the views over Eastbourne; but at the top there is only scrubland and a golf course. Instead, I suggest that the dedicated coastal walker follows the public footpath immediately left, which works its way around the cliff edge by Whitebread Hole and via a steep path rejoins the National Trail at the top of Beachy Head.

At the windy, exposed 'summit' there is a tremendous sense of elevation, unmatched even by the White Cliffs of Kent, although the highest point on the Channel Coast is not actually here (163m) but at Golden Cap in Dorset (191m). Nevertheless the views are panoramic – as far east as Dungeness – and skylarks and seabirds fill the huge sky all around. The name Beachy Head is from 'beau chef' meaning 'beautiful headland', although early Venetian sailors knew it as the 'Devil's Cape' because of the dangerous shallows at its foot. Here sits the famous red-and-white striped Royal Sovereign lighthouse, although the best view of it is not from directly above but a little further west. Nearby is Belle Tout, a former clifftop lighthouse that was made redundant by fog that frequently obscured the high clifftop location and rendered the light useless.

The wonderful clifftop walk now continues along the Sussex Heritage Coast to Birling Gap, where there are refreshments and access to the beach; and after this is the Seven Sisters. For an energetic and uplifting rollercoaster of a romp nothing beats the 2½ miles between Birling Gap and Cuckmere Haven. Unless your legs are tiring it is difficult to resist charging up and down the springy chalky turf of the first couple of Sisters, although by the time you stagger up the final slope of Haven Brow it may be a different story. From east to west the Sisters are: Went Hill, Baily's Hill, Flagstaff Point, Brass Point, Rough Brow, Short Brow and Haven Brow (or Cliff End), but if you keep a careful count as you walk them you may detect an extra crest (called Flat Hill) just before Flagstaff Point – a missing eighth Sister?

The chalk cliffs end abruptly at Cuckmere Haven, where a well-walked track descends steeply to the pebbly beach. This is the only river mouth between Ipswich and Southampton not to be overshadowed by retirement bungalows or industrial development, nor tainted by roads. King Alfred the Great is supposed to have founded a shipyard here; but by the 1800s it was mainly used by violent smuggling gangs moving contraband French brandy upriver to Alfriston. Both the original and canalised River Cuckmere are usually unsuitable to wade, so walk upstream for a mile to Exceat Bridge, or to the Seven Sisters Country Park visitor centre at Exceat, where there are exhibitions showing what has been achieved in the Park since East Sussex County Council acquired the land in 1971. One particular success story is the return of peregrine falcons to the Sussex cliffs, after they had completely stopped breeding here in the 1950s due to the effects of insecticides and poisons.

The return to the shore is along the Vanguard Way, a 63-mile long-distance path that begins rather improbably at East Croydon Station, then crosses the Weald of Surrey and Sussex before arriving at Cuckmere Haven. You will be following the last three miles of the trail as it heads west along the cliffs to finish at Seaford. The trail is named after the mainly London-based Vanguards Rambling Club, who pioneered the route, and who arrived at their name by the fact that travelling back on the train from a ramble in Devon in April 1965 there were so many of them they could not fit into one compartment and so all squeezed into the guards van.

From the low cliffs on the western side of Cuckmere Haven there are classic views of the Seven Sisters, with the seven (or is it eight?) massive ripples of chalk cliff extending out into the distance. It is an easy path to Seaford, culminating in the swelling of Seaford Head, where the fabulous sight of the Seven Sisters may now be rivalled by new views west towards Brighton and the Isle of Wight.

The main part of Seaford is back from the seafront, which is fortunate since it is a frightfully dull place. Continue briskly on to Bishopstone, where a public footpath leaves the road as it turns inland, then runs parallel with the railway for a short distance across meadows, and via Tide Mills into the harbourside industry of Newhaven; or else follow Seaford Bay all the way to East Pier and head upstream.

Pick of the walks

FOLKESTONE – SANDWICH (22 miles): undulating route via some fascinating and diverse scenery and attractions, including several castles and Dover's famous White Cliffs.

EASTBOURNE – SEAFORD (12 miles): another station-to-station route along the invigorating chalk cliffs of Sussex, via Beachy Head and the Seven Sisters. This one will make you puff!

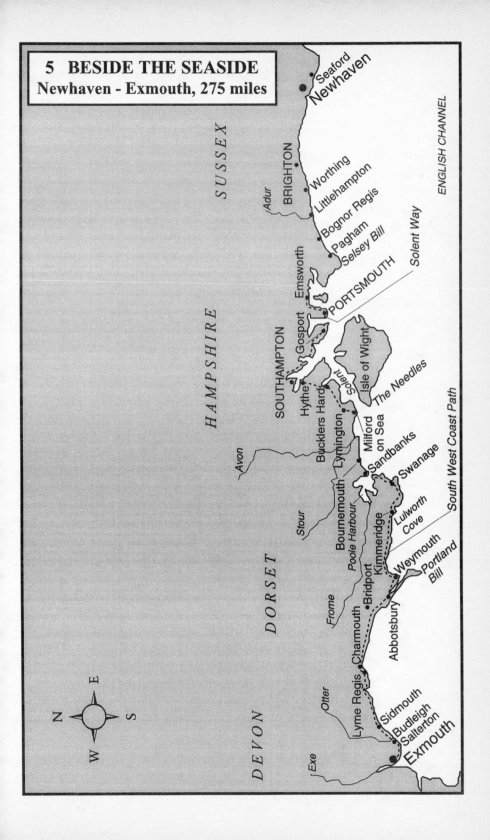

5 BESIDE THE SEASIDE
Newhaven - Exmouth, 275 miles

SUSSEX

HAMPSHIRE

DORSET

DEVON

ENGLISH CHANNEL

Seaford
Newhaven

Adur

BRIGHTON

Worthing

Littlehampton

Bognor Regis

Pagham
Selsey Bill

Emsworth

PORTSMOUTH

Solent Way

Gosport

Hythe

SOUTHAMPTON

Isle of Wight

The Needles

Solent

Bucklers Hard

Lymington

Milford
on Sea

Sandbanks

Swanage

Avon

Bournemouth

Poole Harbour

Lulworth
Cove

South West Coast Path

Stour

Frome

Bridport

Kimmeridge

Weymouth

Portland
Bill

Abbotsbury

Charmouth

Otter

Lyme Regis

Sidmouth

Budleigh
Salterton

Exmouth

Exe

N
E
S
W

NEWHAVEN – WORTHING (21 miles)

The Channel Coast has some common themes: proximity to the Continent has meant that it is well-endowed with ports and ferry terminals, but on the other hand it has meant that it has had to be fortified in the face of attack and threats of invasion. The remains of Roman forts, Napoleonic Martello Towers and Second World War pillboxes can all be found between Kent and Cornwall. However, if there is one feature that typifies this south-facing coast above all others it must be the seaside resort. Although Scarborough was the first, and Blackpool the most popular, it is the Sussex resorts of Hastings, Eastbourne, Brighton, Worthing, Littlehampton and Bognor that typify the bustling, showy, built-up face of modern British coastal development. There are quieter backwaters ahead, around Chichester Harbour and the fringe of the New Forest; but for the next 80 miles or so from Newhaven to the Solent there is no real coast path. Instead there are colourful, noisy promenades; coast roads and seafronts; and endless rows of flats and bungalows. Hilaire Belloc despaired for the lost coast of Sussex, calling it 'a string of London outposts'. But in this relatively recent transformation from fishing villages to booming resorts is the history of the British seaside phenomenon, and that above all else means Brighton.

Newhaven is more a harbour/ferry port than a resort, and seen from the cliffs to the west the massive Dieppe ferry seems to engulf the small quayside. The port owes its existence to huge storms around 1570 which completely re-routed the River Ouse. Prior to this the river met the sea near Seaford.

Perched on a cliff above the harbour entrance is Newhaven Fort, a virtually impregnable 10-acre fortress built to repel the French, and seventy years later made ready again to rebuff a German invasion. Newhaven was also the site of an unusual trade in flints (often known as 'boulders'). These were gathered from the surrounding beaches then loaded into ships for transportation via Runcorn to the Potteries, where they would be ground into pottery material.

Beyond the fort there is a path past a coastguard lookout and along the soft, crumbling cliffs all the way into Peacehaven.

At Peacehaven Heights there are steep steps down to a lower promenade at the foot of the high chalk, but since this leads pretty much nowhere it's not worth the effort. Built ostensibly for returning First World War veterans, Peacehaven was originally meant to be called Anzac-on-Sea, and its construction sparked a bitter struggle between conservationists and developers. Today its ordered rows of bungalows with names like 'Sea View' and concrete lions on the gateposts look like any other dismal seaside sprawl. Perhaps the only feature of interest is that the Greenwich meridian (zero degrees longitude) leaves England at this location, and is celebrated by a monument that lists the distance from this point of various Commonwealth cities (Canberra is 10,564 miles away). However, there is a clear path seaward of the buildings until Saltdean, when you should descend to the Undercliff Walk for the short distance into Brighton (although notices warn against this route in bad weather, and indeed the concrete walkway was awash with storm-tossed beach pebbles when last I walked it). Alternatively, the grassy strip next to the A259 reveals great views over Brighton from the billowing downland crest at Rottingdean. Descend past the famous Roedean Girls' School and prepare to go promenading.

Once upon a time Brighton was a small, unremarkable fishing settlement, and it may have developed little but for the actions of two people. Dr Richard Russell from Lewes first attracted visitors to Brighthelmstone (as it was originally called) when his theories on seawater cures became the fashion. Russell's 'Dissertation on the Use of Seawater in Diseases of the Glands' (1750) was widely admired, and his suggestions for not just bathing in but also drinking seawater (diluted with milk for the very ill!) were readily taken up. Then in 1783 the Prince of Wales (later George IV) visited the resort, and so impressed was he with his reception that he returned many times, bringing with him a loud and stylish entourage and encouraging a whole army of others to make the coach journey from London. George married in Brighton, and later had John Nash design the sumptuous Royal Pavilion in the style of an oriental palace. Late eighteenth-century Brighton was the place to be, and many of the trappings of the modern seaside resort date from that period. For instance, women spectators at the popular Brighton races began parading on donkeys – a seaside association that has endured ever since. Brighton's famous Chain Pier, built in 1823, was the first construction of its kind to be designed specifically for the purpose of promenading (the pier was supported by chains hung between oak piles driven into the sea bed). It is reported that William IV loved nothing more than to stroll up and down it giving out sweets to young children and imagining himself far out to sea. The Chain Pier was swept away by gales seventy years later, but by then the attractions and amusements of Brighton's new West Pier had taken over.

Amid the modern guest houses and arcades Regency Brighton does still exist, as Royal Crescent and other parades testify, and a stroll along the prom is to be recommended. 'London-by-the-Sea' still retains much of the metropolitan flair and flavour that distinguishes it from other resorts. It has been said that couples who have been together for a long while choose Bournemouth for a holiday; but they go to Brighton for affairs.

Brighton merges imperceptibly into Hove, a much more serene place where elderly ladies quietly play bowls on seafront greens. This contrast between neighbouring resorts – one loud and colourful and the other demure and overtly respectable – is not uncommon: Blackpool and Lytham St Anne's, Clacton and Frinton, and Hastings and St Leonards all echo this trend.

Beyond Hove the scene is dominated by the power station at Portslade, and Shoreham Docks. Although not principally a shipbuilding site, Shoreham Docks was where two massive sea forts were constructed by the Navy in 1917. These so-called 'mystery ships' were intended to be the first of six that would form a line of forts across the Channel, between which a huge anti-submarine net would be hung. But the First World War ended before the plan could be enacted. One fort was broken up, and the other is on the sea bed off the Isle of Wight.

Once across the Adur there is much more pleasant walking, and west of Shoreham Beach there is firm sand below the shingle at low tide that continues past South Lancing into Worthing.

WORTHING – PAGHAM (20 miles)
Worthing can be summed up by one guidebook reference: 'Bowls is extremely popular here.' It was even the site of the world championships a few years ago. An uninspiring place, it must be said, so best press on to Littlehampton, about 9 miles away, either along the narrow strip of sand revealed below the shingle at low tide, or the never-ending seafront.

Where the Arun meets the sea, however, there is interest and activity once more. Littlehampton is not as brazen as Brighton, but not as sleepy as Worthing, and its river mouth not as spoilt as the Adur's at Shoreham. The port has been in use for centuries, although it was previously just an outpost of Arundel and until about 1500 the Arun actually entered the sea at Lancing, ten miles to the east. Excavation and new cuts made the mouth of the river more accessible, and the Littlehampton Harbour Act of 1732 allowed harbour dues to be levied in order to finance further improvements and to counter silting, the bane of so many ports.

West of the moored yachts there is open space for the first time in many miles. A public footpath trots across the fields to Atherington, or else you can return to the mouth of the Arun and pass seaward of the golf course. All too soon the bungalows creep up again, and at Middleton-on-Sea (which originally grew out of a First World War seaplane base) the Bognor miles begin.

In the late 1780s Sir Richard Hotham, a well-off London hat-maker, decided to create a new watering place to rival Bath and Brighton. He wanted to call his new seaside resort Hothampton, for obvious reasons, but died before things really got off the ground, and it ended up Bognor. Later, following a visit by King George V, the resort gained a royal suffix. Opinion from the throne is open to debate, however, following His Majesty's curious and much-disputed death-bed gasp. When told by his physician that he would be going back to the South Coast to convalesce after illness King George is supposed to have uttered the immortal dying words: 'Bugger Bognor!'

Continue along the low, monotonous shingle shore as it swings southwards to Selsey Bill. A sizeable diversion is required to skirt Pagham Harbour, around 1,000 acres of natural saltmarsh, lagoon and tidal mudflats. There was a harbour here as long ago as 1345, but by 1875 it had become silted and the land was reclaimed. Then on 16 December 1910 a combination of heavy rain and high tide punctured the sea wall and the waters spilled back. The result is a massive nature reserve that is home to 200 different species of birds, including breeding little terns, shelduck, redshank and Brent geese (which can number up to 4,000 in winter). On most weekends there is a veritable army of twitchers hiding in the long grass. But over 340 varieties of flowering plants have also been recorded here – and even thirteen species of woodlice! From Pagham Spit, a narrow shingle bank by the harbour mouth (where the incoming tide simply zips through), there is a virtually continuous footpath around the edge of the wide expanse of mud and water, spoilt only by a massive caravan park just over the hedge in Pagham. On the far side of the harbour, near Sidlesham, there is an excellent visitor centre; and from near there the waterside path resumes to Church Norton, only a mile away from Selsey.

PAGHAM – EMSWORTH (40 miles)

If you imagine Beachy Head at the eastern end of a massive, gently curving bay that encompasses Newhaven, Brighton, Worthing and Bognor, then Selsey Bill is the western tip. It is actually the southernmost point of Sussex, but far more interesting is the fact that apparently it was once the centre of a thriving mousetrap industry. In late Victorian times as many as 1,000 mousetraps were produced here in a single week, and taken by cart to Chichester for distribution around the world. Unlike the 'break-back' type, the Selsey model never wore out, and remained popular until, well, cats got the upper hand, I suppose. Today Selsey is a quiet and unassuming place, with a pleasant shore walk above the East Beach and for a short distance west of the Bill, otherwise it can be a tedious shingle trudge, and at high tide you must seek a pavement route through the town. One of the most famous residents was St Wilfrid, patron saint of Sussex, no less, and one-time Bishop of Northumbria. He was shipwrecked here in the seventh century, then returned a few years later and founded a monastery. It became a major Episcopal centre for several centuries until the encroaching sea forced a move to Winchester in 1075. The site of Wilfrid's monastery is believed to have been lost under the sea, but it is said that the odd block of the building's original Caen stone has occasionally been recovered.

From the defensive groynes and concrete sea defences of Selsey Bill there is no coast path westwards, just a high shingle bank with a few tawdry holiday camps and empty fields behind. However, choose your moment carefully and at low tide over six continuous miles of firm sand are revealed. Because of strong currents swimming is not recommended, but instead the great sweep of Bracklesham Bay is a walkers' (and horseriders') delight. It even won the Solent Water Quality Award for 1994. Offshore is a flotilla of ferries, naval ships, tankers and yachts approaching and leaving the Solent (technically Spithead), while, on the far side of the water is the bulk of Culver Cliff and Bembridge Down – the first close-up view of the Isle of Wight. Due west is the Portsmouth skyline, steadily approaching as you stride past East and West Wittering to the mouth of Chichester Harbour.

Chichester Harbour, like Pagham before it, is not an industrialised, carved-out basin lined with busy wharves and derricks, but a vast, natural lagoon of creeks, mudflats and marshes. Arms of land extend out into the main area of water, where birds outnumber mariners, and the harbour is said to total up to 50 miles of shoreline and 17 miles of navigable channels. The faithful coast walker will have a long trek, but the rewards are great. After miles of promenades, donkey rides, funfairs and chip shops, touristy Sussex is virtually at an end, and ahead is the many-faced but interesting shoreline of Hampshire.

To begin your circuit of Chichester Harbour first take a short stroll out to the National Trust's East Head, a sliver of low sand dunes that extends out into the harbour mouth like a bent finger. It was stabilised a few years ago by stone-filled gabions (cylinders of woven metal bands), and by the sowing of marram and lyme grass, but until then the spit was gradually changing direction, from south-westwards to northwards. Today some of the delicate duneland is fenced off, and there is a specially laid high-tide boardwalk.

From East Head follow the clear shore path around a marshy lagoon and all the way to West Itchenor. Chichester Harbour sprawls like a huge natural lido beside you, while ahead the curves of the South Downs provide a lovely backdrop.

As you approach West Itchenor, a strip of trees provides welcome protection if the wind is biting, and soon the path leads through a boatyard and out on to the busy hard (a hard is a firm, sloping causeway over a soft foreshore). Hundreds of small vessels either bob about in Chichester Channel, or are being hammered, sawn, painted or polished on legs beside the water. You will not be surprised to learn that the large, popular public house is called the Ship, nor that it serves locally caught fresh fish. Altogether, it is a pleasant, bustling little place, and in spring and summer there is a regular passenger ferry across the narrow channel which enables you to continue the walk to Bosham. The alternative is to follow public footpaths via Chichester Yacht Basin and Dell Quay to Fishbourne, famous for the remains of a first-century Roman palace. Chichester, or Noviomagus to the Romans, is only a few minutes away, and is well worth a visit. Its splendid 900-year-old cathedral has been visible from as far back as Pagham Harbour. The return to Bosham Hoe is via paths and quiet lanes.

Step off the West Itchenor ferry and follow the waterside path until it joins Shore Road into Bosham, a highway that is flooded every high tide (although walkers can dodge the lapping waves without too much trouble). The views across the water to the picturesque village opposite are superb: a huddle of cottages around an ancient church, with the downs rising in the far distance. Shivering in a raw March wind, the old man selling his wife's home-made produce told me it was pronounced 'Bozzum' (whopping chunks of bread pudding and tasty slices of chocolate coconut cake, only 25p each). It was at Bosham that King Canute supposedly tried to turn back the waves, and legend also had it that his young daughter who drowned in a nearby millstream was buried in the church. In 1865 an excavation found a stone coffin containing the bones of a girl of about eight years old. Bosham Church is also depicted in the Bayeux Tapestry, with King Harold and a companion entering to pray prior to sailing to Normandy in 1064.

Some of the public footpath from Quay Meadow to the head of Bosham Channel and the A259 can also be under water at high tide, but it soon becomes a wide and firmer track. After a few strides along the pavement of the former Roman road return to the tranquillity of Chichester Harbour, and an almost continuous waterside footpath around the flat fields of Chidham. The shore and sea wall route rounds Cobnor Point, and approaching the activity centre there are fine views across to Bosham. Further round is Nutbourne Marshes Nature Reserve, and a marsh-side walk on to and around another flat headland. This one is known as Thorney Island, and until 1976 was an RAF base. The ugly buildings remain, but the views outwards across the harbour are excellent, and where the sea wall is crumbling it is easier to walk the foreshore. These final eight miles to Emsworth represent the western terminus of the Sussex Border Path, which follows rights of way along the whole of the county's boundary with Hampshire, Surrey and Kent, to end at Rye, a total distance of 152 miles.

EMSWORTH – PORTSMOUTH (15 miles)

Once upon a time there were large oyster beds in Emsworth

Harbour. Unlike now, oysters were then regarded as humble fare – you could buy 100 for just a shilling at London's Billingsgate Market. In *The Pickwick Papers* Sam Weller remarks that 'poverty and oysters always seem to go together'. In the case of Emsworth, however, the oyster business came to an unfortunate end following a banquet held by the Dean of Winchester in 1903 during which platefuls of Emsworth oysters were consumed. The Dean and a number of guests felt a trifle unwell after the meal; but it turned out that it was more than just passing indigestion. They had all contracted typhoid – and subsequently died. An inquest concluded that the oysters had been infected by the outflow of sewage into Emsworth Harbour, and not surprisingly that was pretty much the end of the local oyster trade.

Emsworth is where a coherent long-distance walking trail reasserts itself. Not that the next 60 miles or so are all quiet and pastoral, mind you. The Solent Way, which follows the Hampshire coast to Milford-on-Sea, takes in the naval heritage of Portsmouth and the natural heritage of the New Forest, and its waymark is what looks like a hovering tern. (Another Hampshire County Council route, the Wayfarer's Walk, also begins its 71-mile journey to Berkshire's Inkpen Beacon from here.) But sticking with the coast, leave Emsworth, where the Ship public house makes another appearance, along the sea wall via the sailing club westwards, joining what is known as Church Path across fields. It returns via the churchyard to the shore and trots around to Langstone (another Ship). The busy bridge before you takes a steady stream of holiday traffic on to Hayling Island, which despite some small nature reserves and a 4-mile-long walk/cycleway along the former 'Hayling Billy' railway line is rather flat and unexciting.

Continue to the edge of Langstone Harbour, a huge tidal lagoon that nearly dries out at high tide, and like Pagham and Chichester Harbours is a mecca for birdlife. Farlington Marshes, in particular, is rich in wildlife. Thousands of the small, gregarious dunlin can be seen huddling by the edge of the water; and more than 300 species of plants have also been found here, including fifty grasses (a third of the British total).

A short diversion is necessary around an inlet near Brockhampton, otherwise follow the obvious sea wall route around Farlington Marshes and southwards by the A2030 towards Spithead. This is the eastern edge of what is known as Portsea Island, upon which sits most of Portsmouth. The Solent Way then weaves through the houses of Eastney to the seafront, passing Eastney Pumping Station which, with the help of its two old beam engines, has been sorting out Portsmouth's human waste since 1887. A turning to the left leads past the eighteenth-century Fort Cumbernauld to the narrow mouth of Langstone Harbour, and a passenger ferry to Hayling Island. But since this is a dead end with limited shore access, carry on westwards along the promenade, past the Royal Marines Museum to Southsea Castle and the fine open space of Southsea Common, only a short stroll away from the heart of Portsmouth.

The history of Portsmouth is inextricably linked with the sea and naval activity. By the harbour there is the salvaged hull and remains of Henry VIII's great warship, the Mary Rose, which sank off Southsea in 1545 with the loss of 700 men, destabilised after water poured through the lower gun ports which had been built too near the water line – and, crucially, which had been left open. Then of course there is Nelson's magnificent flagship, HMS *Victory*, sitting proudly in dry-dock by the waterfront. And as the importance of Portsmouth as a naval dockyard and harbour grew, so did Pompey's defences. A series of solid towers and forts overlooking Spithead were begun in the 1400s. A semaphore extension was added to the Square Tower in 1812, which formed one end of a line of fifteen towers that stretched all the way to London, and enabled a message to be relayed from Portsmouth to the Admiralty in London in as little as fifteen minutes.

From Portsmouth there are regular ferries across to an island that now dominates the offshore view. The Isle of Wight Coast Path runs around this attractive, user-friendly island for about 65 miles. With plenty of accommodation, a variety of terrain and coastal scenery, and even good public transport links, this is a great place to walk. If you hop over from Portsmouth you could easily walk around the whole island in four or five days or less. Walking clockwise, there are the promenades and tea shops of Sandown, Shanklin and Ventnor, followed by a series of chines (deep-cut ravines) where the coast path is sometimes re-routed as the unstable clay slumps, as has recently happened at Blackgang Chine. The western end of the island rises to high chalk downs above the Needles – some of the most dramatic chalk cliff walking on the whole of the South Coast – then beyond Totland the ground is lower and wooded, dotted with old forts and small yachting havens. If you don't want to walk the whole coast, there are many (often waymarked) shorter trails across the island, and because of the island's handy size and shape plenty of potential circular routes (try Freshwater Bay – Needles – Yarmouth – Freshwater Bay as a long day walk). On the other hand, if you're walking this Newhaven–Exmouth section of the Channel coast you could conceivably cross from Portsmouth, walk around the Isle of Wight to Cowes, then take the ferry to Lymington for the Solent Way to Milford and the Bournemouth Coast Path to Poole, and so arrive at the start of the South-West Coast Path – and in so doing miss out all the fuss of Southampton Water and the New Forest diversions. Now there's a thought.

GOSPORT – SOUTHAMPTON (19 miles)

At Portsmouth it makes sense to nip over the narrow harbour mouth on the passenger ferry and resume at Gosport. If you're sticking to terra firma then docks, the M275 and the 'urban marina' of Port Solent prevent any decent waterside access until Portchester. Here you can walk through Castle Shore Park by the imposing Portchester Castle and along the Wicor Path to the edge of Fareham, before crossing the Wallington River for a bankside walk as far as Hoeford then a roadside journey into Gosport.

From Haslar Bridge, amid the hubbub of Gosport, pass the Royal Navy Submarine Museum and the entrance to Fort Monckton before heading off by a golf course and some small lakes to rejoin the Solent. There are terrific views back to Southsea and across to the Isle of Wight, and of the hundreds of ships, boats and craft of all description.

Now it is simply a question of following the sea wall towards Southampton. The earth embankments at Gilkicker Point are the remains of a fort, one of a series of over twenty built in the 1860s under the instructions of Lord Palmerston to encircle Portsmouth, six situated on Portsdown, the thin ridge of chalk downs behind the harbour, and others even in the sea (Spitbank Fort, for instance, which is still a well-known landmark and tourist attraction). Despite all the efforts, not to mention the massive expenditure, none of the forts was ever used in serious combat, and they became known as 'Palmerston's Follies'.

At the far end of Stokes Bay the MOD allows access along the high-water path and established tracks over the shingle of

Browndown Point, which leads to the promenade at Lee-on-the-Solent. Here is the Old Ship (Bass) and the Fleet Air Arm base HMS *Daedalus*, with its own hovercraft slipway. At Titchfield Haven, beyond Hill Head, the rich wetland and marshes of the lower Meon have formed a nature reserve, although the ornithologically friendly conditions were largely created through failed attempts to canalise the river, when the 3rd Earl of Southampton built a sea wall and sluices in the hope of making Titchfield sea-going. When I visited in late February the wardens were getting excited over black-tailed godwits, which had peaked at 1,500, a reserve record. From nearby chalets (where a sign reads 'drive at walking speed' – so why not just walk?) low cliffs take the path on via a caravan park called Solent Breezes. On the far shore of Southampton Water the huge oil refineries of Fawley blink and smoulder; but your pleasant track wanders past Hook-with-Warsash Nature Reserve and up the River Hamble past the College of Maritime Studies, where merchant navy officers are trained, to Warsash ferry.

The River Hamble is home to yachts by the marinaful, with slipways and jetties every way you look. The Royal Thames Yacht Club, formed in 1775 and the oldest club in England, can be found here; Cowes, of course, is just across the Solent; and the TV series *Howard's Way* was filmed at Warsash. But a few centuries ago the Hamble was important for shipbuilding, and the remains of Henry VIII's warship *Grace Dieu* are still buried in the mud upstream.

A plaque on the wall of the Rising Sun Inn, by Warsash Quay, tells that nearly 3,000 hand-picked and highly trained commandos embarked from here on 5 June 1944, the day before D-Day, as the vanguard of the main assault. They were led by Brigadier Lord Lovat, who throughout the operation was accompanied by his personal piper, and the sound of the bagpipes was relayed by loud hailers across the Solent as the troops left Warsash.

If you choose to ignore the river crossing to Hamble there is a very pleasant path over and alongside mudflats up the east bank of the river, past the splendidly named Bunny Meadow to the bridge at Bursledon, then roads and paths back. Otherwise walk across Hamble Common and pass waterside of the large BP oil terminal, and a large works where they have something to do with building aircraft, then enter the peace of Royal Victoria Country Park. It covers 200 acres and almost a mile of shoreline, and is the grounds of a former military hospital (the first purpose-built one in the country). Its construction was partly due to Queen Victoria's horrified pronouncements at the reports of conditions in the Crimea, and for 100 years the massive complex tended the needs of injured servicemen. It even had its own pier and railway halt. The hospital was demolished in 1966, with only the green-domed Royal Chapel (now the Heritage Centre), YMCA building (tea rooms) and officers' mess (private) remaining. The site now comprises open lawns and some fine mature trees, including Corsican, Monterey and Scots pines, plus Holm Oaks and Cedars of Lebanon, and discreetly hidden away behind them a military cemetery whose gravestones read like a roll call of imperial encounters as well as the hazards of travel to outposts of empire for whole military families in some cases.

Beyond are the ruins of Netley Abbey, the last item of interest before Southampton. Founded by Cistercian monks from nearby Beaulieu, it suffered many years of neglect following the Dissolution before being seized upon by the romantic Victorians. Hugh Walpole won the prize for over-the-topness, claiming: 'They are not the ruins of Netley, but of Paradise: Oh, the purple Abbots, what a spot they had chosen to slumber in!'

HYTHE – BUCKLERS HARD (19 miles)

Whereas Portsmouth grew up as the focus for naval activity, Southampton's modern success was based on commercial shipping. From the shelter of Southampton Water, with its unique double high tide, came the famous Cunard liners, and latterly a regular procession of supertankers and container ships. And it was from here that two ships set sail for North America on epic voyages – but meeting rather different fates. In 1620 the *Mayflower* took the Pilgrim Fathers to the New World, a long and rough crossing of sixty-seven days that was made all the more cramped since the sister ship on the voyage, the *Speedwell*, almost immediately sprang a leak and all had to transfer to the *Mayflower* during an unscheduled stop at Portsmouth. Meanwhile in 1912 the White Star liner SS *Titanic* left Southampton on her first and only journey with a crew mostly from Southampton, the vast majority of whom never returned.

Much of the head of Southampton Water is predictably an urban and industrialised affair, typified by the vast Western Docks. Best to take the ferry to Hythe from Town Quay (the alternative is a long, mainly roadside walk via Totton and Marchwood, although there are some public footpaths from the latter to Hythe.) Head south for Langdown, past huge waterfront sheds once used by flying boats, and which in the 1930s and '40s saw regular BOAC and Imperial Airways flights across the Atlantic.

The Solent Way now takes a lane inland, then via a forest track and the B3054 across the heathland of the New Forest to Beaulieu. If the route had been around before 1920 it probably would have kept to the shoreside via Fawley to Calshot, but since then a massive industrial complex of oil refineries has appeared that sprawls for miles along Southampton Water's south-western shore. Trees have been planted to try and disguise the scale of it all; but although it may be part of the area's prosperity, it does little to enrich the Hampshire coast for the walker. However, if you persevere along the road as far as Fawley turn off for Ashlett Quay, where there is a public footpath opposite the Jolly Sailor pub (next to a fabulous old tide mill – now the Esso Ashlett Social Club) which runs waterside of the power station to Calshot Marshes Nature Reserve.

Walk out on to the windy spit, and if you are visiting Calshot Castle, another of Henry VIII's defences, you can go past the outdoor activity centre and former seaplane hangars to the very end. From here there are close-up views of the passing tankers and liners, almost in shouting distance as they enter Southampton Water. Calshot Spit is unusual because tidal drift is causing gradual accretion, not erosion, and very slowly the outer edge and tip of the Spit is expanding.

At low tide it is possible to walk the foreshore from Calshot Beach to Lepe Country Park. At the edge of North Solent Nature Reserve are some raised concrete platforms where sections of the floating Mulberry harbours were made before being towed across the Channel for the D-Day landings. At Lepe Country Park there is a restaurant and information shop; and from here a footpath runs along the shore below coastguard cottages for a mile, although notices warn that this is liable to flood at high tide. Across the Solent the wooded slopes of the Isle of Wight seem very near, while ahead extensive mudflats and creeks at the mouth of the Beaulieu River now block any further pedestrian access. Hampshire has nearly 23,000 acres of this valuable inter-tidal zone of mudflat and marshland, more than any other county on the South Coast.

Now you must take to country lanes via Exbury, and the rhododendrons, azaleas and camellias of Exbury House if you wish, to Beaulieu. This famous, pretty Hampshire village is where King John founded an abbey in 1204 (his only one), although only a few pieces remain. Leave the picturesque scene (and its usual crowds) along a lane by the Montagu Arms (named after the family that owns most of the village), rejoining the Solent Way for a series of direct footpaths across fields and through woodland to Bucklers Hard. Here, 200 years ago, in this small and remote New Forest village, they used to make giant warships for the English navy. These included Nelson's favourite, the 64-gun *Agamemnon*, and it was on this ship off Corsica that he lost his eye. At the end of the eighteenth century there were around 4,000 men employed at Bucklers Hard. After a long lull, the village once more saw frenetic activity building boats and floating harbours prior to the Normandy Landings, and still today a few shipwrights remain.

BUCKLERS HARD – MILFORD-ON-SEA (20 miles)
Sadly, there is no legitimate access along the Solent shore until Lymington, although a few tracks do lead down to the waterside. So it is a question of following obvious country lanes west. The circled '40', by the way, painted large on the tarmac at regular intervals, represents the 40mph speed limit and is part of an attempt to reduce the number of accidents involving New Forest ponies and other animals (including, presumably, walkers).

Lymington is dominated by small boats. It should come as no surprise to find a Ship public house by Old Town Quay and that it offers showers; but this one also quotes its latitude and longitude. Past boatyards, sailmakers and chandlers, the waterside path resumes between the opposing headquarters of Lymington Town Sailing Club and Royal Lymington Yacht Club, near the open air seawater baths (the largest of its kind on the South Coast, apparently) before continuing through a large marina. Jonathan Raban, who sailed the British coast, noted that: 'The clink and jangle of steel rigging against alloy masts rang out over Lymington like the bells of a demented herd of alpine cows.'

For many years Lymington's chief industry was the manufacture of salt, and the obvious path that follows the indented shore beyond the marina passes a series of shallow pools which were constructed to allow the seawater to nearly evaporate, before being pumped into iron pans for the brine to be boiled down into salt. Much of the salt was sold to the naval dockyards at Portsmouth for preserving meat, and at one time up to a tenth of the country's salt was produced from Lymington's salterns.

The coast path continues along the sturdy sea wall above Pennington and then Keyhaven Marshes. Part of the lounge of the seventeenth-century Gun Inn at Keyhaven was known as the Chapel Bar, since it was used as a temporary morgue for drowned corpses recovered on the local beach (they were stored in the cellar). Despite this grisly fact it is still a very pleasant place, even though the toilets are named 'gulls' and 'buoys'. Earlier this century there were plans to dig a tunnel to the Isle of Wight from Keyhaven, and to convert nearby marshland into dockyards. Thankfully neither project got off the ground, and calmness and serenity remain.

A short but rather arduous shingle trek leads to the end of the spit occupied by Hurst Castle, which like Calshot was originally built by Henry VIII but much modified since. Indeed the most arresting features of this powerful fortress are two 38-ton Victorian guns that crouch within the thick stone walls. From the top you can gaze across at the Isle of Wight and the distinctive shapes of the Needles. But although the island is under a mile away (this is its closest point to the mainland), the swirling and unpredictable currents make swimming treacherous, as some of the customers at the Gun have found over the years.

Now it is time to change direction and head for Dorset. Wave goodbye to the Solent and the Isle of Wight and head briskly westwards along the shore and into Milford-on-Sea. The dim shapes of Bournemouth are now visible, with the chalk cliffs of Purbeck beyond. However, after the variety of the Hampshire coastline the next 20 miles may seem a little dull, with a semi-urbanised stretch that lasts until Poole Harbour.

MILFORD – SANDBANKS (20 miles)

The Solent Way officially terminates in the friendly, homely atmosphere of Milford, which has probably been helped by the fact that the railway never quite made it to the town. However, a perfectly pleasant clifftop path continues along the shore to Barton-on-Sea. Although much land has been lost to the waves, Barton's diminishing clay cliffs are famous for fossils, with specimens up to 45 million years old, and the town has even given its name to some fossils and fossil-bearing clays. The narrow, wooded defile of Chewton Bunny was once used to land contraband, but now represents the Hampshire–Dorset border (bunny is a local term for a wooded ravine, although in nearby Bournemouth like the Isle of Wight they are known as chines).

Now walk past rows of beach huts that line the popular sands of Christchurch Bay as it sweeps around to Hengistbury Head. In Saxon times Christchurch was known as Twynham, which means the town between the waters, for it lies at the confluence of the rivers Stour and Avon, but its present name is connected with the 900-year-old Priory. High in the south choir aisle the so-called Miraculous Beam can be seen protruding through an arch, and legend has it that it was originally cut too short but overnight was lengthened by an unknown carpenter (and so the name Christchurch). In the Priory Garden is the mausoleum of a Mrs Perkins, who was so terrified of being buried alive that she had her coffin fitted with a lock that could be opened from the inside in case she suddenly revived! The Priory can be seen if you choose to walk around the expanse of Christchurch Harbour; and indeed the waterside footpaths via the 150-acre Stanpit Marsh nature reserve to the Avon bridge are very pleasant. (The return on the southern side is less well-defined, and there are no decent tracks until you reach the Double Dykes built by the Iron Age defenders of Hengistbury Head.) The other, much more direct option is to take the summer ferry from Mudeford across the mouth of Christchurch Harbour to Hengistbury Head.

Bronze Age barrows dating from around 1500 BC indicate that the relatively low but shapely headland of Hengistbury Head has been popular with visitors for a long time, a fact which probably goes unnoticed by the motorised trainloads of holidaymakers that trundle out to the end and back again. There are numerous tracks across the heath and scrubland, from where the views up and down the coast are simply superb: from the Isle of Wight to the Isle of Purbeck, and inland over the New Forest. Last century iron ore was dug from here, and only the building of a prominent groyne has prevented the whole headland from being slowly washed away.

For almost the next 10 miles the shore is dominated by Bournemouth and its environs, with golden beaches and wooded chines that eat into the dark, low cliffs. Civilised is a word often associated with the resort. Perhaps it's because of the elegant pines, the presence of the acclaimed Bournemouth Symphony Orchestra, or simply because a lot of old folk hang out here. John Lennon bought a house in Panorama Road for his aunt (he is said to have declared of the view: 'Of all the places I have travelled to this is the most beautiful'). The Victorians came to Bournemouth believing that the sweet pine-scented air would cure their tuberculosis, and that the sheltered, southerly climate of the resort 'where summer winters' would send them back to their urban squalor healthy. But so many came that the local paper feared that invalids would begin to outnumber ordinary tourists, and that the place would become 'a very Metropolis of Bath Chairs'!

Continue either along the top of the low, wooded cliffs or across the golden (and very clean) sandy beaches and before long you arrive at Sandbanks, a small community of posh retirement houses on the narrow finger of land guarding the entrance of Poole Harbour. By the Haven Hotel join the regular chain ferry that rattles across to Studland Heath opposite, and there begin the 600-mile South-West Coast Path that will take you as far as north Somerset.

If you want to circumvent Poole Harbour by land then it's a long trip, since it's the country's largest natural harbour. With all its inlets it's over 90 miles round, but of course much of this is inaccessible to the walker. The north side is taken up with Poole itself, then after skirting Wareham the southern side of the harbour is a huge expanse of marsh and heathland, including the RSPB's Arne Reserve, but access to the actual waterside is limited. Out in the middle of the harbour is the wooded lump of Brownsea Island, where Boy Scouts were dreamt up and red squirrels now roam (it can be visited by boat). Before the National Trust acquired the island in 1962 it was the domain of the eccentric Mrs Bonham Christie, who was so determined not to allow visitors that she employed well-built female athletes literally to throw people off the island.

SANDBANKS – SWANAGE (8 miles)

At South Haven Point all the cars speed off across Studland Heath while you return to the sanctuary of the shoreline, and via Shell Bay to Studland Bay. Studland Heath National Nature Reserve is home to Britain's three native snakes: adder, grass and the rare smooth snake. This last is confined to the sandy heaths between Surrey and Dorset, and it is not surprising that the equally rare sand lizard, on which it feeds, is also found here.

Ahead is the bulk of Ballard Down, the easterly point of a long and distinctive ridge of chalk that runs across south Dorset from the Lulworth area (and before the sea broke through it once carried on across to the Needles and the Isle of Wight). In the only major gap in the Purbeck Hills sits the ruins of Corfe Castle, where King Edward the Martyr was murdered in AD 978.

The coast path skirts Studland itself and climbs the chalk headland along a broad track until suddenly below appear the much-photographed white chalk stacks. Nearest is Old Harry, still jutting out of the water, but Old Harry's Wife is now just a sad stump of chalk after she was toppled in a gale in 1896. The cliff-edge path continues to rise towards Ballard Down, and I recommend a brief diversion on to the crest of the hill to enjoy the fabulous views: Poole Harbour, Bournemouth and the Isle of Wight one way; Swanage and the Purbeck coast the other. Like Thanet and Portsea before it, the Isle of Purbeck ceased to be an island some time ago. The chalk downland supports an array of plantlife (as many as ten different kinds under just one footprint, as a nearby noticeboard curiously puts it), including kidney vetch, mouse-ear hawkweed and even the rare early spider orchid.

Descending the edge of the rather crumbly cliff into Swanage you may find that tracks further back from the steep drop are rather more reassuring; and near White Cliffs the path down to the shore is now closed, so that the official route deviates through Ballard Private Estate in order to reach Swanage promenade by road.

Despite recent controversy over a bayside development, efforts have been made to improve the appearance of Swanage, with the use of local stone in some rebuilding works. As far back as the Middle Ages this area was quarried for limestone, and Purbeck marble was used in Salisbury Cathedral and Westminster Abbey. Indeed, before the coming of railway-borne tourists the town's main income was from local stone, shipped to London from masons' yards on the seafront and cliffside quarries to the west. Since the empty sailing ketches were prone to capsizing on the return leg, they were loaded with unwanted street masonry and heavy items from the burgeoning Victorian capital. This is the reason why today you can see various pieces of London street furniture all around Swanage. There are numerous bollards or cannon posts in the nearby Durlston Country Park, for instance. Even the ornate stone façade of the Town Hall originally came from the former

Mercers' Hall in London's Cheapside; and the clock tower was once to be found in Southwark. No wonder Swanage earned the nickname 'Little London by the Sea'.

SWANAGE – KIMMERIDGE (12 miles)

Leave Swanage via Peveril Point, a sloping nose of land that guards the southern approach to Swanage Bay. The coast path then rises above slumped, wooded cliffs and enters Durlston Country Park, with a series of lovely viewpoints from among the trees. The country park, established in 1973 and Dorset's first, has an information centre and a variety of trails; but stick to the clifftop route for Tilly Whim Caves, once popular with smugglers, and whose entrance is decorated with a stone gatepost brought from Pentonville Prison, London, in 1887. The caves are actually old quarry workings, and a whim was a crane used to lower the cut stone to waiting boats below. The once-busy ledges still bear holes where the whims operated, although if conditions were too hazardous the stone was first placed in flat-bottomed craft which were then rowed out to the larger vessels offshore.

Continue along the cliffs of the Purbeck Heritage Coast, and since the footpath sticks close to the edge watch your footing. There is further evidence of past quarrying at Seacombe, and then at Winspit, which was the last site to close, in the 1950s. Further on is St Aldhelm's Head (also known as St Alban's Head), a pleasantly isolated outpost, with none of the noisy charabancs that can choke Swanage and nearby Worth Matravers. The tiny Chapel of St Aldhelm, dedicated to the first Saxon Bishop of Sherborne, is an unusual medieval structure. It is square, not rectangular, and the angles of the building, not the sides, point (very nearly) to the cardinal points of the compass. It is likely that the building was formerly a chantry, and that a priest would say mass for the well-being of those on the sea.

As the path turns northwards, allowing views of Portland and the soaring Kimmeridge and Lulworth coast, it does one of those things that you will simply have to get used to if you walk this exciting but demanding coast. There is a mighty flight of steep steps down and then back up to the crest of Emmetts Hill opposite, which really does test the leg muscles. Further on, keep to the main, waymarked track above landslips near Chapman's Pool, dropping down and then once more heaving back up on to Houns-tout Cliff above huge, dark screes. Carry on along the rolling cliffs until the folly of Clavel Tower signals a descent to Kimmeridge Bay.

At the foot of the steps a stark MOD notice warns both mariners and walkers alike that at the far side of the bay is the Lulworth Firing Ranges, and should red flags be flying then a long inland detour is the only option for the pedestrian. More on this shortly.

Kimmeridge Bay reminds one of Robin Hood's Bay, on the North Yorkshire coast, with dark, bare ledges extending out into the sea at low tide, which most unusually occurs twice a day here. This contrasts with Southampton, a little up the coast, which has two high tides a day instead (something to do with Kimmeridge Bay being close to the English Channel's Amphidromic Point, whatever that may be). The Purbeck Marine Wildlife Reserve's hut by the beach has more details on this, and is also keen for any sightings of the Black-faced Blenny (Tripterytion Atlanticus), a rare black-headed fish found occasionally in these parts.

At the far side of the bay the cliff path passes a small BP oil well. Kimmeridge's oil shale beds have been fairly unobtrusively tapped for the last thirty-five years, with just a bit of barbed wire and a few pumping jacks (the well-known 'nodding donkey' pumps) visible. In the past locals used to gather the bituminous shale from the shore as extra fuel in winter, but the so-called Kimmeridge Coal has an acrid and pungent smell when burnt. Then more barbed wire and fences beyond, with the eastern boundary of the army range.

KIMMERIDGE – WEYMOUTH (19 miles)

Lulworth Range tends to be open to the public most weekends and at other peak holiday times, such as during the month of August, and at Christmas and Easter. It is advisable to check ahead, since the alternative is a lengthy inland detour. When access is permitted you should stick to the clearly designated 'range walks' (indicated between yellow posts), which fortunately for us include a wonderful, invigorating 6-mile clifftop walk to Lulworth, visited by more birds and butterflies than walkers. Inland is the 'lost' village of Tyneham, which under Churchill's orders was seized by the army in 1943 for military manoeuvres. The occupants were evacuated and the tanks moved in (as did local thieves who stripped the vacated church and manor house within days). Today the buildings are still empty, and the village remains in the hands of the Ministry of Defence, despite years of protests. There is now an exhibition centre in the deserted village – but of course you can only visit when firing is not taking place.

Back to the shore, and a pause for breath on top of the mighty chalk whale backs of Gold Down and then Bindon Hill, where you can truly appreciate this stretch of the soaring Dorset Heritage Coast. Overall the South-West Coast Path climbs an average of 45.1m or 148 feet per mile, considerably more than the Pennine Way's 38.7m or 127 feet per mile but still behind the Offa's Dyke 46.6m or 153 feet per mile – compared to just 1.5m or 5 feet on the Thames Path (although a more recent contour count estimated that SWCP walkers in fact climb as much as 60.9m or 200 feet per mile). But if we work on a figure of 45.7m or 150 feet per mile and assume that the South-West Coast Path is about 600 miles long (as the South-West Way Association claims) then between Poole and Minehead you will ascend something in the order of 27,432m or 90,000 feet. What a prospect!

The grassy coastal walk skirts the clifftop and approaches the oyster-shaped Lulworth Cove. There are a number of helpful MOD notices dotted along the route, such as 'Keep to Range Walks'; 'Falling rocks – beware of unstable cliffs'; 'Danger: Keep Out – Unexploded Shells'; and my favourite one, perched above a sheer cliff edge, 'Danger of falling!'

Leave the range and drop down to Lulworth Cove from the crumbling cliffs at Pepler Point. For most of the time you can walk the stony beach; otherwise it's a hike over the dismayingly steep cliffs that tower above the pretty bay – but due to erosion following winter storms the path does not descend directly to the edge of the beach any more.

Lulworth Cove is one of those pretty little places that for much of the year is swamped by a flood of car-borne visitors. Grab an ice cream or tea while they are still queuing to park and either take the metalled lane behind the heritage centre that leads to a steep clifftop path, or the wide and well-worn track from the car park up Hambury Tout. Both meet up above St Oswald's Bay, and from there the fine clifftop path rolls up and down above the famous chalk arch of Durdle Door and on to Osmington Mills.

John Constable came to Osmington Mills for his honeymoon in 1816, which no doubt inspired his famous painting *View of Weymouth Bay*. Westbound coastal walkers will emerge among the massed tables of the beer garden at the Smugglers Inn; then go up the lane a short distance and left by a signpost for a diversion around a recent landslip – follow the signs. Don't confuse it with the other 'alternative' and much longer inland route also indicated, which cuts off the whole of the Weymouth/Chesil Beach stretch.

Beyond the thick vegetation of the slipping Black Head and a couple of holiday camps descend for a long walk into Weymouth, and if the weather is benign the best route is along the top of the sea wall above the busy road.

Weymouth was popularised by George III, who came to bathe in the sea in order to cure his nervous disorder. In fact he made history at Weymouth in 1789, becoming the first reigning monarch to try out the newly invented bathing machine. The townsfolk were so grateful for all the attention that they not only erected a large, painted statue but also cut a figure of him on horseback into the chalk hillside above nearby Osmington. His Majesty loved the place so much that he tried to return each year, but his enthusiasm was not shared by his family. 'This place is more dull and stupid that I can find words to express,' wrote Princess Mary from Weymouth in 1798. Today, on a summer's afternoon, most of the traditional seaside sights are still in evidence: Punch and Judy on the sand, the Salvation Army on the esplanade, fish and chip wrapping on the pavement. However, the well-preserved seafront is an attractive spectacle and simply begs for a spot of promenading, not least to enjoy the views over Weymouth Bay to Lulworth and Purbeck.

WEYMOUTH – ABBOTSBURY (14 miles)
The huge limestone lump of Portland looms out to sea like the hulk of some giant moribund vessel, or a great whale, according to H.V. Morton. It is scarred by years of quarrying, and today houses a large prison and the Royal Naval Air Station HMS *Osprey*, which may not endear it to coastal walkers. It is, after all, an island, reached by Ferry Bridge at the mouth of the Fleet, so you could justify giving it a miss, but that would be a pity. If you tolerate a mile or two of roadwalking on to it, there is a circular walking route of about 8 miles from Fortuneswell. Portland has been compared to Gibraltar – a huge chunk of rock sticking out from the land – and the airiness and feeling of detachment make it worth a visit. So head south, along West Cliffs, past quarries to Portland Bill, which offers great views up and down the Channel and is a good place to spot migrant birds such as redstarts, warblers and chiffchaffs. Then swing northwards above raised beaches to the road near

Southwell, and back via more paths to the edge of the prison near Fortuneswell.

For those not visiting Portland it is worth crossing Ferry Bridge just to inspect the visitor centre below Chesil Beach. Here you will learn that the scaly cricket's only British home is in this area, probably brought to these shores as an unwitting passenger aboard World War II landing craft stored in Portland Harbour after their return from the Mediterranean. Even though it's not your actual route do take a moment or two to scrunch up to the top of the remarkable shingle bank before you. Chesil Beach is 17 miles long, and its beautifully rounded pebbles have been graded by the waves so that they appear as gravel at the western end and as large as a fist near here at Portland. A few pebbles even have natural holes in them, and every fishing boat used to carry one for luck and for a good catch. It is said that a local fisherman landing on Chesil Beach in the fog could tell where he was by the size of the pebble.

Behind Chesil Beach is a shallow and peaceful 7-mile lagoon called the Fleet which contains what must be Britain's oldest nature reserve when protection was given to the famous mute swans of Abbotsbury in 1393. It remains important for a range of other wildlife, and in particular for 150 different types of seaweed. The Fleet is especially famous for its eelgrass, which forms an underwater carpet, and which is both home and dinner to a number of fish and birds. The Fleet has no feeder streams, but maintains its levels by seepage through the beach pebbles.

It is possible to walk along the full seaward side of Chesil Beach during the winter months, but it is an extremely arduous undertaking. At other times access is restricted due to nesting seabirds, so the national trail squeezes past the caravans behind Ferry Bridge for a waterside journey along the Fleet's inland shore until Rodden Hive, from where there is a short inland stretch to near Abbotsbury. A diversion may be necessary at Tidmoor Point if firing is taking place; and you may care to dally at Moonfleet Hotel (formerly Fleet House, built in 1603) named after Meade Faulkner's romantic novel of smuggling times which was set around here.

ABBOTSBURY – CHARMOUTH (16 miles)

Abbotsbury is about a mile inland from the western end of Chesil Beach, although if you have followed either of the two arms of the official coast path you will almost pass through it. On an August weekend this quaint little place is overrun with tourists scoffing over-priced cream teas. But if you choose a quieter moment there is much to see: the ruins of a Benedictine monastery, a fifteenth-century tithe barn and swannery, and St Catherine's Chapel, a lonely and rather romantic refuge sitting on a low hill above the village. It is dedicated to the patron saint of spinsters, and it is said that unmarried women in the area used to meet there and invoke St Catherine's help in finding husbands. The coast path skirts Chapel Hill, although a quick scamper up the grass slopes is recommended for the illuminating views back across Chesil Beach and the Fleet to Portland. At last you can appreciate the length and directness of the shingle bank – and why it seemed like an age to walk past.

This next stretch via West Bexington to Burton Bradstock is easy and uncomplicated. The ground very gradually rises to low cliffs, and it is worth glancing over your shoulder to admire the expanding views of Chesil Beach. The path follows a lane and along some of the Chesil pebbles, passing Labour-in-Vain Farm, so-called because the land needed a large amount of work for little reward. There are seasonal refreshments at Cogden Beach, while a mile inland is Burton Bradstock, an attractive village that grew out of the nineteenth-century cloth industry.

Continuing westwards, the low yellow cliffs of Bridport Sandstone are very attractive but crumble easily, so keep to the main path and stay back from the edge. Ahead the prominent table-top of Golden Cap is getting nearer, but first descend to West Bay near Bridport, a town that has provided the maritime world with quality ropes, twines and nets for centuries. The full story is told in the Harbour Museum, a converted salt house, at West Bay.

The clifftop path might remain grassy and enjoyably open, but the gradients begin to stiffen. The route to Seatown is obvious, then beyond is the relatively short but nevertheless steep ascent of Golden Cap, the highest point on the entire south coast (191m). The reward is worth all the effort, and the popular summit enjoys magnificent views along the whole coast.

Drop down towards Charmouth through bracken and then cross

open fields and, resisting paths inland, skirt a patch of scrub-covered undercliff and amble down to the River Char. The Heritage Coast Centre by the beach has an exhibition of fossils that have been found on beaches locally. Fossils are a big thing around here. In 1811 a local schoolgirl found the complete, 21-foot skeleton of an ichthyosaur, a porpoise-like marine creature from the Mesozoic period. Ammonites can still be found on the beach, and the authorities take pains to discourage fossil-hunters chipping away the unstable cliffs. Charmouth itself is quite a pleasant village these days, now that the A35 bypass has been completed.

CHARMOUTH – EXMOUTH (32 miles)
The two miles from Charmouth to Lyme Regis have been complicated by cliff erosion, and older guidebooks may still show a clifftop route by the golf course that disappeared when the unstable clays and sands began shifting some years ago. It is hoped that a new route will be open by the time you read this, but at the moment the official, waymarked route diverts past Black Ven landslip and via a small section of the busy A35 before returning to paths and lanes and into Lyme Regis. It is possible to walk the shore underneath the cliffs, but this should *only* be undertaken on a falling tide (there are two places in particular where walkers could be cut off), and mudflats also make this passage dangerous.

The famous sea defence known as the Cobb has been witness to much of the history of Lyme Regis. Built in the thirteenth century, it has seen ships set sail to fight (in the Hundred Years War and against the Armada) and to explore the New World (Lyme MP Sir George Summers discovered the Bermudas). In 1685 the Duke of Monmouth landed here and began his ill-fated challenge to the throne of his uncle James II, which ended in bloody fashion at the Battle of Sedgemoor. Twelve of his men were subsequently hanged in Lyme, and the place is now known as Monmouth Beach. It was from the Cobb that Louisa Musgrove took a tumble to blight the romantic prospects of Jane Austen's heroine Anne Elliot in *Persuasion*, while film buffs will also recognise the Cobb from *The French Lieutenant's Woman*, based on the book by Lyme resident John Fowles.

At Lyme Regis you pass from Dorset into Devon. Immediately beyond is a long and potentially tricky 6 miles to Axe Bridge through the Undercliffs National Nature Reserve. This is a series of massive landslips that have been colonised by a jungle of scrub and patchy woodland, and is a fascinating and totally different coastal environment to almost any other along this coast. But in or after wet weather it is liable to be muddy and slippery, and since there is no access to the beach or the land above this stage must be tackled carefully.

Finally descend via a golf course to the River Axe and into Seaton, a compact and lively resort that sits snugly between the cliffs. Tourism, of course, is the main industry here, but I wonder how many of the happy trippers staying in one of Seaton's largest holiday camps know that it was previously used as an internment camp in the Second World War?

From the coast road out of the resort there is a scenic surfaced path that leads along the clifftop and steeply down into Beer (although a beach route from Seaton is also feasible at low tide). This tiny bay is hemmed in by chalk cliffs which afford valuable shelter for the fleet of small fishing boats, most of which are winched up the pebbled shore at night. At the head of the narrow slipway by the Anchor Inn begins the main street, with Beer Brook running down its side. St Michael's Church has the distinction of owning Britain's first ever Wurlitzer, imported from the United States.

The path resumes by fields along the fenced cliff edge, and after rounding Beer Head the coast of South Devon beyond the Exe comes into sight. Before a former coastguard cottage there is the choice of either staying with the high clifftop path, or dropping down a safe track through Under Hooken and rejoining the former at Branscombe Mouth; the latter is recommended for the views. Under Hooken was formed in March 1790 when a trapped underground stream eventually caused a huge slab of cliff to plunge into the sea. Such was its force that it pushed up a mighty ridge in the sea bed, and crab pots left by fishermen several fathoms deep were stranded high and dry above the water.

At Branscombe Mouth the Sea Shanty, a former coal wharf and boat house, serves food and drink in season. Beyond here the coast path continues along the cliff edge to Sidmouth via high, wooded combes. The views remain good, but the going is hard at times.

Sidmouth, like Seaton, nestles among the cliffs. The short seafront is particularly handsome, and the proliferation of Georgian and Regency buildings, plus 'cottage' style houses, reflects an age when fashionably dressed folk strolled the prom and hired bathing machines and sedan chairs.

To leave Sidmouth there is a stiff pull up a lane (a signpost points to a safer short cut across a field), then into woodland and out on to Peak Hill, followed by High Peak. The latter is a high, wooded cliff, with the remains of a hillfort somewhere among the pines. These few minutes under cover provide a welcome respite should the sun be blazing or the wind howling, but the exit south to Ladram Bay can be slippery in wet weather. Seaward are distinctive red sandstone stacks and arches of rock where the crumbling cliff meets the water. Back from the edge a large caravan park adds little to the scenery, but at least it does have a shop and café, and I can report that breakfasts do come very cheap.

Follow the clifftop towards Budleigh Salterton, past a succession of small headlands. As you reach a stand of pines by the River Otter, with Budleigh Salterton on the other bank, a notice warns that it is dangerous to wade and advises a short detour upriver to a road bridge. A wise move, more so since the lower Otter is a nature reserve. There is an abundance of birdlife on and about the river, plus dragonflies and butterflies; and many of the pines above the river support bat boxes. These artificial nests make up for the lack of natural holes in the pines, and provide both temporary summer roosts and sites for hibernation in the winter.

Most local people refer to the town as Salterton, but both names derive from the salterns in the river estuary. The quiet and relaxed surroundings attracted Sir John Millais, who used the town's sea wall as the setting for his famous painting *The Boyhood of Raleigh* (Sir Walter was born only a couple of miles away, at Hayes Barton).

The final 4 miles to Exmouth keep to the top of low cliffs, carefully avoiding the Royal Marines firing range at Straight Point and a massive caravan site (over 2,000 of the beasts) at Sandy Bay. It is difficult to say which of the two is the more unsightly.

Pick of the walks

SWANAGE CIRCULAR (6½ miles): from the resort to the top of panoramic Ballard Down, then down to Studland village and Old Harry Rocks and back along the clifftop.

WEST BAY (BRIDPORT) – SIDMOUTH (26 miles): from Golden Cap, the highest spot on the Channel Coast, to the spectacular Undercliff jungle of Lyme Regis, this two-day walk captures some of the best South Devon scenery.

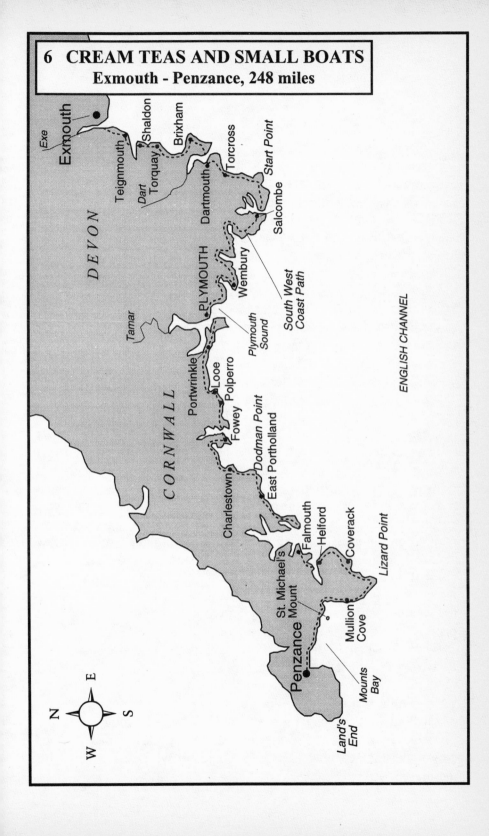

6 CREAM TEAS AND SMALL BOATS
Exmouth - Penzance, 248 miles

Exe

Exmouth

Teignmouth

Shaldon

Torquay

Dart

Brixham

DEVON

Dartmouth

Torcross

Start Point

Salcombe

PLYMOUTH

Wembury

South West
Coast Path

Tamar

Plymouth
Sound

CORNWALL

Portwrinkle

Looe

Polperro

Fowey

Dodman Point

East Portholland

Charlestown

Falmouth

Helford

Coverack

Lizard Point

St. Michael's
Mount

Mullion
Cove

Penzance

Mounts
Bay

Land's
End

ENGLISH CHANNEL

N
E
S
W

EXMOUTH – SHALDON (19 miles)

The ferry from Exmouth across the wide mouth of the River Exe to Starcross runs only in the summer months; otherwise continue along the flat northern shore of the Exe as far as the all-year-round ferry at Topsham. Or you can wander the extra couple of miles into the centre of Exeter if you wish. As far as the old Mussel Purification Station near Lympstone this is along the course of the newly created East Devon Way, a 40-mile inland route that connects the Exe to the Lym, at Lyme Regis. After this it is roadside all the way into Devon's county town. The return to Starcross is along the towpath of the Exeter Canal, then an estuary-side track and eventually a road to Dawlish Warren, home to holiday chalets and caravans galore, but also to a huge double sand spit that attracts vast numbers of wading birds. From here the sea wall can be walked at low tide into Dawlish itself, otherwise stay with the road.

As the prolific and engaging local author Chips Barber points out, Dawlish is probably the only town in England that has its railway station on the seafront and in the town centre at the same time. Along this attractive part of the Devon shore the Brunel-built railway really does hug the beach; its raised course is the actual sea wall. What is now the main Paddington–Penzance line was originally built to a revolutionary 'atmospheric' design, whereby ten pumping houses (one survives as a museum at Starcross) drew air out of a pipe between the rails. This produced a vacuum, which worked on a piston that in turn propelled the trains. Unfortunately there were many teething problems, not least from the effects of the weather and the fact that inquisitive rats and mice jammed the pistons, and the expensive experiment ended in 1848.

From Dawlish Station, parts of which are occasionally swept away by rough seas, the coast path climbs up on to the red sandstone cliffs above the tunnel. The next couple of miles to Teignmouth follows the Old Teignmouth Road, a small burst of clifftop, and the pavement of the A379 until Smugglers Lane deposits you on the end of the sea wall (high tides or bad weather may make the sea wall impassable here, in which case stay with the main road).

Once upon a time Dartmoor granite was shipped from Teignmouth Harbour to build the old London Bridge. Today one of the busiest boats is the regular ferry across the mouth of the Teign to Shaldon, the alternative to which is the nearby road bridge upstream.

SHALDON – TORCROSS (40 miles)

There are great views back over Teignmouth from the Ness, a small but distinctive wooded headland that was planted to celebrate Queen Victoria's Silver Jubilee in 1863. The path up to it from Shaldon and then beyond sticks close to the sea and is reasonably clear, but this whole section around Babbacombe Bay is quite undulating and tiring, and refreshment points are limited.

Approaching Torquay it is worth detouring for the views from near the top of Petit Tor; then shortly after you pass underneath the cliff railway at Oddicombe, past the beach and over Walls Hill or Babbacombe Downs and around Anstey Cove to Hope's Nose. Welcome to Torbay, an area that styles itself the English Riviera, and where you can find palm trees, nightclubs and for much of the year huge crowds of what are known in Devon as grockles, or holidaymakers (in Cornwall they are known as emetts). In fact Torquay is second only to Blackpool in terms of the leading British holiday destination, and its growth stems from the time of the Napoleonic Wars when the affluent classes were forced to look closer to home for their relaxation. Also, since the British fleet was anchored in Tor Bay during the war with France, officers' wives and families came to live in the town, so hastening development. Ironically, the south Devon coast was also admired by Napoleon Bonaparte as he was taken to exile on St Helena aboard the British warship *Bellerophon*. He is said to have remarked 'Quel bon pays' ('What a beautiful country').

The journey from Torquay all the way round the bay via the packed beaches of Paignton to Brixham is mostly urban and noisy, but the ferry across the bay to Brixham provides the ideal way of circumventing these miles of crowds and pavement-walking.

Today Brixham is part of what is collectively known as Torbay (with Torquay and Paignton), but it has a character and history all of its own. William of Orange landed here in 1688 to begin the Glorious Revolution; and in the mid-1800s Brixham was the country's leading fishery. Large-scale commercial fishing was carried out by powerful fishing smacks which carried beam trawls, devices which simply allowed nets to be kept wider and so give a greater trawl.

Beyond Brixham the coast path visits Berry Head Country Park. The short, high headland was fortified during the Napoleonic Wars and remains a fine lookout point. Portland can even be seen on a clear day. The next ten miles to Kingswear are quite tough: there are no refreshment points (so stock up in the Berry Head café) and some of the gradients are severe. However, this is also one of the most attractive sections, as the path hugs the clifftop past Sharkham Point and follows the unspoilt and dramatic coastline south. No bucket-and-spade mob here!

Near Outer Froward Point there are views inland of a prominent tower built among the fields on the hilltop. Known as a Daymark, it acted as a navigational aid for passing shipping that in times gone by probably wondered where on earth the narrow mouth of the River Dart had got to. It was built in 1864, and the National Trust noticeboard says that it is still in use today. (Nice to know that even in this modern, technological age mariners still rely on spotting an 80-foot stone tower through a telescope.) Inner Froward Point affords more spectacular views, especially of the yachts and other shipping heading for Dartmouth and Kingswear. This is now your destination, too, as the path heads through pines and lovely rich undergrowth that on a hot afternoon in late spring and summer can have almost a tropical air. There is a sudden drop down to the picturesque Mill Bay Cove, with the return climb up a steep zig-zag path by the edge of bluebell woods. A plaque at the top explains that this piece of the path by Warren Woods is dedicated to the memory of Lt-Col H. Jones, who died in battle in the Falklands.

After this it is a gentle wander through the Dart's steep and wooded eastern shore opposite Dartmouth Castle, and down to the hurly-burly of Kingswear and Dartmouth Harbour. Celebrate completing a wonderful piece of the South Devon coast with a sumptuous tea at the Brunel Buffet, at the terminus of the preserved Paignton and Dartmouth Steam Railway.

There are numerous ferries to take you the short distance across the Dart, but if you insist on walking around the river be prepared for a long, long journey mainly via roads as far north as Totnes, the river's navigable head.

Dartmouth is a place steeped in history. Over the centuries merchants have traded English wool for wine from Bordeaux; then later taken supplies out to settlers in Newfoundland, returning with salted cod to trade for fruit and wine in the Mediterranean before sailing home to Devon. However, Dartmouth has also been the embarkation point for armed expeditions, from the Crusades to the D-Day landings, when 485 American amphibious craft left the harbour. And on the hillside above are the imposing shapes of the Britannia Royal Naval College.

Follow the path back out to the sea via Dartmouth Castle. Built around 1480, this was the first in Britain to be designed for artillery, although a much simpler ploy also used was to hang a chain across the harbour mouth to Kingswear Castle. Continue beyond the fortifications and along a rocky shore of dramatic promontories and hidden coves. Shags and cormorants can often be seen perched on rocks above the waves. At Warren Cove walkers have to head inland, and the South-West Coast Path turns into the South-West Road Path for a while to Stoke Fleming; and then after a short footpath again from near Blackpool Sands to Strete. Follow the official signs, but it is a most unsatisfactory detour. Perhaps one day a true coast route will be negotiated?

Since crossing the Exe there have been many miles of soaring cliffs and headlands, but the next couple of miles into Torcross are very different. Walk by the road, or walk on the beach, but Slapton Sands is very straight and very flat. Behind the long shingle bank is Slapton Ley, a national nature reserve, and the largest natural (freshwater) lake in the West Country. This area was used by the American military in 1943 as a practice for the Normandy landings, and the whole village was evacuated for the exercises. One of the two memorials to that time includes a Sherman tank that was pulled from the sea.

TORCROSS – WEMBURY (40 miles)
Start Bay continues in a straight and uncomplicated manner via Hallsands. Below today's settlement are the remains of the former village. It was 'lost' to the sea in 1917, after years of uncompromising offshore dredging for raw material for the Devonport Dockyard removed the protective shingle bank at the southern end of Start Bay and left the village totally exposed. It succumbed to the sea very quickly.

The path climbs gradually to Start Point, whose lighthouse you have probably seen blinking from as far back as the approach to

Kingswear. It has been warning ships of the dangers of this jagged south Devon shore since 1836. The low headland of dark schist takes its name from the Anglo-Saxon word 'steort', meaning tail, and from here the path sweeps around Lannacombe Bay to the other major headland, Prawle Point, the most southerly point in the county and Devon's equivalent of the Lizard. In between you drop down to Lannacombe Beach, after which the path makes use of raised beaches as it skirts fields to reach the Point. The coastguard station used to be a Lloyds signal station and had a direct telegraph link with the head office in Leadenhall Street, London. This is certainly the place from which to take in the views, of ships big and small, and of migratory birds and insects blown off the Atlantic.

The remainder of the route to Salcombe is straightforward, most of it a stirring march across and along the top of rough cliffs that tumble into the surf. The rugged coast may be bracing to walk along, but is not friendly towards seagoing folk. Just beyond Prawle Point are the remains of the *Demetrios*, which ended up on the rocks in 1992. Meanwhile at Gammon Head two Spanish galleons separated from the Armada came to a sticky end; and the fully rigged *Meirion* from Liverpool ended her days on Rickham Sands in 1879.

There is a regular ferry across Salcombe Harbour from East Portlemouth, otherwise it is a lengthy walk along lanes to negotiate the huge Kingsbridge Estuary, whose numerous watery arms extend deep into the low, green countryside.

In the 1860s Salcombe fruiters were a common sight around here. These were not a local dessert dish or weird cocktail but a type of schooner that sailed from the port to trade in citrus fruits with the Azores. Largely due to the shelter afforded by the estuary, Salcombe remains popular with mariners, and a large number of yachts and small craft are always to be found here.

Follow the narrow road out to the popular beach of South Sands, below Overbecks House, where the coast path resumes in earnest once more along Courtenay Walk. Here is another great stretch of walking and another fabulous headland, this time Bolt Head. Starehole Bay, just before the head, was where the last working tall ship was wrecked, in April 1936. After hitting rocks the four-masted Finnish *Herzogin Cecilie* came aground at Starehole Bay. It was almost two months before she broke up, and her cargo of rotting corn could be smelt for miles around. An infinitely greater tragedy occurred in 1760 when HMS *Ramilles* was dashed on the rocks below Bolt Tail, a little further along this treacherous shore. Up to 800 seamen perished.

Now stride on to Bolt Tail, past the two Hopes (Inner and Outer), Thurlestone Golf Course and a series of sandy bays to reach the mouth of the River Avon. At low tide the wide expanse of sand and narrow river channel looks harmless enough, and you may be forgiven for thinking that it is the easiest thing in the world to wade across to Bigbury-on-Sea. Think again. Even the Secretary of the South-West Way Association will not risk it, for as well as the patches of soft sand the various river channels are also liable to vary in depth. Walkers have waded the Avon successfully, but if you want to avoid the possibility of getting yourself and all your belongings totally immersed in cold water take the seasonal ferry from Bantham. Should this not be running follow the suggested route of the SWWA upstream via Aveton Gifford, in fact a very pleasant 7-mile countryside ramble.

Burgh Island, just off Bigbury, is worth a visit at low tide. Above the art deco hotel is a hut once used by lookouts. But they were not seeking smugglers or distressed ships, but pilchards. Today we might view the supermarket tins of the little fellows in brine or tomato sauce with a certain amount of indifference or amusement, but 100 years ago the pilchard industry of the South-West was big business. The inshore fishing of pilchards was known as 'seining', after the type of nets, and at its height millions could be landed in just one day (no wonder the shoals disappeared earlier this century). Continue along the cliff-edge path to the next river mouth, that of the Erme, but since there is no ferry here you must wade or else walk inland via lanes to Sequer's Bridge. The advice for those wading this quiet, unspoilt river is to stick within one hour either side of low tide, along the course of the old ford.

This is a quiet and by and large undeveloped stretch of coast. The few centres of activity, such as Bantham and Bigbury, are little more than villages and, once clear of them, likely as not you will have the cliffpath to yourself. In fact west of the Erme the coastal track marches around Stoke Point and Gara Point towards Noss Mayo in splendid isolation. The views across the approach to Plymouth Sound to Cornwall are magnificent. Better still, this lofty walk is firm and level, since it is along an old coach drive laid out by Lord Revelstoke at the end of the last century. It extends for nine miles in total, and was cut simply so that he could impress his visitors with a tour of his land, which is as good a reason as any, I suppose.

A mile before Noss Mayo there is a seasonal ferry from the foot of Ferry Wood to Warren Point, across the River Yealm, or else a long road journey via Newton Ferrers and Yealmpton.

WEMBURY – PORTWRINKLE (27 miles)

The 7 miles from Wembury to Turnchapel stick to the coastline, and the only problem is if HMS *Cambridge*, the Royal Navy Gunnery School, is in action. There are prominent notices if firing is about to take place, and an alternative route is given.

As you swing into the Sound Cornwall seems tantalisingly close, but you will have to negotiate Plymouth first. The official coast path stutters to a halt amid the houses at Turnchapel, and to enter the city centre a walk or bus ride of several miles is necessary in order to cross the Plym at Laira Bridge (water taxis are also available). The South-West Way Association give detailed directions for walking through the city, via the Barbican and the famous Hoe, to the ferry for Cremyll from Admiral's Hard, Stonehouse. Take your time, for there is plenty to see, including the Mayflower Steps, from where the Pilgrim Fathers finally set sail, and the Hoe, with the Sir Francis Drake Memorial and Smeaton's Tower. The latter is the upper part of John Smeaton's famous Eddystone Lighthouse, built in 1759, and the third of four lighthouses that have been constructed over the years to warn ships of the three deadly Eddystone reefs 14 miles offshore from Plymouth. It was the earliest rock light built in Britain, but after the first two lasted barely sixty years the distinguished engineer John Smeaton was brought in to devise a longer-lasting model. He introduced a revolutionary new system of interlocking masonry, and experimented with hydraulic mortar which set underwater, in an effort to resist the power of storm waves that regularly reached 30m high. His model lasted 123 years, and now marooned on the Hoe you can climb the spiral staircase for views of the present Eddystone Lighthouse. In 1994 Smeaton was finally commemorated by a plaque in Westminster Abbey, joining Telford, Brunel and Stephenson in the 'Engineers' Corner'.

Those who want to stay on dry land will leave Plymouth by the Tamar Bridge and rejoin the coast along lanes via St Germans, otherwise most walkers will enter Cornwall from the ferry at Cremyll Point. The coast path now passes through Mount Edgcumbe

Country Park, sticking close to the shore, but if you have time a diversion into the deer park or to the Orangery café is worthwhile. Apparently both the house and grounds were to have been given to the Duke of Medina Sidonia if the Spanish Armada had been victorious. Now via Heavitree Road and into the twin villages of Kingsand and Cawsand, where Lord Nelson and Lady Hamilton were regulars at the Ship Inn. Until the breakwater in Plymouth Sound was built the Royal Navy often anchored in Cawsand Bay, although one of its most famous visitors was a defeated enemy (Napoleon, after Waterloo). Over the years the casual observer on Cawsand waterfront, or better still in Mount Edgcumbe Park, will have seen much of Britain's maritime history unfolding. Sir Francis Drake's fleet sailed to meet the Armada from the Sound; James Cook and Francis Chichester both sailed the world from here; and today naval craft still regularly use the dockyards at Devonport, which were established in 1691.

The path wanders out to Rame Head, affording fine views of the south Cornwall coast towards Dodman Point and the Lizard; then from Polhawn Cove to Portwrinkle there is a delightful low-tide walk along the beach – about 5 miles – although to begin with it is rather rocky. However, this route will also be impeded if firing is taking place at Tregantle Fort, in which case stick with the path along the cliff which is forced to join the road for an inland detour around the range. The fort itself was another in the series that were built in the 1860s and '70s to defend the Channel Coast.

PORTWRINKLE – CHARLESTOWN (30 miles)
The route through and beyond Portwrinkle stays close to the sea, using an unofficial path for a while to Battern Cliffs, among the highest in south Cornwall. After a steep drop to Downderry you can either walk through the middle of the strung-out village or along the beach and sea wall to the road through Seaton. Once more uphill, and left along a high track past the Amazonian woolly monkeys at the Murrayton Monkey Sanctuary, and via Millendreath and quiet lanes into Looe (the approach is rather fiddly, so look to the relevant guidebook for directions if needed).

Daphne du Maurier found Looe claustrophobic, as the buildings huddle together on the steep sides of the narrow valley overlooking the busy harbour and tight river mouth. A bridge has linked the communities on either bank since 1411, although today there's a summertime ferry across the harbour as well. Walkers should in particular seek out the Quayside Pantry in West Looe, highly recommended for superlative sausage rolls and other home-made delicacies; and there's also the Ship Hotel.

The path resumes where the road finishes at Hannafore. Offshore is St George's or Looe Island, which was inhabited by a pair of monks in the twelfth century, then much later by the notorious smugglers 'Black Joan' and her brother, 'Fyn'. They kept a huge stash of contraband, and it is said lived on a diet of rats and rabbits, which may account for the lack of rodents on the island. During the Second World War the island was bombed by German pilots who mistook it for a warship.

The route is straightforward all the way along to Polperro, erstwhile haunt of smugglers and fishermen, and now very popular with tourists. The much-photographed whitewashed cottages benefit from the exclusion of traffic, but it can become equally congested with slow-moving pedestrians.

The next stretch to Polruan is stimulating but exacting. The gradients are severe in places, and it is easy to underestimate the time needed for completion. Facilities are also few, since the clifftop track meets no more villages or ice cream vans until Fowey is in sight. Pull your socks well up, check the sandwiches and flask, and enjoy some fine coast walking away from the crowds.

Habitation is reached once more at Polruan, from where there is a regular ferry across to Fowey (pronounced Foy). The Ship Inn (St Austell Ales) and the pink-washed King of Prussia both provide hearty fare, the former built in 1570 and home of the Rashleigh family. John Rashleigh sailed with his cousins Sir Francis Drake and Sir Walter Raleigh in his ship *Frances of Fowey*, which the pub name commemorates.

Once more out to the coast, and at Readymoney Cove there are signs for another recreational footpath. The black Celtic cross denotes the 26-mile Saints Way, which crosses the peninsula on paths and lanes from Fowey to Padstow. The Saints Way heads up leafy Love Lane, while the coast path strides out to the low cliffs above the harbour mouth. Here, by the ruins of St Catherine's Castle, you can watch the ships laden with china clay leaving for far-off places, escorted out of Fowey Haven by pilots.

After bouncing along the clifftop turf for a mile or so the track descends to the serene and sheltered surroundings of Polridmouth.

Here, by two small, sandy coves, is a neat cottage with lawn and artificial lake (coast path walkers are allowed to cross by the dam). It was the inspiration for Daphne du Maurier's *Rebecca*, ('Last night I dreamt I went to Manderley again . . .') since for many years she lived up the valley at Menabilly.

Ahead, up a short pull to Gribbin Head, is the huge, 25m-high barber's shop-striped Daymark, which it must be said could do with a lick of paint. It was built in 1832 to aid ships entering Fowey. New views open up across St Austell Bay, and of the smoking chimneys of the china clay works ahead, and this is now the direction as the straightforward cliff path heads north via the former pilchard-fishing village of Polkerris. The Saints Way makes another appearance near here, and at Polmear (the Ship Inn, once more), by the clay-whitened Par Sands; but as it wanders off inland you should bear west around Par Beach and negotiate the china clay processing plant at Par. This means walking the white-dusted pavements around the industrial plant. It is unlikely to be the most scenic part of your trip.

The reason for all the fuss is kaolin, a fine white clay produced by decomposed granite, and only found in the UK in Devon and Cornwall. Inland, around St Austell, the so-called sky dumps of waste clay and quartz have produced an odd lunar landscape, but the 'Cornish Alps' are not for climbing.

Regaining the sea at Spit Point turn right, past the more familiar sight of a golf links, although the ugly boxed shapes of Cornish Leisure World at Carlyon Bay could easily be construed for an extension of the industrial complex. You then arrive at Charlestown, originally a tiny fishing village but then transformed by Charles Rashleigh, whose name it bears. Another of the prominent Rashleigh family, Charles was born in 1747 at Menabilly – where, as we have seen, du Maurier subsequently lived – and over the years built up a thriving export industry, first in copper and then china clay. John Smeaton, the lighthouse chap, was employed to design the harbour, which was cut out of solid rock, and a gun battery was built on cliffs to the south in case of attack by the French. Today the place still retains its stark, eighteenth-century appearance, which has been used by the likes of *The Onedin Line* TV series.

CHARLESTOWN – EAST PORTHOLLAND (17 miles)
With all the mess safely behind, the coast path resumes its pleasant shoreline passage to Porthpean. Beyond here the going gets tougher,

with a high and wild track out to Black Head, once an Iron Age fort and latterly a rifle range – but now safely in the hands of the National Trust.

Keep to the clifftop path as far as Pentewan, where a harbour and jetty built in 1744 were silted up within a short time by the constant stream of waste washed down from works and claypits upstream. Specially built reservoirs that allowed water to wash through the harbour had little effect, and ships were even trapped in the harbour by fast-forming sandbanks. Then from the road by the huge beachside caravan and camping site return to the cliffs and via Penare Point to Mevagissey. The name comes from the two saints to whom the local church is dedicated: Memai and Iti, which later became Meva and Issey. Today it is another picturesque fishing village, with another Ship Inn and more narrow streets choked with summer traffic and pasty-eating families from Woking.

The road climbs out of the village southwards, giving good views of the harbour and the colourful collection of fishing boats. Leave the tarmac at Portmellon for the path to Gorran Haven, once a fishing centre that outstripped Mevagissey in importance but now residential, via Chapel Point and the well-named Turbot Point. Here you will find Bodrugan's Leap, which is supposed to be where Sir Richard Edgcumbe chased Sir Henry Trenowth (aka Bodrugan) into the sea. Edgcumbe had supported Henry VII at Bosworth, and as his reward was offered most of the Bodrugan estate, the family having sided with the doomed Richard III. Legend has it that Sir Henry rode off the cliffs into the waves, then clambered on board a waiting boat and escaped to France.

The route continues in an uncomplicated manner to the superb headland of Dodman Point, often known as the Dodman. The name may derive from 'tomen', the Cornish term for bank or dyke, since Iron Age ramparts are evident. However, it is more natural to assume that it means, quite simply, 'dead man', since the rocks below the high, dark promontory have accounted for numerous ships and men over the centuries, with one of the most recent being the pleasure cruiser *Darlwin* which sunk in 1966 with the loss of all thirty-one passengers. At the tip of the headland is a massive granite cross erected by the Revd G. Martin in 1896 as a navigational (and presumably spiritual) aid, but despite the rector sleeping beside the cross the first night the shipwrecks continued. At the time of writing the National Trust, who own the headland, are allied with local fishermen and other groups, opposing plans by the military to create an offshore firing range near Dodman Point. One has to hope this ridiculous idea will be seen off.

Past the white sand of Hemmick Beach, a sunny hideaway that cars can't quite reach, the path drops down to Porthluney Cove and the foot of thick woodland (a rare sight in Cornwall) surrounding Caerhays Castle. It was designed in 1808 by John Nash, who also designed Buckingham Palace and the Brighton Pavilion, but the cost of the construction and landscaping the grounds eventually ruined the Trevanion family. Matters were not helped by the fact that Nash used papier-mâché in the roof, which soon disintegrated in the Cornish rain.

EAST PORTHOLLAND – COVERACK (38 miles)

On through the two Portholland hamlets, joined by either the road or seawall, the coast path reaches the narrow harbour of Portloe, where the attractive Ship Inn (which I believe is known locally as 'the Drinking Kitchen') can be found up the hill. Like East and West Portholland, it is pleasant to find little commercial development brought on by the demands of tourism.

It's up and down once more to Nare Head. A little way out to sea is Gull Rock, a popular nesting site for kittiwakes and guillemots, and used in the 1950s film *Treasure Island*. Then there are some more steep gradients before rounding Gerrans Bay, where you can dip your feet in the shallows at Carne and Pendower beaches at low tide before the swing south to Portscatho.

The rest of the route to Place, via Porthmellin Head and Zone Point, is well-walked and quite easy. There are good views over Falmouth Bay and the entrance to Carrick Roads, including St Mawes and Pendennis castles, and south to the mouth of the Helford River. However, it is likely that those on more than a leisurely day walk will be more concerned with the availability of water-borne transport to Falmouth at this stage, since two ferries are usually necessary to make the full crossing (it is advisable to ring ahead from Portscatho to check times and so on). The St Mawes–Falmouth ferry is year-round and usually no problem, but the boat from Place to St Mawes has a seasonal and more limited timetable. There is an alternative 8-mile land route to St Mawes from Place via St Gerrans – see the South-West Way Association's guidebook; but should you be an absolute purist the inland route around the many tentacles leading off Carrick Roads will take you as far inland as Truro.

Libby Purves aptly describes Falmouth as the Piccadilly Circus of the coast, when she and her family stopped off there on their voyage around the coast of Britain in 1988. It's a safe, deep-water anchorage, famous over the centuries for its fast mail packet service, and a stopping-off point for homeward-bound vessels keen to learn which European port would offer the best market for their cargoes.

Follow roadways out to Pendennis Point, where you can marvel at the boats, the docks, the sea, and more boats. And, of course, the castle. Pendennis Castle was another one built under the orders of Henry VIII, and later strengthened by Elizabeth I. But when the attack eventually arrived it came not from the sea but the land – 900 men were besieged for six months during the Civil War, and they only gave themselves up to the Roundheads when famine-point was reached. The premises now contain a youth hostel.

Via the back of Swanpool Beach to Pennance Point, and the cliff path continues until it drops to the sandy cove of Maenporth (even though the name means 'rocky cove' or 'stone cove'); then on to Rosemullion Head. In spring the ground is covered in bluebells, plus gorse and early purple orchids. A little further on are the cliffs of Mawnan Shear, dark with oaks, then swing west to Helford Passage. If you gaze across the Helford's wide reaches and wonder why the number '6' is painted 10 feet high on circular boards at regular intervals, it is because you are in Helford's Voluntary Marine Conservation Area, and vessels are requested not to exceed 6 knots.

The peaceful, tree-lined Helford River is the ideal place to slip down a gear or two and take things easy, and the shelter is especially welcome if a prevailing westerly is battering the coast. Technically it is not so much a river estuary but a ria, or drowned river valley. Although there is little direct riverside access upstream from Helford Passage, a network of mostly empty country lanes and public footpaths will help you explore, and when you reach the groans and barks emanating from the seal sanctuary at Gweek you can return to Helford itself via the National Trust-owned Frenchman's Creek – the du Maurier connection once more, although it is not widely known that in fact Sir Arthur Quiller-Couch set a short story of the same name here forty years before. (Needless to say most coastal walkers will cut all this out by taking the ferry from Helford Passage.)

To return to the sea follow the clear track though shaded bluebell woods of the Bosahan Estate and out to the scrubby headland of Dennis Head. Below is St Anthony in Meneage, whose church has a small-scale model of itself outside, next to the collection box. The stepping stones to Gillan are walkable an hour either side of low water, but they can be very slippery so take care; otherwise stick to the minor road around Gillan Creek.

Follow the cliffpath to Nare Head and then south for a scenic stretch to Porthallow, where you will find a pub called the Five Pilchards. After this the official route cuts inland to reach Porthoustock and Rosenithon, then emerges at Godrevy Cove. Offshore you will see the Manacles, a group of treacherous rocks spread over a mile, and which it is believed has claimed getting on for 1,000 victims. You may wish to keep staring out to sea in order not to dwell on Dean Quarry, which you have to walk through in order to rejoin the main coast path that will take you to Coverack.

COVERACK – MULLION COVE (17 miles)

By now you are well into Lizard country, that famous peninsula reaching out far into the Channel. If Land's End is the toe, then the Lizard is the hefty heel. To reach the Point follow the obvious cliff path via Chynhalls Point to Black Head. Here a coastguard once kept watch, his gaze sweeping from Lizard Point all the way to the Dodman.

Further along is Kennack Sands, and at low tide you can walk across both beaches if you wish; then at Poltesco a brief diversion may be made to view a former serpentine works. The Lizard is well-known for its hard, polished serpentine stone, and even today a small industry continues to mine the attractive, durable and easily trimmed green-reddish rock to sell as ornaments to visitors. Walkers should note that older stone stiles on the Lizard are made out of serpentine and are liable to be very slippery when wet.

The coast path sticks rigidly to the clifftop, passing through the picturesque fishing village of Cadgwith. Lobsters and crabs are now the main catch, but previously it was pilchards. South of Cadgwith is the Devil's Frying Pan, a natural rock crater caused by the collapse of a sea cave; then a relatively easy cliff walk leads around the ever rockier Lizard Point.

The most southerly spot in Britain is surrounded by a frightening array of rocks and reefs lurking up to some distance offshore. In 1720 the military transport carrier *Royal Anne* sank near here, and 200 bodies from the tragedy were buried in a mass grave nearby. Earlier this century the Lizard lifeboat and three others took part in what a notice describes as 'the greatest ever rescue operation undertaken by the RNLI'. It took a day and a half for the four boats to lift all 524 people off the White Star liner *Suevic* when she became stranded on rocks in thick fog and heavy seas. Lizard Point is crowned by some rather uninspiring cafés and a serpentine-selling shop, but overall it is far less commercialised than Land's End which you will meet shortly – and which is now visible if the weather is good. The actual settlement of Lizard is only a few minutes inland, but since it is little more than a shabby, scattered collection of buildings and shops stick with the coast.

Mind you, if you do venture inland you will get a better idea of the make-up of this wide, flat peninsula, with the surprisingly bare expanses of Lizard and Goonhilly Downs. Its southerly position and mild climate, plus a combination of unusual rocks and soils, have encouraged a rich spread of plants and flowers. You will see this as you leave Lizard Point for Mullion, with the path dropping through colourful meadows and natural rockeries. In the sheltered valleys the flora is especially rich, including sedges, orchids, Cornish heath and even wild asparagus.

The well-walked clifftop track to Mullion Cove is via the National Trust's Kynance Cove, a much-visited beauty spot with an underlying serpentine outcrop that extends for nearly eight square miles and which is responsible for the distinctive rocky outline above the sand.

MULLION COVE – PENZANCE (20 miles)

Mullion Cove is one in a series of pleasant west-facing and mostly sandy coves linked by the coast path along this stretch. On Angrouse Cliff, between Polurrian and Poldhu Coves, is the Marconi Monument, which marks the spot where Guglielmo Marconi arranged the first wireless message to be transmitted across the Atlantic in 1901. He had gone across to Newfoundland in order to pick up the pre-arranged signal (an 's', repeated three times). This western side of the Lizard is also notorious for shipwrecks, some involving the loss of valuable cargo. An unnamed Spanish vessel wrecked near here in the 1780s is supposed to have been full of silver dollars, and strenuous but mostly unsuccessful efforts were made in subsequent years to recover the treasure (nowadays identified wrecks are protected by Historic Wreck Protection Orders, in case you get any ideas).

Eventually you drop down to Porthleven Sands, and a fairly short shingle trudge across the Loe Bar towards Porthleven. The bar plugs Cornwall's largest freshwater lake, the Loe, and a 5-mile circular walk around the pool is possible. Until a spit developed around the mouth of the Cober in the thirteenth century Helston was an important river port, but a combination of natural drift and possibly storms began to block the estuary, a process aided by silt brought down by the river from the tin mines upstream.

Near Bar Lodge leave the beach for a route inland of some cliff erosion then via a road into Porthleven. The harbour was built mainly to service the local mining industry, and belonged to a mining company until 1961.

As you leave Porthleven there is a cross commemorating all those lost when the frigate *Anson* was wrecked on Loe Bar in 1807, and who were subsequently buried in unnamed graves and unconsecrated ground – the toll was over 100. Then on westwards, via some cliffs that are not always particularly stable, to the lovely burst of Praa Sands, which really should be walked if the tide permits. A little further is Prussia Cove, named after John Carter, a notorious eighteenth-century smuggler and so-called King of Prussia (the name of the inn he ran). The name can be found elsewhere in Cornwall. We have already passed the prominent King of Prussia in the centre of Fowey.

The trail continues along the cliffs, and soon the fairy-tale shape of St Michael's Mount draws near. There is a walkable causeway at low tide, otherwise a regular fleet of small boats ferry the crowds across to one of the National Trust's star attractions. Edward the Confessor founded a Benedictine chapel on the rocky summit, and the castle was added three centuries later. Like so many of these places it's best to choose your moment carefully – if it's August Bank Holiday then it may be more prudent to admire the view from the mainland, with a splendid backdrop of Mount's Bay and the Penzance-Newlyn spread.

From the pleasantly unspoilt main street of Marazion it is a long, level embankment or beachwalk next to the railway (the main line from London Paddington) until just past the heliport, when you should hop over the footbridge and enter Penzance. This stretch is part of St Michael's Way, a walking route of around 12 miles that links St Michael's Mount with the Church of St Uny at Lelant, on the north Cornwall coast. It is part of the European network of Ways of St James, which comprises various routes used by pilgrims over the centuries that all lead to St James's Cathedral in Santiago de Compostela, Spain.

Pick of the walks

BRIXHAM – KINGSWEAR/DARTMOUTH (11 miles): surprisingly remote, wooded sea cliffs away from the crowds, with a handsome harbour ending (and an optional steam train ride back to Torbay).

HELFORD – MULLION (30 miles): a coastal tour of the Lizard, England's most southerly spot; from lazy tree-lined inlets to exposed headlands.

III THE ATLANTIC COAST

7 ENGLAND'S CAPE
Penzance – Ilfracombe
218 miles

8 SEVERN SEAS
Ilfracombe – Swansea
232 miles

9 THE CLIFFS OF WALES
Swansea – Cardigan
290 miles

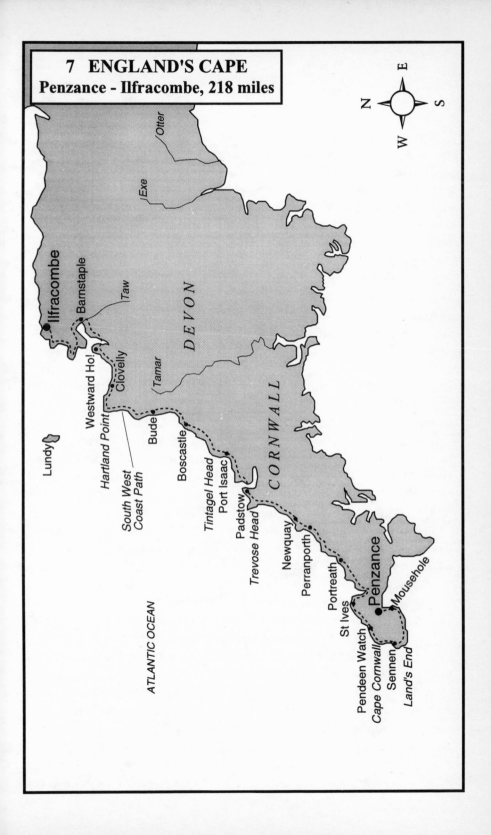

7 ENGLAND'S CAPE
Penzance - Ilfracombe, 218 miles

N E S W

Otter

Exe

Ilfracombe

Barnstaple

Taw

DEVON

Westward Ho!

Clovelly

Tamar

Hartland Point

Bude

Boscastle

South West
Coast Path

Tintagel Head

Port Isaac

Padstow

Trevose Head

CORNWALL

Newquay

Perranporth

Portreath

Penzance

Mousehole

St Ives

Lundy

ATLANTIC OCEAN

Pendeen Watch

Cape Cornwall

Sennen

Land's End

Penzance, from the Cornish 'pen sans' meaning holy headland, was the first port in Cornwall to have a lifeboat. However, the craft never saw action even once in the whole of the nine years that it was stationed here, and was sold to cover debts in 1812. But the influence of the sea is all-pervasive, from the Museum of Nautical Art to the National Lighthouse Centre housed in the old Trinity House depot, which a century ago produced the granite blocks for the Wolf Rock Tower and regularly serviced navigational buoys. Penzance was also the birthplace of Humphry Davy, gifted chemist and well-known as the inventor of the famous miner's safety lamp, and who is commemorated by a statue outside the Market House.

Penzance promenade soon gives way to the fish quays of Newlyn, leading port in the South-West and popular with artists since the early 1880s. From here the road is followed to Mousehole, another quaint fishing village with narrow streets blocked by parked cars. The name is pronounced 'Mowzel', and may come from a cave on the foreshore which has the appearance of a large mousehole. A mile inland is the village of Paul, and in its churchyard is a memorial to Dolly Pentreath. She died in 1777 and is believed to be the last person to speak solely Cornish.

The route finally leaves the tarmac after Mousehole for a track to Lamorna Cove, then quite a wild and unspoilt burst via St Loy's Cove and Penberth Cove to Porthcurno. The accessible and urban miles around St Mount's Bay are quickly forgotten as you inch nearer to the far tip of the Land's End peninsula. If the wind is blowing off the Atlantic all the way from North America these miles can be bracing to say the least; and if you are walking in anything other than summer, facilities will be limited so make sure that you are well supplied.

Porthcurno is one of several tiny and idyllic sandy coves hiding among these cliffs. Given some peaceful, August sunshine the golden sands contrast with the deep and clear blue waters to create a scene that is almost tropical. And there is a sort of link actually under your very feet, since Porthcurno was where the first ocean cable from overseas (Bombay, to be precise) came ashore in Britain. Since the 1870s cables from all around the world began to arrive here, facilitating the modern international telephone call, although Cable and Wireless now use the location for a training college (hence the huge car park and out of place buildings).

Leaving Porthcurno the path passes the famous Minack Theatre, a small, open-air amphitheatre carved out of the rock face in the 1930s, and where productions are still staged each summer. Unfortunately, coast path walkers will have to pay in order to get in just to view the arena.

Continue around the windy and exciting cliffs, accompanied only by jackdaws and gulls if you are lucky, and soon – although it's not really perceptible – the route swings around to the north and to the end of the land.

You can tell that you're nearing Land's End: the tracks get wider and more numerous and litter starts appearing. On top of the mean, jagged cliffs the Land's End complex offers welcome pots of tea and expensive beds, plus displays and 'experiences' for all ages and intellects (check out 'The Legendary Last Labyrinth: the No 1 Multi-sensory Experience'). Some of it is quite interesting, including a small exhibition on the Land's End – John o'Groats record breakers. Outside is the famous signpost, and for a sum you can have a destination of your choosing fixed to the post for you to pose by. John o'Groats is given as 874 miles, while New York is a mere 3,147 miles distant.

The coastal path squeezes seawards of the hotel complex and walkers should have no trouble with access, despite reports of problems a few years ago. Out to sea is the Longships Lighthouse, and in the far distance the Scilly Isles may even be visible.

Leave the First and Last House for the first and last time and continue along any number of clifftop tracks to Sennen Cove, and to one of the most delightful bays in Cornwall. Whitesand Bay, in fair weather as bright and dazzling as its name, curves gently out before you to a line of tumbling cliffs that culminate in the distinctive cone of Cape Cornwall. At low tide the best place to walk is alongside the Atlantic breakers, often being ridden by surfers, but before long you must veer towards the grassy slopes in order to regain the cliff path northwards.

Land's End beats Cape Cornwall by barely half a mile as England's westernmost point, but as many people have noted it is the latter that really feels like the end of the country, and in fact until the fourteenth century it was mistakenly believed to be the point furthest west. It is also notable for being the only cape in England, and comprises a small grassy lump that rises almost conically from the waves. To round it all off the Cape is capped by an old mining tower, restored in 1986, and since it is all now National Trust land it can be explored at your leisure.

One mile south-west of Cape Cornwall are a couple of menacing-looking rocks called the Brisons. In 1851 the *New Commercial* had the misfortune to end up on them, but Captain Sanderson and his wife stayed aboard the sinking vessel as six attempts were made to rescue them. By this time a crowd estimated at almost 6,000 had gathered on the clifftop. They saw Mrs Sanderson pulled off at the sixth attempt, but unfortunately she died before reaching the mainland and was subsequently buried at Sennen churchyard.

The 17 miles from Cape Cornwall to St Ives are among the toughest on the whole of the South-West Coast Path. Even the strongest walkers underestimate this section, according to my landlady at Sennen Cove who has seen a few overconfident coast walkers set off from her doorstep over the years. As far as Pendeen Watch the problem may be a confusion of tracks through the former tin workings dotted about the clifftop. Some have been restored and can be visited, but most are derelict and should not be entered.

PENDEEN WATCH – PORTREATH (24 miles)
This is certainly a breathtaking stretch of coastline, but with next to no facilities until St Ives, and very little off it, make sure you pack your sandwiches and thermos before you start. It is what the South-West Way Association call a 'severe' section (rather than just plain 'strenuous'), and they should know, with additional problems of inadequate waymarking and sometimes a confusing choice of tracks. Although the official coast path sticks reasonably close to the edge of the wild cliffs it is not unlikely that now and again you will unknowingly deviate from the proper route, and should you suddenly find yourself staring down a sheer drop or faced with some dangerous scree I suggest you turn promptly around and retrace your steps. The climbing is best left to the folk with ropes on Bosigran Cliff.

If weather or fatigue force you inland you may well head for Zennor. D.H. Lawrence stayed here for a short while in 1915, but the locals suspected his German-born wife Frieda of being a spy (she was, after all, related to no less than the Red Baron). The couple were harassed so much by the authorities that they were finally forced to leave. According to the stuff of legend a local man once fell under the spell of the Mermaid of Zennor and was lured to a watery grave (the sixteenth-century 'Mermaid Chair' can still be found in the local church). But with luck you will only be lured to the Tinners Arms for a pint of St Austell ale and a sandwich.

Now a major tourist centre, St Ives was once the home of pilchard fishermen and miners. They all used to live in narrow streets behind the quay, with the former in what was known as the 'downalong' and the miners in the quarter above them called the 'upalong'. The pilchard shoals disappeared towards the turn of this century to be replaced by an influx of artists, and in particular the distinguished sculptor Barbara Hepworth. Today the handsome Tate Gallery St Ives continues this fine tradition, and includes works from the St Ives school. It has a commendable policy of community-wide accessibility, which extends to providing a rack for surf boards in the gallery entrance.

For the next few miles the route keeps company with the railway, landwards of it until Carbis Bay then along the edge of the white Porth Kidney Sands to Lelant. From here it's a dull and unpretty roadside affair around the estuary to Hayle and back out past a large caravan park to St Ives Bay. The official route is now indistinct and often heavy-going across a wide band of dunes as far as Gwithian. If the tide is low walk the beach.

Beyond Gwithian Bridge the path makes a tour of the low and rocky Godrevy Point and Navax Point. Southwards are good views of St Ives, while the lighthouse on nearby Godrevy Island was the inspiration for Virginia Woolf's *To the Lighthouse*. It was on these rocks that the ship carrying the personal possessions of the deposed Charles I was supposedly wrecked while attempting to reach the continent.

Hell's Mouth is a spectacular and well-known vantage point high above the waves, especially popular with car-bound tourists whose presence has at least encouraged a seasonal café. The coast road now sticks close to the sea, but for the most part walkers will be untroubled and can thank the National Trust for an unspoilt 6 miles into Portreath.

PORTREATH – NEWQUAY (24 miles)

Beyond Portreath the route passes seawards of an RAF establishment and through an area dotted with old tin and copper workings
via Porthtowan to St Agnes Head. It's best not to stray off the
path along this stretch, for the cliff edge is particularly crumbly
and dangerous, although overall the gradient is reasonably flat and
not too strenuous.

North Cornwall is particularly popular with surfers, and in many
of the bays around Porthtowan, Perranporth and Newquay energetic
young bodies ride and fall into the Atlantic waves with much
enthusiasm. It's certainly not as easy as it looks. Try walking
around for a while with a full-size Malibu board – let alone try
standing upon the thing in the swell – and you may think that the
rise and fall of the coastal path is infinitely preferable.

The power of the sea is amply demonstrated at Trevaunance
Cove, where all three harbours built since 1699 to serve the nearby
settlement of St Agnes have been washed away. More forlorn
chimneys of bricked-up and fenced-off engine houses accompany
you all the way to Perranporth. Around Cligga Head tin, tungsten
and copper have all been mined at various times. In the middle of
the nineteenth century Cornwall produced two thirds of the world's
copper (and together the tin and copper industry employed 50,000
men in just this one county). But competition from abroad meant
that by the end of the century production had fallen from 160,000
tons to as little as 500, and thousands of miners were forced to
emigrate to the likes of Australia and South Africa.

Perranporth is named after St Piran, patron saint of tinners, who
is supposed to have floated over to Cornwall on a millstone from
Ireland in the sixth century. He founded a chapel on Gear Sands, to
the north of present-day Perranporth, which was overrun by shifting
sand and only rediscovered following a storm in 1835. Known as St
Piran's Oratory, it proved to be in such an exposed position and in
such a state of ruin that it has been allowed to return to the sands.
Meanwhile, the nearby St Piran's Church which was built after the
Oratory disappeared has also been engulfed by sand (the third and
current church is safely located a mile or so away at Perranzabuloe).
There is a public footpath to the marked sites of the two buildings
from the coast path alongside Perran Beach, a 3 mile golden strip
that at low tide presents a perfect sandy surface for the walk towards
Ligger Point.

The route skirts an ugly army camp, then after Penhale Point and the lovely Holywell Bay there are a couple of small headlands before the approach to Newquay. However, the walker's passage is blocked by the Gannel, not a large piece of water but one with a number of options for crossing depending upon the time of day and year: ferry to Pentire (summer only), a tidal ferry or tidal footbridge near Crantock, or failing that via the road bridge near Trevemper.

NEWQUAY – PORT ISAAC (34 miles)

Cornwall's premier resort is described as 'the golden gateway to fun and relaxation', which really just means beaches, cafés, gardens, crazy golf, chips, beer, amusement arcades and so on – except in greater quantity than all the other places. Newquay really comes to life, however, on its beaches, or more specifically in the rollers. Fistral Beach and, a little further north, the long sweep of Watergate Bay, offer first-class surfing, and international competitions are held here.

Once the last outposts of Newquay are left behind the cliffs reassert themselves, and it is a pleasant walk above the golden sand to Mawgan Porth, where surf hire shops and hotels cater for the needs of most guests. Beyond here is Bedruthan Steps, several dramatic granite stacks rising out of the waves that were once used as stepping stones by a giant, or so it goes. It is a popular tourist attraction, and the National Trust who own land overlooking the Steps have recently completed rebuilding a staircase down to the beach after years of worsening erosion.

Continue along the clifftop to Park Head, a rugged headland also in the safe hands of the National Trust. Altogether the National Trust owns about 200 miles of the seaboard of Devon and Cornwall, more than one third of the coast of the two counties combined, and part of the ongoing Enterprise Neptune appeal to save Britain's coastline. It was launched in 1965 at a time when it was reckoned that six miles of coast were being lost to developers every year, and by 1994 nearly 550 miles of the coast of England and Wales had been delivered into their care. Enterprise Neptune has now raised over £20 million, which has helped to purchase Lizard Point, Orford Ness, the Needles and many other important coastal sites for the nation. As you roam around the unspoilt 200 acres of Park Head with its tumuli and cliff castle and look down at the seabirds and the rocky islets below, gratitude must be tempered by a lingering unease and indignation at just how easy it is, and has been, for our precious coastal heritage to be wrecked by oil refineries, caravan parks, marinas, nuclear power stations and the like.

After the small settlements of Porthcothan and Treyarnon the national trail makes for the windy outpost of Trevose Head, with terrific views back along the north Cornwall coast. Beyond Trevone the path hugs the high grassy clifftop until Padstow Bay and the mouth of the Camel, where as recently as May 1995 the *Maria Assumpta*, then the world's oldest operating wooden sailing ship, was driven on to the rocks with the loss of three lives. In calm and sunny weather the estuary glistens, the turbines of a large wind farm far inland spin lazily, and at low tide a massive expanse of sand is revealed. However, the treacherous nature of this spot is given away by the name of the very sandbar that has grown slowly across the estuary mouth. The Doom Bar has finished off hundreds of vessels over the centuries, and the various Padstow lifeboats have saved over 620 people, although sometimes at considerable cost to the rescuers. In 1867 five crewmen drowned when going to the assistance of a stricken schooner; then in 1900 the steam lifeboat capsized and eight men were lost.

The easy, open path drops into Padstow, a medieval town and former pilchard-fishing centre that thankfully has been little spoilt by modern or vulgar development. Padstow celebrates May Day with the 'Obby 'Oss festival, claimed to be the oldest fertility dance in the country, when local men dance around the town in fiercesome masks. Past the fish-processing halls on the quayside a bankside route along the River Camel begins that until 1967 was a railway branch line and is now a popular walk/cycleway known as the Camel Trail. The route extends as far as Poley's Bridge, near Bodmin Moor, but coast walkers can cross the river at Wadebridge and return by road and footpath. Of course the easiest option is to catch the ferry to Rock from Padstow.

At low tide the beach can be walked from Rock to Daymer Bay, but make sure to save a few minutes to visit St Enodoc Church, reached by a marked path across a golf course. The tiny building, which was once engulfed by windblown sand, is where the former Poet Laureate Sir John Betjeman is buried, a Londoner by birth but, since childhood holidays, a devotee of North Cornwall.

Hayle Bay at Polzeath is another popular venue for surfing, while beyond is the magnificent viewing station of Pentire Point

(Pentire means 'head of the land'). More high, stern and impressive cliffs follow, until after Portquin the path plunges down into Port Isaac, an old fishing village tucked away in a cleft in the cliffs with steep and muddled streets. One such, commonly known as Squeeze-ee-belly Alley, once made it into the *Guinness Book of Records* as the 'narrowest public thoroughfare in the world'.

PORT ISAAC – BUDE (29 miles)

The next eight miles to Tintagel are rigorous, to say the least, with a series of dismayingly steep climbs and descents. Conditions underfoot can also be very rough and sometimes eroded; this is not a stage for flimsy footwear, but proper walking boots whose strong moulded soles offer a decent grip and ankle protection. Trainers or sand shoes are fine for the beach but loose rock and angled scree are another matter.

Also make sure you carry adequate provisions, for there won't be any refreshments until Trebarwith Strand. From here the cliff path passes above old slate quarries until reaching Tintagel Head, a wild location with some awesome cliffs and a dramatic island that can be visited via a footbridge. There are certainly traces of a fifth-century monastery here, quite possibly England's first, and the remains of a castle once owned by the Black Prince, the first Duke of Cornwall. And there is conjecture that there may also have been a Roman signal station, or perhaps it is even the place that the Romans called Durocornovium, whose precise location has never been established. But it's the King Arthur legend that pulls in the crowds – and they are there in force during the summer – even though there is no evidence to support Arthur's connection with Tintagel. Not that those in charge of Merlin's Gift Shop or the King Arthur Car Park are too bothered.

Continue along the cliffs, and ignoring a large caravan and campsite at Rocky Valley, admire the wheeling seabirds about Long and Short Islands, which often include puffins. Sometimes known as the sea parrot, puffins return to the coast in late February and March after spending the winter out at sea. Following mating a single egg is laid not on cliff-ledge nests but in burrows on grassy sea cliffs, islands and hillsides. The chick is fed on small fish, which are held crosswise in the adult's famous multicoloured bill, sometimes as many as fifteen at a time.

Eventually drop down to the narrow, snaking inlet at Boscastle.

A wonderful little place, completely hidden from the sea, and in days gone by rowing boats known as hobblers used to tow small ships into the harbour. Today the waves almost lap the doors of the youth hostel (a former stable) by the tiny harbour; and there is also a National Trust shop (the old forge) and an interesting Heritage Coast Centre. The young Thomas Hardy often came here, and it's still a fascinating place to explore.

The remaining sixteen miles to Bude are demanding. Apart from at Crackington Haven, there is little in the way of refreshment, something that you might find you need since this is a strenuous section. The approach to High Cliff, Cornwall's highest at 223m, is dismayingly steep, and is also preceded by some loose scree that should be watched. The clifftop is best avoided altogether in galeforce winds. Before descending the well-walked track to Crackington Haven there is some more precipitous cliff at Cambeak that, quite frankly, will make anyone slightly worried about vertigo quiver in their boots.

After a well-earned cup of tea, or something stronger, at Crackington Haven, prepare for more huffing and puffing up Pencannow Point, Castle Point and then Chipman Point. The path levels out for a while and passes some scrub oak forest at Dizzard Point, where sessile oak have been kept stunted by the fierce, salty winds. When you finally descend to Millook Haven pause and admire the amazing zig-zag strata of the cliffs. This is where the sandstone and shale formed around 300 million years ago in the Devonian period were folded and twisted as a result of the collision of land masses further south. Between here and Widemouth you will have to follow some of the road, the coast path having disappeared through erosion.

From the inviting sands of Widemouth Bay the coast is lower and less exacting, and the route is easily followed along the clifftop and the backs of small beaches into Bude, entering the town via the sea lock gates.

BUDE – CLOVELLY (24 miles)

Bude Canal was built in the 1820s and the original intention was to take sea-going craft all the way to Launceston, 35 miles inland. But it turned out that at Helebridge, only a couple of miles south of Bude, all the cargo had to be transferred from barges to smaller, wheeled tug boats which were then hauled up a railed incline of over 400m using either water or steam power. Ironically the usual incoming cargo was nothing more exotic than sand, and on the way back out it was often slate. Bude Canal enjoyed some success for a while, but by 1912 the waterway was closed and today much of it is dry and untraceable.

Leave the surfers and sunbathers of Bude behind and resume another remote, challenging and quite superb piece of the South-West Coast Path. North of Duckpool, in particular, there are plenty of steep ups and downs, leaving you gasping both at the views and for breath. A brief diversion inland to Morwenstow may reward you with seasonal refreshments by the lovely old church; and make sure to locate Parson Hawker's hut on Vicarage Cliff nearby. This wooden, turf-covered hut was where local parson Robert Stephen Hawker spent much of his time meditating, writing poetry and keeping a lookout for shipwrecks, since he was concerned that the bodies of all those washed up must have a Christian burial. Vicar at Morwenstow from 1834 until his death forty years later, Hawker was engagingly bonkers. He used to stride about the village in wellington boots, a thick fisherman's jumper hung with holy medals, and a purple overcoat; and at other times he dressed up as a mermaid. It is also reported that he excommunicated one of his ten cats for catching a mouse on the Sabbath. In his driftwood hut he enjoyed the occasional opium pipe, and among his writings is 'The Song of the Western Men', which became the Cornish national anthem.

Among these formidable cliffs – Henna Cliff is second only to Beachy Head as the highest sheer cliff in England – the county border is crossed at the rocky and remote Marsland Mouth. Four miles away rises the River Tamar, which separates Cornwall from Devon, and which we last saw all those miles back at Plymouth.

At Speke's Mill Mouth there is a fine waterfall that tumbles 15m in a staircase of falls down to the rocky beach; then in less than a mile is Hartland Quay which was once a thriving port and even authorised to print its own bank notes at one time. The small museum has more details, and about the awful toll of shipwrecks along this coast which have continued recently with the loss of the Dutch cargo ship *Johanna*, smashed into pieces on the rocks below the headland.

If it's blowing hard off the Atlantic you will have every sympathy for the poor mariners as you round the exposed Hartland Point, and it will come as no surprise to learn that this part of North Devon was known as the wrecking coast and that the lighthouse out on the Point has one of the strongest beams of any British lighthouse. Be prepared for mountainous autumn seas, and be careful.

And so the direction abruptly changes from north to east, and some straightforward cliffwalking to Beckland Bay, where a small memorial recalls the loss of the crew of a Wellington bomber which crashed into the cliffs on 13 April 1942. Now the cliffs become wooded, and after passing through the grounds of Clovelly Court the route stays high up on the Hobby Drive, built by local landowner Sir James Hamlyn Williams a couple of centuries ago as a hobby, as well as giving employment to out of work local fishermen and French POWs. Alternatively you can join the tourist trail down to the picturesque fishing village of Clovelly.

Until the mid-nineteenth century Clovelly was known as a safe north coast anchorage, but essentially not much more than a small fishing and farming community. Then the Victorians 'discovered' it, fell in love with it, and came in ever increasing numbers to pester it. Luckily the estate owner, Christine Hamlyn, kept new development strictly under control, and even today the visitor centre (that quaint twentieth-century invention) is tucked away behind trees at the top of the village. Next to it is a huge car and coach park since cars are not allowed on Clovelly's steep, cobbled streets, although a Land-Rover does provide a taxi service to the Red Lion Inn on the quayside. Local people use home-made sleds to transport items, although how they tolerate the daily invasion of camera-clicking tourists eager to capture the chocolate box village baffles me.

CLOVELLY – BARNSTAPLE (28 miles)

After another quite demanding passage of cliff walking the route levels out and you join the course of a former railway line into Westward Ho!, which comes as something of a disappointment for a place with an exclamation mark after its name. Its Victorian property developers took the title from Charles Kingsley's story of Elizabethan sailors; but he was not a supporter of the project. Today it resembles little more than an untidy collection of chalets and holiday camps. It was also a poor choice in terms of location, since in no time at all buildings were being washed away by the sea, and even the 500-feet-long pier disappeared.

After miles of undulating cliffs conditions now level out, and the next few miles to the lovely old fishing village of Appledore are around Northam Burrows, where the beach or pebble ridge offers quiet walking. The running of the Appledore–Instow ferry across the Taw/Torridge estuary is dependent on both the season and state of the tide; otherwise you must continue for about 6 more miles along the riverside to cross by Bideford's famous Long Bridge.

Bideford is a charming old place, especially since the A39 (the ridiculously nicknamed Atlantic Highway) takes a lot of the traffic away. It was once important for the export of woollen goods, and even today some commercial shipping can be seen. The most notable local feature remains the twenty-four-arch stone bridge, although each arch is slightly different in size. Before the present stone construction took shape in the sixteenth century there had been an oak bridge here since 1285.

From the former Bideford Station, now home to the Hartland Heritage Coast Service, the national trail takes to the former railway line downriver to Instow, where the old station building houses the North Devon Yacht Club and the preserved signal box is occasionally open for viewing. A footpath traverses the river's edge past the old Yelland power station before rejoining the railway line near the RSPB's Isley Marsh reserve and into Barnstaple. Today the line is a joint walk/cycle route, and part of the Tarka Trail, a 180-mile walking route that forms a figure of eight around North Devon and is named after Henry Williamson's book *Tarka the Otter*, which is set in the surrounding countryside.

Barnstaple is one of the oldest towns in Britain, and one of only four Devon boroughs recorded in the Domesday Book. Although its importance as a port ceased when the Taw silted up it remains a major regional centre, and off the High Street the lively Pannier Market continues to be held each Friday.

BARNSTAPLE – ILFRACOMBE (29 miles)

Barnstaple is also a useful place from where to explore the North Devon coast on foot, being at the end of a railway line and having ample shops and services. There are still one or two tourist leaflets about that refer to this region as 'Devonia', and upon enquiring why I was told by a chap from the tourist board that they thought that people might be deterred from visiting by the less sunny north-facing coast, and that – like South Devon's 'Riviera' – North Devon needed a tag. Sense has now prevailed, and North Devon it is once more, and a jolly good place it is too. Wide beaches and sandy coves contrast with mighty cliffs and wooded combes where Exmoor plunges into the sea. (And it's not all that cold, either.)

Some flat land first, however, as a dismantled railway leads to the edge of Braunton, then follow the estuary wall out to the southern edge of the vast Braunton Burrows. This massive area of bumpy, scrub-covered dunes has recovered from extensive damage caused fifty years ago by American troops practising for the D-Day landings, and now visitors come to this national nature reserve to enjoy the botanical delights of over 400 species of flowering plants. They include the deep blue viper's bugloss, and biting stonecrop, with its clusters of bright yellow star-shaped flowers. There are also large numbers of marsh orchids and marsh helleborines (delicate whitish-pink petals), a typical plant of damp dune slacks. But you should also be aware of local newspaper reports that lately some visitors have been arriving at the burrows and have promptly taken all their clothes off, after a naturist magazine mistakenly claimed that the area included a nudist zone.

Either make for the sea and follow Saunton Sands north, a route possible at all but the highest of spring tides; or take to a series of long tracks via the burrows and a golf course until you reach the village of Saunton. The path out to Croyde Bay along the side of Saunton Down above the road offers superb views back over Braunton Burrows, the Taw/Torridge estuary and Bideford Bay. Quite the place to pause for a sandwich.

Cross the road and follow the path round the back of Croyde Bay, a beautiful spot at the beginning or end of a summer's day when the crowds are thin. A detour to the village above will allow an inspection of the Gem, Rock and Shell Museum; whilst down in the water both here and at Woolacombe surfers will be out in force, should conditions be right, since these west-facing bays can funnel the rollers in like nobody's business. Separating the two bays is Baggy Point, high sandstone cliffs popular with climbers but where HMS *Weazle* came to grief in 1799 with the loss of 106 lives. From the top there are probably the closest views you will get of Lundy Island. Boats from Bideford and Ilfracombe make day visits to the inhabited, 3-mile-long island, which takes its name from the Norse for puffin; and its unspoilt 154m-high cliffs remain a great place for ornithologists – over 390 different species of birds have been seen here. In the hot, dry summer of 1995 the Royal Marines were called in to help evacuate the majority of Lundy's farm animals to the mainland by landing craft as the island's water dried up and grazing withered.

From the high cliffs of Baggy Point follow the uncomplicated path down to the seemingly endless white strip of Woolacombe Sand. Although the official route follows the downs behind, if tide conditions allow make sure to follow the edge of the water all the way along to the cafés and bucket-and-spade vendors at Woolacombe itself. But, as with nearly all of these places, turn up out of season and you will have the place virtually to yourself. Don't be surprised if there is nothing open at all.

The remainder of the coast path to Ilfracombe is enjoyable and straightforward, but may tax tired legs that have already plodded many miles. Morte Point is a particularly fine viewpoint where, if the weather is clear, the coast of South Wales opens up. Now there is a definite swing to the east and perhaps, if you have embarked on a long-distance walk, a faint thrill at finally getting stuck into the Bristol Channel and approaching the Severn. Of course, Bristol is many miles away yet, and there's still the splendid Exmoor coast to come. And a fellow called the Great Hangman, by the way.

Pick of the walks

SENNEN COVE – ST IVES (22 miles): Cornwall's cliffs at their finest, including England's only cape. This is a breathtaking but rough and isolated stretch, and for most people a two-day walk.

PORTREATH – PERRANPORTH (13 miles): a grassy clifftop route via St Agnes Head, past long-idle tin mines, sandy bays and surfers.

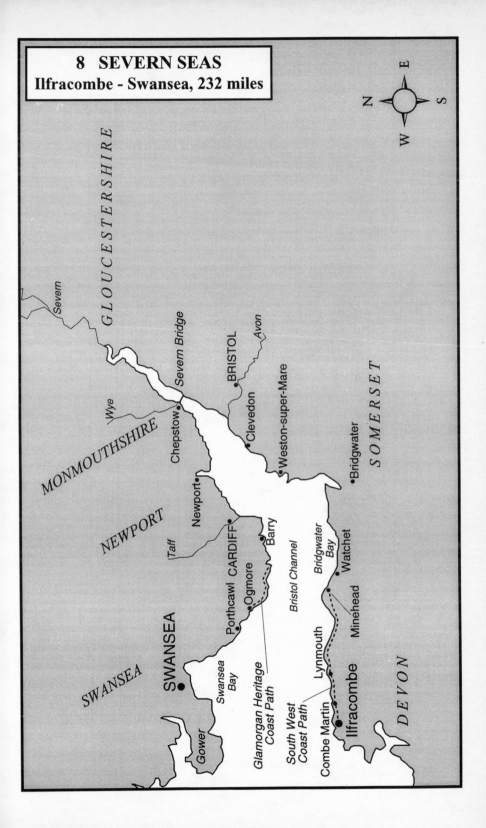

8 SEVERN SEAS
Ilfracombe - Swansea, 232 miles

N E S W

Severn

GLOUCESTERSHIRE

Severn Bridge

BRISTOL

Avon

Clevedon

Weston-super-Mare

Wye

SOMERSET

MONMOUTHSHIRE

Chepstow

Bridgwater

NEWPORT

Newport

Taff

CARDIFF

Barry

Bridgwater
Bay

Watchet

Porthcawl

Ogmore

Bristol Channel

Minehead

SWANSEA

SWANSEA

Swansea
Bay

Glamorgan Heritage
Coast Path

South West
Coast Path

Lynmouth

Ilfracombe

DEVON

Gower

Combe Martin

ILFRACOMBE – LYNMOUTH (18 miles)

Once in Ilfracombe, saunter out to Capstone Point and take a look down on this fine old Victorian resort. There are pleasure gardens, an attractive and busy harbour, and even tunnels through the cliff to beaches (dug by South Wales miners). Above the harbour is Lantern Hill, where the light in the chapel of St Nicholas has guided sailors since the fourteenth century. In the 1870s future German Emperor Kaiser Wilhelm II was sent to Ilfracombe to be educated. Apparently he was punched on the nose by an English boy after he threw stones at a bathing machine, and it has been suggested that his hatred of the English stemmed from this childhood incident.

The coast path leaves Ilfracombe for the steepish green slopes of Hillsborough, once an Iron Age hillfort and now a nature reserve, then at Hele there is a little roadwalking until the path resumes its clifftop passage before dropping down to Watermouth, a scenic inlet with a mock Gothic castle and fun centre across the road. The foreshore can be crossed at low tide, otherwise follow signs through a holiday park and around the shore until rejoining the main road into Combe Martin.

Don't be deceived by the crowd of holidaymakers thronging Combe Martin's tight little beach, squeezed between the rocks, or packed around the Foc's'le Inn, for there is much of interest here. For a start, the village is strung out for over 2 miles along the Umber valley, making it one of the longest village streets in England. Silver was mined here as early as 1293; local strawberries are much sought after; and as well as an Exmoor National Park visitor centre, since you are entering the national park now, make sure to see the Pack of Cards Inn (it has four floors for the four suits, each with thirteen doors for the cards in the suit) and the motorcycle museum, that numbers amongst its exhibits one owned by Lawrence of Arabia.

It's 13 miles to Lynton, and 13 remote and demanding miles they are too. The terrain is sometimes rough and the ground high and stimulating with stunning views, although there is some welcome woodland towards the end. Best of all there is no coast road and no caravan parks; no burger vans and no olde worlde tea shoppes. This is the South-West Coast Path at its best, a section to walk and to enjoy. But make sure to pack some lunch first.

Follow the signs to Lester Cliff and then on to Little Hangman (218m). Great Hangman, you will not be surprised to learn, comes next, and is 100m higher. As the National Trust leaflet to this area points out, albeit in imperial measurements, nowhere else in the West Country does the 1,000 ft contour get so close to the sea. It is the highest point on the entire South-West Coast Path, and if the wind is keen you will have quite a battle on your hands.

Next the route skirts the huge slopes of Holdstone Down, then returns to the clifftop until it zigzags steeply down to the narrow valley of the River Heddon. Half a mile upstream there is respite and refreshment at Hunter's Inn, a secluded hotel sheltering in the woods and which offers hot food and accommodation. Perhaps you might be tempted to visit, for soon you leave the shade of the oaks and climb steeply once more for a fine walk around the cliffs and into the trees of Woody Bay. Beyond Inkerman Bridge you must join the toll road down through the woods all the way to the Valley of the Rocks; but it is neither a wide nor busy road.

The Valley of the Rocks is the most curious thing you will have seen all day, save for the peacocks trying to snatch the crisps off your table outside Hunter's Inn. It feels as if it would be more at home in Dartmoor and not Exmoor, with the entirely dry, narrow valley – complete with cricket pitch and picnic site – encircled by a ring of jagged tors. They have odd names like Devil's Cheesewring and Rugged Jack, and the valley is also home to a herd of wild Cheviot goats. Time to leave the traffic behind for the moment, though, and take to the surfaced North Walk seawards of the tors and around to Lynton. It was originally constructed in 1817 as a promenade for Lynton's new visitors, and an early guide reassured them that although the cliffs below may be rather on the steep side 'there is no occasion for giddiness'.

Before reaching the town – which needn't be entered if it's not your destination – you pass just below the top of the famous cliff railway, which when built in 1890 was the steepest railway in the world, with a gradient steeper than one in two. It works using the weight of water in the 700-gallon tank of the downward car to power the simultaneous upward-moving car, and on the twisting path down to Lynmouth you pass over the railway several times.

In its early days it carried freight as well as passengers, including even motor cars.

LYNMOUTH – MINEHEAD (22 miles)

Until the late eighteenth century clifftop Lynton was a farming village and Lynmouth, some 150m below at the mouth of two rivers, a port dealing in coal and limestone from South Wales. But then the Romantic movement discovered the beauty of this coast. Wordsworth and Coleridge both visited; Southey likened Lynmouth to a Swiss village; and Gainsborough even described Lynmouth as 'the most delightful place for a landscape painter this country can boast'. Meanwhile Shelley rented a cottage at Lynmouth for nine weeks with his seventeen-year-old bride, but spent much of his time writing inflammatory leaflets criticising the government which he then sealed in bottles and threw into the Bristol Channel (over which he eventually had to flee to Wales as the authorities began to get annoyed). Lynmouth also came to people's attention through R.D. Blackmore's novel *Lorna Doone*, which was set on this suitably romantic Exmoor coast. Today Lynmouth is better known for the disastrous floods in 1952 which killed thirty-four people, since when new flood barriers have been installed and river widening has taken place. A memorial hall stands on the site of the former lifeboat station which was washed away in the surge of water and debris.

Climb out of Lynmouth by the edge of the coast road until a track veers out towards Foreland Point, and then along the edge of Countisbury Common above the waves. Foreland Point is the most northerly spot in Devon, a great hulk of a headland with steep and crumbly cliffs that must be respected. If you want to venture out to the Point then it is safest to stick to the lighthouse track.

The national trail now weaves its way through and around wooded combes for several miles, crossing into Somerset and passing the isolated Culbone Church, reputedly the smallest parish church in England (roughly 35ft x 12ft). There have been a number of landslips along this stretch so be prepared to follow official signs on the ground should a diversion be in place.

Eventually the track emerges from woodland and drops through fields to the picturesque fishing cottages at Porlock Weir. Once a bustling port sending tan bark, charcoal and pit props to South Wales, its tiny harbour is now frequented by just a few yachts and the occasional fisherman, while the Anchor Hotel and next-door Ship Inn do good business in tourists. Along the lane is Porlock itself, famous for its steep hill which regularly terrifies A39 motorists, and also for the 'person from Porlock', whose visit to Coleridge caused him to forget the intended ending of 'Kubla Khan'. But Coleridge is also believed to have stayed in the village, at the sixteenth-century Ship Inn in fact, where he composed some of 'The Ancient Mariner'.

The final 9 miles of the South-West Coast Path begin with a few minutes' trudge along the shingle, or far more satisfactorily a path along the back of the beach. This location has been the source of local dispute over the last few years, when the authorities proposed to stop shoring up the sea defences and let the sea take its own course. After much acrimony residents managed to overturn the policy of retreat, and limited coastal defence work has once more been carried out. How long the shingle bank will hold out is another matter.

After a brief excursion to visit the tea rooms at Bossington, take the well-walked path up to Hurlstone Point, with great views back across Porlock Bay, but a hellishly windy spot in rough weather. The cliffs of the Glamorgan Heritage Coast will be visible on a clear day. Now the route wanders away from the sea and across some high and fairly level moorland to Selworthy Beacon. It's scenic and straightforward, and with no severe climbs it will be just what you want if, heaven forbid, you've walked all the way from Lynmouth in one day. (There is an alternative but more strenuous track closer to the cliffs, not marked on most maps.)

Finally descend quite steeply from North Hill through Corsican pines to be greeted with the sight of Minehead sitting neatly below, and Bridgwater Bay extending beyond towards the narrowing Severn. The path drops down to what is known as Quay Town, the oldest part of Minehead, although few really old buildings remain following a disastrous fire in 1791 when a miller lobbed a blazing barrel of tar out of his door and into a stream, only to see its flames set fire to the overhanging thatch of neighbouring cottages. Over ninety buildings were destroyed. Gazing across at the huge Butlin complex, Somerwest World Holiday Centre, on the far eastern end of Minehead seafront, it is hard to imagine that this was once a small Saxon port, belonging in fact to the son of Lady Godiva.

Eventually emerge from behind the Red Lion Hotel on the seafront, opposite which there is a brown footpath sign with what must be one of the longest mileages given on a public pedestrian sign in this country: 'Start of S.W. Coast Footpath to Poole (Dorset) 500 miles'. 500 miles? If you've made it all the way from Poole you will probably agree with the South-West Way Association that it's more like 600 miles. Basically, it's a very long way, and an exceptionally good path. Go try it!

MINEHEAD – BRIDGWATER (33 miles)
The national trail may have ended but the coast path continues around the golf links by Blue Anchor Bay, which at low tide is one huge mass of mud and shingle. But the distant views are much more impressive: the Exmoor hills beyond Dunster, North Hill crouching over Minehead, and out across the Bristol Channel with its various islands to South Wales. You emerge by the handsome Blue Anchor station on the West Somerset Railway, a preserved and very popular steam line. The level crossing is the last one in the West Country to be operated by the signalman.

Blue Anchor is not much more than a short strip of seafront backed by an endless caravan park. The Driftwood Café provides welcome refreshment, while at the far end is the Blue Anchor Hotel itself. A litle way up the road both a public footpath and then a permissive path return you to what have now become colourful cliffs, and follow the top as far as Warren Bay Caravan Park, where you must return to the road for less than a mile into Watchet.

For a small but on the face of it undynamic-looking town Watchet has had quite an illustrious maritime past. Once, Vikings sailed in and did their stuff; and much later the busy port was the focus for the export of local produce, including ore from the nearby Brendon Hills which came all the way to the quayside via a mineral railway. Coleridge supposedly drew inspiration for 'The Ancient Mariner' after chatting to an old sailor at Watchet who explained how ships' boys trapped albatrosses while at sea by dangling a triangular brass frame in the waves. Coleridge went on to write this, plus 'Kubla Khan' and the first part of 'Christabel' while staying a few miles away at Nether Stowey, on the Quantock Hills. Make sure to visit Watchet Museum in the former market house for much more in the way of interesting local history and anecdote; but whether the old harbour will still be the same when you visit is uncertain, since work is due to start on a 250-berth marina in 1997. 'These are exciting times for Watchet,' the official noticeboard outlining the development proclaims. I wonder what Samuel Taylor would have thought?

Beyond Watchet the coastline is blocked by a couple of holiday camps, that perennial coastal disease, the first of which states very clearly that both the road and footpath to it are private, and with the unstable if extensive foreshore providing a poor alternative you will have to follow the road to West Quantoxhead. After a thankfully short burst of the A39, descend to the tranquillity of East Quantoxhead, a pretty hamlet where the most disturbance is likely to come from the reedy duck pond that sits in front of the centuries-old Court House. To the east of here a signposted footpath leads once more down to the low, rocky shore, which can then be followed all the way via Hinkley Point to the mouth of the Parrett, and along to Bridgwater. Not necessarily the most stimulating stretch of coast compared to what has gone before, as nuclear power station gives way to mudflats and man-made riverbank, but at least there is virtually unrestricted access and few people about.

For the geologically minded, Kilve beach has cliffs of blue lias and shale, with ammonite fossils dotted throughout. At Lilstock, where the shelving beach is popular with windsurfers, you could pick your way along the foreshore, tide permitting; or better still follow the coast path up through a field and on to the low cliffs that wander out to and quickly around the giant blue boxes of Hinkley Point power station to Stolford and Catsford Common.

Bridgwater Bay National Nature Reserve is famous for its birdlife, and in particular large numbers of shelduck which not only winter here but also gather in mid-summer to moult. Access to the Steart peninsula is limited at certain times of the year because of nesting birds. Just across the muddy mouth of the Parrett is Burnham-on-Crouch, but the walker will have a long journey to reach it, following the monotonous and twisting river embankment all the way to Bridgwater before returning. At Combwich (pronounced 'Cummidge'), opposite the Anchor Inn (but also near the Old Ship Inn, you will be glad to hear) is a rusty old sign which reads: 'Somersetshire Drainage Act 1877. Notice is hearby given that any person or persons found removing sand or shingle or in any way interfering with or damaging the sea defences will be prosecuted.'

As I write these words I have learnt that a new walking trail along the length of the River Parrett from its source in Dorset is opening. Further details from Bridgwater Tourist Information Centre.

BRIDGWATER – WESTON-SUPER-MARE (26 miles)

Bridgwater was formerly a busy sea port, although today the open waters seem far away. Turn off the A38 just north of the town, at Dunball, and follow the Parrett's raised northern bank back out to the Bristol Channel. There's a momentary diversion around the lower reaches of the River Brue via Highbridge, but overall it's an unobstructed public right of way the whole distance. It's a flat, rather featureless place, the western edge of the Somerset Levels, with the Quantocks steadily retreating over your left shoulder and the distant ridge of the Mendips ahead to the right.

A former tiles works has been flattened and relandscaped as Apex Park, a hopeful attempt at conservation among the holiday chalets and council flats. From here the Brue's embankment leads you on to the prom of Burnham-on-Sea. Not to be confused with Burnham-on-Crouch, in Essex, which is equally dull, the small resort soon gives way to an extensive strip of duneland that stretches all the way north to Brean. In 1607 Burnham was inundated by a huge tidal wave which flooded the countryside for 20 miles around and submerged over thirty villages. There were many fatalities, and predictably some saw it as divine intervention. A London pamphlet appeared as a result, entitled 'God's Warning to his People of England'.

At low tide it is an easy walk seawards of the dunes and golf course, but there are paths across the scrub, and in particular a visit should be made to St Mary's Church at Berrow. Calling itself the 'Church on the Sand Dunes', it is one of very few churches to depict a cat in a scene of its stained glass window. According to local legend, Joseph of Arimathea landed on these shores, on his way to Glastonbury. The actual area used to be known locally as Paradise, and according to the local church warden the precise spot is now occupied by Chestnut Terrace Post Office.

Brean is a long, flat, stretched-out sort of place where cars park on the huge, golden sands, and overweight couples from Wolverhampton sit in their caravans all day watching TV. At the far end the coast road is halted most abruptly by the huge carboniferous limestone lump of Brean Down. This fine headland juts fiercely out into the sea, the final gasp of the Mendips, although stranded from the main body of the hills. After panting up the steep concrete steps you can bound along the airy, elevated top of the downs in the company of pipits and skylarks all the way out to its tip, then return via a track along its sloping northern side that overlooks Weston Bay. Brean Down is a fine place for a circular walk, with terrific views of Steep Holm and Flat Holm perched in the Bristol Channel, and Glastonbury Tor and Brent Knoll rising from the Somerset Levels like huge mole hills. Not unnaturally Brean Down has also proved a useful defensive position. There are the remains of a fort at the seaward end, originally built in 1867 to counter the threat of French invasion. But it came to an inglorious end on 4 July 1900 when Gunner Haines accidentally fired his carbine down a ventilator shaft into the magazine and blew the whole place sky-high. Little of Gunner Haines, or indeed the fort, remained. It was later rebuilt during the two World Wars, when an anti-aircraft unit was added.

A public footpath descends to Brean Down Farm and along the floodbank of the River Axe to a ferry point south of Uphill. The small passenger ferry operates in the summer months, but with current uncertainty over its future it is worth checking ahead.

Uphill is where the West Mendip Way, a splendid 30-mile walk from Wells, finishes. It was formerly a Roman port, where lead and silver from mines in the Mendips were shipped out. From here Weston-super-Mare is only a mile away along the edge of the beach.

WESTON-SUPER-MARE – SEVERN BRIDGE (39 miles)

My brother, a resident of Bristol, tells me that Weston-super-Mare is known to some as Weston-super-Mud. A little uncharitable, perhaps, but at low tide quite accurate. As at Burnham, the golden sand gives way to a huge expanse of grey-brown mud when the sea retreats. However, Weston is a resort of mixed charms. The Grand Pier is quite becoming, especially when it glows bright green at night; and there are some very elegant Victorian buildings. But there are also tacky souvenir shops and garish-looking guest houses. In 1872 the Revd Francis Kilvert, he of the famous diaries, visited Weston, but poured scorn on the popular Bath House at Knightstone. Instead, he preferred 'the delicious feeling of freedom in stripping in the open air and running down naked to the sea, where the waves were curling white with foam and the red morning sunshine glowing upon the naked limbs of the bathers'. Above the northern end of Weston Bay is Worlebury Hill, once a massive late Iron Age hillfort but now disguised by a thick covering of trees. There are tracks through Weston Woods should you wish to explore or want to avoid walking the edge of the toll road around to Sand Bay.

The third of the three spurs that jut out into the Bristol Channel is Sand Point, reached by the beach or dune-top path by Sand Bay. Together with Middle Hope, Sand Point was purchased by the National Trust in 1964, an early acquisition for Enterprise Neptune. After wandering out to the grassy headland retrace your steps to Middle Hope, gorse-covered downland that rolls invitingly above the sea, and which offers new and stimulating views across to the South Wales coast.

Although not marked on maps, there is a permissive path from the National Trust land at the eastern end of Middle Hope down to Woodspring Priory, run by the Landmark Trust. Built in 1230, it occupies a site of a chapel founded by the knight Reginald Fitzurse, one of the assassins of Thomas à Becket, and the martyrdom of the archbishop is depicted on a Priory seal. After lengthy restoration the Priory was rehallowed by the Bishop of Bath and Wells on 29 December 1970, the 800th anniversary of Becket's death.

Beyond the Priory the sea wall extends around Woodspring Bay and on to distant Clevedon. However, it is not a public right of way, and although a route may be confirmed at some stage in the future the surer way forwards at the moment is along paths and quiet lanes inland, via Ebdon, Bourton and west of Kingston Seymour. Approaching Clevedon the sea wall behind the new golf course is very popular with locals out for a stroll, although again this is not strictly a right of way. It crosses the mouth of the Blind Yeo below Wain's Hill, where a few boats are usually being tinkered with, and from here there are some steps up to the low, rocky promontory, and to a welcome bench.

Now follow the so-called Poets Walk around the edge of the lovely, wooded headland. Not surprisingly this has long been a popular place with artistic folk, hence the name. Thackeray, Coleridge, Rupert Brooke and John Betjeman all visited or lived near here; and Tennyson came to pay his respects to his friend Arthur Hallam buried in the twelfth-century Church of St Andrew, an occasion that inspired his poem 'In Memoriam A.H.H.' ('Break, break, break, On thy cold grey stones, O sea').

Soon the surfaced path drops down to Salthouse Field, Clevedon, a very respectable kind of place. Notices ask you not to cycle or skateboard on the prom, and to clean up doggy mess. Clevedon Leisure Centre is about the size of a large bus shelter, and looks as if the National Trust probably maintain it. In the middle of the last century Clevedon's Local Board of Health were even inspecting the donkeys on the beach for fleas. On the north side of Clevedon Bay are elegant Victorian and Regency buildings, and here you will find the pier, a short and stumpy sort of thing built in 1869. As late as 1969 it was used by 50,000 people, but the following year it partly collapsed as, rather worryingly, it was being tested for loading to fulfil insurance requirements. The pier is currently being restored, and paddle steamer trips may be had from here. A short distance beyond is what is known locally as Lovers' Walk, the beginning of a 5-mile shoreside track to Portishead, and one of the most pleasant stretches of continuous coastal walking since Minehead. Except for a patch of erosion at Redcliffe Bay, the track is easy and enjoyable, weaving its way through quiet copses and along low, open cliffs behind sedate bungalows, passing the slipway of the Portishead Yacht and Sailing Club and seawards of a few caravans.

The Severn estuary is one of the largest in Europe, and enjoys the second highest tide in the world – a remarkable range of 12.5m or 40 feet. (The highest is the Bay of Fundy in Canada with a staggering 21m or 70 ft.) This partly accounts for the large amount of mud suspended in the water – estimated at 10 million tons – which results in the deposition of silt further down the Bristol Channel and hence Burnham and Weston's huge mudflats. The estuary is home to 10 billion shrimps, eighty different kinds of fish, and around 50,000 migratory birds. For the walker, after so many miles of open sea on your left, the estuary has steadily narrowed so that Wales is no longer a distant blur. Instead, the buildings and chimneys of Cardiff and Newport flicker and smoke quite clearly now; and even the vehicles on the M4 can be seen on a clear day. Closer to hand large container vessels and tankers make their way to Avonmouth; while upstream the two elegant, gleaming bridges span the powerful river.

After skirting a golf course the path joins Portishead's short waterfront by the boating lake and seasonal café. Continue around the open air swimming pool at Battery Point, as the name suggests a former Napoleonic fort, and across open ground to a nature reserve at Eastwood. This is one of the few patches of ancient coastal woodland along the Severn Estuary.

Large commercial developments hog the Avon's mouthparts, including the Royal Portbury Dock, so that any route into and around Bristol is likely to involve some pavement walking. At the time of writing a permissive route is being sought through both Portbury and Portishead Docks, so look out for official signs in the future. Cross the River Avon by the M5 bridge (there is a safe walk/cycleway), after which the vast industrial sprawl of Avonmouth has to be negotiated before reaching the waterside once more.

For those interested in visiting Bristol cross the M5 for Pill and join the Avon Walkway for a riverside trip into the city centre. This excellent 30-mile walking route links the lower Avon and Bristol with Bath and the Kennet & Avon Canal at Dundas Aqueduct. Bristol's importance as a port dates from Saxon times when it traded with Ireland and southern Europe. This was eventually supplanted by the opportunities of the New World, and in particular the profits from the so-called triangular trade involving the transportation of slaves from West Africa. Bristol's seafaring tradition is relived at the Maritime Heritage Centre, and with the restored SS *Great Britain*, the world's first propeller-driven ocean-going steam ship, designed by Brunel.

The path along the Severn resumes at Chittening Warth, near ICI's huge chemical works, and with the gigantic spans of the Second Severn Crossing looming. Opening in 1996 and strictly vehicle-only, construction of the new bridge is predictably making the walking via Severn Beach and Redwick a messy and noisy affair at present. Continue along the path to the original Severn Bridge at Aust, although the riverside route continues much further. This is in fact the Severn Way, a long-distance footpath that begins at Tewkesbury, in Gloucestershire, and follows the eastern bank of Britain's longest watercourse downstream towards Bristol. Officially it finishes at Pill, after a final inland diversion at Avonmouth, and you will have been walking it for a few miles by now. However, there are optimistic plans to extend the Severn Way via Portishead and Clevedon as far as Weston at some point in the future (and at the other end it may be continued as far as

Shrewsbury). Clearly, the benefits in terms of new access, and greater and better signposting, would be of enormous benefit to coast walkers – so keep your eyes open.

SEVERN BRIDGE – NEWPORT (20 miles)

Like the mighty Humber Bridge, the pedestrian crossing of the Severn Bridge is a memorable experience. Here, though, the sheer volume of extra motorway traffic seems to make the bridge reverberate even more, which can be an unsettling experience halfway across. Particularly oversized individuals may like to know that a bar restricts the height and width of walkers to 2.3m.

Once across the river some may be tempted by a wander into Chepstow, where the Wye Valley Walk begins; and near to where the Offa's Dyke Path starts its 177-mile journey to Prestatyn. However, coast walkers will turn west and begin the long haul back out to the Atlantic, and what turns out to be a diverse and often a surprisingly attractive South Wales seaboard. Not that it's too stimulating to begin with. Access to the Severn's northern bank is achieved near Portskewett, but power lines, the railway, and construction of the new bridge do not make this a particularly scenic section. Regardless of this there is a public right of way along the river embankment for a considerable distance, and even where this technically finishes past Redwick the wide, grassy bank is still walked by local people and fishermen. The latter turn up in droves, parking their cars and vans at the end of farm lanes and hurrying with their rods and boxes to stake out their place above or on the gooey mud. By and large they're a cheerful lot, although I can't remember seeing any of them catch a thing, so bid them a suitably encouraging greeting.

There is no legitimate access beyond Gold Cliff, where beside the small lightbox and massive marooned anchor on the grass cliff you can gaze across the widening river to Portishead, Clevedon and an attractive Mendip backdrop. Ahead it must be lanes towards the chimneys of Newport in order to cross the Usk.

On foot it is a rather unglamorous, industrial journey in and back out of the town, with the power station and enormous transporter bridge dominating the skyline. In the centre is John Frost Square, named after one of the leaders of a Chartist uprising which occurred here in 1839 and which was ended by troops with over twenty demonstrators killed.

NEWPORT – BARRY (25 miles)

From Newport more embankment walking is possible as far as Cardiff, past St Brides and Peterstone Wentlooge. It should be pointed out that along here the Severn's grassy, marshy shore does not actually incorporate many public rights of way, but this does not stop caravanners, anglers and the regulars at the Lighthouse Inn near St Brides from enjoying a waterside stroll.

Cardiff, capital of Wales, once exported 10 million tons of coal a year from the valleys of South Wales to the rest of the world. Today the docks handle tourist coaches, not coaltrucks, and the renovated Inner Harbour features Techniquest, a science arena, plus a massive tube-like visitor centre. Rather surprisingly you will also find a black and white timbered Norwegian Church. Originally built in 1867 as a place of worship for visiting seamen, it fell into disrepair, but in 1987 author Roald Dahl, who was baptised in the church, helped set up a trust to rebuild the splendid building. And on 8 April 1992 it was officially reopened by Princess Martha Louise of Norway. But perhaps the most ambitious scheme of all is an 8-mile barrage across the bay, which will create a massive freshwater lake and lead to more waterfront development.

At Cardiff's Bute West dock basin, overlooking the Inner Harbour, there is a large bronze sculpture called 'the Ring'. It looks like a giant earring, or perhaps a partially eaten doughnut, and marks the start of the Taff Trail, a 55-mile walk and cycleway that follows the River Taff upstream via Merthyr Tydfil to the Brecon Beacons. A little way along, near the fairytale castle of Castell Coch, the ambitious could strike westwards on the Taff Ely Ridgeway, which in turn joins the Ogwr Ridgeway Walk and then the Coed Morgannwg Way to end at Margam Country Park, a few miles from the coast near Port Talbot.

But perhaps the long-distance paths of inland South Wales can wait for another day. Coastal walkers should head out of Cardiff for the smart promenade and Victorian pier at Penarth. Inland is a former limestone quarry and refuse tip that is now Cosmeston Lakes Country Park, and next to it a reconstructed medieval village ('see the Middle Ages come to life'). A coastal track and road leads all the way to Barry, and on the way you may notice a memorial plaque on the church wall at Lavernock Point which records Marconi's first radio transmission across water made between here and Flat Holm island in 1897; while at Sully

Island Bronze Age burial mounds and other ancient defences are evident.

There is clearly much of interest and variety along this South Wales coast, but until now the walker has had to rely on individual research and routefinding, and apart from the Glamorgan Heritage Coast stretch there are few waymarks. However, things may change thanks to the energetic Cardiff group of the Ramblers' Association who are planning a continuous walking trail all the way along the coast between Chepstow and the Gower. As I write their plans are at a very early stage, and there are probably years of lobbying and consultation ahead before (or if) the so-called 'Seascape Trail' can be realised – but watch this space.

BARRY – PORTHCAWL (25 miles)

Barry Island has long been a centre of loud and gaudy family fun, not so much an island but a peninsula with a safe and sandy crescent bay protected by short headlands. The town itself dates only from Victorian times when entrepreneur David Davies decided to build a rival port to Cardiff. Nowadays there are funfairs and fried food, and Ship pubs.

West of Barry Island is the Knap, a gentle stretch of pebble beach with gardens and a boating lake, from where a path climbs high limestone cliffs to the woodland and meadows of Porthkerry Country Park. A public footpath continues along the coast past the quarries and airport of Rhoose to East Aberthaw, although you will have to take to the road to avoid the massive, coal-fired power stations. (Its enormous chimneys are even visible from the North Devon coast on a clear day.) But beyond West Aberthaw things brighten considerably as the Glamorgan Heritage Coast begins, which with one small break provides a continuous 14-mile coastal walking route along a cliffline surprisingly wild and remote. It makes for a great day's walk, or a more leisurely weekend's exploration, with a succession of sheer and formidable cliffs overlooking narrow bays and rocky wave-cut platforms and storm beaches. However, since the layered limestone and shale is also dangerously unstable make sure that you not only watch your footing but also keep away from the immediate foot of the cliffs.

Close by inland is Llantwit Major or 'Llanilltud Fawr', meaning the great church of Illtud. Here, about 1,500 years ago, St Illtud is said to have educated the likes of St David, the patron saint of

Wales, and made this monastic centre a respected seat of learning. You will also pass St Donats Castle, bought in 1925 by American newspaper tycoon William Randolph Hearst and much renovated. Today it is known as Atlantic College and houses the world's first international sixth form school.

Beyond St Donats the cliffs bulge out at Nash Point, an unspoilt promontory which although not in the same league as Start Point or St David's Head still provides a stimulating walk. There is a nature reserve and access to the beach at low tide, absorbing views across the Bristol Channel, plus two lighthouses built to warn shipping of the treacherous Nash Point sandbank. The passenger steamer *Frolic* came to grief here in 1832, with the loss of forty lives, after which the two light towers (one full- and one half-sized) were built so that they could be carefully aligned by vessels sailing up the Bristol Channel. Only one of the two is now operational.

Although the coast path continues a little further along the shore, to the wooded Cwm Nash, it is then forced inland to the road at Monknash, but soon returns via Dunraven Park to enjoy one of the best viewpoints along the whole of this coast. The spectacle of the savage and unbroken limestone cliffs south of Trwyn-y-witch (Witch's Point), with a grooved, rocky platform below it at low tide, is quite superb. The views from the headland north are also arresting, of Ogmore and distant Porthcawl. Follow permissive paths past the remains of a castle and walled garden down to the sands of Dunraven Bay, where at low tide you can enjoy a close-up view of the geology of the cliffs. Horizontal bands of hard Liassic limestone, created about 180 million years ago, are sandwiched with layers of soft shale, over a bed of much older carboniferous limestone. Folding has produced some fascinating anticlines and synclines, but since the shales in particular are prone to erosion the cliffs are constantly unstable and should be treated with respect.

Back from the beach there is also a Heritage Coast visitor centre, where you can find out more about Glamorgan's largely undiscovered jewel. Heritage coasts were established by the Government in the early 1970s, and Glamorgan was one of the very first. Today they cover one third of the coastline of England and Wales (40% in Wales), although like national parks and areas of outstanding natural beauty none is owned by one specific body. Most heritage coasts have their own officer and management service which coordinate conservation projects, recreational facilities, and so on, and you can find out more about Glamorgan's from the Dunraven office.

Now you can continue walking along the rocky shore of Ogmore-by-Sea, with Porthcawl growing nearer across the bay. But first there is a river crossing, by stepping stones over the usually benign Ewenny by the ruins of Ogmore Castle (below a pub called the Pelican). The steps are only covered at the highest tides, but watch your footing nonetheless. At the end of the lane from Merthyr Mawr, a leafy, English-style thatched village, the vast Merthyr-mawr Warren extends across to Porthcawl, an expanse of sands and shifting dunes offering any number of paths and tracks. The older, stabilised and scrub-covered ones towards the back lie against a low escarpment and form the second highest dune system in Europe.

PORTHCAWL – SWANSEA (20 miles)
Stroll around Porthcawl's seaboard and you will see two very different sides. On the eastern flank is Sandy Bay and Trecco Bay, whose popular golden coves are topped by Coney Beach Pleasure Park and what Porthcawl's holiday brochure describes as 'one of Europe's greatest caravan holiday home parks' – which is enough to make any walker shudder. But a short walk around Porthcawl Point is Lock's Common and the appropriately named Rest Bay, which offer a more peaceful prospect. A track by the Royal Porthcawl links course leads along the edge of the bay and over Sker Point to Kenfig Sands and Burrows. R.D. Blackmore, set *The Maid of Sker* at the isolated Sker House nearby.

A track known as Haul Road will safely take you across the sand dunes above the high-water line to the reserve's northern boundary. But Kenfig National Nature Reserve is famous not only for its wildlife – especially the rare fen orchid – but also for what it hides. Seven hundred years ago a prosperous medieval borough existed on this site, but a series of storms overwhelmed the settlement and by 1600 the walled town was almost covered by sand. Today the only visible remnant of the town is part of the keep of Kenfig Castle which can be seen near the M4 bridge inland.

And inland is the direction that you will shortly be heading if you choose to continue on foot to Swansea. Although the Gower should already be visible across Swansea Bay there is a long and distinctly off-putting coastal strip of industry and roadways immediately ahead that is dominated by Port Talbot steelworks, a complex so huge and overwhelming that poor Kenfig is rather overshadowed. I suppose dogged walkers could tramp alongside the A48, with a short detour along Aberavon prom, then the busy A483; or perhaps a much longer but scenic route would be through the wooded hills inland, possibly via Margam Country Park. Or simply catch a bus to Swansea.

At the time of writing there are plans to extend the Swansea Bike Path, which presently runs from the city centre to Mumbles, eastwards to the city council's border with Neath at Crymlyn Bog. Much depends on the redevelopment of the docks and the Tennant Canal, whose towpath is mostly walkable but not a public right of way. However, with luck this route should one day be a useful means of approaching and entering Swansea.

Pick of the walks

COMBE MARTIN – LYNMOUTH (13 miles): a stimulating day's walk along the beautiful north Devon coast, including plunging cliff and rich woodland scenery.

LLANTWIT MAJOR – OGMORE-BY-SEA (12 miles): breezy tour of Glamorgan's rugged heritage coast, to the east of Porthcawl.

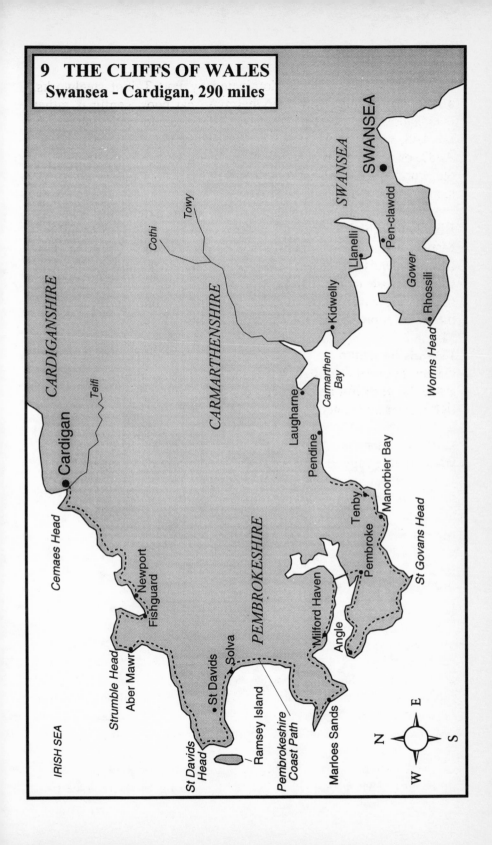

9 THE CLIFFS OF WALES
Swansea - Cardigan, 290 miles

IRISH SEA

CARDIGANSHIRE

CARMARTHENSHIRE

PEMBROKESHIRE

SWANSEA

SWANSEA

Gower

Pen-clawdd

Llanelli

Rhossili

Worms Head

Kidwelly

Carmarthen Bay

St Govans Head

Laugharne

Pendine

Manorbier Bay

Tenby

Pembroke

Milford Haven

Angle

Marloes Sands

Ramsey Island

Pembrokeshire Coast Path

St Davids Head

St Davids

Solva

Aber Mawr

Strumble Head

Fishguard

Newport

Cemaes Head

Cardigan

Teifi

Cothi

Towy

N
E
S
W

SWANSEA – PEN-CLAWDD (39 miles)

Swansea, so-called 'Gateway to the Gower', is named after the Scandinavian King Sweyn Forkbeard, having been settled as early as Viking times. Nowadays trendy cafés and a sparkling marina have replaced derelict dockland, and here in Swansea's award-winning Maritime Quarter you will come across Dylan Thomas Square, complete with obligatory statue – but more on the city's famous son when we reach Laugharne, further on. From the Maritime Quarter the Swansea Bike Path runs for an uncomplicated half a dozen miles out to Mumbles Head, following the route of the former Mumbles Railway, and for the whole distance there are tremendous views across the huge sweep of Swansea Bay, with the waterfront developments and old docks ringed by lines of houses stretching up to the hills.

Near Blackpill a spur of the Bike Path heads off into Clyne Valley Country Park, but it is hard to tear yourself away from the activity in and around the bay. At the western end this is focused on Mumbles, where the Victorians once dressed up and promenaded and a century later their descendants dress down and jet-ski.

Then all of a sudden you turn abruptly westwards at the rocky limestone islets of Mumbles Head and most of the hubbub is left behind. Ahead is a glorious walk around the Gower, which became Britain's first area of outstanding natural beauty in 1956, and then in 1973 was awarded heritage coast status. It is almost certainly the best coastal walking you will have enjoyed since Devon, but perversely although there is a fairly continuous walking route along the cliffs and bays of this small peninsula no one has chosen to make it an official long- (or short-) distance footpath, even though there was talk of something called the Gower Heritage Coastal Path at one time. Perhaps this is a good thing, since you may find that some of the quieter cliffpaths tend to attract just the odd casual wanderer rather than the boots and cagoule brigade; plus waymarking hasn't got completely out of control. Erosion, too, has largely been kept at bay.

Stern notices warn you not to attempt to cross to the lumpy outcrops of Mumbles Head due to fast-rising tides. Instead pick up what a notice calls the Gower Cliff Walk at Limeslade Bay and follow its unsubtly surfaced course to Langland Bay – where the tatty beach huts are protected by conservation area status and cannot be pulled down – and then around a golf course to Caswell.

How pleasant to be back on a firm, high clifftop walk once more! Towards Pennard Cliffs the path passes Bishop's Wood Local Nature Reserve and an ancient promontory fort on Pwlldu Head, from where there are fine views across Oxwich Bay, and on a clear day across to the lofty Exmoor coast. Limestone was once quarried in this part of the Gower, with boats known as 'limestone tars' transporting the huge blocks of stone across the Bristol Channel to ports in Devon. Remains of quarries and kilns are still evident in Bishopston Valley. But the rocks have also yielded other prizes, for in caves below the cliffs the remains of bison, reindeer, soft-nosed rhinoceroses and even lions have all been found.

Soon the huge golden floor of Three Cliffs and Oxwich Bays open up at your feet. If the tide is low or falling it is possible – in fact immensely pleasurable – to walk the firm sand all the way to Oxwich. To cross Pennard Pill and Nicolaston Pill (pill is the local term for a stream) you may be required to roll your trousers up a little, but generally this is a place to wander happily amid the kite-fliers and cricketers, the rock climbers scrabbling up and down the cliff's jagged teeth, and general all-round idlers up to nothing much at all. If, however, the weather is rough or the tide is high keep to the safe paths at the back of the beach that criss-cross the dunes and burrows; and also bear in mind that dangerous currents can make swimming off Three Cliffs Bay risky.

If you walk among the burrows at Penmaen and Oxwich respect the plants and wildlife and keep to the established tracks, especially as efforts are being made to counter the persistent problem of sand dune erosion.

The ground out to Oxwich Point is steep and thickly wooded with oak and ash, and above sits Oxwich Castle, rather a Tudor fortified manor house than a castle. The path now clings to the heights all the way to Worms Head, via the lovely Port-Eynon Bay, and these remote, rugged 300-year-old limestone cliffs contain a string of ancient forts and caves where many clues to the past have been unearthed. In 1823 a prehistoric, headless skeleton was found at Paviland Cave, along with the remains of a mammoth and other animals. The Red Lady of Paviland, as she became known, was thought to have lived in Romano-British times, but later tests discovered her to be male and Cro-Magnon.

Locally it is called the Worm, and from any angle Worms Head can be imagined as a giant serpent wriggling out of the water (the name comes from the Old English for dragon), especially in stormy weather when the Atlantic rollers thunder in, and when it's a good idea to keep well back from the unprotected cliff edge. 'The rock at the world's end', according to Dylan Thomas, can be reached for two-and-a-half hours either side of low tide, although the public are asked not to walk on to Outer Head between March and August when seabirds nest. It is here that a famous blow hole periodically produces a noise that ranges from a moaning to a booming when the sea is forced up through it, and has given rise to the local saying: 'The old Worm's blowing, time for a boat to be going'.

The neat National Trust track leads to the even neater shop and visitor centre at Rhossili (the Trust own around three quarters of the Gower coastline), from where there are stunning views north to your next destination, Burry Holms. The wide sandy strip of Rhossili Bay (or the grassy ledge behind) is a popular and obvious route, reached by a path from behind the tea shop; but a far more stimulating walk is over the 193m-high Rhossili Down, the highest point on the Gower and a magnificent viewpoint. The long, level outline of south Pembrokeshire juts out across Carmarthen Bay, and according to the indicator by the Gower Coast Reserve Centre overlooking Worms Head, Tenby is only 19 miles away. (Land's End is 122, apparently, and South America is just to the right of this.) There are megalithic remains up here, plus usually a fair number of brave hang gliders who throw themselves into the sky and hope to end up on the sands below (although some have had to be plucked from the sea before now).

How far and exactly where you choose to walk on Gower's north-west tip is up to you, since the burrows, flats and marshland extend for a large and sometimes indistinct area. I advise you arm yourself with the Ordnance Survey's Gower Explorer map (1:25 000) and go off and be an explorer, carefully bearing in mind tide times and nesting birds. A national nature reserve important for both wintering and breeding birds extends out to Whiteford Sands, and is reached by a 2-mile track from Cwm Ivy. In January 1868 this was the site of a mass shipwreck, when sixteen large colliers fresh out of Llanelli were driven on to the shore overnight. The victims were buried in local churchyards.

Whatever your route, in order to circumvent the wide estuary of the River Loughor you will have to walk through Llanmadoc and Cheriton by lane, then after the latter turn off for a public footpath via Landimore to Llanrhidian. The narrow strip of woodland overlooking the creeks and marshland is welcome after many miles of treeless, windswept cliffland. This is a low, sometimes bleak landscape, much less frequented than the cliffs and bays of south and west Gower. Writer Charlie Pye-Smith calls it 'one of the most forlorn, desolate and inspiring landscapes in Britain'.

From Llanrhidian to Crofty you must follow an unfenced and generally quiet lane along the southern side of the National Trust's Llanrhidian Marsh that is liable to flood at high spring tides. The landscape is flattening out by now. Semi-wild ponies graze out on the rough pasture and marsh, but notices warn that if you wander from the highway leave odd-looking objects well alone, since this area was once used by the military. Across the water the urban skyline of Llanelli becomes clearer, and you know that your Gower journey is at an end. At Crofty the pavement of the B4295 leads into Pen-clawdd.

PEN-CLAWDD – KIDWELLY (29 miles)
Swansea Market still prides itself that you can buy both national and regional delicacies from its stalls. There is Welsh lamb, of course, and laverbread, which is a sort of boiled-down edible seaweed. Then there is seafood, and one of the best-known local items is Pen-clawdd cockles. The cockle beds are out in the wide, tidal estuary, and the shellfish are still picked by hand when they are about five to six years old (I am told that their age is denoted by the number of rings on their shell).

From Pen-clawdd there is no alternative to roads until over Loughor Bridge, when a public footpath leads across the railway and around the shore to the Wildfowl and Wetlands Centre near Llanelli. This 200-acre saltmarsh site has been transformed into a residency for over 1,000 wildfowl, and some of the more unusual occupants include Hawaiian geese, Hottentot teal, and white-winged wood ducks from Asia.

A former steel-producing town, Llanelli is known to many who have probably never even been to Stradey Park as a centre of Welsh rugby. You are now entering a Welsh-speaking part of West Wales, though notices will have been bilingual since crossing the Severn. But now you may be accosted in Welsh in Boots, which is the real test. As far as coast walking is concerned, extensive land reclamation and coastal protection work is currently taking place along Llanelli's shore as a huge, £29 million Millennium project to develop a coastal park begins to take shape. It is planned to stretch for over 12 miles, and give walkers and cyclists unhindered access to the coast from Loughor Bridge all the way along to Pembrey Country Park – what should be a superb walk around the estuary. At the time of writing the only decent access is to Llanelli's promenade, which leads to the Water Park (where a steelworks once stood); then via the A484 past the site of the former Carmarthen Bay power station to Burry Port. For the present the coast walk resumes at the Burry Port Yacht Club, which is located on the west side of the harbour mouth. Near to it a rather daunting notice forbids access to certain local mussel beds, in accordance with a piece of legislation that glories in the title 'Food Safety (Live Bivalve Molluscs and other Shellfish) Regulations 1992'.

A duneland walk past caravans and Ashburnham Golf Club brings you to Pembrey Country Park, a huge area of pine forest, beach and open spaces that was once the site of a Royal Ordnance factory. The remote coastal location was ideal for the manufacture of explosives, begun in earnest for the First World War, and after the factory finally closed in 1965 there followed fierce controversy before the various plans for a gunnery range and caravan site were defeated at a public inquiry and Llanelli Borough Council purchased the land in 1977 for public recreation. Today there are forest walks, miniature railways, conservation and picnic areas, and the seemingly endless golden beach of Cefn Sidan (or 'silken ridge') which extends for almost eight miles – a fine beach to rival those on the Gower and in Pembrokeshire, and in fact parts of both these areas can be seen from this point.

If bombing is taking place at RAF Pembrey Sands you will be stopped from walking all the way along Cefn Sidan. This is of limited consequence, since there is no legitimate access around the marshes north of the pine forest to Kidwelly anyway, and the only proper access to the country park is the road to Pembrey itself. Whether you are only passing through or can devote a

The cliffs of Cornwall and Devon make the South West Coast Path a stunning and demanding trail: at Bedruthan Steps (*above*) and Tintagel from Barras Nose (*below*).

Even sterner cliffs can be found along the Glamorgan Heritage Coast east of
Southerndown (*above*). Rhossili Bay, Gower (*below*), with the wreck of the
Helwick still partly visible in the sand.

The beginning of the Pembrokeshire Coast Path at Amroth (*above*); and St Non's Bay, near St David's (*below*).

Bilingual signposts on the Pembrokeshire Coast Path; and at the delightful Whitesands Bay, near St David's Head (*below*).

While the crowds flock to Snowdon, there will be little to disturb your view of Bardsey (*above*) from the Lleyn Peninsula. Meanwhile local residents near Nefyn become curious (*below*).

The Ribble estuary (*above*) is a haven for wildlife, even though Blackpool Tower is in sight centre skyline. But the promenade is not always such a safe option, as at a galeforce Morecambe (*below*).

Silverdale Cove and its cave, with Morecambe Bay extending into the distance (*above*). A view of St Bees Head on the wild and for the most part empty west Cumbrian coast (*below*).

Despite a multitude of signs, keep the sea on your left and you should not go wrong!

whole day to its pleasures, do go out and explore Pembrey Country Park.

The best way to enter Kidwelly is the longest: from the south take the path over the railway and follow it to the picnic site by the renovated quay, once busy with ships from foreign ports. Then follow the road into the town, and make sure to visit the heavily defended castle, a powerful medieval fortress where two dozen archers and local townsfolk withstood an attack by Owain Glyndwr's army in 1403.

KIDWELLY – PENDINE (38 miles)

Beyond Kidwelly the Rivers Tywi and Taf do their damndest to thwart the determined walker keen not to lose sight of the sea or the momentum of knocking off the coastal miles. First the Afon Tywi wriggles its way inland to Carmarthen, necessitating a there-and-back detour to Llansteffan; then the Afon Taf requires a further diversion almost as far as St Clears.

It wouldn't be so bad, but a great deal of this foray into deepest Carmarthenshire has to take place on surfaced roads – although the smaller thoroughfares tend be very quiet. From Kidwelly the railway hogs nearly the whole of the east bank of the river via Ferryside, but your route along deserted lanes and a few short, linking paths should not be too taxing. Once over the unlovely modern road bridge south of Carmarthen, busy market town and supposed birthplace of the wizard Merlin, the roadside return to the estuary at Llansteffan is less attractive.

The Georgian architecture and peaceful streets of Llansteffan are worth the effort, though. Climb to the remains of its hilltop castle and enjoy the views south over the sandy estuary to the Gower, and also of warplanes plunging out of the sky over the bombing range nearby. The twelfth-century defence was built on top of an Iron Age fort, and guarded the entrance to the Tywi.

As with the approach to Llansteffan, there are no cohesive public rights of way along the shore, and so it is a question of threading together country lanes and the occasional linking footpath over the Afon Cywyn in the direction of St Clears. Then follow the A4066 back towards the sea, turning off left just before Laugharne for a lane and then a narrow farm track down to the pretty farmhouse of Delacorse. Local authority waymarks now point you across meadows by the Taf to a high, firm woodland track – the so-called

Dylan Thomas Walk – which brings you out by the poet's attractive home, the Boat House.

Dylan Marlais Thomas, explaining why he settled in Laugharne (which is pronounced 'Larne', by the way), said that one day he simply 'got off the bus and forgot to get on again'. It's generally a quiet, retiring sort of place, surrounded by hilly fields and a leafy shore, and solely visited because the poet lived there until eighteen straight whiskies finished him off in a New York hotel in 1953. Brown's Hotel looks much the same as it did fifty years ago, apart from the sign that bears his chubby face, and it was where Thomas would sidle in most mornings to share the gossip and some of the hard stuff with the other villagers. After some acrimony, his widow, Caitlin, is now commemorated alongside him in the churchyard.

Another pleasant riverside path leaves the township (the burgesses of Laugharne were granted a charter as far back as the time of Edward I) by the Strand, near the ruined castle, although it can be under water at high tides. Follow it around the wooded slopes of St John's Hill, and at Salt House you can cut across the reclaimed pasture and join a minor road past the handsome Hurst House to Laugharne Burrows. If there are no red flags and the military are not firing, and they tend to limit it to weekdays here, then you may walk westwards along the vast expanse of Pendine Sands – otherwise follow the road inland.

PENDINE – MANORBIER BAY (20 miles)

Pendine Sands extends for as far as the eye can see. It seems as if you could land a couple of space shuttles on it. Such is its smoothness and flatness that it was the venue for attempts at land speed records earlier this century. In 1926 Parry Thomas set a record speed of 171.02 mph, which was extended by Sir Malcolm Campbell in his famous Bluebird to 178.88 mph. But in an effort to regain the record Thomas and his car Babs met a tragic end. With the consent of his family villagers buried the wrecked vehicle in the sand, but forty years later it was dug out and restored. Pendine's Museum of Speed has more details.

Ahead, finally, are firm and continuous coastal walking trails once more. First of all there is the short but welcome Carmarthen Bay Coastal Path, a 4½-mile route that takes the walker from Pendine to the district council's boundary near Amroth, which is conveniently only 300 yards from the beginning of the Pembrokeshire Coast Path.

The Bay Path begins by the Cliff Snack Bar at Pendine, then climbs Gilman and Ragwen Points and crosses Marros Sands beneath the hefty Marros beacon. It passes Top Castle, a motte and bailey design now just an outline, before joining the road as it enters Amroth. The route is indicated by finger posts and, since it is relatively new and a number of diversions have had to be made, follow official waymarks on the ground and not necessarily tracks indicated on the map.

The Pembrokeshire Coast Path, an idea conceived in 1953 but not opened until seventeen years later, was originally intended to be 167 miles long. I have used the national park's mileage chart published in 1991 (total: 179.6 miles), but latest estimates put the current length at around 186 miles. It is not the longest nor the most demanding national trail, but the occasional firing range and oil refinery notwithstanding it contains some of the finest cliff scenery in England and Wales, with numerous hidden coves and golden bays to enjoy. The route is generally easy to follow, although be prepared for 515 stiles and 2,500 steps; and away from the honeypot sites you can walk it in freedom and peace.

The route begins at the quiet little spot of Amroth, and rather ingloriously disappears into woods behind the public conveniences. But after a short, sharp climb there are tremendous views over the pebbly beach from among the pines, and the path soon takes to an overgrown lane before joining the road down to Wiseman's Bridge. Here Churchill, Montgomery and Eisenhower surveyed a full rehearsal of the D-Day landings in 1943. At low tide (only) the beach route to Saundersfoot is possible, otherwise stick to the cliff path which follows the trackbed (and through several tunnels) of a former narrow gauge railway that was used to carry local coal for export via Saundersfoot. Since the 1930s the revenue has come from tourist traffic. From Saundersfoot the high, wooded track via Monkstone Point and some pretty stiff cliffs makes for Tenby, and should routefinding become uncertain among the larches look out for the official coast path signs.

As you approach the resort from North Beach it is difficult not to find the combination of unspoilt stone harbour set against a backdrop of pleasantly clustered, elegant colour-washed houses anything less than picturesque. Tenby's pubs may heave like any other's on a Saturday night, but generally the medieval walls enclose a genteel sort of place, with a distinct lack of the garish and a definite feel of respectability. It should come as no surprise to learn that Tenby was a founder member of the International Walled Towns Friendship Circle (others include Limerick and St Malo). The artist Augustus John was born here in 1878 (the seafront Belgrade Hotel bears a plaque), and he once said of his birthplace: 'You may travel the world over, but you will find nothing more beautiful; it is so restful, so colourful, so unspoilt.' (John conducted an intermittent relationship with Dylan Thomas's wife Caitlin, though the philandering John was later described by her as a 'hairy monster' and 'old goat'.)

By far the best way to leave Tenby is to stride down South Beach to Giltar Point, with ever-improving views back to the town. Be careful not to stray out on to Whiteback sandbank where people have been stranded by incoming tides. At high water the alternative route to the beach is landwards of the golf course alongside the railway line.

As the deep, sandy track plods up to the headland there are close-up views of Caldey Island, where a religious community founded by St Pyr in the sixth century is today maintained by around twenty monks of the Reformed Cistercian Order who sell perfumes and toiletries that they make from wild flowers found on the island. Also evident will be the less than welcoming notices from the MOD, warning of the Penally Range. Red flags and bangs will already be evident if firing is taking place, in which case there is an inland route via the village of Penally.

From the folded limestone cliffs and blow holes (collapsed caves) of Proud Giltar the track descends via a holiday park to Lydstep Haven and a small peninsula owned by the National Trust. Now the coast path skirts a succession of lovely coves, plus a former army camp, to reach Manorbier Bay.

MANORBIER BAY – ANGLE (27 miles)
Manorbier Bay, crowned by the remains of a fine Norman castle, is another attractive, sheltered sandy spot, popular with both swimmers and surfers although, as on many of these Atlantic beaches, you must be aware of the danger from currents and undertows in heavy seas.

Continue along the clifftop to the caravans and cafés of Freshwater East, then a long and mostly remote section leads via Stackpole Head to Broad Haven. Near Stackpole Quay you may notice how the grey carboniferous limestone takes over from the lighter red sandstone.

The dunes behind the open sands of Broad Haven hide a series of delightful lily ponds, created by the Earl of Cawdor 200 years ago; and if the military are active to the west you will be forced to walk via the ponds to Bosherston whether you like it or not.

Military activity along the coast of south-west Pembrokeshire has long been a source of bitter dispute between the authorities and outdoor groups (principally walkers and climbers), and the main bone of contention is over access – or rather the lack of it – to the Castlemartin range. At Broad Haven you may be turned inland if the red flags are flying, so denying a chance to visit the ancient chapel built under the cliffs at St Govan's Head, and the nearby feature known as Huntsman's Leap, named after a horseman who jumped the narrow chasm – and supposedly looked back afterwards and died with fright! If Range East is open you can follow the wild, plunging clifftop for another couple of miles to Elegug Stacks, two huge limestone teeth protruding from the waves, and close to the much-photographed Green Bridge of Wales, a huge sea arch. This is an area teeming with seabirds, who nest on the isolated cliffs and stacks. However, from this point the coast is completely out of bounds. There are guided walks in the range with 'approved' leaders on occasional weekends, although participants have to sign a so-called 'blood chit' indemnifying the military in the event of any injury. But in reality the Pembrokeshire *Coast* Path effectively ceases here; and instead NATO tanks roar around and shoot at things. To find out when Range East and the Penally Range are likely to be active contact the national park office or tourist information centres.

Wherever you are forced to turn inland you will end up on the road via Castlemartin that finally returns to the shore at Broomhill Burrows, a frustrating tarmac journey of either six or eight miles.

Back by the sea once more, and make sure to inspect the preserved seaweed collector's hut on the southern edge of Freshwater West. Here edible seaweed was gathered to be made into laverbread and sold in Swansea Market. Laverbread is still a very popular local delicacy along the South Wales coast. After being washed and exhaustively boiled the seaweed is reduced to a black mush not unlike puréed spinach; it is sold sometimes coated in oatmeal and can be gently fried and eaten with bacon and cockles. If you want to try some, look out for it in village fishmongers or the markets of Llanelli and Swansea. I am told there is nothing like it, which I can well believe.

Walk across or behind the golden sweep of Freshwater West, since most of it is covered at high tide, but although the Atlantic rollers are popular with surfers the strong currents do not make this a particularly safe place to swim.

The coast path now climbs to round the rocky Angle peninsula, and gives the first views of Milford Haven. Angle was once a busy fishing village, but if you stand on Angle Point today the ships you will see are very different, and not least in size, as massive tankers slip in and out of the Texaco refinery across the water.

ANGLE – MARLOES SANDS (42 miles)

The coast path follows the shore of Angle Bay as far as the picnic site by the former BP pumping station. From here a private, surfaced drive takes you out to Popton Point. Fort Popton was built last century to defend Milford Haven, and now looks over the oil refinery jetties which serve the huge Texaco plant to your right. Leave the shore and pass south of the power station and underneath its towering pylons and into Pembroke. Not altogether a scenic stretch, but still oddly fascinating, and in bad weather when the tops of the chimneys are in cloud it can be very eerie.

Pembroke is dominated by the magnificent Norman castle, the walls of whose keep are 22½m high and 6m thick. It was where Henry VII, Henry Tudor, was born, and it was further along the Pembrokeshire Coast Path near Dale that he landed in 1485 to wrest the English crown from Richard III.

After crossing the Pembroke River the national trail wanders downstream close to its northern bank before a tarmac trudge through Pembroke Dock until crossing the Daugleddau by the Cleddau Bridge. The views from its lofty spans are worth pausing over, with the winding, wooded shores upriver contrasting with the confusion of ferries, container ships, yachts and launches downstream in Milford Haven. Until the toll bridge was completed in 1975 the Pembrokeshire Coast Path National Trail could not be continuously walked.

Where the A477 crosses Westfield Pill turn off left and return to the havenside via the marina at Neyland. Whereas Pembroke Dock used to be an important naval base, Neyland had commercial connections; Brunel's *Great Eastern*, the world's largest ship when she was launched in 1858, had a special berth here.

The shore road leads to Hazelbeach, from where a path takes you past the Gulf Oil Refinery and into Milford Haven itself. From Hamilton Terrace you can look down on all the activity on the busy waterway below, from the gleaming, modern yachts in the new marina to the huge supertankers nosing their way towards the fragile-looking jetties. The waterfront street takes its name from Sir William Hamilton, who together with his nephew Charles Greville developed the town virtually from scratch. In 1790 an Act of Parliament empowered Hamilton and his heirs to 'make and provide quays, docks, piers and other erections', and Greville extended this to setting up new industries. At his invitation Quaker whalers from Nantucket established themselves at Milford Haven, and their sperm whale oil was used to light London's street lamps and thus the oil industry had its first splutterings. On a visit in 1802 Lord Nelson declared Milford Haven one of the finest natural harbours he had ever seen, but he may have been in a benign mood as he stayed at the New Inn (now the Nelson Hotel) in the company of Sir William Hamilton and his second wife, Emma – who ended up as Nelson's mistress.

Beyond the houses of Hakin the route follows a road then shore path around the former Esso refinery, once the second largest in Britain, but which closed in 1983 after only twenty-three years in service. Finally the oil industry is left behind at Sandy Haven, a quiet and sheltered spot with attractive woodland on the far side. Sandyhaven Pill can be crossed by a walkway at low tide, but otherwise there is a detour of about four miles upstream via Herbrandston. The same applies for the crossing of the Gann, a little further on, which is a small river that empties out into the gravelly bay near Dale. It, too, can be crossed for about four hours around low water.

The West Wales Windsurfing and Sailing Centre is responsible for much of the frenzied activity that takes place out on Dale Roads. For those intending to stay dry, and especially if the Dale Peninsula is being battered by some typically rough weather, then the best place to watch is from the Centre's sumptuous bar.

The clifftop path around St Ann's Head to Marloes Sands is easy to follow and allows plenty of time to study the supertankers and other traffic using (or sheltering in) the Haven. The lighthouse at

St Ann's Head was built on the site of St Ann's Chapel, possibly constructed by Henry Tudor who landed at nearby Mill Bay en route for Bosworth. The flat, exposed headland is a windy spot to say the least. I have read that gale-force winds are experienced here on an average of thirty-two days in every year. But now it's time to turn north and leave the shelter of Milford Haven. Pembrokeshire's finest coastal scenery of all lies ahead.

MARLOES SANDS – SOLVA (24 miles)

The gorgeous sands of Marloes Bay are studded with rocky outcrops, while at the far end Gateholm Island can be reached at low tide. The cliffs above you are worth a closer examination, particularly the Three Chimneys. This is where the horizontal beds of Silurian rock (400–450 million years old) have been virtually up-ended into 'chimneys' of eroded sandstone and mudstone.

Where the peninsula ends a cluster of islands extends into the sea, culminating in the birdwatchers' mecca of Skomer Island. Here, and on Skokholm to the south, puffins, petrels and Manx shearwaters nest in large numbers, and there are boat trips for the curious. You can wander the deer park beyond Martin's Haven for a closer look, but otherwise the coast path heads around the clifftop edge of St Brides Bay in a very obvious manner to Little Haven. The bay takes its name from Bridget of Kildare, a sixth-century saint, and the small church above the pretty cove of St Brides Haven is dedicated to her (although she is not believed to have ever set foot here). It was here at St Brides Haven that an 18m juvenile female fin whale was stranded for a while in October 1994 before later being washed ashore dead at Newgale beach. The fin whale is second only to the blue whale in terms of size, and females can grow up to 24m long and weigh as much as 80 tonnes. If you come across a live stranded porpoise, dolphin or whale contact the RSPCA immediately; and if they are already dead contact the local authority.

At Little Haven the Swan Inn features 'cawl' among its bar meals, a traditional Welsh lamb and vegetable soup; plus 'Swan Upper', which consists of sardines, spinach and egg, topped with mozarella and grilled until piping hot. It is possible to walk across the sand from here to Broad Haven at low tide, otherwise you must take the steep lane. Notices warn of the 'red sea', which is not a geographical mix-up but a red algal bloom that occasionally occurs near this beach in the warm summer months. It is caused by the death of large numbers of tiny fish and shellfish which turns the sea a reddish brown, and it is advisable not to venture out into the water when this is the case.

Continue north along the eroded cliffs of St Brides Bay via Nolton Haven to Newgale Sands, another of Pembrokeshire's fine golden beaches, a mile and a half long and backed by a high shingle bank. In January 1990 the combination of a fierce storm and high tide swept the pebbles across the coast road, blocking it for a week and destroying a telephone box and toilet block.

Brandy Brook is supposed to represent the western end of the Landsker, the dividing line between the English-speaking south and the Welsh northern Pembrokeshire. Then it's cliffs once more to Solva, with regular national park signs reminding walkers '*Mae clogwyni'n lladd – cadwch at y llwybr*' (or 'Cliffs kill – keep to the path'). Behind you the chimneys of far-off Milford Haven are finally disappearing from view, while ahead the path wanders through the National Trust's St Elvis estate, and then along the distinctive ridge known as Gribin and into the picturesque village of Solva.

Lower Solva is vaguely reminiscent of Boscastle, in north Cornwall, for the way in which the narrow finger of water creeps into the land between the high ground. It has offered shelter from the pounding Atlantic for vessels over many centuries, and on the quayside remain a few relics from the building of the Smalls lighthouse, the first version of which was built in 1775 to warn shipping of the treacherous Smalls rocks.

SOLVA – ABER MAWR (30 miles)

Refreshed at the Ship Inn, or next-door at the Anchor Café, you leave the quayside for a straightforward clifftop passage out to the magnificent peninsula of St David's. When I walked around this high, remote headland the sun shone and the gulls hung lazily in the sea breeze. It wasn't quite warm enough to swim at Whitesands Bay, mind you, although that never stops the surfers. But how different it can be when the exposed rocks are battered by another roaring gale blown halfway across the Atlantic.

Working your way around from the south, the ruined chapel at St Non's Bay was where St David was supposedly born during a great storm in about AD 462; and a little further on near Porth Clais tradition has it he was baptised. Like Solva, this drowned lower valley or ria has long been important for sea trade, with coal and other commodities imported for St David's.

At St Justinian the lifeboat station sits raised on stilts below the cliffs, pointing out across Ramsey Sound towards the treacherous rocks surrounding Ramsey Island called the Bitches. Further out is an equally dangerous collection of reefs known as the Bishops and Clerks. The list of vessels and crewmen lost in this area is extensive, and in 1910 three members of the St David's lifeboat also drowned attempting to help a stricken ketch. But the high turnover of wrecked ships benefited some people, and whenever an ailing vessel was spotted a large crowd of onlookers would soon gather. Sometimes, however, it literally backfired on them. When a ship returning from the West Indies laden with gunpowder was wrecked at Druidston beach in 1791 there was a free-for-all as people struggled to grab the valuable cargo. Some powder was spilt as barrels were being thrown from the wreck to people waiting below, and when a musket was dashed against a rock the spark caused the gunpowder to explode. Eight people were killed, and around sixty burnt. The local rector later spoke of the fire as 'providential judgement'.

Follow the Llwybr Arfordir (coast path) on to Whitesand Bay, another popular stretch of sand, and from here up a well-walked path to St David's Head itself. Seawards from the promontory the waves crash over the outlying islets and reefs, and it makes you glad to be safe on dry land. Inland is Britain's smallest city (only given the Queen's formal seal in 1995), destination for missionaries and pilgrims for many centuries. The cathedral was built in a dip in order to hide it from invading enemies.

Now it is time to shift direction and head north-eastwards for Cardigan Bay and the Cambrian coast. The next 25 miles or so to Fishguard are among the most remote of the entire national trail, since after St David's Head you lose the vestiges of tourism and can enjoy a wild and little-walked stretch of tremendous cliff scenery. From the heather and rocky outcrops of St David's Head you plunge through a host of wild flowers that, depending upon the time of year, may include endless clumps of thrift or sea pink, plus small blue clusters of sheep's bit. Then there are oxeye daisies, foxglove, bluebell and fern, gorse and kidney vetch, and the blue-grey cushion of sea campion.

The towering dark cliffs are home to peregrine falcons, while on the rocks below you may see seals. In particular, grey (or Atlantic) seals, almost half of the world's population of which frequent Britain's shores, enjoy the undisturbed Pembrokeshire coves and bays. 'The old grey music doctors of the ocean' (as L.A.G. Strong called them), they can be told from common seals by their elongated muzzle and tremendously varied coat colour pattern. Although they choose inaccessible ledges and bays, grey seals are nothing if not inquisitive. Peer down at them from the clifftop and in all likeliness they will sit in the water and peer back at you (a habit sometimes referred to as 'bottling'). Seal pups swim and fish within weeks of birth, and a pup tagged off Ramsey Island reached Brittany within seventeen days.

At Abereiddy there are the remains of a former industry in slate, and a nearby flooded quarry known as the 'blue lagoon' is worth seeing. The black-stained sand is also popular with fossil-hunters, as the slates and shales around here are rich in graptolites (small, colonial marine mammals that lived in the Palaeozoic era). Didymograptus bifidus, known as the 'tuning fork' fossil, which lived about 500 million years ago, was first discovered at this site. There are more industrial relics at Porthgain, a little further around the deserted shore, with a derelict brickworks and remains of local granite quarrying that ended in 1931. Then, with refreshment facilities in sparse supply on this north coast, it is likely that you will call in to Trefin, which although only a village is the largest settlement between St David's and Goodwick, before continuing to the hamlet of Aber Mawr.

ABER MAWR – NEWPORT (24 miles)

Since St David's Head the Pembrokeshire Coast Path has followed a wild and rugged course that has left the holidaymakers and hoverers behind. These north cliffs are among the finest in the whole of Wales, perhaps even more inspiring than those of Cornwall in terms of remoteness and adventure; and with no sprawling caravan sites or garish holiday camps to wreck the view. The grand swelling of Penberry, back towards St David's, is daunting enough, but as you approach Strumble Head the rocky lump of Garn Fawr closes in on your right. Below it the coast path sweeps around Pwll Deri, a small bay containing a wonderfully sited youth hostel. Behind is an Iron Age hillfort and former World War II radar post; below, the wheeling seabirds and groaning seals in the bay.

With tremendous views back along the cliffs towards St David's the track reaches Strumble Head, resplendent with white lighthouse (its 4.5 million candlepower is visible from 29 miles away) and flocks of ornithologists. They come here because Strumble Head is the top sea-watching site for birds in Wales, as well as the fact that it's also a most delectable place. An old Second World War lookout point provides shelter – often needed here – for twitchers and hikers alike, perched on the cliff edge and now decorated with information boards on the wildlife you can see out of the window. Among the more curious summer visitors that sometimes arrive in the warmer currents are basking sharks, Risso's dolphin and sunfish. The last is a bizarre customer. It has a large, round and compressed body, no tail, and feeds on jellyfish.

Continue along the clear and straightforward cliff path to Goodwick, with the occasional ferry from Rosslare chugging past bound for Fishguard. Among the bracken and heather, on the bare and completely deserted clifftop of Carregwastad, is a memorial stone commemorating the French Landing of 1797, the last occasion that Great Britain was invaded, and an odd event it was too.

The invasion force consisted of less than 1400 men (most of them freshly released convicts, ill-equipped and unreliable) and four ships. It was led by an elderly American privateer, General Tate, who had already got himself into trouble for stirring up revolution back home, and the plan was to knock out the ports of Bristol, Chester and Liverpool, encourage the downtrodden natives to rebel, and hopefully trigger an invasion by the Irish. In the event they ended up outside Fishguard, were scared off by three rounds of blanks fired by the local fort (all the ammunition they had, in fact) and subsequently made a difficult landing on the cliffs at Carregwasted. Tate took over a farmhouse as his headquarters, and his hungry men scoured the neighbourhood for food. What they found, however, was a great deal of smuggled liquor – a thriving local business in those days – and in no time at all most of his force were blind drunk and totally incapable. The French fleet sailed off, fearing that the Royal Navy might show up, and when Tate's orders to advance were totally ignored by his own men he gave up the struggle and surrendered to the nervous local militia in Fishguard. (Eventually Tate returned to the United States; although the French authorities expressed no desire to receive their own sorry citizens back.)

Descending to level ground at Goodwick, pass the quay for the

Rosslare ferry – where the liner *Mauretania* once berthed – and a short promenade of colourful flags from around the globe, then take the Marine Walk around to the lovely harbour at Lower Town. The main body of Fishguard is above and includes the Royal Oak where the hapless Tate signed a document of surrender at a table now in the front bar. It is Lower Town, however, that is the older and far more picturesque site. The Normans landed here and did battle with the Welsh; and in 1971 it was briefly renamed Llareggub for the film version of Dylan Thomas's *Under Milk Wood*, starring Richard Burton and Elizabeth Taylor.

After a few easy clifftop miles the path lurches up on to Dinas Island, although it's been 8,000 years or so since it was separated from the mainland. Dinas Head, or Pen y Fan (142m) more precisely, has been in view for some time, a high headland that towers over the far eastern side of Fishguard Bay. But the height is soon lost, and as you descend the potentially slippery grassy slope make sure to join the lower path that skirts the cliff above Needle Rock, a stack often teeming with guillemots and gulls. Emerging at Cwm-yr-Eglwys, an attractive east-facing cove, it is clear that St Brynach's Church is not what it used to be. Mostly destroyed in the great, two-day storm of October 1859, which saw 114 ships sunk off the coast of Wales (including the *Royal Charter* off Anglesey with 450 lives), the church was further damaged in a gale in March 1979, so that only the belfry and part of the west wall remain.

The remainder of the route to Newport is straightforward, including a diversion around a major cliff-fall that occurred a few years ago.

NEWPORT – CARDIGAN (17 miles)
The National Trail Guide claims that at low tide you can wade the Nyfer to reach Newport Sands, but the safe route via the Iron Bridge is not much of a diversion. The golden sands are justly popular, but from here until Poppit Sands and the conclusion of the trail (just under 13 miles) the walking is elevated and strenuous. In fact these wild cliffs are the highest on the whole of the Pembrokeshire coast (they reach 175m approaching Cemaes Head), so be prepared for some windy conditions.

Just before Ceibwr Bay is a steep valley with a dramatic collapsed cave, called the Witches' Cauldron; and further along at Pen yr Afr there is some fascinating folding of the rock strata that took place

400 million years ago when today's landscape was being formed. Elsewhere the rock has slumped and slipped, due partly to the effects of marine erosion and the unreliable nature of the shales and sandstones.

At Cemaes Head take a last look back at the Pembrokeshire coast, then turn towards the Teifi estuary and Cardigan. The trail takes to the road to end at St Dogmaels, but of course you will continue a little further on to cross by the road bridge into Cardigan. At Poppit Sands there is a plaque announcing the opening of the national trail by Wynford Vaughan Thomas in May 1970 (there is another at Amroth), who nicely described the coast path as a 'silver girdle' around Pembrokeshire. If the sea has wandered away stroll out on to the sandy river mouth by the Poppit Sands Lifesaving Club and reflect on the splendour of another fine coastal trail under your belt. Perhaps next time you might return and sample the delights of the Landsker Borderlands or the Preseli Hills, a little inland. So much to see!

Pick of the walks

GOWER CIRCULAR (7–8 miles): figure of eight from Rhossili, one loop over the great viewpoint of Rhossili Down, and the other to Worms Head and field paths back from the south-facing cliffs.

SOLVA – ST DAVID'S (30–35 miles): the heart of the Pembrokeshire Coast National Park, and among the finest sea cliffs in Wales, with views of islands, seabirds and grey seals. If time allows finish with a tour of St David's Head.

IV THE IRISH SEA COAST

10 A CAMBRIAN VOYAGE
Cardigan – Bangor
216 miles

11 PROMENADE MILES
Bangor – Lancaster
189 miles

12 THE OTHER LAKE DISTRICT
Lancaster – Gretna
221 miles

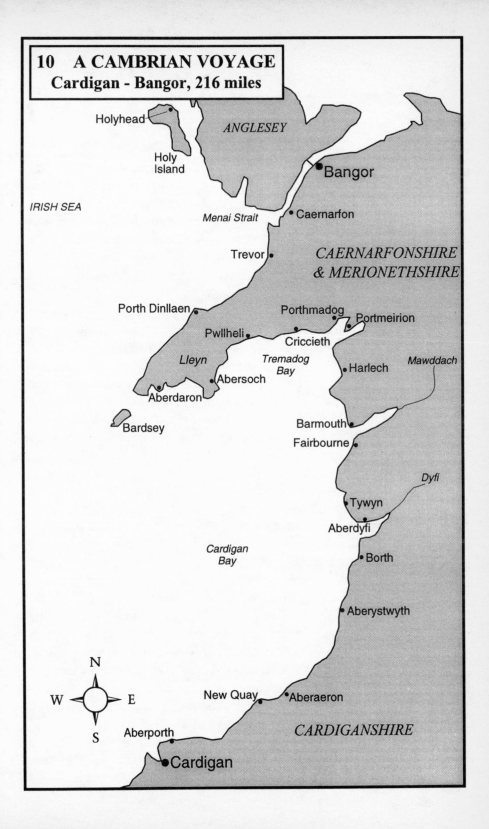

10   A CAMBRIAN VOYAGE
Cardigan - Bangor, 216 miles

Holyhead

ANGLESEY

Holy
Island

Bangor

IRISH SEA

Menai Strait

Caernarfon

Trevor

*CAERNARFONSHIRE
& MERIONETHSHIRE*

Porth Dinllaen

Porthmadog

Portmeirion

Pwllheli

Criccieth

Lleyn

*Tremadog
Bay*

Harlech

Mawddach

Abersoch

Aberdaron

Bardsey

Barmouth

Fairbourne

Dyfi

Tywyn

Aberdyfi

*Cardigan
Bay*

Borth

Aberystwyth

N

W   E

S

New Quay

Aberaeron

Aberporth

CARDIGANSHIRE

Cardigan

Cardigan is a fine old market town, whose battered castle walls are testimony to the centuries of strife that once occurred in these parts. Indeed, both the Normans and the Welsh held the town at various times during the twelfth century. Rhys ap Gruffudd, Lord of South Wales, staged the first recorded National Eisteddfod here in 1176 (although its origins go back much further with the Druids), a date celebrated when the great cultural festival visited Cardigan in 1976 to mark its 800th anniversary.

For the coast walker it's not so easy from now on, since there's not another official long-distance path along the coast until Bangor. You have been spoilt by Pembrokeshire, by the proliferation of tracks around the beautiful Gower, and now it is time to get the Ordnance Survey Landranger or Pathfinder maps out and start doing some exploring for yourself. It may be piecemeal, but there's a surprising amount of enjoyable and extremely scenic coast walking ahead. You may not have a continuous path, but you won't have the hordes or the repetitive signposts.

The tour of the Cambrian coast, or the Cardigan Bay shore if you prefer, begins at Gwbert, a small settlement named after a wandering saint on the north bank of the Teifi estuary (Cardigan is Aberteifi in Welsh – the mouth of the Teifi). An inland route via lanes and footpaths leads to nearby Mwnt, a delectable sandy cove sheltering beneath a grass headland. Above is the tiny, whitewashed Church of the Holy Cross, where medieval pilgrims used to pause for prayer on their way to Bardsey Island. Until about 1800 local people used to celebrate 'Sul Coch' (Bloody Sunday) on the first Sunday in January, remembering an encounter in 1155 when a Flemish attack was violently repulsed. Today the peaceful site is in the capable hands of the National Trust, who have relocated the car park away from the church.

With no access to the clifftop, Aberporth is reached by more inland lanes and paths, but from this popular holiday spot there is a fine walking route along a Heritage Coast path to Tresaith. It's not much more than a mile, admittedly, but it's still an excellent there-and-back stroll above rocky inlets and with beaches at either end. From the waterfall at the eastern end of Tresaith Beach it is possible to walk along the shore to the lane or paths up to Penbryn – but only when the tide is out. From the village of Penbryn the coastal walking route continues, with a signposted footpath from the top of the farm lane (opposite the National Trust car park) that leads along the cliffs via Castell Bach to Llangranog.

Llangranog huddles by the beach, another hidden sandy pocket that perhaps surprisingly was a flourishing shipbuilding site as late as 1875. From the village a popular cliff path extends across National Trust property to the distinctive headland of Lochtyn, which together with Pen y Badell, a hill fortified in Iron Age times, comprise the symbol of the Ceredigion Heritage Coast. The island at the tip of the peninsula can be reached at low tide, but the rugged cliffs to the east can only be walked a little further before you must turn inland and follow lanes down to the narrow valley mouth at Cwmtudu, a secluded spot once favoured by smugglers bringing illicit brandy over from Ireland and France. The cliff path resumes for a breezy 2-mile jaunt into New Quay, above sheer cliffs and a stack called Birds Rock, home to razorbills, kittiwakes and a host of other seabirds.

Dylan Thomas once lived in New Quay, and it is thought likely that 'the cliff-perched town at the far end of Wales' was the basis for Llareggub, the setting of *Under Milk Wood*. The terraced houses above the quay once looked down on various sea-going activities, with at one time over 300 shipwrights busy here; while New Quay boats have landed herring, mackerel and more recently shellfish. New Quay now deals in tourists, and you may step over some of them as you walk the lovely crescent-shaped beach at low tide for the beginning of a 3½-mile cliff walk from Cei-bach to Aberaeron. Despite a small holiday camp and some caravans, there are a succession of quiet leafy river valleys and some up and down cliffs to enjoy.

Aberaeron is rather different to what has gone before. No clustered village this, but rather a neat and open town with carefully laid-out rows of coloured terraced houses and a wide stone-walled harbour. Many of the Georgian buildings are of special architectural interest, and this deliberate, planned design is wonderfully at variance with all the other places along this coast that seem to sprawl and squeeze haphazardly about and above the shore. In the summer months you can cross the harbour on something called the Aeron Express, a sort of mini cable car extended high above the water and hand-operated by pulleys.

The mapped path along the low cliffs to beyond Aberarth has completely eroded into the sea in some places, so the beach is a better bet. The foreshore may be followed as far as Llanrhystud, but at low tide only, after which the cliffs rise dramatically. There is a rough public footpath for most of the way over these high and wild slopes to Aberystwyth, although at one point you will have to detour to the road and back in order to rejoin the right of way via the campsite at Morfa Bychan down to the mouth of Afon Ystwyth.

ABERYSTWYTH – ABERDYFI (29 miles)

Victorian Aberystwyth was once touted as the 'Biarritz of Wales' to early trainloads of visitors, which when viewed from Constitution Hill on a grey and blustery day in mid-February is stretching the imagination just a little bit. The modern town is the focus for all serious shoppers in mid Wales and houses a university and the National Library of Wales. The library holds around 5 million items, with a priceless collection of Welsh language books that includes the 'Black Book of Carmarthen' written in the twelfth century and the oldest surviving manuscript in Welsh. Steam train enthusiasts come here too, to ride the Vale of Rheidol Railway up into the hills at Devil's Bridge and back. But period Aberystwyth still survives, especially with the short promenade, at the end of which is another throwback to what was at the time a traditional sort of seaside attraction. Built in 1896, the Electric Cliff Railway is the longest of its type in Great Britain (I am hard pressed to name many others, though) and whisks you up the one in two gradient in no time at all. From the café on top of Constitution Hill Aberystwyth is spread out at your feet, and you are immediately struck by how the bulky hills and high cliffs crowd around the town.

From here to the mouth of the Dyfi (Dovey) there is a well-defined, walkable route that contains several sections usually bereft of people, which is just how we like it. First, choose either a cliffedge or hilltop path over and down through dense conifers to Clarach Bay. There's a small and uninspiring leisure park, and a few dozen caravans arranged in rows like prison huts; but this is soon left behind for a cliffedge path that runs unhindered all the way to Borth. It's good to see that there's some new stiles and a fresh coast path sign at the remote Wallog, and also that steps have been maintained where the path steepens dramatically on cliffs near Upper Borth. With a good track, superb views to the Lleyn and elsewhere, and even access to the beach for a picnic at a couple of points, it proves that there is indeed more to discover and enjoy than the set number of official national trails may suggest.

The World War I memorial on the exposed clifftop above Upper Borth was damaged by a lightning strike in 1983, but after a whip-round by locals it was soon repaired, though with the sensible addition of a small lightning conductor. Below is Borth, a remarkable-looking one-street village that is strung out for over a mile towards the Dyfi estuary. At the far end of the coastal lane is Dovey National Nature Reserve, where a visitor centre explains how the dunes and vast flats are home to a diversity of wildlife; while the extensive raised bog of Cors Fochno to the east is equally fascinating, although access is limited and beware the squelchy peat that can be as much as 30 feet deep.

Across the narrow mouth of the River Dyfi is Aberdyfi, which at low tide seems tantalisingly close. With the backdrop of southern Snowdonia, and the Dyfi working its way into the hills to the east, this is a breathtaking setting. The river is the traditional boundary between North and South Wales, and for many centuries a ferry plied the estuary. As long ago as 1215 the Princes of Wales were crossing here after being summoned by Llywelyn the Great to attend the Great Council of Aberdyfi. Much later a refuge tower was even built on the sands as a means of escape for waiting passengers at risk from the incoming tide. But return to this location when the waters have risen and the wind is getting up and you will see how dangerous the fast-flowing currents are, which is why the only option for the foot-bound traveller is a long roadside hike upstream to Machynlleth and back. But there are other, far more attractive options. The obvious answer is to catch the scenic Cambrian Coast Railway, changing at Dovey Junction; or else explore paths around the valley. One possibility is to follow some of the Dyfi Valley Way, a 109-mile walking route created by local rambling enthusiast Laurence Main that stretches all the way up and back down the lovely Dyfi valley from Borth to Aberdyfi.

ABERDYFI – HARLECH (37 miles)

Aberdyfi clings to the foot of the steep hillside, wrapping itself around the shore rather than cutting far inland. Boats are moored by the short quay, and many more out on the Dyfi. Once ships took slate from here to Cadiz, then sea-salt on to Newfoundland, from where cod was brought back to Britain or Spain. Aberdyfi presents an unhurried and agreeable scene, although you may care to listen out for the fabled 'Bells of Aberdyfi', which according to legend is the ringing of submerged bells of a city lost underneath the sea. Aberdyfi is also in Snowdonia National Park, and the grand mountains of North Wales will soon become a familiar and irresistible sight for coastal walkers.

First, a short scamper along the beach or a path behind the dunes to Tywyn, whose name actually means sand dune. Not a flashy place, although it does boast a narrow-gauge steam railway (the Talyllyn), and St Cadfan's Church, against the wall of which is a stone pillar rescued from a farmer's field. It dates from early eighth century, and has one of the earliest known inscriptions in Welsh.

The railway bridge across Broad Water at the mouth of Afon Dysynni has been used by naughty walkers in the past to reach the opposite bank, even though it is intended for trains only. So those on foot should properly follow footpaths upstream to Bryncrug before returning to the sea via lanes at Tonfanau. With no coast paths it is probably best that you avoid a direct water's edge route until Fairbourne. Although there is a foreshore, people have been cut off by rising tides along this stretch, since there are few escape points. The railway runs close to the shore all the way, and before too long the ground rises steeply as Pen y Garn tumbles down to the sea. From the road, and of course from hill tracks further inland, there are great views of Barmouth and Afon Mawddach with a stunning mountain backdrop.

The miniature railway at Fairbourne enjoys a gauge narrow in the extreme (only 31.11cm or 12.25 in). It runs for 2 miles out along the estuary spit to Porth Penrhyn, from where a ferry service operates across to Barmouth depending both on the season and the weather. A far better option is to follow the marshside path to the famous Barmouth Bridge for a toll walk alongside the railway over the river. Track and pedestrian walkway are separated, naturally, and you may have to dodge a fisherman or two. But it's a stimulating and usually very windy ten-minute crossing with fine views up the wooded Mawddach to the Cader Idris range, overall resembling a Scottish sea loch as much as a Welsh valley. And only 30p, too!

Perhaps only once you've walked it should you know that this is the last wooden railway bridge still in use in Britain, and that over the last few years the authorities have had to deal with the problem of marine worms nibbling away at its legs. (To explore this lovely area further try the Penmaenpool–Morfa Mawddach Walk along the estuary's southern shore, which follows a dismantled railway from Barmouth Bridge to the RSPB's reserve and nature information centre at Penmaenpool.)

Barmouth is a cheerful and attractive seaside location, the start of the Three Peaks Yacht Race, whose competitors sail to Caernarfon to climb Snowdon, then Ravenglass for Scafell Pike, and finally to Fort William in order to scale Ben Nevis. In 1895 four acres of the steep, craggy hill behind Barmouth became the first piece of land to be purchased by the newly formed National Trust for Places of Historical Interest and Natural Beauty. Octavia Hill, one of the founders, wrote at that time: 'We have got our first piece of property. I wonder if it will be the last?' The National Trust has since bought more land around Dinas Oleu, that first plot, and it is possible to follow a steep but waymarked trail up through the town to enjoy what Octavia Hill once called 'open-air sitting rooms for city dwellers to have a place to breathe'.

Ahead is a long beach walk via Llanaber to Tal-y-Bont. By the railway station at the former is the attractive thirteenth-century Church of the Sts Mary and Bodfan, with an elaborate South doorway and five-bay arcades dividing the aisles. 'Llan' originally meant the consecrated ground devoted to prayer and burial, where some sort of building would usually be built, from which today it has simply come to mean the church of some saint. There are grand views of the Rhinog hills as you walk north, past a Royal Aircraft Establishment base to Shell Island (or Mochras). Up to 200 types of shell can be found washed up after high tides or storms, and if you are into them make sure not to miss the shell shop in Barmouth. There is a small holiday complex on the semi-island, but only car-bound visitors are charged admission; and to leave follow the causeway or footpath that leads inland to Llanbedr. Soon there is a path back through riverside fields to the tiny Church of St Tanwg hidden among the dunes. Although the present building dates from the early Middle Ages it replaced an even older, maybe sixth-century church, making St Tanwg's one of the oldest sites of Christian worship in Wales. The diminutive

building has sometimes been completely buried by shifting sand
and abandoned on occasions, and even today renewed efforts are
being made to save the church from being engulfed by the dunes
once more.

A notice in the nearby café warns beach-goers of the danger of
weever fish. These nasty, ugly little fish lie under the sand with their
sharp and poisonous dorsal spines exposed, and the sting that they
can give to bare human feet can be excruciatingly painful. The best
remedy is to put the affected foot in a bowl of hot water as soon as
possible, otherwise I have read that the effects can last as long as
a fortnight. Where you see such warnings do take heed and protect
your feet with boots, trainers or sand shoes.

Tide permitting, and in appropriate footwear, walk along the
foreshore to the extensive sandy beach below Harlech. Across
Tremadog Bay is the bumpy outline of the Lleyn Peninsula, while
more immediately the arresting shape of Harlech Castle grabs the
attention. If no one else is in close hearing I suggest you stride
boldly along the beach bellowing the words (which you probably
won't know beyond the first line) to a famous Welsh anthem (the
tune of which you almost certainly will). 'March ye men of Harlech
bold/Unfurl your banners in the field/Be brave as were your sires
of old/And like them never yield!' Stirring stuff.

HARLECH – PWLLHELI (26 miles)
Harlech always seems such a small place in comparison to the size,
grandeur and sheer power of its castle. It was another in Edward I's
'iron ring' intended to subdue the Welsh, finished in 1290 after just
seven years. Since then it has endured all manner of attackers and
defenders. In a nicely ironic twist Owain Glyndwyr seized it briefly
for the Welsh; then much later it was held by Welsh Lancastrians
during the Wars of the Roses (when 'March of the Men of Harlech'
supposedly dates from). During the Civil War Harlech was the last
Royalist stronghold to fall, but afterwards the order to demolish the
castle was luckily never carried out.

Although the wide beach seawards of the Royal St David's
golf links can be walked much further, and it is rewarding for
the solitude, views and wildlife, if you're intent on reaching
Porthmadog it is easier to leave the coast road beyond the town
for paths across the rough dunes and plantations of Morfa Harlech
to Llanfihangel, even though they may be indistinct in places.

A path around the creeks and saltmarsh of Glastraeth finally allows you to cross Afon Dwyryd by road, and further on enter Porthmadog via the long embankment above the Glaslyn estuary. Before you do, however, it is worth pausing not so much for the views of Snowdonia but the oddities of Portmeirion. Designed and gradually built by architect Sir Clough Williams-Ellis during the years 1925 to 1972, it is a village straight out of southern Italy, with statues and fountains, fake façades and rare shrubs and trees. Williams-Ellis once said: 'I wanted to show people, with a sort of light-opera approach, that architecture could be fun, could be entertaining, interesting, intriguing.' He could hardly have guessed, however, that his creation would become familiar to millions as the setting for one of the greatest television cult serials of all time, *The Prisoner*. Escaping from the village was the hero's problem. You will have less difficulty in moving on to Porthmadog.

Another ambitious individual, William Maddocks MP, was responsible for building the original town of Porthmadog, created from 10,000 acres of reclaimed estuary. This involved building the mile-long bank known as the Cob, along which runs another of the Great Little Trains of Wales, the Ffestiniog. Opened in 1836 it was designed to carry slate down from the quarries in the hills to the quayside for export around the world. Returning ships dumped their ballast overboard outside the harbour, forming an island shown as Cei Ballast on OS maps.

To the south the town merges into the quiet and respectable Borth-y-Gest, after which the smooth Black Rock Sands of Morfa Bychan offer good walking conditions past a golf links and holiday camp ('Morfa' in a Welsh place name is the equivalent of 'on-Sea' in English). Beyond the caves of Graig Ddu walk into Criccieth, and to the distinctive promontory landmark of the ruined castle. It was captured from the Welsh rather than built by Edward I, only to be subsequently besieged by Owain Glyndwr who eventually tried to scorch it. From the pleasant seafront either side, which faces south and so catches a good amount of sunshine, there are absorbing views back across Tremadog Bay. Harlech Castle, in particular, stands out dramatically above the shore, and must have been even more arresting once upon a time, since its walls were originally painted a dazzling white.

A shoreside path can be walked as far as the Afon Dwyfor, but beyond the stream there is virtually no public access to the coast until after the roller coasters of Butlin's Starcoast World. The complex includes a long chairlift which takes happy campers out to the headland of Pen y chain, near where you can resume a public footpath along Morfa Abererch and then along the unbroken sands towards Pwllheli. For an interesting diversion on the way from Criccieth you might consider visiting the Lloyd George Museum at Llanystumdwy, the village where the Liberal Prime Minister grew up.

PWLLHELI – ABERDARON (23 miles)

Even if you can't pronounce it, Pwllheli is well worth visiting, with long sand and shingle beaches, a new marina and harbour development, and even dune restoration work being carried out near the modest promenade. Best of all, Pwllheli is a great launch pad from which to explore the Lleyn (or Llŷn) Peninsula, the 'Land's End of North Wales'. This surprisingly secluded finger of land boasts no huge resorts, few obvious tourist trappings, and while the various tracks up Snowdon may be heaving it is likely that the much lower but equally beautiful summit of Mynydd Rhiw towards the tip of Lleyn will have far fewer takers. Virtually all the Lleyn is a designated heritage coast, which gives some indication of its unspoilt nature, but although there is a coastal track along some of the northern shore you will be hard pressed to find any continuous coastal path elsewhere. Rather, this is a place for selective dips: a tour of the Llanbedrog headland, to the National Trust's Mynydd Penarfynydd and back, around Porth Dinllaen bay, or over and through the twin summits of Yr Eifl to Trefor.

From Pwllheli's South Beach it is possible to walk the foreshore to Llanbedrog, but only when the tide is low and there is no danger of being cut off at Carreg y Defaid. Most of Llanbedrog is situated up the hill, including the Ship Inn (Burtonwood Beers), although the Galley café by the beach is perfectly placed. Go beyond the Boating House, underneath the heavily wooded cliffside, for a public right of way which climbs by endless flights of steep steps through the foliage to the open heather and gorse headland. There are handrails and you will need them. But it is worth it, for the broad igneous headland offers dramatic views towards Trwyn Cilan and St Tudwal's Islands beyond Pwllheli, as well as back to Snowdonia and the Cambrian coast. And if you catch sight of a tall, thin and weathered-looking man staring intently across the bay, then look a little closer. This is the Tin Man, a lifesize figure with spear built out of flotsam from the bay to represent the Celtic warriors of old, by local artist Simon van de Put.

There are paths to the low moorland summit and back around to Llanbedrog (this is an excellent circular walk), or else continue down to the sandy beach in front of caravans and into Abersoch. Very popular with sailing enthusiasts and surfers, Abersoch's fine sandy surrounds extend south to Marchros, then paths lead across the peninsula to allow a visit to the tiny strip of sand beneath the cliffs at Porth Ceiriad. Nearby the National Trust's Mynydd Cilan offers grand views to the end of the Lleyn, and from it a path descends to the eastern end of Porth Neigwl or Hell's Mouth. Here is a narrow 3-mile strip of sand, a bay entirely unspoilt by twentieth-century development, and backed only by low and crumbling clay cliffs. When the conditions are right it is popular with surfers, but notices warn of the dangers of a strong undertow and cross current, and others that cliff falls and landslides make walking directly below the cliffs hazardous. All the same, because Hell's Mouth is devoid of any major car parks or cafeterias, walking it is a joy.

A heritage coast circular waymark guides you on to the steep road up to Rhiw, where Mynydd Rhiw can be scaled to your right, or else turn seawards for tracks across further National Trust land to the windy, rabbit-nibbled grass headland of Mynydd Penarfynydd. Another sublime viewpoint, especially of Bardsey Island, this steep, narrow promontory from Rhiw is also rich in historical remains, with hut settlements, a fort and standing stone. From Penarfynydd you can link with empty lanes above the cliffs (or drop down to visit the bay at Porth Ysgo if you wish) which lead to Aberdaron. In the fields above Porth Cadlan King Arthur fought his last battle, according to a recent book. After painstaking research the authors claim that it was here that Arthur defeated his enemy Mordred, but in so doing he was badly wounded and afterwards was taken to be healed at the Isle of Avalon – which they suggest is in fact Bardsey.

ABERDARON – TREFOR (28 miles)

Aberdaron sits behind a headland that partly protects it from the worst of the winter gales, but in summer it is a popular place, when the Ship does a good trade. This remote fishing village was the last stopping point for pilgrims en route to Bardsey. They would visit a building that still exists today, Y Gegin Fawr or 'the large kitchen', for rest and refreshment before making the short journey over to the island where it is said that 20,000 saints are buried. They needed the sustenance, however, for Bardsey's Welsh name is Ynys Enlli, or the isle of currents, and the passage across what was formerly known as Bardsey Race was often very difficult. The focus of their pilgrimage was the sixth-century Abbey of St Mary, founded by St Cadfan, although today little remains.

Your land-based passage should not be too awkward, however, save for a little rough ground and varying degrees of breathlessness as you follow the clifftop path south to Pen y Cil, then across the promontory for the imposing summit of Mynydd Mawr, from where I have read that you can even see the Wicklow Mountains of Ireland on an exceptionally clear day. These sheer, dark mainland cliffs opposite Bardsey don't have any sort of continuous cliff-edge path, but there's plenty of connecting public footpaths and lanes, and access to the cliffs is possible in the large pockets of National Trust land. It's high and quite wild, an almost treeless countryside thanks to the harsh winds, with bumpy heathland and rough pasture that can only be properly explored on foot. Below Mynydd Mawr there are the outlines of an open field system, dating from medieval times, while inland are the smaller irregular fields that followed afterwards, with finally the larger, ordered layout of the nineteenth-century enclosure movement visible. But all the time you will be drawn towards the sea, which at some places surrounds you on three sides, and especially by the seabirds that enjoy these inaccessible cliffs and grey seals who may be seen reposing on the rocks below. In particular look out for choughs, the Lleyn Heritage Coast emblem you will see displayed on their waymarks. This crow-like bird, with distinctive red feet and bill, inhabits sea cliffs and mountains but is now virtually absent from England. Over 5% of British choughs nest on Lleyn's remote cliffs, and if you are walking here in April/May you may see their impressive aerial performances.

Finally back on the north-facing coast, walk the stirring clifftop down to Porth Oer (or Porthor) where the sand is supposed to whistle. The odd sound is thought to be caused by the crunching together of the uniformly rounded quartz grains underfoot. From here follow lanes parallel with the shore until a path leads to Porth Witlin. From this point there is a continuous public footpath along the heritage coast for over 10 miles to Morfa Nefyn. Unspoilt but gradually lower cliffs and bays now replace the wilder scenery of further west. The sand can be walked and the sea surfed at Traeth Penllech, beyond Porth Colmon. While Porth Ysgaden was where lime and coal were once brought ashore (the coal yards are still evident). At the same time, butter, cheese and salted herrings would all be exported. There are occasional heritage coast waymarks along the route, but you should not really need their guidance.

The uninterrupted pathway culminates at the narrow grassy promontory by Porth Dinllaen and, despite the all-encompassing golf course, you still have a right of way around the clifftop. Porth Dinllaen was once considered as a site for a full-scale ferry port (with railway terminus) for Ireland. Today it is little more than a lifeboat station, a few cottages and a pub ('no golfing shoes and strictly no wetsuits in the bar'). A peaceful, unhurried and extremely pleasant spot. Fairly recently most of Dinllaen was purchased by the National Trust, and so we can now rest much easier in the knowledge that it will not turn into another Holyhead.

The short beach walk to Morfa Nefyn, then a clifftop track to Nefyn itself (with perhaps a visit to the Historical and Maritime Museum at St Mary's Church) is the last proper coast walking that you will be able to enjoy for some time. From Porth Dinllaen there will have been distant views of Anglesey, but rather more arresting will have been the sight of Yr Eifl (The Rivals), a two-pronged mountain that rises a dramatic 560m from the sea and makes any shore route impossible. But the alternative is not all road. A mile out of Nefyn a path branches off left to Pistyll, and passes the Church of St Beuno, a simple building often strewn with dried, medicinal herbs and rushes. St Beuno was a well-known Celtic saint, famed in particular for restoring the severed head of his niece, St Winifred.

Above Llithfaen your path becomes a wide, unmade access track to the former granite quarries that scar the seaward of the two peaks. While most of North Wales mined slate, the Lleyn produced granite. Neolithic men quarried these hills long before nineteenth-century miners toiled away to pave the streets of new, industrial Britain. Crouched in a valley on its own by the sea far below is Porth y Nant, built in 1870 to house the miners, which became a ghost village for a few years after its abandonment in the 1950s. It was then taken over by hippies for a while, but is now a residential Welsh language centre. The track passes directly between the two peaks, revealing tremendous views of the coast in both directions, before you must join a path between the heather and bracken that falls away steeply down to the village of Trefor.

TREFOR – BANGOR (27 miles)

Apparently Trefor was named after Trefor Jones, who once worked for slate supremo Samuel Holland. Near the renovated quayside, where granite used to be shipped out from the quarries above, signs warn of soft mud, and although there is a little sand further on it's not a particularly appetising or easy foreshore to walk. Nor, at times, is there much of it. This is a shame, since there is no proper coast path of any length until Bangor, save the odd mile at Pontllyfni. Beyond here the hills retreat somewhat and a low coastal plain develops towards Anglesey and the mouth of the Menai Strait, which is where a short but interesting ramble by the sea is possible.

The approach is along the sandy beach at Dinas Dinlle which leads to a former World War II air base that is now home to Caernarfon Air World. It was here, incidentally, that the first RAF mountain rescue team was formed. The sandy spit beyond the airstrip ends at Fort Belan, built by the first Lord Newborough to defend the Menai Strait from Napoleon's forces and not open to the public. A public footpath returns along the western edge of Foryd Bay, a popular haunt of waders and other waterfowl, while in the distance the summit of Snowdon is visible on a clear day. Short, connecting paths and lanes are necessary before a scenic, unfenced lane hugs the shore all the way around to the pedestrian swingbridge into Caernarfon.

Without doubt this must be the best position from which to view the most awe-inspiring of Edward I's fortresses. From across the mouth of Afon Seiont the castle walls seem utterly impregnable, modelled according to some on those of Constantinople (although the Romans built a fort on the castle site 1,000 years before Edward). The castle was begun in 1283 and took forty years to complete, and such was its strength that a force led by Owain Glyndwr was twice beaten off, the second time by a garrison of only twenty-eight men. It was here that the English set up base, and was where Edward crowned his eldest son Prince of Wales in 1301. At the same spot exactly 668 years later the investiture of the current Prince of Wales took place. A small section of the original town wall also remains intact, and today's visitor can also enjoy Caernarfon's maritime museum, situated at Victoria Dock.

For the coast walker it is frustrating that the attractive, often wooded shore of the Menai Strait contains virtually no public footpaths at all. However, there is a dismantled railway turned walk/cycleway parallel to it which can be followed from Caernarfon's Victoria Dock all the way to Port Dinorwig, with one small break by the roundabout for the new Anglesey road. (And this popular route may even be extended in due course.) The only decent access to the shore is at the National Trust's Vaynol Park, where you can walk waymarked footpaths opposite the Marquess of Anglesey's fine stately house of Plas Newydd, also in the Trust's care. But even these paths end before Britannia Bridge, a double decker structure with the road on top and the railway below; although if you are keen to visit the island or see its bridges, it will be Telford's graceful suspension bridge of 1826, a mile further on, that will appeal the most. Its height reflects the need to allow 30m-high fully rigged sailing ships of the day to pass below.

In between the two bridges – right in the middle of the Menai Strait – is Ynys Gored Goch (Red Weir Island). The inhabitants of this tiny island used to make a living out of fish traps, the only ones in Britain that used the natural water pressure of the tide to prevent the herring, sole and other fish escaping. Such is the tremendous power of the tide through the Strait, one of the strongest in the country in fact, that periodically it sweeps through the ground floor of the main house on the island. The occupants have become accustomed simply to retire upstairs for a couple of hours then carrying on as before.

If, by now, the Menai Strait is beginning to appear no more than a wide river and Anglesey a part of the mainland, then let's take a closer look at the largest island in England and Wales. Ynys Mon, the island of Mon (the Romans called it Mona, or mother), is easily reached by bridge, although there were once five ferries operating. There is much fine scenery for walkers to enjoy around its long and varied shore (three separate sections of heritage coast) and, although there is no official waymarked coast path as such, several guidebooks do describe similar routes that each total around 120–130 miles. A few sections of continuous coast footpath exist, but mostly the routes link together existing public rights of way with roads. Perhaps Anglesey is better suited to a series of day or weekend walks. For extensive dunes and an unspoilt beach wander head for Aberffraw or Benllech; while for a stunning section of rough and wild rocky shore nothing beats the Cemaes–Amlwch stretch (9 miles). But if a truly invigorating though strenuous day's outing is what you want, then try a circular route around (and over) Holyhead Mountain on the northern tip of Holy Island.

Pick of the walks

LLEYN CIRCULAR – LLANBEDROG (up to 5 miles): short wander around the heathy headland, though one steep climb (see main text).

LLEYN CIRCULAR – RHIW (5–7 miles): optional figure of eight from Rhiw inland to the top of Mynydd Rhiw, and seawards to the National Trust's unspoilt headland of Mynydd Penarfynydd, with fabulous views of Bardsey Island.

FAIRBOURNE – BARMOUTH (5–7 miles): Little train or lane walk to estuary mouth; then shore path and dramatic railway bridge to Barmouth. For the energetic the steep tour of the National Trust's Dinas Oleu is a further extension. Back to Fairbourne by train.

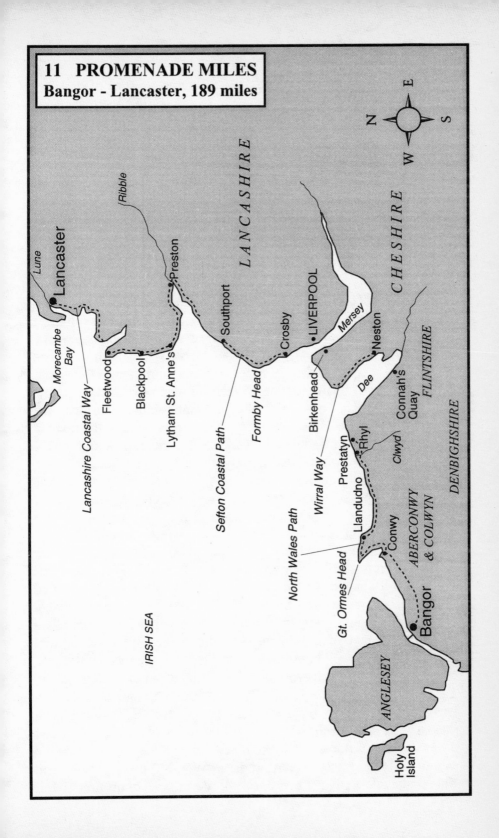

11 PROMENADE MILES
Bangor - Lancaster, 189 miles

N E S W

Ribble

LANCASHIRE

Lune

Lancaster

CHESHIRE

Preston

Morecambe Bay

Southport

LIVERPOOL

Mersey

Neston

Fleetwood

Crosby

FLINTSHIRE

Lancashire Coastal Way

Blackpool

Formby Head

Birkenhead

Connah's Quay

Lytham St. Anne's

Sefton Coastal Path

Dee

Prestatyn

DENBIGHSHIRE

Wirral Way

Rhyl

Clwyd

Llandudno

Conwy

North Wales Path

ABERCONWY & COLWYN

Gt. Ormes Head

Bangor

IRISH SEA

ANGLESEY

Holy Island

St Deiniol established a church at Bangor in the sixth century, seventy years before Canterbury. There's still a cathedral here today, and although it may not be a great religious centre Bangor is still a busy place with a university and a handsome, restored Victorian pier, the first you will have seen for a long time. It is also the start of a new long-distance trail, the North Wales Path, which runs for 48 miles between Bangor and Prestatyn. Opened in 1995, there is currently only a leaflet guide, but some waymarking has taken place along a route that very sensibly tries to keep clear of the A55. Unfortunately, since this busy highway hugs the shore and coastal strip for long periods the North Wales Path is forced inland, which to an extent excludes it for the purposes of this book. From Bangor it heads for the towering hills above Lavan Sands, and via Aber Falls and an established track over Cefn Coch the trail passes through Sychnant Pass to reach Conwy. For the dogged coast walker there is in fact a very pleasant walk from Aber Ogwen, by the huge neo-Norman Penrhyn Castle just outside Bangor, along both a shore path and the shore itself through several small nature reserves as far as Llanfairfechan. Large numbers of waders enjoy the extensive mudflats, while typical saltmarsh plants such as sea aster and sea spurrey can also be found. After Llanfairfechan the road and railway completely dominate the shoreline, and you will be forced on to the mud or sand, or inland.

Telford's suspension bridge over the River Conwy, opened in 1826 but closed in the late 1950s when a modern, steel construction took over, has reopened to allow foot travellers the most elegant of crossings. Once threatened with demolition, the bridge and toll house were restored by the National Trust in 1995, and from it you can gaze up at the battered castle. Edward had it built in just four years, another formidable fortress with which to try and bully the Welsh. But ironically it was the King himself who was besieged in the winter of 1294 when the river flooded and stranded him at the castle over the whole of Christmas. Today it is a World Heritage Site, and the medieval walled town is well worth spending time over, especially as the new road tunnel has eased town centre traffic congestion.

Once across the river turn left and follow the estuary shore from Deganwy to Llandudno, or tracks alongside the golf course if you prefer, until the splendid prospect of Great Orme rises above. The North Wales Path follows Marine Drive around the edge – the nearest route to the sea – but it is far better to wander through the centre of the country park to the 207m summit for excellent views of Anglesey and Snowdonia National Park. And for a celebratory ice cream, despite the presence of those lazy sods who have ridden the tram all the way up from the resort. This fine, nipple-shaped limestone headland is an ideal place for a day's wander, with nature trails, an acclaimed bronze age mining centre, and a large area of open hilltop and rough pasture that is home to a few Kashmir goats. The lonely, exposed church on the far side is named after the sixth-century St Tudno, who had a small retreat on Orme (the old Norse word for sea monster).

With Great Ormes Head on the west, Little Ormes Head guards the eastern end of Llandudno's curving promenade, and on summer evenings both are floodlit to dramatic effect. In between is the classic Victorian seaside resort, developed in the 1840s when a sudden mining boom proved short-lived. The original well-ordered street planning is still evident, and how refreshing it is that the handsome seafront buildings have not been swamped by vulgar, modern hotels or blighted by endless amusement arcades and food stalls. On the West Shore is the White Rabbit, a statue commemorating the fact that it was here in the 1860s that the visiting Lewis Carroll (the Revd Charles Dodgson) met a little girl called Alice Liddell, who proved to be the inspiration for *Alice in Wonderland.*

Little Ormes Head may be the younger brother, but his sea cliffs are just as good as his elder. And it is more unlikely that the Great Unfit will make it up there, since there's no tramway or cable car to take the weight off their feet, so enjoy the wild headland and some fine views over the Dee estuary towards the Wirral and Merseyside. The seafront road to Colwyn Bay passes the miniature chapel of St Trillo, the smallest in Wales, actually set into the sea wall at Rhos Point.

Colwyn Bay is another classic old Victorian resort, with a long promenade severed from the town by both the railway and A55 dual carriageway, the latter eventually taking its place. It's not a particularly walkable bit of coast, and the North Wales Path also arrives at my conclusion that there is little alternative but to head inland on country lanes to Llysfaen before returning to the sea at Llanddulas. From here to the River Clwyd crossing at Rhyl it is a straightforward journey along the sand, sea wall or shoreside tracks. The hilly ground slowly retreats, at least until the abrupt end of the Clwydian Range at Prestatyn, and the widening coastal plain is full of holiday camps and caravan parks. Towyn seems to consist of almost nothing else. It is a dismal place.

The North Wales Path shies away from entering Rhyl, perhaps no bad thing, and instead heads inland to Dyserth and the limestone pinnacle of Graig Fawr before joining a former railway line turned walkway back to the coast where it ends at Prestatyn.

Rhyl is yet another centre that likes to style itself North Wales's premier family resort. After a steady period of decline, which saw the pier and pavilion vanish, determined investment in the 1990s has resulted in the likes of Sun Centre. This is a massive indoor complex of pools and palm trees which generates the feeling of constant warmth and sunshine – something, it must be said, that is occasionally lacking from the not-always-tropical beaches of the Irish Sea.

RHYL – NESTON (32 miles)

For most of the time you can walk the broad swathe of sand from Rhyl all the way along past Prestatyn to Point of Ayr, at the mouth of the Dee estuary. If you don't there are promenade and tracks alongside the golf courses and holiday camps that are walkable if dull. Dull is not a word you could ever use to describe the Offa's Dyke Path, which comes down steeply off the Clwydian Range to finish at Prestatyn after its glorious 177-mile journey from Chepstow.

At Talacre, by Point of Ayr, there are even more caravan parks and shoddy pubs. The lighthouse closed some time ago, and would have opened as a visitor centre had not vandals set fire to it. There are a few waymarked paths through the dunes, and some good views over to the Wirral, but unfortunately here the North Wales sands end and should you want to continue on foot the southern edge of the Dee estuary is not an attractive proposition. Unless you forge a route by path and lane along the hillside above – perhaps via Holywell

and including a visit to the remains of Edward I's castle at Flint –
you will be faced with a long and tedious walk along the A548, bar
a section of sea wall beyond Mostyn. If you're on a long-distance
coast walk and have a mind for your sanity and not your scruples
then catch the train from Prestatyn to Connah's Quay. I drove it.

Connah's Quay is hardly a walker's mecca, either, although the
ice rink at Queensferry is the National Centre for Ice Sports in
Wales. At the time of writing a power station is being built on
the riverside, which will nicely complement the unsightly Shotton
steelworks opposite. There's also a new road bridge in the offing,
so a different walking route to the Wirral may eventually be
possible. At the moment cross the Dee by the blue girder bridge
at Queensferry, and after a burst of the A550 cross into England
and branch off left for the mercifully quiet hamlet of Shotwick,
then a path to sleepy Puddington and lanes via Burton across the
railway to a marshside track into Neston.

NESTON – BIRKENHEAD (20 miles)

Now the walking begins in earnest once more, and ahead is the
attractive if understated Wirral shoreline. It may not exactly be a
wilderness, and certainly has its fair share of prom, but nevertheless
there's plenty of interest. Plus the walker can enjoy 20 miles
of virtually uninterrupted shoreline from Neston to Seacombe,
opposite Liverpool's fine waterfront, and which after Thurstaston
is waymarked as the Wirral Coastal Walk (the blue discs show a
local shrimping boat known as a nobby).

Unlike the Dee's southern shore, where the hillside forces the
main road down to the waterside, this opposite bank is peaceful
and generally unspoilt, with fields and footpaths and huge patches
of saltmarsh extending out into the estuary. Most of this is
contained in Wirral Country Park, opened in 1973 as Britain's
first country park, a delightful rural strip that accompanies the
shore for many miles and through which runs the 12-mile Wirral
Way. A waymarked, multi-user route, it follows the course of
the old Hooton to West Kirby branch line, and tends to take a
leafier line away from the shore – but ideal as part of a circular
day walk.

Neston is on the commuter line to Liverpool, but down on the
promenade at Parkgate it feels nicely detached, almost elegant; and
of course there's the Ship Hotel. Two of the other pubs include the

Boat House and the Old Quay, which is an indication of Parkgate's past, and the fact that once the lucrative Dublin Packet even sailed from here. But fifty years ago the sea went out and never properly came back, so ending the port's prosperity.

There is a path along the old sea wall beside the golf course. If it's high water join the Wirral Way for a bit, through the edge of Heswall, otherwise you can safely and easily walk along the foreshore below a few houses and by the side of the creek-ridden marsh. Across the estuary the Clwydian Range rises green and steeply, and the further you walk the more peaceful it becomes. Soon low cliffs develop, and you may want to climb to the path along the top in order to visit the excellent country park visitor centre at the end of the Thurstaston lane, with café and campsite. From here the Wirral Way continues into West Kirby, where the cliffs disappear and the sailboarders on Marine Lake hold the attention. A popular track then runs seawards of the golf course, and swings round to leave the Dee estuary for Liverpool Bay. Offshore are the tiny Hilbre Islands, a popular site for waders who roost here when much of the Dee's vast flats are covered at high tide. They incorporate a few private residences, plus a bird observatory and old telegraph station, and tides allow access on foot for six hours out of every twelve, although groups of six or over need permits (available from the country park offices). During the winter months the 31,500 acres of the Dee estuary are home to over 80,000 waders (10% of the British population), and as many as 24,000 ducks and geese. Knot, dunlin, shelduck, sanderling, curlew, oystercatcher, redshank – all can be found beak-down in the Dee's yummy mud.

From the walkable if dull, residential seafront at Hoylake (Ship Inn) you may see grey seals basking on offshore sandbanks; then at Dove Point the prom gives way to an uninterrupted shore footpath through the North Wirral Country Park to Kings Parade at New Brighton, virtually at the mouth of the Mersey. Four miles long, this is another splendid linear country park that hosts all manner of recreational activities. At Leasowe Common (Leasowe is the Old English for coastal grassland) there is a distinctive white-painted lighthouse that was built in 1763 by the Mersey Docks and Harbour Board. Closed since 1908, its last keeper was a Mrs Williams, the only woman lighthouse-keeper of her time. Today it houses the country park ranger service.

From New Brighton's promenade it is pavement all the way to

Seacombe, or if you prefer to Birkenhead, from where the ferry across the Mersey (good moment to hum along perhaps?) is a must. Join commuters, shoppers and tourists for the best view of Liverpool; there's even a separate cruise up and down the river past the famous old docks and other sights.

If you fancy walking around the River Mersey then good luck. Eastham Country Park and Frodsham Marsh may offer some respite, but otherwise there is no alternative to miles of roadwalking and some grisly industry around Ellesmere Port, Runcorn and Widnes. The return on the north bank is a different prospect, however, along the as yet incomplete but promising Mersey Way. It's currently possible to walk the riverbank between Hale and Garston past Liverpool Airport, and at Otterspool, and it is hoped that further redevelopment will allow even greater access, so check locally.

LIVERPOOL – SOUTHPORT (26 miles)

Windswept headlands and deserted bays are all very well, but there's another aspect to the coast of England and Wales that can and should be explored on foot, even though there might be no public footpath signs and few walking boots about. Grimsby's National Fishing Heritage Centre, the historic seafront at Southsea and Dover's clifftop castle, Plymouth Hoe and the Cardiff Bay development – all these places tell of the history and heritage of our coast, and there's nowhere more fascinating than the waterfront of Liverpool to enjoy a lesson in maritime history. Forget football and the Beatles for a moment and step off the Mersey Ferry in front of the famous Royal Liver building, with its two main towers topped by mythical Liver birds from which the city is supposed to have taken its name. Turn right for Albert Dock, opened by Prince Albert in 1846 but largely redundant only fifty years later when it proved too shallow for the new steamships. It closed in 1972 but after extensive renovation has reopened to become one of the country's top tourist attractions, home to the likes of the Beatles Story and Tate Gallery, as well as the excellent Merseyside Maritime Museum. Here are exhibitions on the slave trade and emigration to the New World, on the era of the grand ocean liners, and even performances by a group specialising in shanties and sea songs. It is also home to the HM Customs and Excise National Museum.

The country's first modern commercial wet dock was built at Liverpool in 1715, and despite recent decline Liverpool was still the second busiest port in Britain as late as 1966. Then London was at the top, but look how its docklands have changed. A recent promotional leaflet (*50 Great Merseyside Facts*) observes wryly that the Thames Barrier 'that stops Londoners from drowning' was built on Merseyside. Liverpool's working docks and shipyards once stretched for almost ten miles, and today are concentrated mostly along the Bootle waterfront, so that there is no public access to the shore for five grimy miles until clear of the Mersey's mouth near Seaforth. At Crosby Marine Park, however, the 21-mile Sefton Coastal Path begins. It's an attractive, waymarked route that weaves its way through dunes and coastal pines, along promenade and seafront as far as Crossens, north of Southport. It must be said that with a diversion around the mouth of the River Alt near Hightown, the vast sands off Crosby, Formby and Southport can be walked quite easily instead – at low tide at least – without once losing sight of the Irish Sea. But not surprisingly it's a bit dull, and I suggest the more imaginative official coast path as a far better option.

Follow the promenade past Crosby, keeping an eye on the busy shipping heading for Liverpool Freeport to your south, and the Wirral and the mountains of North Wales in the far distance. Beyond the coastguard station a waymarked dune track leads to Hightown, then alongside the railway to Hoggs Hill Lane before returning seawards. The detour is necessary to skirt Altcar Rifle Range as well as to negotiate a safe crossing over the River Alt.

Formby is a quiet and up-market commuter outpost of Liverpool, and the coast path passes the edge of the semis before heading seawards through the dunes behind Formby Point. Although long vanished, Britain's first lifeboat station was built at Formby in 1776, and although it was soon replaced by a second this too eventually closed, in 1918. After enjoying something of a renaissance as a tea room the building finally succumbed to the sand. Such is the problem with sand dune erosion along here that wooden fences have been introduced along the shore in an effort to trap the sand and so prevent the dunes disappearing further. In fact the Formby that you see today is a relatively modern version, the ancient town having been swallowed up by shifting sand by the beginning of this century.

Through the dunes the coast path can sometimes be arduous because of deep, soft sand, but this is short-lived, and turning inland on the so-called Fisherman's Path you are rewarded by acres of cool, shaded pinewoods that on a scorching hot day are bliss. Better still is the range of wildlife that you can hear and see, and foremost are Sefton's red squirrels. Although there is an actual squirrel reserve off Victoria Road, where they are almost as tame as their more bullying grey cousins (thankfully absent here), there will be fewer people about in these woods further north. Walk quietly and patiently and you will be rewarded by the fine sight of a couple of red bushy tails scampering up and down the tree trunks.

The pinewood is not a natural habitat, having been planted at the beginning of this century. It is part of Ainsdale Sand Dunes National Nature Reserve, and the coast path emerges by the railway along its eastern edge – although on the other side of the trees there is also a waymarked track across the dunes and dune slacks (damp hollows between the dune ridges that are often home to orchids and marsh plants). At the corner of the reserve the Sefton Coastal Path goes underneath a road and trudges alongside some dreary houses to Ainsdale-on-Sea. Forget that! Before the road turn left and take what's called the Pinfold Trail into Ainsdale Local Nature Reserve and across the scrubby dunes of Ainsdale Hills to Ainsdale-on-Sea (but do stick to the white-posted tracks, since this habitat is important for the rare natterjack toad and sand lizard).

Ainsdale-on-Sea is a bit of a dump, not helped by a less than beautiful Pontins camp whose high perimeter fence conjures up memories of *The Great Escape*. From here the official route is past Royal Birkdale Golf Course and over the Birkdale Hills ('no motor cycling, no horse riding, no fires, no nude sunbathing'), although this stays landwards of the noisy coast road all the way. If the tide is out then walk the great fat beach instead, a massive yellow sweep that widens as you reach Southport (it even includes a runway for light aircraft that put on tourist flights in the summer). This popular resort has a pier second only to Southend's in terms of length and, like its equivalent in Essex, it has a train to the end for the lazy. Southport's attractive main street still enjoys some trappings of its Victorian past, with glass-topped frontages and wide pavements, while north of the 100-year-old marine lake is an RSPB reserve that attracts large numbers of wildfowl in winter. Ahead is Lytham and further on the distinctive shape of Blackpool Tower, but first there is the small matter of crossing the River Ribble.

SOUTHPORT – PRESTON (22 miles)

The Sefton Coastal Path finishes at the roundabout at Crossens, where you should turn off for Banks. In less than a mile, at Fiddler's Ferry, Merseyside is swapped for Lancashire, and there is an embankment path opposite the old Crossens Pumping Station which allows a walk along the edge of Banks Marsh. Although you have to return to the lane there is almost immediately another right of way alongside Hesketh Out Marsh. Across Banks Marsh, in particular, there are wide views of the Ribble estuary, a tremendously important site for birdlife. Pink-footed geese graze on the fields, gulls and terns breed on the marshes, while huge flocks of waders such as sanderling, dunlin and knot are usually to be found on the water's edge. The River Douglas foils any further advance up the Ribble, necessitating a detour via Hesketh Bank and Tarleton before a bridge is reached.

At the moment this long section between Crossens and Freckleton, the latter actually quite close as the crow flies across the marshy mouth of the Ribble, is one of two missing gaps on the Lancashire Coastal Way that are presently being tackled. As yet unfinished, the trail will eventually span the entire seaboard of the red rose county – around 137 miles – and it is likely that when you walk at least from Southport to Preston the county council will have put in place signposts and even made some improvements in the route.

For the moment the route from the River Douglas to Preston comprises small sections of two other established long-distance paths. At Carr House Bridge leave the A59 to follow the Douglas Valley Way along the eastern bank of the Douglas out to the Dolphin public house at Longton. Here a disc with a wavy blue line signifies the beginning of the Ribble Way, which tracks the river for 73 miles to its source at Gayle Moor in the Yorkshire Dales. There may be Stainforth Force and Pen-y-Ghent further upstream, but here at Longton the Ribble is flat and a little listless, forced into a narrow channel between reclaimed pasture. But at least the firm and unswerving embankment makes the walking easy, and before long you arrive in the middle of Preston, 'a fine town, and tolerably full of people' according to Defoe.

PRESTON – FLEETWOOD (30 miles)

At present there is no legitimate access to the Ribble's northern bank between Preston and Freckleton. Things may change when the Lancashire Coastal Way is completed, but at the moment it's a bus ride or a long and unpleasant roadwalk.

The Ship Inn on Bunker Street, Freckleton, is a welcome and by now familiar coastal sight, and is where the walking resumes. For the first few miles it's more of the marshy, languid Ribble, via Naze Point and the edge of Warton Aerodrome, home to the USAF during World War II and subsequently British Aerospace. As the open sea approaches you must weave your way through the streets of Lytham to gain the pleasant promenade, backed by a wide grassy strip and bordered not by gaudy shops or cheap hotels but by smart private town houses. It's an elegant, respectable kind of place, typified by the uncluttered front where instead of an amusement arcade there is a well-preserved windmill that contains displays on local history and an information centre; plus the well-behaved headquarters of the Ribble Cruising Club. Continue to Granny's Bay, where depending on the time of day bird-watchers may outnumber senior citizens as they focus their binoculars on the mudflats and sandbanks out in the estuary. Next to it is Fairhaven Lake, with an RSPB information centre; then go further along the sea wall and around the edge of the popular sands of St Anne's, and as the coast swings north Blackpool is almost upon you.

From the Irish Sea the Fylde Peninsula must look like one gigantic promenade. In the south is Lytham St Anne's (two places for sure, but one borough since 1923), genteel and refined; while ahead of you the more brash and colourful Golden Mile eventually peters out in the residential buildings of Fleetwood. But follow the shore on foot and yet again the inquisitive walker will be rewarded, as nestling quietly off the coast road is Lytham St Anne's Nature Reserve, established in 1968 and containing the best preserved sand dunes in the region. The uncommon dark tussock and portland moths are among the wildlife found in the reserve.

And so to Blackpool. Back in the 1750s there were a few modest lodging houses by an attractive sandy beach. But developers saw the potential, and the lure of cheap holidays for the thousands of low-paid Lancashire mill town families, and when the railway link was achieved in 1846 there was no stopping the resort's rise. Black and white photographs from the turn of the century show the promenade completely thronged with holidaymakers (all, without exception, wearing hats of course). At the Empress Ballroom 3,000 people danced in elegance; while in dozens of pubs there was just plain singing and dancing – from 9.30 in the morning until 11 at night. Nowadays Britain's premier resort boasts a glitzy seafront that extends for six miles or so, lined with arcades, funfairs, take-away food joints and a large number of cheap and cheerful guest houses. A staggering total of 17 million visitors pour into Blackpool each year. As with other resorts, the holiday season has been craftily extended by seafront illuminations that are switched on in September. But without doubt it's an enthralling scene, with the famous tower resembling a lighthouse decorated for Christmas. Opened in 1894, the 155m-high Eiffel lookalike gives great views over the seaside spectacle, and inland over the flat coastal plain to Preston and the Forest of Bowland.

If you have never really experienced a big resort then a walk along Blackpool promenade is an illuminating experience, if you excuse the awful pun. But it will not be most walkers' idea of a relaxing day out, and on a sunny summer's day it may be hellish. If the latter is the case the sand is also likely to be swarming with fat white flesh turning bright red, in which case an ideal if bone-shaking journey to Fleetwood can be had on one of the old trams that have plied the seafront now for 100 years.

A word of warning. You may see huge crowds on the sand and in the sea at Southport and Blackpool, but the Irish Sea beaches of north-west England are among the most polluted in the whole of Britain. Industrial and radioactive contamination, untreated sewage outfall and oil spillages continue to mar what is nevertheless a very attractive seaboard; but enjoy it from the safety of the coast path.

The high spirits of Blackpool slowly give way to the more sober Fleetwood, which earlier this century was the chief West Coast fishing port. It was originally the brainchild of wealthy landowner Peter Hesketh-Fleetwood, who employed the services of his architect friend Decimus Burton (so-called because he was the tenth child). The promenade walk extends all the way around to the mouth of the Wyre, from where there are the first views of the vast Morecambe Bay, with the fells of southern Cumbria beyond; and in exceptionally clear weather the tall cranes and shipyard halls at Barrow-in-Furness are even visible.

FLEETWOOD – LANCASTER (19 miles)
For much of the year there is a regular ferry service from Fleetwood across to Knott End, a short hop away. But an interesting dry land

alternative is the 16-mile Wyre Way, a waymarked trail through Wyre Estuary Country Park. The first part in fact follows the promenade south via Rossall Point, so eliminating the need to walk the road past Fleetwood docks; then cutting inland it reaches the river near ICI's Hillhouse works, and follows the Wyre's bank via the Wyreside Ecology Centre to Skippool and Shard Bridge. The return to the sea along the east bank is on lane and footpath, via Barnaby's Sands and Burrows Marsh, both designated Sites of Special Scientific Interest (SSSIs). Altogether it is a fine day's outing and, with the ferry at the Wyre mouth, here is a splendid circular walk around a pleasant river that many outside Lancashire will never have heard of.

The Lancashire Coastal Way resumes at Knott End and follows the uncomplicated sea wall all the way to Fluke Hall, where it joins a lane for half a mile before returning to Pilling Embankment. The enormous expanse of sand and mudflat revealed to your left may not be picture postcard stuff (especially with Heysham power station on the horizon), but it makes Morecambe Bay one of the largest and most important inter-tidal areas for birds in north-west Europe, and is fed by five separate rivers (Wyre, Lune, Keer, Kent and the Leven). All this from the official noticeboard opposite the Knott End Café. What it doesn't say is that when the wind blows hard and rain is threatening the best place to be is in fact inside the Knott End Café with a steaming mug of coffee. Beyond Lane End there is no public access to the embankment, and the official coast path takes to an inland lane via Moss End (although the Lancashire Cycle Way curiously stays on the busier A588 nearer the shore). Over Breck's Bridge, then over the Cocker and the main road for a marshside path out to the remote Cockersand Abbey. Isolation being everything, Hugh the Hermit (yes, really) lived here for some years on his own, and although it later became a leper hospital, in 1190 a Premonstratensian abbey known as St Mary of the Marsh was established on the site. It became one of the richest in the county, and covered almost an acre. After the Dissolution the abbey fell into ruin and the masonry ended up in local farm buildings and in the sea wall. Today all that is left is the octagonal chapter-house, and that only because subsequent landowners decided to use it as their family vault.

Continue along the shore track by the mouth of the Lune until Crook Farm. What seems a stone's throw away across the river is the village of Sunderland, whose river traffic was stolen when Glasson Dock – which you arrive at along Marsh Lane – was developed in the mid-eighteenth century. It's a quiet and attractive spot which still receives boats today, albeit mostly pleasure craft, and since it is connected to the Lancaster Canal the docks are kept locked.

From Glasson to Lancaster coastal walkers follow what used to be the bed of the Lancaster–Glasson Dock Railway, built in the 1880s to encourage trade but closed in 1964 after its one goods train a day stopped running. It's also known as the Lune Estuary Path, and whatever the name it's a very attractive route that is also popular with cyclists. There is a picnic spot at Conder Green, where a notice says that the first phase of the Lancashire Coastal Way was opened here in September 1991. Nearby the Stork public house offers more serious refreshment. At Aldcliffe Marsh the coast path veers off to the left, sticking as close as possible to the river, then loops back round into Lancaster to end up at the handsome St George's Quay.

From being a Roman harbour, by the late 1700s Lancaster was one of the foremost ports in the country, with St George's Quay handling cargo from places as far afield as the West Indies. But increasingly larger vessels and the silting of the Lune meant that ships had to dock downstream. The tree-lined quayside is now quiet but still very well-preserved, and the old Customs House is home to the award-winning Maritime Museum. Elsewhere, the traditional county town boasts a formidable medieval castle and handsome Priory Church, both perched on the hilltop above the river; while on the hillside opposite is Williamson Park, with a butterfly house and the gleaming Ashton Memorial, a massive folly described by Nikolaus Pevsner as 'the grandest monument in England'.

Pick of the walks

SEFTON COASTAL PATH (Crosby – Southport, 21 miles): level route via beach, dune and pine forest. Plenty of opportunities for circular walks, plus excellent Merseyside rail links along the whole route.

PARKGATE/NESTON CIRCULAR (9 miles): a low-tide walk along the Dee estuary to Thursaston Country Park visitor centre, and back along the Wirral Way (or a linear route on to Hoylake, 9 miles).

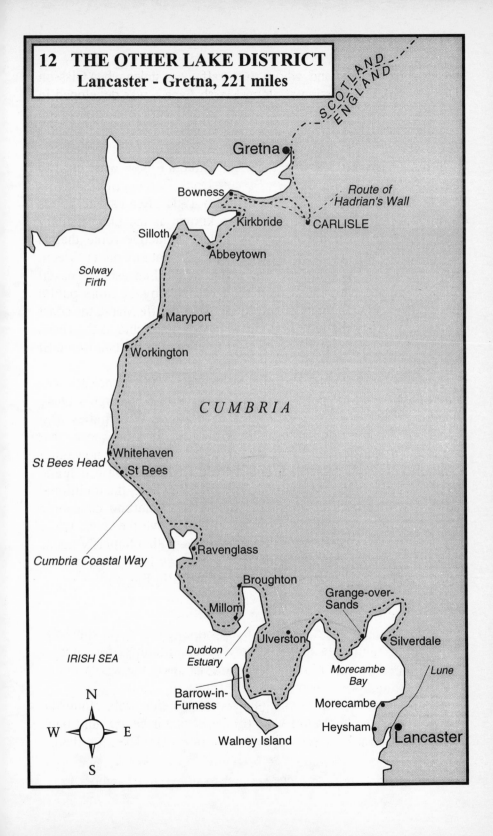

12 THE OTHER LAKE DISTRICT
Lancaster - Gretna, 221 miles

SCOTLAND
ENGLAND

Gretna

Bowness

*Route of
Hadrian's Wall*

Kirkbride

CARLISLE

Silloth

Abbeytown

*Solway
Firth*

Maryport

Workington

C U M B R I A

Whitehaven

St Bees Head

St Bees

Ravenglass

Cumbria Coastal Way

Broughton

Grange-over-
Sands

Millom

Ulverston

Silverdale

*Duddon
Estuary*

IRISH SEA

*Morecambe
Bay*

Lune

Barrow-in-
Furness

Morecambe

Heysham

Lancaster

N

W E

S

Walney Island

LANCASTER – SILVERDALE (25 miles)

From the north bank of the Lune in Lancaster the Lancashire Coastal Way currently joins a footpath/cycleway that follows the old North Western Railway from Carlisle Bridge straight into Morecambe. At some point a proper coastal route is to be developed via Overton and Heysham, but until such time we will have to make our own. So steam along the former railway line for a mile before turning left, near the superstore, and return to the riverbank on a lane that floods at high tide. The tide also cuts off the Golden Ball, a mouthwatering Mitchell's pub whose car park wall has a blue-painted marker showing the high water level (it is up to car roof height). This was an occasional haunt of mine during my years at Lancaster University, when the prospect of being stranded in a pub at high tide was irresistible.

There is no access on to the grazing marsh, so follow the quiet lane as far as Overton and the Ship Hotel (Thwaites), where a public footpath leaves Chapel Lane for a short circuit of Bazil Point. At its conclusion join the unfenced tidal road across the creeks and saltmarsh to the village of Sunderland, but do make sure that tide conditions are safe before setting off. Here at the peaceful mouth of the Lune life is slow and unhurried. A few desultory yachts and grazing cattle are set against the backdrop of the dark Bowland Fells and the distinctive Williamson Memorial above Lancaster; while out on Sunderland Point large flocks of waders regularly gather. Two hundred years ago, however, Sunderland was a thriving port for Lancaster, with hemp, tar, flax and other shipbuilding materials arriving from the Baltic, and mahogany from the West Indies. The latter linked Lancaster's wealthy Quaker merchants to the infamous slave trade, and for a while it was not unusual for young black boys to be found as servants in the large houses of the Lune valley. The most famous if sentimentalised case relates to Sambo, a captain's servant who arrived in 1736 and who supposedly died of a broken heart when he thought his master had left him. His grave in a nearby field is still much visited.

From the quayside cottages take the signposted bridleway past the Mission Church (services subject to tides) and Sambo's grave to Potts Corner. The dismal man-made lump ahead is Heysham Nuclear Power Station, which has been despoiling the views since as far back as Fleetwood. Take to the lane inland, past the grounds of uninspiring holiday camps, and by the one that sports the silhouette of a ship with mock funnels and port holes there is a waymarked footpath to the left. This eventually leads through Ocean Edge Caravan Park (which ocean, I wonder?) to join either a lane or a permissive path through the Nuclear Electric-sponsored nature reserve to a busy five-road junction with traffic lights.

Go half left and down to the edge of the sea, with the huge power station and Isle of Man ferry port on your left. This is the regular sailing to Douglas, Isle of Man, and opens up the enticing prospect of a fabulous island coast path: Raad ny Foillan, or the Gull's Road, whose 91-mile route encircles the whole of Man. Continuing on the mainland, stride purposefully along the tidal shoreside track to the surprisingly peaceful spot known as Lower Heysham – the original village, which is pronounced 'Heesham' in these parts. There are cafés and a few shops, and below the ruined ninth-century St Patrick's Chapel a wonderful panorama across Morecambe Bay to Grange-over-Sands and the south Cumbrian fells.

From Lower Heysham it is promenade all the way through Morecambe, a famous resort that is struggling to retain the few trappings of its proud past, in particular the graceful if now a little run-down Midland Hotel on the seafront, built in 1933 and one of the first modernist public buildings. Lacking any decent beach, Morecambe is introducing new gimmicks like the Polo Tower, which joins Frontier Land, in an effort to keep up with the Blackpools of this world. At least the views from the prom are much better here, even though the state of the seawater is equally revolting.

Approaching the railway at Hest Bank, leave the roadside for a short footpath by the sea to the Shore Café next to the level crossing. Mindful of the tides, you can continue by public footpath around the edge of the marsh, past caravan and campsites, until you join a lane that eventually turns inland to emerge by the Steamtown railway museum at Carnforth. But there is another, much quicker way to reach the Cartmel Peninsula, and that's to follow an old right of way directly across the bay itself. From the thirteenth century until the 1850s the regular route for travellers from Lancaster to Barrow and west Cumberland was across the sands of Morecambe Bay, and for those keen to try the crossing – an invigorating if rather damp outing that cheats the tide and dodges the quicksand – you must join a party led by a man who rejoices in the title of the Queen's Guide (not that Her Majesty makes the journey very often). The first official guide to the sands may have been appointed in the fourteenth century, after Edward III funded the Abbot of Furness to appoint a coroner to look into the high number of fatalities on the Kent and Leven sands. Nowadays guided walks begin at Arnside or Silverdale, rather than from the traditional Hest Bank (an 8-mile crossing), since the older route has developed a deep channel across it. Contact Morecambe Tourist Information Centre for further details. *On no account should you attempt the crossing on your own.*

Since this final, northern stage of the Lancashire Coastal Way is still being developed – route finalisation and signposting is taking place as I write, with a new permissive route lately agreed through the RSPB's reserve, for instance – it is best you follow signs on the ground and obtain the County Council's official booklet guides. From Carnforth I would have said follow the Silverdale road as far as Crag Foot, by Leighton Moss reserve, and take the short path across to the small but exquisite wooded limestone hills of Silverdale. But by the time you read this I may be wrong.

SILVERDALE – GRANGE-OVER-SANDS (19 miles)
The Arnside and Silverdale Area of Outstanding Natural Beauty is a haven of peace and tranquillity, where small, jumbled and tree-covered hills rise out of the moss and marsh above the sea. From the slopes of Arnside Knott there are fine views over the muddy flats of Morecambe Bay, and in the distance growls the M6 traffic creeping towards the Lakes.

As you follow the linking lanes and footpaths from Silverdale to Arnside you cross into Cumbria, the last county on our epic journey. In addition, you join the last major long-distance footpath of the Walk, the Cumbria Coastal Way, which stretches an impressive 150 miles from Silverdale all the way around the Lake District's forgotten but often attractive shore to Gretna. Although planned for some years, it's a relatively new trail, and in some places a final route is still being negotiated. Don't expect waymarks all the way, either. In the next few miles you will also touch upon the Furness Way, a 75-mile route from Arnside to Ravenglass via Coniston, that begins by looping around the River Kent to Cartmel.

Cliffside tracks through the yew and ash bring you into Arnside, a shy little village sheltering by the mouth of the River Kent. The tides are incredibly fast and strong, and the short stone pier you see today replaced an earlier version washed out to sea.

A short distance away is Grange-over-Sands, reached by the railway viaduct – but only if you are a train or one of its passengers. Unless the Queen's Guide accompanies you across the sands, there is the prospect of a long detour to cross the Kent upstream near Levens, which begins with a sea wall walk to Sandside, and the Ship Inn, then a lane and a short burst of the A6 to cross the river at Levens Bridge. Next to it is Levens Hall, a handsome Elizabethan building famous for its topiary garden (that's clipped ornamental shrubs and hedges to you and me), and where falconry displays, steaming traction engines and the like are often to be experienced.

For a while you can enjoy a couple more quiet lanes off the main road by the Kent until you enter the Lake District National Park at Sampool Bridge, which is where the A590 is left behind for a long and deserted track to the edge of Milnthorpe Sands. Cut inland to the hamlet of Meathop, perched below a tiny wooded hill, then follow a lane that drops down to accompany the railway from Arnside into Grange-over-Sands, crossing over to begin the promenade walk at Blawith Point.

Grange underwent the usual transformation from an unknown village into a popular Edwardian resort when the railway arrived at the end of the nineteenth century, and until then it featured mainly as the northern terminus of the bay walk (hence the '-over-Sands' bit). There are still some fine old hotels set into the unspoilt hillside, and some dignified shops and gardens, but stand on the prom at low tide and you will realise that 'golden miles' it ain't. A vast sea of mud extends almost endlessly out into the bay, so much so that it is incredible that there is time in the day for the sea to find its way back again. But comes in it does, and so fast at times that many people have been overtaken and perished. Cartmel Priory alone records over 140 people who never made it to the other side alive. William Wordsworth survived the trip, and wrote 'the stranger, from the moment he sets foot on the sands, seems to leave the turmoil of the world behind him . . .' De Quincey was a little more realistic, reporting that 'partly from the daily variations of the tide, partly from the intricacy of the pathless track which must be pursued, and partly from the galloping pace at which the returning tide comes in, many fatal accidents are continually occurring'.

GRANGE-OVER-SANDS – ULVERSTON (21 miles)

Grange is only seven miles from Windermere, but the Cartmel and Furness Peninsulas seem a world apart from the throngs of Bowness and Ambleside. There are no queues for the mountains here, but instead a network of quiet rural paths and country lanes that allow you to explore the hidden delights of Cartmel, for instance, and the windy summit of Hampsfell, with its curious hospice built as a refuge for weary travellers and terrific views of Morecambe Bay, north Lancashire and the Yorkshire peaks.

From Kents Bank station there is a low-tide route around the shore to Humphrey Head, a fascinating limestone promontory that is now a nature reserve and was where, legend has it, the last wolf in England was killed. Here are the only sea cliffs of any real size between the Dee and St Bees Head, further round the Cumbrian coast.

Lanes take you back towards Flookburgh, then out to West Plain Farm, next to an old airfield, from where there is an embankment track alongside Low Marsh to the edge of Cartmel Sands, then back inland to Cark. Ordnance Survey maps depict a right of way across the Leven estuary to Canal Foot, near Ulverston, but as previously, you *must* first contact the official guide for more details of the three-mile route. In this case he is known as the Ulverston sand pilot.

The safer, if much lengthier route, either involves a long stretch of the narrow B5278 past the grand Holker Hall; or preferably a footpath route above it and across the fellside east of Ellerside ridge and via Bigland Tarn. Both routes make for Haverthwaite, from where steam trains chuff lazily up to Lakeside and back, but before crossing the Leven Bridge take the private road, then public footpath along the bank to Roudsea Wood and Mosses National Nature Reserve. This is a wonderful haven to all manner of wildlife, including red squirrels, deer and otters, but you must obtain a permit before entering.

The track continues beyond Roudsea Wood to finally cross the river by footbridge opposite Greenodd, with its Ship Inn and busy

A590 dual carriageway. Unfortunately the latter has to be followed for a short distance until a minor turning to the left leads down to Plumpton Hall and a shore walk to Canal Foot.

ULVERSTON – BARROW-IN-FURNESS (14 miles)
If you have never visited Ulverston then follow the towpath of the mile-long canal (England's shortest?) into the cobbled town centre. First granted a charter by Edward I in 1280, this pleasant market town contains a mix of old and new, was where Hartley's beer originated, and also boasts a museum dedicated to Laurel and Hardy, since Stan Laurel was born here on 16 June 1890 and lived in Ulverston until he was five. The town is also the starting point for the 70-mile Cumbria Way, which heads north for Carlisle via Langdale and Borrowdale. Fine places, certainly, but not for us the crowds of Tarn Hows and Keswick. Instead, the Cumbria Coastal Way reveals Cumbria's shy, quiet shoreline. It gives us new and exciting views of Lakeland's Southern and Eastern Fells, a host of charming estuaries and soon a burst of cliffs; and before too long the magnificent vista of the Solway Firth and southern Scotland will appear. The coastal route from Ulverston is over twice as long as the mountain route (the Cumbria Way) but it is still an excellent way of reaching Carlisle – and maybe the really ambitious have a ready-made circular route around the county?

From Canal Foot take to the road past the giant Glaxo works until branching off left for a track back to the estuary side. Now stay by the low shore past Conishead Priory, the original building constructed by Augustinian monks in the twelfth century, but the nineteenth-century Gothic pile you see today is now home to monks of the Mahayayana Buddhist order of Tibet. Beyond is Bardsea Country Park, a popular spot for family recreation, and at Sea Wood a few of the oaks originally planted for the Barrow shipbuilding industry still survive, although many of the trees along this shore have been bent and battered by the wind off the Irish Sea.

From Bardsea to Rampside the best course of action at anything other than high tide is to walk the foreshore. It is safer than the road, which is never very far away, and although it is debatable if it is more taxing on the feet it is certainly much less wearing on the nerves.

The southern tip of the Furness Peninsula comprises several low and fascinating islands. From Rampside a causeway leads out to

Roa Island, now joined quite firmly to the mainland it must be said. Immediately east is Foulney Island, really just a small spit of shingle but important for breeding terns. More popular is the tiny Piel Island, due south, which is reached by ferry and contains both a ruined castle and a pub, the Ship Inn (what else?), whose landlord is known by the grand title of 'King of Piel'. Apparently he has the power to confer the title 'Knight of Piel Island' on visitors, although I gather the price of a Piel knighthood is to buy everyone present a drink. The castle was built by the monks of Furness Abbey to safeguard incoming cargoes, although they found it useful for smuggling in wine as well. Piel Island today forms the western end of the Cistercian Way, a 33-mile walking route from Grange-over-Sands that visits the sites of Cartmel, Conishead and Furness Priories. Before the Dissolution the monks of Furness, together with the Cistercians of Cartmel, were second only to those at Fountains Abbey in terms of wealth and power, and have left their stamp on this land. Cartmel and Furness are fascinating parts of Cumbria to explore – the mountains can wait till another day.

From Roa Island a track leads waterside of the gas terminals and alongside Roosecote Sands into the centre of Barrow-in-Furness. Little more than a village until the middle of last century, Victorian Barrow was a planned development that at one point boasted the largest iron and steel works in the world (even dubbed 'the Chicago of England'), plus a thriving shipbuilding industry. Today they put together nuclear-powered submarines, although there's a question mark over the long-term future. Surrounded by a small forest of cranes, the gigantic submarine sheds rise out of the town centre like some ghastly urban monoliths. The Dock Museum, sited in the docks area, has more details on Barrow's fortunes.

Nearby a lifting bridge leads to the 8-mile long Walney Island, a flat and windy landscape looking on the map like a piece of mainland Barrow that is in the process of being prised off. A round-island walk is about 20 miles in length. Nature reserves grace either end, with the north home to natterjack toads and the Walney geranium, which is found nowhere else in the world, and huge colonies of nesting gulls in the south. In between is Vickerstown. Originally planned as a resort, it was taken over by Vickers, the Barrow shipbuilders, and developed as a model estate along the lines of Port Sunlight on Merseyside. The venture never really worked, but many of the cheap houses are still inhabited and it has even been designated a Conservation Area.

BARROW-IN-FURNESS – MILLOM (21 miles)

I think it fair to say that the southern section of the Cumbria Coastal Path is not suited to those long-distance footsloggers to whom distance across the map is everything. Already we have made detours around the Kent and Leven, with optional island diversions about Barrow, and now there is a long inland sweep to negotiate the lovely Duddon estuary.

Leave the Dock Museum for the road to Ormsgill, there crossing the railway for a shoreline path around Scarth Bight and Sandscale Haws nature Reserve. Here you can see more natterjack toads, and further out a host of waders enjoy the wide and unspoilt, sands. Sometimes the high-water route may be altered to protect nesting birds.

The path continues to Askam, today a nondescript sort of place that grew up to serve the old ironworks that closed in 1918. The iron ore was known as haematite, sometimes seen as a blood-red stone in pieces of jewellery, and you may spot occasional waymarks for the Haematite Trail (a circular, 18-mile walk) on this Barrow–Askam stretch. From the slag banks of Askam Pier head for the dramatic limestone outcrop of Dunnerholme and alongside the railway to Kirkby-in-Furness, which owes its existence to mining. From the buildings at Sand Side (Ship Inn), it is best to ignore what can be treacherous rights of way across the sand and instead follow safe and quiet lanes via Foxfield to Broughton-in-Furness. A good place to take an overnight halt, the attractive Georgian market square contains unusual fish slabs about the obelisk in the centre, where fish used to be laid out on market day.

The Duddon is finally crossed at Duddon Bridge, after which, leave the main road for a lane to Lady Hall, and then Causey Lane will take you back to the edge of the marsh. High across the estuary the slate quarries on Kirkby Moor are a reminder of the past, while the small, white forest of wind turbines are perhaps an indication of the future. Cross the railway by stiles and walk the embankment all the way above Millom Marsh into the town.

MILLOM – RAVENGLASS (22 miles)

Follow the coast path out to Hodbarrow Point, and by a large area of enclosed water which was caused by subsidence following the closure of the iron ore mine in 1968. Happily it is now an RSPB reserve, home to grebes and tufted ducks, but the short iron lighthouse on the embankment remains. Ahead is a 4-mile walk beyond Haverigg along sand and shingle to Silecroft. The tentacles of Morecambe Bay are now replaced by the smooth and curving coast of west Cumbria, and the overall progression northwards is slowly resumed. From the mouth of the Duddon it is 45 miles to Whitehaven, the next place of any size on this coast, and as the bare Black Combe and Muncaster Fell fall down almost to the sea edge it can be a long and solitary stretch. There are huge, high dunes at the back of the beach, and it is likely that you will have mile upon mile virtually to yourself.

There is a fine low-tide walk along the sand from Silecroft, then at Gutterby Spa ascend low clay cliffs in order to join permissive paths past Annaside and around Selker Farm. The route soon joins a minor road above the out-of-bounds beach at Eskmeals where the military periodically test ammunition. Incidentally, this pleasant and usually deserted coastal lane is also the route of the Cumbria Cycle Way, which provides an exhausting 259-mile journey around the county.

Since the lower Esk is crossed only by the railway, walkers bound for Ravenglass will have to detour upstream on paths through the hamlets of Newbiggin, Hall Waberthwaite and Roughholme in order to reach Muncaster bridge on the main road. If you have a moment, and you should really make the time, wander into the nearby village of Waberthwaite and visit Richard Woodall's shop. Here, by Royal Appointment no less, you can buy delicious cured ham, bacon, and the famous Cumberland sausage.

Once across the Esk, turn left in under half a mile at Hirst Lodge and follow the drive through the attractive grounds of Muncaster Castle. It's worth taking a few minutes to explore the surrounds of what is for the most part a nineteenth-century construction. Apart from the lush gardens, full of azaleas and rhododendrons, there is an owl sanctuary run by the British Owl Breeding and Release Scheme, and most British varieties can usually be seen. Open on most afternoons, there is a turnstile and an honesty box for your honest contributions.

The clear, wooded track returns you to the edge of the Esk, from where a bridleway weaves its way out around the edge of the saltings and into Ravenglass.

RAVENGLASS – WHITEHAVEN (21 miles)

The Romans built a fort, Glennavanta, just south of present-day Ravenglass, and across the railway Walls Castle rises from the remains of a Roman bathhouse. In fact its walls are believed to be the tallest surviving non-military Roman structure in the country. It's a very pleasant spot, where three rivers drain into the Irish Sea (Irt, Mite and Esk), and where the Ravenglass and Eskdale Railway has its southern terminus. This charming narrow gauge steam railway, known affectionately to many as 'Ratty', was originally built to carry ore from local mines, but when they closed in 1912 the line was soon reopened and has ended up a popular tourist attraction. For the walker the 7-mile railway provides the perfect opportunity to devise a circular walk back to the coast, either alighting at Irton Road Station for a walk back across Muncaster Fell; or possibly exploring further up the Esk valley.

Fortunately the railway bridge over the Mite incorporates a pedestrian section, and on the far bank take the track through Saltcoats for a deserted lane across fields. Cross the railway, then look for the track off left to Holme Bridge, an old packhorse construction, which arches over the River Irt. Continue up through more fields to join the road at Drigg.

You won't be surprised to learn that Shore Road will lead you back to the sea, and to the northern end of a sizeable nature reserve. The extensive area of sand dunes support the largest British colony of black-headed gulls, many thousands strong, which gathers every March/April to indulge in a spot of 'neck-stretching' and 'head-flagging', as one nature book engagingly describes it.

After a shoreline ramble to Seascale you will approach what has sadly been visible for some time already. Sellafield's grim collection of huge concrete towers, boxes and domes, was home to the world's first commercial nuclear reactor, although then it was simply known as Calder Hall. Next, the growing complex became Windscale, then after an accident in 1957 it transformed into Sellafield (its original name, actually), and now it reprocesses nuclear waste and wants to bury some of the stuff underneath the surrounding countryside. Sellafield Visitors Centre breezily promises a family show '. . . with hands-on interactive scientific experiments'. But what about

native south Cumbrians, who may prefer not to be so interactive
with Britain's atomic expansion? The late Norman Nicholson, one
of Lakeland's best-known modern writers and poets, and who lived
all his life at nearby Millom, wrote that Calder Hall 'darkens the
landscape like a threat'.

The coast path continues along the shore by the railway, with
the nuclear plant on your right. There's no point beating about the
bush. As at Bradwell and Dungeness, the sense of remote natural
beauty has been ruined; and barely a mile from the edge of the
Lake District National Park, too.

The beach walk will take you past Braystones, with its chalets
and caravan park thoughtfully set against the picturesque backdrop
of nuclear reactors and cooling towers. Approaching St Bees you
can walk along the cliffs if you don't fancy the beach.

St Bees dates back to the seventh century, when St Bega
established a nunnery; although in more modern times St Bees
became known for its prestigious grammar school. Today the
place is known to the walking public at least as the beginning of
Wainwright's Coast-to-Coast Walk, a scenic if over-used route that
he described as 'harmless and enjoyable'. So popular has it become
that an official sign has been erected by the beach outlining the
190-mile route to Robin Hood's Bay. From it you can watch eager
if heavily laden walkers stride down to the beach and dip their boots
in the waves, a ceremony that is repeated if the participants make it
all the way to the other side of England. I must say that it struck me
as a rather daft thing to do at the time, especially early on a grey and
drizzly Monday morning watched by some sorry-looking seagulls
and a brother who clearly thought I was off my trolley. I wondered
that, too, when the drizzle turned to driving rain once I climbed on
to the cliffs, and found that the path was uncomfortably close to
the slippery cliff edge. (The weather got better, by the way.)

For the next three miles the Coast-to-Coast and Coastal Walk
follow the heritage coast around St Bees Head, whose handsome
sandstone cliffs rise to almost 100m and are the highest in
North-West England. From the cliff edge – or where it has
disappeared the field edge – you can look down on shearwaters
and guillemots, probably not seen since Wales. On a clear day
the Isle of Man is visible, about 30 miles away, and the neat little
lighthouse on the headland was the last to use an open coal fire as
a light source (it caught fire, unfortunately).

As Whitehaven approaches the Coast-to-Coast Walk heads inland to Sandwith, and you should continue around Saltom Bay and down into Whitehaven.

WHITEHAVEN – MARYPORT (14 miles)
Whitehaven may not be on most visitors' itinerary, but it is a place with history and variety. On the one hand there is the sprawling Albright and Wilson chemical works as you descend off the cliffs from the south, plus of course the legacy of coalmining that is still visible. Saltom Pit was Britain's first undersea coalmine, sunk in 1731, although a more visible memorial is the unmissable Candlestick Chimney, which ventilated Wellington Pit (the last colliery in the area, closed in the mid-1980s). But on the other hand Whitehaven boasts a number of handsome Georgian houses built around a planned street grid, plus a fine pier. And, as a busy mid-eighteenth-century port, Whitehaven was not far behind the likes of London and Bristol in importance. The main export was coal, from the West Cumbria coalfield, while inwards came tobacco and rum from across the Atlantic. There are other American connections, too, since George Washington's grandmother lived here, and is buried in St Nicholas Gardens; and the energetic American privateer John Paul Jones, whom we last met battling with the Royal Navy off Flamborough Head, landed at Whitehaven in 1778 and ran amok for a short while. John Paul Jones was actually born at Kirkbean, just across the Solway Firth near Criffel, and served an apprenticeship at Whitehaven.

Leave Whitehaven on the clifftop alongside the railway, crossing over beyond Parton to walk the road through Lowca, past former collieries. Lowca's bizarre claim to fame is that in 1915 it was attacked by a German U-Boat that surfaced close inshore and fired somewhat ineffectually at a chemical works, the first time a submarine had ever targeted a dry land location.

Turn off left for Park House and at the end of the lane join a former mineral railway to Harrington Harbour where you can walk the shore for a little way until the steelworks at Workington forces you inland. In its heyday Workington produced vast quantities of iron and steel – as much as 600,000 tonnes of pig iron a year, or one tenth of Britain's total output – assisted by a revolutionary new steel-making process invented here at Workington by Henry Bessemer.

Mary Queen of Scots fled here (to Workington Hall, not the
steelworks) after defeat in Scotland, and the ruined mansion, once
home to the landowning Curwen family, is still worth a visit and
sometimes the venue for opera pageants.

From Siddick, just outside Workington, the coast path treads
the narrow but safe strip between sea and railway all the way to
Maryport.

MARYPORT – KIRKBRIDE (27 miles)
The Romans established a fort on the clifftop at Maryport (Alauna),
the most southerly in a palisade and turret defence system that
extended 26 miles down the English Solway Firth coast. Excavated
last century, the remains are on display at Senhouse Roman
Museum next to the site of the original fort, and comprise the
largest collection of Roman military altar stones and inscriptions
from any site in Britain.

Down at the harbour old mixes with new, but not altogether
harmoniously. The Maritime Museum by the bridge has displays
of Maryport's seafaring history, on Fletcher Christian (he of
Mutiny on the Bounty) who was born nearby, and on Humphrey
Senhouse II who built the town and named it after his wife, Mary.
Across the River Ellen at Elizabeth Dock there are also guided
tours around two restored steamships, *Flying Buzzard* and *Vic
96*. But when I visited last the talk was of harbour redevelopment, with Victorian reproduction street lighting and waterfront
offices – which I hope won't look as bad as some of the new
housing developments which currently spoil Maryport's harbour
area.

Follow the promenade north, and where it ends at Bank End
Farm walk the easy, raised beach, or if conditions allow you
may follow the water's edge virtually all the way to Silloth.
It is a flat and relatively easy passage, waymarked even, which
allows you the chance to gaze out across the Solway Firth to the
hills of Galloway, and in particular the shapely granite lump of
Criffel, south of Dumfries. There is a tremendous sense of space
and distance, with the outline of the Lake District mountains
also presenting an impressive spectacle over your right shoulder.
Near Crosscanonby and Allonby you pass former saltpans where
saltwater was first converted into salt crystals as long ago as Norman
times. At Maryport you will have also joined the route of the 54-mile

Allerdale Ramble, which begins in central Lakeland and ends beyond Silloth at Grune Point.

As Silloth approaches there are a few caravan sites but overall this is an empty and peaceful coast. Not many people make it to England's far north-western outpost. Oystercatchers enjoy the undisturbed shingle, while on the sand dunes you will find Isle of Man cabbage.

Silloth has wide, cobbled main streets, a couple of old Victorian hotels, and glorious flower beds bordering a wide seafront green. Next to the solitary amusement arcade is a stand of pines which, since it has the Solway Firth and the Scottish hills beyond, is every photographer's dream. The sunsets are particularly good from here. But Silloth's on-the-edge location has been the barrier to its expansion, despite mid-nineteenth-century efforts to turn it into a railhead and port. Today, although it can get reasonably bustling over high summer, it is seldom thronged.

Walk along the edge of the minor road to Skinburness and out to Grune Point, an isolated spit extending into the mudflats of Moricambe Bay. Another valuable feeding station for migrants, it forms part of the larger Solway Firth estuarine zone and is home to the entire Spitzbergen population of barnacle geese and a fifth of Britain's pink-footed geese each winter.

There is a walking route across Skinburness Marsh at all but the highest tides (see the guidebook listed in the Appendix for specific directions), and then a path from the River Waver into Abbeytown. Surfaced lanes via Calvo offer a safer alternative.

The abbey of Abbeytown was Holme Cultram, which Robert the Bruce sacked in 1319, despite his father being buried there. Leaving the town, follow the road across the flat Solway Plain via Newton Arlosh to Kirkbride.

KIRKBRIDE – GRETNA (37 miles)
After crossing Whitrigg Bridge the official Cumbria Coastal Way turns right, and by the meandering Wampool leaves the road for a mossland footpath to Drumburgh. However, the only reason that this cross-country route is in place is because the route around the lonely Cardurnock Peninsula is a road affair. Not exactly a busy road, mind you, past former wartime airfields now home to a forest of transmitters, and an RSPB reserve offshore at Campfield. It's worth walking this stretch to enjoy the shifting views of the

Solway Firth, with Annan less than three miles away, and of course
to visit Bowness-on-Solway. Just before this you may notice a minor
headland at Herdhill Scar, which is where a former railway crossed
the firth by a viaduct. Eventually undermined by the weather, the
structure was closed in 1924 and demolished a decade later, which
was a blow for some local Scots who used to walk over for a drink
on Sundays.

Bowness is the unsung and relatively unvisited western end of
Hadrian's Wall where a large Roman fort used to stand. And yet
why end the Wall here and not on the Eden at Carlisle? The reason
seems to be defensive, since the Solway and its tributary rivers are
all fordable at certain points, and it would have been quite easy
with local knowledge to turn the Wall. This also explains the extra
Roman fortifications south along the coast to Maryport, of course.
Despite the fact that little of the Wall is actually standing today,
the sheer size and scale of what is now a World Heritage Site is
compelling, and in the next few miles you can walk its course
towards Carlisle. But why stop there? Whether you fancy nipping
up to Gretna or not (and you won't be missing much if you choose
not to), there will soon be a continuous walking route of about 75
miles along the whole length of the Wall to Wallsend, Tyne and
Wear, on the North Sea Coast. The Hadrian's Wall Path may not
always follow the exact line of the Roman Wall, but as the newest
national trail it will provide a scenic, fascinating and of course
waymarked walking route – and a perfect way of switching from
coast to coast.

From Bowness follow the road eastwards via Drumburgh, after
which its straight-as-a-die direction indicates the line of the original
Wall. Beyond Burgh by Sands (which is not by any sand) the Wall
walking route leaves the road for a track to Beaumont, then follows
the Eden upstream via Grinsdale and along the riverbank into
Carlisle. An alternative, attractive maybe to the Welsh and the
Scots, is to branch off left at Burgh for a path to Old Sandsfield and
the memorial to Edward I, Hammer of the Scots, who died at this
spot whilst on his way to mete out some rough treatment to Robert
the Bruce in 1307. But take note – this route is not recommended
at high tide or when the Eden is in flood.

The last major centre on our epic Coastwalk is Carlisle, with its
distinctive red sandstone cathedral founded in the twelfth century
that was previously a Priory for Augustinian monks. Carlisle Castle

has a dour and resolute look, reflecting centuries of border raids and repeated conflict over the long-disputed English-Scottish border. Robert the Bruce, for instance, followed up Edward's sudden exit by not just seeing off his son at Bannockburn but also rampaging around northern England.

Carlisle's determined constable, Andrew de Harcla, did his best to defend the region from these incursions, but in the end was forced to parley with the invaders in order to save innocent lives. This action was later judged treasonable, and de Harcla was executed. Pele towers and reiver raids, sieges and feuding, this 'Debatable Land' has a complex and at times desperate history.

Presuming you are not immediately dashing off east along Hadrian's Wall, or even south on the Cumbria Way to Caldbeck, there is the relatively small matter of 12 miles to polish off before reaching Scotland. It's not an astounding final stage, but if you've come all this way, what's a dozen miles?

For the most part it is a pleasant if uneventful walk, since the north bank of the Eden can be walked all the way from the outskirts of Carlisle to Rockcliffe, and then from farm to farm along connecting lanes off Rockcliffe Marsh. A footpath via Garriestown Farm leads to Metal Bridge, an oddly unimaginative if accurate description of Thomas Telford's original construction of 1815 (the present concrete version replaced it in 1920).

With no pedestrian access to the shore the final two miles are along the very busy and very fast A74, and if you insist on walking it take care. There are buses back to Carlisle from Gretna, which sits just over the border and is surprisingly quiet if not particularly exciting. Gretna Green, the other side of the railway, is where most visitors head, and unless you have a sudden impulse to get married or feel the need to mingle with brain-dead tourists wander down to the edge of the Solway Firth and simply relax. After all, it's what the coast is there for, isn't it?

Pick of the walks

ST BEES – WHITEHAVEN (8 miles): a pleasant day's ramble around the red sandstone cliffs of St Bees Head, west Cumbria.

SILVERDALE – ARNSIDE (5–10 miles): a further station-to-station route on lanes and paths through the quiet wooded hills above Morecambe Bay. The ascent of Arnside Knott is a must.

APPENDIX I

Walking the Coast

If you have rarely wandered much further than the promenade or beach there are a few points to bear in mind when exploring the coast on foot. Where an official long-distance path exists, like the South-West Coast Path, there is usually not too much trouble with route-finding, since waymarks are fairly regular, the track is often well walked, and if an obstruction should occur an alternative route is sooner or later established, whether it is a temporary route around a landslip, or whatever. But the absence of an official coast path does not mean that the coast is not worth walking, or that there's nothing to see – quite the opposite in some instances. Despite the proliferation of official coast paths there are many still beautiful and fascinating places to explore along our shores, particularly in Wales. However, do take into account a few factors.

In some places the foreshore offers the best walking route, but now and then this can be tricky. First, soft sand and shingle banks are awkward, tiring and time-consuming to walk upon, so don't plan a long shingle walk – your legs will never forgive you. Firm sand is a lovely walking surface, often found near the water's edge, but check locally and with the OS map in case of soft sand or dangerous mud, and always watch the tide (see below). I have deliberately avoided certain danger spots, and suggest you do the same. Second, many of these habitats are home to birds, plants and other wildlife, so respect nature reserves and follow any instructions or waymarking for visitors. Third, the law as regards walking along the inter-tidal zone is not altogether clear. Technically the public has no legal right to walk the foreshore (the land between high and medium low water) unless a public right of way has been created. However, since the foreshore is usually owned by the Crown – and also since we are dealing with a strip of land covered by the sea twice a day and whose upper limit constantly shifts – by and large it is unlikely that the bona fide walker will be prevented from walking the inter-tidal strip (but don't necessarily count on it).

The fourth – and perhaps most crucial point of all – involves tides. Every year without fail people are drowned because they simply did not read the tide correctly, if at all. Always know what the tide is doing.

Learn the signs to recognise the state of the tide on a shoreline – how far up the beach is the water? Is there a large area of drying sand above the surf? – but don't rely on this knowledge because you will not know the speed at which tides in strange places come in and out. Tide tables are widely available from local post offices, some newsagents, tourist information centres – or ask any lifeguard, coastguard, harbour master, etc. NEVER walk into a potentially restricted space – such as a small cove or the foot of cliffs – when the tide is rising, and even if it is falling make sure that you know when it will turn and whether you can safely get to your destination in time. (It should go without saying, of course: wear a watch!) Occasionally high tides, and in particular high spring tides, may either cut off a foreshore route or make it altogether impassable; and even coast roads can be under water at peak times. If this is the case then find a safe inland route (I have indicated several instances of this in the text), or wait for the water to retreat.

Similarly, resist the urge to ford the mouth of every small river that you come across, since there are often perilous patches of soft mud, hidden channels and strong currents that can easily topple even the most careful of walkers, and especially a top-heavy, rucksacked type. Some rivers can be forded, and often there is a safe 'wading window' at and around the time of low tide, but do seek the advice of local experts first. When the South-West Way Association's guide employs capitals and bold type to assert that even their senior officers won't wade the River Avon near Bigbury-on-Sea, Devon, then take note.

On the other hand there may be times when you want to dive in, and a dip on a hot summer's afternoon can be particularly refreshing. But if you do fancy a swim, it may be wise to check that it is a safe area, since many bays and estuary mouths (especially on the West Coast) have potentially dangerous currents and tides that can quite literally draw you under and out. It is also a good idea to check with the *Good Beach Guide* or take the advice of user groups like Surfers Against Sewage before you tear off into the surf. Although efforts are being made to clean things up there's still some way to go, and too many beaches still suffer from quite unacceptable levels of pollution. We may laugh at the idea that physicians once advocated drinking seawater for medicinal purposes, but at least the stuff was cleaner then than it is today.

In rough weather the coast can be an invigorating and stunning place, especially off-season when the crowds have dispersed and the cafés and beach huts are all closed, and when you can walk for miles virtually alone. But don't forget that sudden, freak waves do occasionally wash people off promenades or sea walls, and that high and gusting winds can make cliff walking hazardous.

Prolonged periods of heavy rain can also undermine what can often be already unstable ground and hasten cliff erosion, particularly on the North Sea Coast. Always obey official notices and be mindful of signs such as those placed by the National Park authority all along the Pembrokeshire Coast Path: '*Mae clogwyni'n lladd – cadwch at y llwybr*', (or 'Cliffs kill – keep to the path').

All these dire warnings aside, coast walking is fun and full of surprises. Simply use your common sense and avoid taking unnecessary risks. In addition, coast walking requires very little in the way of specialised gear. The underlying principle is dress for the terrain and weather you're likely to meet. In spring or autumn that means taking waterproofs and a spare jumper; but even in summer it is worth taking light waterproofs if you are going for more than a firm forecastable couple of days. In hot, sunny weather shorts are desirable and a hat essential, and since much of the coast is open and exposed always make sure you apply plenty of protective sun cream, since you can get windblown burnt as well as sunburnt all too easily. Spare food and drink is always useful, and of course a map to identify where you are, what you are looking at, and where you want to go. Long-distance walkers will naturally be thinking of rucksacks and maybe camping gear, but there again we're not talking about the Cairngorms, are we? I am reliably informed that backpacking the South-West Coast Path is a wonderful experience, but try ascending the Great Hangman or Golden Cap carrying a tent, sleeping bag, cooking utensils, wet weather gear, spare clothes, food and drink, and so on, and you may end up appreciating the views a little less.

As far as footwear is concerned, one of my most relaxing couple of miles walking was barefoot in the shallow waves between Sandsend and Whitby, a perfect end to a warm day's hike along the Cleveland Way. But there again, the cliffs behind me were the highest on England's East Coast, and I found a stout pair of walking boots essential to grip the sometimes rough ground and prevent a twisted ankle. Ultimately it comes down to personal choice, and precisely what kind of ground you're walking on. Training shoes or sports sandals will be ideal for beaches, marshland, a concrete sea wall, etc, but a harder and rockier terrain such as cliffs will require something a little more robust.

APPENDIX II:

Further Reading, Guidebooks and Useful Addresses

FURTHER READING
— *Turn Right at Land's End* by John Merrill (JNM Publications, 1988, available from Footprint Press, 19 Moseley Street, Ripley, Derby)
— *Land's End to John o'Groats* by Andrew McCloy (Hodder & Stoughton, 1994; Coronet, 1995)
— *And The Road Below* by John Westley (Meridian Books, 1994)
— *The Walker's Handbook* by Hugh Westacott (Penguin, 1978; Pan, 1991)
— *The Rambler's Yearbook & Accommodation Guide* (Ramblers' Association)
— *The Long Distance Walkers' Handbook* (Long Distance Walkers Association)
— *Out in the country: where you can go and what you can do* (Countryside Commission)
— *AA Book of the Seaside* (Collins, 1972)
— *Walking Britain's Coast: An Aerial Guide* by R. Sale, B. Evans & M. McClean (Unwin Hyman, 1989)
— *The Natural History of Britain's Coasts* by Eric Soothill & Michael Thomas (Blandford Press, 1987)
— *In Search of Neptune: a Celebration of the National Trust's Coastline* by Charlie Pye-Smith (National Trust, 1990)
— *The Good Beach Guide* compiled by the Marine Conservation Society (David & Charles, 1995)
— *Lighthouses* by Lynn Pearson (Shire Publications, 1995)
— *Martello Towers: a brief history* by Geoff Hutchinson (1994). Available from local bookshops and some tourist information centres on Kent/Sussex coasts.

– *Photographic Field Guide: Birds of Britain and Europe* by J. Flegg & D. Hosking (New Holland, 1993)
– *Collins Nature Guide: Wild Flowers* (Harper Collins, 1994)
– *The MacDonald Encyclopaedia of Fossils* (MacDonald, 1986; Little, Brown, 1993)
– *Collins New Generation Guide: Butterflies and Day-flying Moths of Britain and Europe* by M. Chinery (Collins, 1989)
– *Eyewitness Handbooks: Shells* by S. Peter Dance (Dorling Kindersley, 1992)

GUIDEBOOKS TO LOCAL COASTAL WALKING
Most of the guidebooks listed below are available from bookshops or libraries, or from the addresses given. In addition, a wealth of informative booklets and leaflets exists that will help you walk and explore the coast, many produced by local experts, rambling groups and official bodies. Before you set off pay a visit to the nearest tourist information centre, National Trust shop, Heritage Coast centre or bookshop.

The map numbers given below refer to the Ordnance Survey's Landranger series (1:50 000) unless indicated otherwise.

THE NORTH SEA COAST
1 Berwick – Hull
Maps: 75, 81, 88, 93, 94, 101, 107, 113; OS Outdoor Leisure 27
Northumberland Coastline by Ian Smith (Sandhill Press, 1988)
Durham Coast Path (leaflet) from Easington District Council or Durham County Council
The Teesdale Way by Martin Collins (Cicerone Press, 1995)
National Trail Guide: Cleveland Way by Ian Sampson (Aurum Press, 1989)
Walking the Cleveland Way and the Missing Link by Malcolm Boyes (Cicerone Press, 1988)
Cleveland Way Information & Accommodation Guide from North York Moors National Park Office
Cook Country Walk from North York Moors National Park Office
Countryside Walks: Flamborough Head (leaflet pack) from Humberside County Council
Wavelength Wanderings Along the Humber Estuary by Larry Malkin (1992). Available from local bookshops and tourist information centres.

2 Hull – Felixstowe
Maps: 107, 113, 122, 131, 132, 133, 134, 156, 169
Wavelength Wanderings along the Humber Estuary (above)
Nev Cole Way by Wanderlust Rambling Group (1991). Available from local bookshops and tourist information centres
The Peter Scott Walk (leaflet) from Lincolnshire or Norfolk County Councils
National Trail Guide: Peddars Way & Norfolk Coast Path by Bruce Robinson (Aurum Press, 1992)
Walking the Peddars Way and Norfolk Coast Path with the Weavers Way by and from the Peddars Way Association (1994)
Suffolk Coast Path from Suffolk County Council (1995)

3 Felixstowe – Tilbury
Maps: 169, 168, 178
The Essex Way from Essex County Council (1994)

THE CHANNEL COAST
4 Gravesend – Newhaven
Maps: 178, 179, 189, 199, 198
Saxon Shore Way (set of 10 route cards) by Kent Area Ramblers' Association. Available from Ernie Kingstone, 22 The Goldings, Rainham, Kent
Coastal Walks in Kent: Wantsum Walks, and *White Cliffs* (leaflet packs) from Kent County Council
Royal Military Canal (leaflet) from Kent County Council
National Trail Guide: North Downs Way by Neil Curtis (Aurum Press, 1992)
National Trail Guide: South Downs Way by Paul Millmore (Aurum Press, 1990)

5 Newhaven – Exmouth
Maps: 198, 197, 196, 195, 194, 193, 192; OS Outdoor Leisure 15, 22, 29
Isle of Wight Coastal Path (4 leaflets) from Isle of Wight County Council
Isle of Wight Coast Path by John Merrill (JNM Publications, 1990)
Exploring the Solent Way by Ann-Marie Edwards (Countryside Books, 1994)

The Bournemouth Coast Path by Leigh Hatts (Countryside Books, 1985)
National Trail Guide: South-West Coast Path – Exmouth to Poole by Roland Tarr (Aurum Press, 1989)
South-West Way by South-West Way Association (plus separate Poole – Minehead 'other way round' supplement available)
Exploring the Dorset Coast Path by Leigh Hatts (Countryside Books, 1993)
Purbeck Coastal Walks by Rodney Legg (Dorset Publishing Company, 1995)
Isle of Portland: a guide to walking and exploring the island (Dorset Books, 1994)

6 Exmouth – Penzance
Maps: 192, 202, 201, 204, 203; OS Outdoor Leisure 20; OS Explorer 8, 7
National Trail Guides: South-West Coast Path – Falmouth to Exmouth by Brian Le Messurier; *Padstow to Falmouth* by John Macadam (Aurum Press, 1990)
South-West Way (above)

THE ATLANTIC COAST
7 Penzance – Ilfracombe
Maps: 203, 200, 190, 180; OS Explorer 7, 9
National Trail Guides: South-West Coast Path – Padstow to Falmouth by John Macadam; *Minehead to Padstow* by Roland Tarr (Aurum Press, 1990)
South-West Way (above)

8 Ilfracombe – Swansea
Maps: 180, 181, 182, 172, 171, 170; OS Outdoor Leisure 9
National Trail Guide (above)
Explore the Coast of Devon by Paul Wreyford (Sigma Leisure, 1995)
South-West Way (above)
The Severn Way from Northavon District Council

9 Swansea – Cardigan
Maps: 159, 158, 157, 145; OS Outdoor Leisure 35, 36; OS Explorer 10
Walking Around Gower by West Glamorgan Ramblers' Association (1991)

National Trail Guide: Pembrokeshire Coast Path by Brian John (Aurum Press, 1990)

Walking the Pembrokeshire Coast Path by Patrick Stark (Gomer Press, 1990). From Gomer Press, Llandysul, Dyfed

The Pembrokeshire Coastal Path, by Dennis Kelsall (Cicerone Press, 1995)

Accommodation list and mileage chart from Pembrokeshire Coast National Park Office

THE IRISH SEA COAST
10 Cardigan – Bangor
Maps: 145, 146, 135, 124, 123, 115, 114; OS Outdoor Leisure, 23, 18, 17; OS Explorer 12, 13

Guide to the Dyfi Valley Way by Laurence Main (Bartholomew Kittiwake, 1988)

Walks on the Llŷn Peninsula by N Burras and J Stiff (Gwasg Carreg Gwalch, 1995). From Gwasg Carreg Gwalch, Iard yr Orsaf, Llanwrst, Gwynedd

Walking Anglesey's Coastline by John Merrill (Trail Crest Publications, 1993)

11 Bangor – Lancaster
Maps: 115, 116, 117, 108, 102, 97

North Wales Path (leaflet) from Clwyd or Gwynedd County Councils

A Walker's Guide to the Wirral Shore Way (Chester to Hoylake) by Carl Rogers (Mara Publications, 1994). From Mara Publications, 22 Crosland Terrace, Helsby, Warrington, Cheshire

Walks on the Sefton Coast from Sefton Metropolitan Borough Council (1995). Covers the Coastal Path.

Ribble Way by Gladys Sellers (Cicerone Press, 1985/1993)

Wyre Way (leaflet) from Wyre Borough Council

Lancashire Coastal Way (4 leaflets) from Lancashire County Council

12 Lancaster – Gretna
Maps: 97, 96, 89, 85; OS Outdoor Leisure 6

Isle of Man Coastal Path by Aileen Evans (Cicerone Press, 1988)

Cumbria Coastal Way by Ian & Krysia Brodie (Ellenbank Press, 1994)

Furness Way by Paul Hannon (Hillside Publications, 1984/1994)

USEFUL ADDRESSES

Camping and Caravanning Club, Greenfields House, Westwood Way, Coventry CV4 8JH

Countryside Commission, John Dower House, Crescent Place, Cheltenham, Glos GL50 3RA

Countryside Commission Postal Sales, PO Box 124, Walgrave, Northampton NN6 9TL

Long Distance Walkers' Association, 117 Higher Lane, Rainford, St Helens, Merseyside WA11 8BQ

Marine Conservation Society, 9 Gloucester Road, Ross-on-Wye, Herefordshire HR9 5BU

National Trust, 36 Queen Anne's Gate, London SW1H 9AS

Ordnance Survey, Romsey Road, Maybush, Southampton SO16 49U

Ramblers' Association, 1/5 Wandsworth Road, London SW8 2XX

South-West Way Association, Windlestraw, Penquit, Ermington, Ivybridge, Devon PL21 OLU

Surfers Against Sewage, The Old Counthouse Warehouse, Wheal Kitty, St Agnes, Truro, Cornwall TR5 0RE

Youth Hostels Association, Trevelyan House, 8 St Stephen's Hill, St Albans, Herts AL1 2DY